Changeling Press, LLC

ChangelingPress.com

Crash/Razor Duet
A Hounds of Hell MC Romance
Jamie Targaet

Crash/Razor Duet
A Hounds of Hell MC Romance
Jamie Targaet

ISBN: 978-1-60521-942-4

Publisher:
Changeling Press LLC
315 N. Centre St.
Martinsburg, WV 25404
ChangelingPress.com

Printed in the U.S.A.

Editor: Treva Harte
Cover Artist: Bryan Keller

The individual stories in this anthology have been previously released in E-Book format.

Table of Contents

Crash (Hounds of Hell MC 5)
A Hounds of Hell MC Romance
Jamie Targaet

She vanished once, leaving scars I can't forget. Now she's back, hiding secrets I may never forgive.

Helena -- Returning to Mercy was supposed to be a fresh start. As a therapist, I've made it my mission to help others find strength, even when I can't always find it for myself. But when Crash walks back into my life, bringing all the pain and passion of our past, I know this town holds more than just memories -- it holds secrets I can't outrun. He's fierce, wounded, and the last person I thought I'd ever see again. And while he's still everything I want, he's also everything I should fear. Especially when he finds out what I'm hiding.

Crash -- The Hounds of Hell gave me purpose when I had nothing but rage. My loyalty runs deeper than blood -- until they betrayed me. Losing Perry, my only brother, has made me question everything I believed about the family I chose. But when Helena returns, the woman who vanished after one night and still haunts my dreams, my anger flares in ways I can't control. I wanted answers, and now I'm in too deep. She's hiding something, and whatever it is, it's tied to the pain that put me on this path. This time, I won't let her slip away, even if it means facing demons I swore to bury.

Prologue

The bar was packed with people seeking shelter from the cold October rain lashing the windows. The steady hum of conversation, the clink of glasses, and the crack of pool balls colliding blended with the muted beat of the jukebox. Whoever kept it playing had good taste in classic Southern rock. The air was thick with cigarette smoke and the smell of beer and leather, all mingling together under the dim, yellow glow of the overhead lights.

Charlie Ford, called Crash by the Hounds, leaned onto the pool table, cue stick in hand, lining up his next shot. Next to him, Outcast stood casually beside the table, his sharp blue eyes scanning the bar as he waited for his turn. Player, always the loudest of the three prospects, was talking with a couple of girls at the bar, his laughter carrying over the noise. All three of them were still earning a place among the Hounds of Hell MC. The weight of it was heavy on Crash's shoulders, the unspoken pressure to prove himself. He was still an outsider -- almost in, but not quite.

The rain continued to pour outside, making the bar feel like a cozy hideaway from the world. The regulars sat at the bar, nursing their drinks, while a few couples danced in the next room, swaying slowly to the music. Outcast smirked at him from the other side of the table. "You going to make that shot tonight?"

The crack of the cue ball echoed through the air and Crash watched the solid ball roll smoothly across the table and drop into the pocket. Outcast grinned, stepping up to take his turn and Player hollered encouragement from across the bar. Crash stepped back to let Outcast have his turn and that was when he saw her for the first time that night.

Helena walked by him to a nearby table, carrying a tray of beer mugs and shots. Fuck, it made him hard just looking at her. There was something so magnetic about her -- a quiet confidence in the way she carried herself, serving drinks with quick, steady motions while keeping a watch on the room to meet her customers' needs. Her long black hair floated around her shoulders in waves, catching the light when she moved. It shimmered with a hint of midnight blue, occasionally falling into her face when she leaned down to grab a bottle or glass. She'd tucked it behind her ear with a casual flick of her hand, revealing high cheekbones and a soft but mischievous smile that caught the attention of more than a few patrons.

Despite the hustle and noise of the bar, she stayed calm, like she could handle whatever came her way. And when she laughed, low and sweet, it was enough to make even the most distracted biker at the pool table turn his head. When she focused those striking green eyes on him, Crash froze. She took his breath away. She stopped at their table as Outcast missed his shot, her black low-cut shirt calling attention to the tops of her full breasts. The short skirt showed off shapely, white thighs that had to be soft as silk. Helena was slender, but she had a figure that had his engine revving every time Crash had laid eyes on her. "Can I get you guys anything?" Helena asked, smiling.

Crash didn't like it when Outcast gave her the once-over. Outcast was a bad motherfucker with a pretty face and hair as black as hers. The girls usually went for him first and he wasn't one to turn away pleasurable company. But her gaze was firmly on

Crash. And he wasn't turning down an opportunity to talk to her. "Can you bring me a bourbon? We have a tab started."

"I know," she said with a smile. "Anything for you?" He knew she was asking Outcast, but she was still looking at *him*.

Outcast winked at her. "Same."

"I'll be right back." Helena headed to the bar.

Outcast unapologetically ogled her ass as she did. "Are you going to do something about that, brother?" he asked Crash once she was out of earshot.

Lining up his next shot, Crash shrugged. "I don't know." Crash sank that shot too.

Outcast shook his head. "She's been hinting at you for weeks. Make a move."

"Maybe," Crash said as Outcast took his turn. Player was still chatting up the two girls at the bar. Helena had disappeared from sight and he didn't immediately realize Outcast was watching Crash stand there like a hopeful puppy.

"If you don't do something," Outcast warned, "someone else will."

That got Crash's attention. "The fuck you say?"

Outcast made his next shot, his grin wide at Crash's response. The fucker was baiting him. Electing to ignore the remark, Crash concentrated on his next shot. He tried to take his focus off the girl he wanted so much.

"I don't even know why I play against you," Outcast told him, leaning his cue stick against the table and draining the rest of his bourbon from a glass balanced precariously on the edge of the pool table. "I don't have a snowball's chance in hell."

Crash winked at him. "No, you don't."

"Here you go." Helena came out of nowhere,

placing fresh glasses of bourbon on the table next to where they were playing pool. The smile she flashed Crash was so sweet it had his cock jerking in his jeans. Crash watched her check on her other tables, running through clever ways to ask her out in his head. Maybe he *should* do something about his attraction to her. Sex, yes. But she was just the sort of woman he'd want for his old lady one day when he became a member of the Hounds. Helena looked like a bad bitch, yet she was sweet as summer honey. He'd love to taste her honey. Every inch of her...

Feeling a brush of cold air, Crash turned to the side door behind him. The second the small group of Cottonmouths strolled through the rear entrance, the easygoing atmosphere gave way to tension and dread. It was like the cold autumn wind had blown something sinister into their midst. Crash wasn't the only one watching them walk in, their cuts marked with the unmistakable coiled snake. The Cottonmouths weren't exactly strangers to *Sackett's*, but they weren't welcome either. *Sackett's* -- Mercy itself -- was Hound territory. Everyone in the bar knew what the Cottonmouths' presence meant: trouble.

Leading the group was Baby Face, and despite the nickname, there was nothing innocent about him. The fucker was almost unnervingly pretty for someone with a soul as dark as his. His sharp jawline and dimples drew women to him by the dozen but didn't match the kind of violence he was known for. The wicked glint in his eyes made it clear that beneath that handsome exterior was a monster. Word around town was Baby Face liked to cut up the women who got too close --"club sluts" was the term the Cottonmouths used. He treated it like sport, his twisted idea of fun. And since his father Eli was the president of that chapter of the Cottonmouths, he was untouchable.

Baby Face scanned the room, a smile forming on his lips that didn't reach his eyes. It turned Crash's fucking stomach and sent a ripple of unease through the crowd. Conversations quieted, laughter faded, and the energy that had once filled the room evaporated. The heavy tension was palpable. The regulars at the bar and the pretty girls sitting with Player exchanged nervous glances before gathering their things and going out the same side door the Cottonmouths had just walked through. Crash and Outcast stiffened at the pool table, hands instinctively flexing toward their weapons.

Taking his time, Baby Face let the silence stretch as he sauntered into the bar, his men trailing behind him like shadows. Every step he took felt like a threat, a subtle promise of violence lurking just below the surface. Even old Amos, the bartender, who'd seen his fair share of rough customers, hesitated for a moment before continuing with his work. The Cottonmouths didn't have to say a fucking word to make their presence felt. *Sackett's* had become a powder keg, and with Baby Face in play, it felt like the match was already lit. Taking a seat in the back corner, Baby Face sat facing the pool table. His eyes lit up in unholy interest on spotting Crash and Outcast who, along with Player, were the only Hounds there at the time.

Player returned to the pool table, his gaze moving between the booth where their rivals sat and his fellow prospects. "What the fuck are they doing here?"

Crash shrugged, electing to act like he didn't give a shit. He drew them back into their game, watching the rival MC members here and there out of the corner of his eye. It all seemed fine until Helena moved hesitantly toward their table to do her job. Her body language changed, her shoulders rising to hover just under her ears. It was obvious she was afraid of them, and she should be. Baby Face's attention was riveted to her and Crash couldn't hear what he was saying. It just pissed him off when the four of them started laughing and her reaction to the fuckers' words stained her pretty face with red. Crash didn't realize his fists had clenched as he watched. Leaning his cue against the table, he kept watching, making no secret of it now.

"Don't," Outcast said, standing behind him. "It'll just start some shit."

Crash didn't care. To defend Helena, he'd do exactly that. The big, shaggy asshole sitting next to Baby Face, Big Dog, was closest to where Helena stood. She looked like she was praying the floor would open and swallow her whole. Big Dog ran a fast-moving hand up the back of her thigh. She skittered away from that touch, stepping back. Turning, Helena raced for the bar. Her green eyes were glossy with tears, causing him to snap.

Before Outcast or Player could get to him, Crash marched in their direction. Yeah, he wasn't officially a Hound yet. But he sure as fuck was going to act like one. His gaze locked with that of Baby Face, who looked amused to see him coming. Before he could reach their table, a strong hand grabbed his upper arm, got his attention. Turning in fury, he expected to see Outcast or Player behind him. He found the club's tall, formidable VP instead who must have just arrived with the twins. Snow's white hair reflected the lights, his cold gray eyes determined.

"We've got this," Snow told him with the twins behind him. Axel's gaze was fastened on the group of Cottonmouths and Ryder couldn't keep the grin off his face. Ryder loved a good fight and not many could beat him in hand-to-hand combat.

Frustrated to be sidelined, Crash nodded his understanding, letting the three of them move to that smoke-filled corner where the enemy sat. When he headed back to the table, Outcast and Player were watching the scene play out. Looking around, he didn't see Helena. Yeah, maybe he hadn't been allowed to champion her. The least he could fucking do was to make sure she was okay. Walking out the side door, Crash marched into the cold rain, looking around.

At the back of the building was the door the employees used, a floodlight illuminating the area. Beneath a huge black umbrella, Helena stood smoking a cigarette, shaking. Crash knew it wasn't from the cold. Not caring about the rain, he approached her slowly. Stopping in front of her, Crash waited until she looked up to meet his gaze. "Are you okay?" he asked, carefully.

Helena nodded, a quick, nervous movement.

"They're not supposed to be here," Crash explained. "We're taking care of it right now."

"Thank you," she said so quietly he almost didn't hear it over the patter of the rain. "I should have handled it better. That's all."

Shaking his head, Crash said, "Honey, there are grown ass men afraid of Baby Face and his scum. You have nothing to be ashamed of. Do you know that?" Helena shook like a leaf. Crash couldn't take it anymore. "Hey, come here," he whispered, ducking under her umbrella to take her in his arms, trying to comfort her. He was prepared for her resistance, and he would have let her go. But she clung to him like she was trying to burrow into his strength. The umbrella wobbled above them, and he took it from her trembling hand, holding her tightly with his free arm. It broke his heart a little because he couldn't help but feel there was something more to the situation. Had the fucker done something to her in the past?

It was cold with the rain soaking into the parts of them that the umbrella didn't shelter. "Why don't we get you back in where it's warm?" he asked.

Helena shook her head, tightening her grip on him. Her slender arms slid inside his jacket; her body pressed to his. "I can't. I can't go back in there with him."

Fucking Baby Face. "Want me to drive you home?" Crash offered. "You probably don't want to ride on the back of my bike in this rain, but I'd be happy to drive you in your car."

After a moment, she lifted her tearstained face to look him in the eye. "You… don't have to."

"I'd feel better knowing you made it home safely," he said. "It's raining and you're upset. Least I can do."

Helena nodded. "Okay."

And just like that, she started walking to the parking lot, not going back in to get things or clock out. Crash followed her to her small blue sedan, taking the keys she handed him and walking her to the passenger side with the umbrella. Marching back around to the driver's side, he folded the umbrella and tossed it in the back and got in. There wasn't a lot of space for him because the seat was pushed up close to the wheel. Chuckling, he moved the seat back and started the engine. "Where am I going?"

She directed him to Vermilion Street, and a tiny duplex that was one half of a small brick ranch. Pulling up in the driveway, he killed the engine and sat there in the dark cabin with her. The rain was still coming down hard. "Thank you," Helena said. "I appreciate this."

Crash smiled. "Glad to do it."

"Wait," she said. "How will you get back?"

"I'll text one of the guys to come and get me," he said with a shrug. "I can just wait out here in the car." Helena nodded in the darkness but, still trembling, didn't seem to be in a hurry to go anywhere. "Hey." She didn't look at him. With careful fingers, he tipped her chin up, urging her to look at him. "Are you going to be okay?"

"I… I don't want to be alone tonight," she said slowly. Then she leaned in and kissed him, catching him completely off guard. When he didn't kiss her right away in return, she pulled back. Her gaze searched his face. With a shaking hand, she carefully caught the back of his head, pulling him to her to kiss him again. Her fingers slid into his hair and her mouth opened for him.

Crash wasn't turning that down. Kissing her back, his hands ran all over her. She tried to move closer as if his kisses were something she needed, his touch something she craved. It was a challenge with the hard plastic of the center console between them. Breaking the kiss, his breath came fast. "Do you want to do this out here?"

"No," she whispered.

In a rush, they got out of the small car, running through the rain to the front door of her duplex. Helena's shaking hand fumbled with the key in the dark. She finally managed it, letting them into the living room. Crash didn't have much of a chance to look around. Helena grabbed his arm, pulling him from the room and down a short, narrow hallway. Once she'd guided him into the small room, she shut the door firmly behind him, locked it.

The bedroom was barely big enough for the single bed pushed against the far wall. The air was chilly, and the only light came from the streetlamp just beyond the window, casting a pale glow that slipped through the thin curtains, shining off the tracks the rain left on the glass. It painted soft pools of light across the floor, illuminating the edges of the worn, wooden furniture and the rumpled blanket draped over the bed. The room felt like a refuge from the world, a place meant for hiding. Shadows gathered in the corners, stretching and shifting gently as the wind stirred the branches outside. There was no clutter he could see, just the basics -- a dresser, a small nightstand, and a painting of the local lake on the wall. The rain was almost the only sound that broke the almost unnerving silence along with the occasional gust of wind or hum of a passing car. The low light lent the room an ethereal, almost dreamlike quality, where time seemed to slow down and the outside world felt a hundred miles away.

Helena stretched on her toes to kiss his mouth, her small hands pushing off his cut and working to pull his T-shirt free of his jeans. She pushed his shirt up and he grabbed it, yanking it off in a single motion. Staring at him appreciatively, she backed toward the bed, pulling her own shirt off to reveal a lacy black bra that matched her panties.

Crash took the hint. Undoing the button of his jeans, he pushed them down and kicked off his boots. When he joined her on that narrow bed, he was just in his boxers. Allowing her to push him onto his back, he couldn't have been happier when she straddled him, running her hands over his body. Crash hoped she liked what she saw. He could smell the rich scent of her own personal musk as she bent to claim his mouth for a heated kiss.

His hands moved over her soft curves, reaching behind her to unhook her bra. When he pulled it off her, his hands covered her breasts, loving their soft weight. Her nipples were diamond hard against his palms and she kissed him with so much passion, burning him down with her need. She had him. He'd give her anything she wanted.

Breaking the kiss, she painted his skin with her lips until she reached his ear. "Please," she whispered. One of her hands slid into his boxers, her fingers carefully seeking out his cock. It was like stepping on the gas. Crash was already rock hard, and the smell of her excitement went to his head, made him insane. Rolling her under him, he grabbed her wrists and held them to the bed. His hold was tight enough to restrain her but not enough to hurt as he claimed her mouth in a blazing kiss. Then his lips burned a trail down her neck to her chest. He couldn't resist teasing her tiny nipples with his lips, tongue, and teeth, with her breathy cries a sinful chorus that drove him on.

Crash released her only long enough to tear those little black panties from her. Grabbing her hips in his hands, he got his mouth on her. From the source, she smelled like heaven and tasted like tangy lemonade. In all the pornos he'd ever played in his head where she was the star, nothing was as sexy as the way she circled her pussy in his face, that weeping flesh begging for more of what he had to offer. He didn't have a vast amount of experience, but he paid attention. It didn't take him long to figure out how to use his tongue on her clit, how to trace her opening with a gentle finger and explore her until he found that secret place inside her pussy that had her crying out in the dark as an orgasm shook her.

Helena lay dazed on the bed above him, mouth open, trying to catch her breath. It gave him a minute to fish his jeans off the floor, to pluck a condom out of his wallet and smooth it on with Olympic speed. Her hands cupped her breasts as he ran the head of himself up and down her slit to get good and wet, to rekindle her excitement. She writhed beneath him on the bed, holding her breasts, watching him with those beautiful green eyes. "Please," she whispered again.

Crash pushed into her, trying to go slow because she was so fucking tight. Lost in the experience, it was all he could do not to come when he slid home inside her. Her pussy wrapped around him tight as a vise, the smell of her all over him. Once he got a grip on himself, he started moving slowly. Easy strokes. If he did a good job, Helena might want to keep him around. So far, she was everything he'd dreamed she'd be.

Lowering himself to his forearms, Crash thrust faster, harder. Helena moved her hips with him, urging him on. Crash gave her what she wanted, loving the way her hips danced against his, the way her nails scored the skin of his back. Her heels pressed insistently at his lower back. His hold on her tightening, he stole slow, sensual kisses from her. His heart pounding in his chest, he slid a hand between them, his fingers teased her clit. He must have done something right because her body jerked beneath him, her hold on him brutal.

"Fuck me harder," she rasped. "Please, harder…" Crash literally pounded her into the mattress, pinning her between him and the bed as she screamed and clawed at him, release ripping through her. As much as he wanted to hang on, he couldn't. His orgasm slammed through him, and he growled. The room spun, the rain outside forgotten. There was just her against his body, their hearts beating together. He didn't want the moment to ever end.

He rolled onto his back, struggling to breathe. Helena snuggled up to him in the darkness, catching her own breath. There was the slightest chill as each of them left the warm sanctuary they'd found for a quick trip to the bathroom. After that, he spooned behind her under the thin blanket from her bed. The scent of her hair was magic, the feel of her body next to him all he'd ever need.

"If I didn't tell you already," her voice was barely a whisper, "thank you for everything."

Crash chained kisses over the delicate skin of her neck. "You don't have to thank me for anything."

"But I want to," she said. "You don't know it, but just being there at the bar over the last few weeks? You gave me something to hope for. You reminded me that life can be… good."

Crash held her against his heart, so happy in that moment, until they drifted off to sleep.

Chapter One

Crash
Five years later...

Sackett's looked like a war zone. The usual warmth of the bar, with its smoky air and dim lights, was replaced by the stark reality of the aftermath. Tables had been overturned, chairs had been knocked on their sides, and glass from shattered bottles and mugs crunched beneath his boots. The usual hum of laughter and music had been replaced by the low murmurs of tired voices, mingling with the sirens of the police cars that had arrived. Flashing red and blue lights from the sheriff department's cruisers parked outside flashed through the windows to light up the walls.

Crash wiped a smear of blood from his cheek -- he hadn't even been sure if it was his -- then leaned against the pool table, scanning the room. A few Cottonmouths were still there, milling around like vultures looking for scraps. Several looks were exchanged with the Hounds, sizing them up even now. But no one moved. The fight had burned itself out.

The Mafia guys, Bianchi's men, lay scattered across the floor, their slick jackets and nice clothes torn and stained with blood, a sharp contrast to the ruthless image they had carried when they showed up at *Sackett's* earlier. Now defeated, because the Hounds and the Cottonmouths had beaten the living shit out of them, they looked smaller, stripped of the power they thought they held over everyone else in the room. Some groaned in pain; others were unconscious. A few remained still, beaten beyond recognition. Their guns were kicked aside, useless once the Hounds got close enough. The authority the New Jersey fucks once commanded was shattered, replaced by the cold realization they had underestimated the Hounds. The mistake cost them more than just pride.

The sheriff's deputies walked into *Sackett's* and moved through the bar, talking quietly as they assessed the damage. Sheriff Sawyer stood near the entrance, arms crossed, his eyes cold and calculating as he spoke with the Hounds' president, Razor. Crash could feel the tension in the room still buzzing like a live wire -- as though the fight wasn't really over -- just paused. With the cops' appearance, the Cottonmouths started making their exit. Crash knew they were looking for an excuse to start something again with the Hounds, but not with the law hanging over them.

Glancing at the overturned table near the bar where the fight had started, Crash shook his head. The place didn't feel like *Sackett's* anymore, not with the stench of the Cottonmouths lingering and the deputies keeping their distance like they also weren't convinced everything was over.

Of course, it hadn't felt like home for him since *she* had left…

The air was thick with the smell of sweat, blood, and spilled beer. Crash's entire being was still wired for the fight, but he forced himself to stay calm. *Sackett's* wasn't just a bar, it was home turf. He didn't like sharing it with the enemy and wondered why the fuck Razor had allowed *that* to happen. His gaze flicked to the last two Cottonmouths as they walked out, part of Baby Face's old crew, whispering amongst themselves. It was hard not to imagine how different things would have turned out if that psycho were still alive.

Sheriff Sawyer's voice cut through the haze. "We'll need statements," he said, loud enough for everyone to hear. The deputies started herding people into groups, separating Hounds from Cottonmouths and Mafia. There were others there even though Sawyer and his men had no idea how they were connected to any of it.

Crash was just grateful the shit was over. He was exhausted and pretty sure he had a couple of broken ribs. He hadn't seen his younger brother the entire time and he wanted to know where the hell Perry had gotten off to. Most of all, like the rest of his brothers, he wanted the Mafia the fuck out of Mercy for good.

Not wanting to talk to the fucking police, Crash went out the back entrance. The cool night air hit him, a balm to flush out the bloodlust of the last couple of hours. Closing his eyes, he savored the moment, trying to be still.

Out behind *Sackett's* in the field was an old barn that had been there as long as he could remember. Beams of light flickered around the inside of the old structure, telling him someone was out there. Sheriff Sawyer walked out of the bar behind him, walking past Crash and heading in that direction. Curious, because he hadn't seen the twins since the middle of the fight, he decided to follow him. After thinking about it, he hadn't seen Snow or Hero since then either. Even though his body ached with each step he took, he followed the sheriff. His injuries kept him from moving too fast.

As he drew closer, some instinct stopped him, whispering he should go back. *What the fuck*?

Deputy Dawson -- he hated that prick -- raced past him to get to the barn. Fighting whatever instinct gripped him, Crash kept walking. He was almost there. He might as well see what was going on.

Crash followed Sheriff Sawyer out to the barn,

his heart still pounding from the fight. The adrenaline was fading, leaving only the weight of what had just happened. The distant hum of the sheriff's cruiser lights flickered through the trees. The field stretched ahead of them, the grass damp beneath his boots, and in the distance, the barn loomed -- an old, forgotten relic that suddenly felt heavy with meaning.

As he got closer, the shadows around the barn seemed to thicken, the structure barely illuminated by the glow of the sheriff's flashlight. The door hung slightly ajar, swinging gently with the breeze, creaking like something out of a nightmare. The air felt different, heavier, and every step closer sent a chill down Crash's spine. He stopped, a sense of foreboding threatening to overwhelm him. Was it an aftereffect of the fight? Was he tired enough for his mind to play tricks on him?

Hearing the sheriff's booming voice pulled him out of his head. Other deputies ran past him, darting into the barn. The sheriff walked back out with Margot Donner. Crash fucking knew she'd show up. Yeah, she was one of Sawyer's deputies, but she also was with Ryder now. Perry told him he hoped Ryder would broom her fast, like he did all the other girls he went around with, but Crash defended her. Maybe it was because she let him go without a speeding ticket one night... and he'd certainly deserved it. As far as he could tell, Ryder was different with her. If she made their brother happy, what the fuck business was it of theirs?

Margot walked back in. Neither Margot nor Sawyer saw him as he reached the barn. Hero was walking out with Jade as Crash reached the entrance, and she was in tears. Hero's eyes widened in alarm.

"Hey, Crash," Hero said in a calm tone that

didn't match his expression. "The deputies are wrapping everything up here. Let's head back to the bar and find Razor."

A spike of fear pierced his heart as that sixth sense returned. Crash shook his head. "What's in there?" He pointed to the barn.

Jade's tear-filled eyes filled with fear as she looked from Hero to him and back. Something was in the barn. Why didn't they want him to see it? When Hero tried to block his entry, Crash shoved him to the side rougher than he should have. He passed a deputy with one of Bianchi's men in handcuffs and was greeted with the sight of Bianchi himself, a crumpled, bloody heap on the dirty straw floor. Scanning the room, he spotted Emily and Snow, Axel and Sadie. Margot was in Ryder's arms until he whispered something to her, the words prompting her to spin around and gaze at him with concern.

What the fuck *was going on*?

"Crash," Margot's tone was gentle. "Hey, why don't we go back up to *Sackett's*?"

His jaw clenched tightly. Pulling his phone from his jeans pocket, he turned on its light, the faint beam sweeping across the scene -- the broken bodies of Bianchi's other men, still sprawled where they'd fallen. The smell of blood hung thick in the air, mingling with the musty scent of old hay and dust.

His phone's light flickered across a dark space at the back of the barn, illuminating something lying on the dirt floor. Staring at it hard, he wasn't sure at first, just what he was seeing. As he moved closer, he realized there were bodies lying on something wooden. When realization hit, the sight hit him like a punch to the gut. There were three wooden crosses. Two of the crosses held bodies -- actually fucking nailed to them. One was Chance who was last seen tailing Bianchi's men out of town after they did a number on the garage.

The other was Perry. His fucking little brother, nailed to a cross.

It took Crash a minute to realize the horrible wail that filled the barn was his. Dashing to his brother's side, he checked for a pulse, for anything. Maybe he wasn't dead. Maybe... Crash's breath caught in his throat, his vision narrowing to just that terrible scene. Perry's lifeless body lay there, nailed to the wood like some twisted, cruel joke.

His little brother, who had followed him into this life, was now gone. Crash had fought so hard to keep him safe, to make sure he had a good life. His fists clenched at his sides, knuckles white. The devastation hit him in waves, like something too big to grasp all at once.

Crash had failed. All those years protecting Perry, shielding him from the worst of their stepfather's rage, only for him to end up here crucified like an offering in this godforsaken barn. His eyes burned, but he couldn't tear them away from Perry. Every memory of their childhood came flooding back, every promise to keep him safe shattered in this awful moment.

Chance's body lay limp on the cross, his skin a sickly, grayish hue, mottled with patches of dark bruising. The blood had long dried around the nails that pierced his hands and feet, and his clothes were torn and dirtied, clinging to his lifeless frame. His face was gaunt, lips cracked and pale, eyes half-lidded and hollow. He looked like he'd been dead for days -- left to rot as a message, the stench of decay faint but unmistakable.

And the empty cross between them, with Sadie's name on it, only twisted the knife deeper.

"I'm so sorry, Crash." Margot's voice was soothing. But it sounded like it came from miles away.

Crash felt the weight of everything settling on him. His past, the violence, the broken barn -- all of it. A hand pressed his shoulder. "Come on, brother." Snow's voice was low by his ear. "We'll do everything we can for him."

Blinded by tears and fury, he threw his VP's hand off. Jumping to his feet, he got in Snow's face. "He's dead. He's fucking dead! There's nothing we can do for him. He's just fucking gone!"

Snow put his hands up defensively, his expression sympathetic.

"When did this happen?" Crash pointed to his brother's lifeless form. "Was it before the fight?"

Searching the room until he spotted Ryder, he turned his anger on him. "I asked you where Perry was right before the shit hit the fan. Did you know he was dead then?"

Ryder had a decent poker face, but not that good. He'd known. Crash fucking knew he did, the sting of betrayal pushed his anxiety and grief higher. Before Ryder could speak, Crash shined the light of his phone on the bodies. "Look at Chance. Look at him! He didn't just fucking die. Looks like he's been fucking dead for days. And I haven't seen Perry since yesterday."

Only Axel remained silent, and it told him everything he needed to know.

Margot moved closer to him and regarded him like a cornered animal. Crash spun on her. "Get away from me!"

Crash ran out of the barn, running back to *Sackett's*, to his bike that had been knocked over into the dirt during the fight. Starting the engine, he raced out of the parking lot, spinning rocks as he went. His brother had been brutally fucking murdered by Bianchi and his men before the fight and the Hounds had known it. They hadn't told him. Why? *Why*? What had happened to the brotherhood?

Riding off into the night, the pain in Crash's heart was more than he could bear.

* * *

Crash slowed his bike. At the end of a cracked, weathered street in Oak Grove stood the old house, sagging under the weight of years of neglect. The paint, once a pale blue, had long faded to a dull gray, peeling in long strips, leaving the wood beneath exposed and cracked. The windows were dark, a few of them boarded up with new planks while others remained cracked, their glass spider-webbed with fractures.

The front yard was overgrown, tall grass and weeds swallowing the path that had once led to the front steps. Rusted remnants of a chain-link fence barely held together, leaning into the yard as if even it had given up trying to stand. The white front door was new, replacing the old one that had been swollen from years of rain and moisture seeping into the frame.

It was the house Crash and Perry had grown up in, a place haunted by memories of rage and violence. It sat at the edge of a poor neighborhood; the kind of house people avoided looking at as they passed. The faint scent of rot clung to it, like the tragedy of their mother's death and the years of neglect had seeped into the very bones of the structure.

Inside, there was plenty of evidence that Perry had been working on it, fixing the place up in hopes of selling it. His efforts were scattered -- half-patched walls, buckets of paint left abandoned, tools covered in a thin layer of dust. And the house still felt broken, like no amount of repair could ever erase the history etched into its walls. Still struggling with all its dark memories, Crash hadn't been able to bring himself to help with the house. Besides, his mind was always elsewhere, too wrapped up in trying to earn his place with the Hounds, and trying -- and failing -- to forget about Helena.

Now, the house stood empty, abandoned but not forgotten, a worn testament to everything they had lost.

Absently swiping at his tears, Crash wandered down the hallway that led to the bedroom they'd shared. The same twin beds that had been there since before he could remember remained, situated with an old, worn nightstand in the middle. The lamp that sat on it didn't have a lampshade, the light bulb jagged glass pointing upward from the socket. There were old clothes on the floor, underneath all the shit Larry had dumped into the room that he didn't want to deal with. Garbage bags filled with their mother's clothes, her books. There was also a bag of straight up garbage in there and Crash scoffed at that. Fucker was probably so high off his ass he didn't know what he put where. The room beneath all the boxes and bags dumped in it honestly didn't look a lot different than it had the day he took his little brother and left.

Crash had been seventeen, going through the motions of high school and not doing so hot. He'd really fucking wanted to drop out of school, but he knew the minute he did, Perry would do the same and he couldn't have that. Perry had smarts, did well in school. He knew their mother, Kelly Ford, wanted them to have something of an education and Crash was determined to honor her wishes.

Their lives had been anything but easy. Crash barely remembered his father. His parents had both been teenagers when they learned they'd be parents. Their families encouraged them to marry, set them up with a trailer that someone owned but wasn't using. Crash couldn't remember which side of the family provided that. They'd both dropped out of high school to keep their family afloat, and he knew it hit their mother hard.

She cried at night sometimes and it broke his heart when he'd been just a child. She'd let him crawl into her lap, play with his hair as he sat with her. When he asked her why she was so sad one night, her stomach huge with Perry, he was afraid it was his fault. Smiling through her tears, she told him that she was sad because she missed school and her friends. He could still feel her kiss on his forehead if he tried hard enough, the way her arms tightened around him. She'd whispered "I love you," in his ear, telling him that he was the best thing she'd ever done in her life. The baby, she explained, would be just like him and she hoped he'd always protect his little brother. She'd known she was having a boy.

Crash promised her he would. Fuck, he'd been three, but he meant it from then until today.

His father worked long hours, pushed through the injuries and wear and tear on his body. Crash didn't understand why at the time but when they'd moved out of the trailer and into a small house? His mother had been so proud of their new home. Seeing her happy meant a cheerful home for him and Perry, even though money was tight.

Marcus Ford fell on a construction site, died instantly, when Crash was six and Perry almost three.

It had been a dark day that colored the rest of his young life, still bleeding into his nightmares, and he woke up screaming sometimes. It was one of the reasons, no matter how fucked up he got at parties at the clubhouse that he refused to stay at the house once it was theirs. Crash wouldn't allow his depressing past to cross the barrier of his life as a Hound. Wasn't happening.

While their families had pushed their parents into marriage, Crash couldn't remember anyone offering to help. Their father had been their sole financial support. They'd had some lean times, including occasions when what little they had would be given to him and Perry. He still found it hypocritical to insist people get married and have a child that was an accident and then tell them they're on their own when they struggle with a life they weren't prepared for.

Yeah, Crash had family living still in Oak Grove. And they could all go fuck themselves.

Their mother had no choice but to find a job after their father died, and life was hard. Crash was in elementary school at the time, but Perry was only three. After a couple of dark months of eating whatever their mother could beg for or find at food pantries, she got a job at a small local day care facility. It didn't pay much but Perry could be there in return for half of her pay and Crash took the bus there after school and stayed quietly until she got off work. They made it work.

If only it had stayed that way.

Maybe their mother was just lonely. The first few boyfriends were one thing. Most of them were freeloaders who needed a place to couch surf. Their mother would share what food they had with them, clean up after them, take orders like she was a fucking maid. When Larry Canty came along, well, Crash hated him the most. At first, he seemed okay. He had a job, brought groceries home. Their mother let him move in when Crash was nine, and they married when he was ten. There were already warning signs before he put a ring on her finger. Larry would be fine one minute and snap the next, lost in a fit of pure rage that had him trashing the place and throwing their mother around like a rag doll.

After they married, their lives turned into a living hell. His mother gave up her job at the day care a little while later, but she hadn't wanted to. That left her dependent on Larry who came home looking for something to be out of place or not to his liking. His mother stayed covered in bruises and started taking them to their rooms after dinner each night. Crash could remember so vividly her tearful pleas for them to stay in their rooms, to work on homework and be quiet so Larry wouldn't be upset.

Their fight took a very ugly turn one night, while he and Perry sat huddled together on the floor between their beds. Perry had to go to the bathroom and since Crash couldn't find anything in their room to use as a receptacle, he led his brother out of the room to the bathroom. It had been terrifying because Larry raged in the kitchen. God only knew what was being thrown around, thrown at their mother. Her tearful pleas broke his heart, made him wish he was big enough to protect her, to beat Larry's ass and throw him out of their house.

He at least tried to protect Perry. They made it across the hall to the bathroom, quiet as they could be. Crash flushed, hoping the fit Larry pitched in the kitchen would mask the noise. They were afraid not to flush because that would blow him up too. As they made their way out of the bathroom, they turned in horror to see Larry marching down the hall in their direction.

"You were told to stay in your fucking room," Larry shouted, knocking Crash down with a sharp blow.

Their mother tried to pull Larry back, her nose bleeding. Crash just made it off the floor when Larry picked Perry up by the back of his shirt and the seat of his pants and slung him into their bedroom with so much force that the boy had rug burn on half his face for a week. His younger brother was eight. Crash ran into the room to his brother, standing as a trembling guard even though he knew there wasn't a lot he could do.

Larry, his face a mask of red fury, pointed at them. "Either one of you two little shits leave this room again tonight and I'll fucking knock you out!"

Kelly Ford Canty died when she was twenty-nine, a freak accident. She'd fallen in the shower and broke her neck. That's what Larry told the police who showed up. When one of the officers asked about all the other bruises on her body, Larry told them she'd been having really bad seizures over the last few weeks. He'd been trying to convince her to go to the doctor, he explained, but she didn't want to leave her "baby boys." Crash remembered the skepticism on one cop's face, but he let it go.

Within a week, their mother was buried and gone. Crash and Perry were left completely at the mercy of the monster who'd killed her. At the funeral, Crash saw the concerned faces of so many aunts, uncles, cousins who asked him and Perry if they were okay, if Larry was nice to them. Crash didn't try to answer. They all knew he'd been beating the shit out of her for the last four years. They didn't step in to save her. Why did they give a shit now?

What doesn't kill you makes you stronger, someone had said. It was the fucking truth. Because for the next several years, Larry trashed their parents' home, bringing in an endless parade of hookers and drug-addicted women, fucking them wherever he wanted in the house without a care for what either he or Perry saw. Yeah, their parents had done some weed from what he remembered. Their mother had done weed with Larry. But it hadn't taken long after their mother died that Larry branched out. Cocaine, meth, a river of alcohol.

When he brought women home, at least they kept him occupied. It was the days when Larry came home alone that terrified Crash. The beatings he and Perry took. Larry would trash the kitchen, get high, and forget he'd done it, blaming him and Perry. Crash took the beatings he could for Perry, but he wasn't always there.

That last year in the house, Crash got a job at a local burger joint. It was a big deal because most of Larry's money went to drugs, not food, and once again, Crash and Perry were starving. Everything he made went for food, other needs they had. Larry ate their food, so they found places to stash things that didn't need to be refrigerated. Larry took his money too if he could find it. They'd come home to find their room ransacked and he just knew the fucker had been looking for it, needing to pay for a fix.

And then that last day --

Crash's phone chimed. With a shaking hand, he fished it out of his jacket pocket. It was Razor. Yeah, he knew his Prez wanted to talk about everything. They had some explaining to do. Perry had been nailed to a cross in a barn behind *Sackett's*. Dead. Crash hadn't been able to save him. But he wasn't Perry's only brother now. Sure, his little brother was just a prospect for the Hounds. But as his brother, with Crash being a full member, he was supposed to be under the club's protection.

The club had failed Perry. They'd failed them both.

Crash sat on the edge of the old bed that had once been his for a long time.

Chapter Two

Helena
December

"How did your first week go?"

Helena Benjamin glanced up from her notes to see Margot Donner standing in her doorway, her brown uniform neat and pressed. Mercy's lone female deputy had kind dark eyes, a smile that could melt snowmen, and a presence big enough for someone twice her size. Helena didn't remember her from the first time she lived in Mercy, but she was grateful to have her as a friend now.

Pulling off her glasses, Helena smiled. "It's been a crazy, busy week but good. Yeah."

Wandering into her office and pulling off her hat, Margot motioned to one of the chairs on the other side of Helena's desk. "May I?"

"Of course," Helena said. "Excuse the mess. I thought I'd be able to get everything unpacked over Thanksgiving break and set up by now, but I've hardly been able to catch my breath."

"I'm sure it won't be as bad when Daphne gets back from maternity leave." Margot's expression was knowing. "You just look so tired."

In Helena's first week as a new therapist, she'd talked to two women just out of domestic violence situations, several recovering alcoholics and drug addicts, and a few kids from the high school dealing with everything from eating disorders to depression. Her worries about job security in such a small town quickly evaporated. If it stayed like this, she had nothing to worry about even when the practice was back to full staff.

It wasn't the sole reason she was tired though.

She'd been back in Mercy exactly two days when the nightmares returned. Visions of the handsome biker she'd fallen for haunted her dark dreams every night until she woke up soaked in sweat, tangled in her sheets. If she was lucky, she maybe had ten hours of sleep under her belt total, and she'd been back in town exactly eight days. Fatigue was her constant companion and nights when she was just trying to sleep were excruciating. She knew she needed to see someone about getting a script for something that would help her sleep, but the new job had been so busy.

"Have you given any thought to helping out with the children's Christmas party this year?" Margot asked, changing the subject. "It'll be my first year helping out too. They do such a good job."

"When's the initial meeting?" It was already the beginning of December.

"Knowing Emily, they've probably met up already. But they'll need lots of help."

Helena just hoped she be *able* to help. If her schedule stayed this insane... "How has your week been?"

"Crazy. At least I have this weekend off. I need it."

"You deserve it," Helena agreed.

"On top of our collective crazy week," Margot said, "I was wondering if I might ask for a favor. And if it's not okay, I'll understand."

"Sure. Name it."

"A friend of mine is having a really hard time," Margot explained. "His brother was murdered back during the summer and he's... shut out everyone around him. He still goes to work, goes home. He's just walled himself off and it's pretty obvious that he's struggling."

"I mean, if you can get him to show up for an appointment, I'd be glad to talk to him," Helena offered. "Is it someone in the sheriff's department?" Police work was filled with trauma from the situations officers were placed in and the horrible things they saw. In her first therapist job back in Charleston, she'd had more than a few police officers as regulars.

Margot shook her head. "No. He's one of the Hounds of Hell. If that poses a problem, believe me, I'll understand. And I haven't mentioned the idea to him or anyone else."

Helena froze. Margot's friend was a Hound? The last time she'd lived in Mercy, lots of bikers crossed her path when she was a server at *Sackett's*. If she hadn't made the mistake of getting involved with one, she wouldn't be verging on panic right now. She'd be able to tell Margot that she was glad to help.

Placing her hands in her lap, she hoped Margot didn't notice they were shaking. Almost like a warning, the scar on her jaw burned beneath the makeup that covered it. Her mind scrambled for an excuse to offer. But what was she going to say? She'd prefer not to have any biker as a patient because she'd been stupid enough to have an abusive relationship with a Cottonmouth and then hooked up with one of the Hounds years ago? She'd barely survived Jared Crizer, who most people knew as Baby Face. She hoped Margot couldn't tell how fast her anxiety was escalating.

If she didn't agree to try and help anyone, what kind of therapist did that make her?

Wait. "I'm curious," Helena said slowly. "*You* have a friend who's in a MC?"

Margot grinned. "Oh, it's worse than that. My

boyfriend is a Hound too. But he's not the one I'm trying to get in here to talk to you."

What? "Your boyfriend is a Hound?" Helena tried to wrap her mind around that. "How does that work with you being a deputy?"

Margot laughed. "One day at a time, honestly. But he's worth it."

"That's what matters." Helena blew out a breath. While her own history with Baby Face made her leery of having anything to do with any biker, at least neither Margot's friend nor her boyfriend was a Cottonmouth. They were Hounds and from what she remembered, most of them were decent. Especially...

No, you're not thinking about Crash *or that night you spent with him.*

Helena knew if she wanted to establish herself as a therapist in Mercy, she couldn't let her personal views or fears influence her job in any way. She was there to help people improve their mental health and cope with life's challenges. A good therapist's door was open to anyone barring those she had personal relationships with. She couldn't cherry pick her patients. And Crash? He'd just been a prospect five years ago when she knew him. What were the odds it was him?

"Yeah, if he thinks it would help and is willing to come in for an appointment, I'd be glad to see him," Helena said, making her decision. "We also do telehealth appointments. But I ask to see new patients in person on their first visit. If they're able."

Margot's dark eyes lit up. "Thank you. I really appreciate it. He's not listening to any of us and I'm just worried that the longer he lingers like this, the worse it's going to get."

"That's often the case," Helena replied.

"Mourning a loved one is hard. If you can get him to agree, text me and I'll put him on the schedule myself. But with Christmas right around the corner, and since the holidays are hard on a lot of people, my schedule is filling up pretty fast."

"I'd be glad to." Rising from the chair, Margot grabbed one of Helena's business cards and tucked it into her pocket before putting her hat back on. "His name is Charlie Ford."

The name wasn't familiar to her. The bikers Helena had known years ago, she'd known by their club names. The only reason she knew Baby Face's real name was from the police reports she'd had to file against him. Quickly, she scribbled the name on her notepad. "I've got it down." Helena watched the deputy walk back to her office door. "Let me know."

"Have a good weekend," Margot told her.

A beat later, one of the ladies at the desk let her know her next patient was there. The timing was good because it left her no time to wonder if she'd made the right choice in agreeing to help Margot.

* * *

Crash

It was a cold ride on his bike to the clubhouse. His body hurt from a long day on the construction site. Their client was pushing hard at them to finish the project by the end of the year but neither Crash nor Beast, their company's foreman, saw how that was even fucking possible. When Beast offered up weekends the client had balked at paying extra for that. And they wanted time and a half if they were going to sacrifice their weekends.

Crash had been spending his weekends at the house in Oak Grove. He owed it to Perry to finish what he'd started in fixing up the house they grew up in. It had been several weeks now, and he was making good progress on repairing what he could fix and replacing what he could afford. Dwelling there with the memories and pain that lived in that house now was an exercise in masochism, but it didn't deter him. Not anymore.

When he pulled up to the clubhouse, he wasn't surprised to see a squad car in the lot. It took most of them a while to get used to seeing the police in their private space. Normally, that wasn't a good sign. But it was just Margot, now Ryder's old lady. It wasn't uncommon for her to stop in when she knew he'd be there. But today, she was just sitting in her car. Waiting. Was Ryder meeting her there?

Parking his bike and killing the engine, Crash intended to go to his room, grab his shit, and ride out to Oak Grove. Out of the corner of his eye, he saw Margot emerge from the squad car as he climbed off the bike. Margot was headed his way. *What was this*?

"Hey, Crash." Her greeting was casual. "How are you?"

Taking a deep breath, Crash steeled himself for what was coming. Since Perry's murder, the Hounds handled him carefully because they didn't know what else to do. The day after the battle at *Sackett's*, Crash met Razor, Snow, Hero and the twins. They'd explained to him the timeline of events from the discovery of the Mafia's message to the battle at *Sackett's*. The crosses with two of their prospects, one of them Perry, along with the one left for Sadie, had been set up behind the clubhouse. The macabre scene had been left there as a message.

Logically, Crash understood why they didn't call the police when the discovery was made. He got why they moved their fallen brothers until after the skirmish where they planned to deal with Robert Bianchi and his Mafia army. They left Chance and Perry nailed to the crosses because they still had to deal with the police at the end of the day, and saying they'd tampered with the scene was an understatement.

But Perry wasn't just some scrappy prospect that ended up at the wrong place at the wrong time. Perry was his fucking brother. *His birth brother*. Their Hound brothers didn't know a lot about their backstory. They had no idea of the vow Crash had made long ago to protect his brother with his own life. And yeah, Perry hadn't been a member of the club yet. But as Crash's brother, that put him under the club's protection. They'd all had an obligation to protect Perry. Yet no one could tell him how Perry ended up there, what led up to his death.

Surely, even with all the Bianchi shit going on, someone had some idea of why Perry had been on his assignment alone. The assignments were supposed to have been in pairs. Crash couldn't decide if they were hiding something from him or if they just didn't fucking know. Either way, it had put him at odds with the Hounds and these days they treated him like he was a ticking bomb.

"What's up?" Crash asked, cutting to the chase. He was tired and wanted to get to Oak Grove.

"Look, you know everyone is concerned about you," Margot started carefully.

Holding up a hand to cut her off, Crash shook his head. "Save it. I'm not in the mood right now."

"You never are." Margot walked with him as he marched toward the front door of the clubhouse. "I just had an idea and if you don't like it, you can just tell me to fuck off like you always do."

That was one of the few things he appreciated about Margot. He *could* tell her to fuck off and she didn't take it personally. "I'll save us both some time." Crash grabbed the doorknob and opened the door. "Fuck off." He shut the door in her face as he walked in. That was the end of it.

But he made it maybe four steps when Margot walked in behind him. Speeding up, she got in front of him, stopping him. Crash blew out a breath, staring her down. He really wasn't in the fucking mood for whatever it was she thought would help. He didn't *want* to be helped.

"Crash, there's a new therapist in town and she's really good," Margot said, patient and calm. "She said if you were willing to come for an appointment, she'd be glad to talk to you."

Crash scoffed. "Not interested, Margot." He lived every day with his memories and scars. How the fuck was stopping and explaining it to someone else going to fucking help? He didn't want therapy. Fuck that. Walking around her, Crash marched in the direction of his room.

"Just think about it," Margot called after him. "Helena's really great."

Helena? It couldn't be. Crash stopped, turning around to see Margot walking back for the door. "What did you say?"

She stopped instantly. Her dark eyes lit up with hope. "I said Helena's really great."

When he didn't move, Margot walked back to him. "She just moved back to town. She's willing to talk to you if you think it might help. She said she likes to see people in person at least on the first visit. After that, you can do it over video chat so it's convenient.

What do you say?" Reaching into the pocket of her jacket, she fished out a business card and handed it to him.

Helena Benjamin was stamped at the top in elegant, bold lettering. *It was her.*

"If you want to talk to her, let me know what day and time is good and I'll let her know," Margot said. "She said her schedule was filling up with the holidays coming up so…"

Crash nodded, hanging onto the card. "I'll think about it."

It was comical the way her already big dark eyes widened. "Great! Just shoot me a text or something to let me know. Okay?"

With a nod, he turned and headed for his room, his mind spinning. Shutting himself in his room, he barely gave any thought to the items he shoved into his backpack. Clothes, toiletries, a phone charger. He went through the motions while his head and heart fought.

Helena Benjamin was back in town. And now she was a therapist?

Crash hadn't seen her since that rainy fall night when she took him back to her place and rocked his world. Memories of that night still played in his mind, reminding him of the last time he'd taken a chance on happiness, only to have it turn into another painful chapter in his life.

Crash had hung around *Sackett's* for months that year. Hanging out at the bar was what a lot of the Hounds did when they had downtime. It wasn't really his scene but one night he went with Outcast and Player to play a little pool, have a few beers. He could still remember perfectly the first time he saw her. Like an image from a dream, he saw her in his mind's eye walking his way. Her raven hair framed her face in soft waves that reached her shoulders, showing off a beautiful face with big green eyes. It always made him weak in the knees when she turned those eyes and that gorgeous smile on him.

Helena often wore tight jeans and modest tops that showed off her petite figure. She barely reached his shoulder but her long, slender arms and legs made her appear to be taller. Her ass was small, firm. Her breasts were generous, always filling out the tops she wore. He still remembered that first night how she introduced herself to the three prospects, her gaze lingering on Crash. She checked in on them a few times that night and kept the beer and whiskey flowing. They'd closed down the bar that night, Crash somehow managing to play with an aching cock and eyeful of Helena. He'd hoped maybe she'd walk out with him, come home with him. But nothing happened. Not that night and for many that followed.

Crash hadn't given up and he hadn't seen her go around with anyone else. He thought maybe he had a chance.

That night she'd taken him home with her. It was burned into his memory. He remembered how she shook out in the rain behind the bar, smoking and in tears under a huge black umbrella. He easily recalled the scent of her perfume in her car as he drove them back to her place. The way she kissed him was heavenly, accented with need. His memory of the way she invited him to stay the night with her never failed to make his heart fly. Crash hadn't wanted the night to end. Everything about her felt right. The way she touched him. The way her body felt. If he tried, he could still remember how the silk of her hair felt against his cheek, the little sighs she made in her sleep. Crash had fallen asleep happy, hoping that maybe there was something there.

Shaking his head, he shoved the rest of his shit into the backpack and slung it over his shoulder as he marched back out into the clubhouse. He thought Razor shouted something to him from his office in the back. Crash didn't even pause. He just barked "I'm out!" as he slammed the door behind him.

It had started to rain as he guided his bike out of the clubhouse lot. It was cold but he didn't feel it. The painful memories of the next morning crowded into his brain as he drove. When he'd woken up, Helena was gone. Just gone. No note with her phone number. He'd checked his phone to see if by any chance she'd put her number in it. Nothing.

There hadn't been a lot of light the night before in the room where she'd had him, but in the light of day, the room was pretty bare. He would have expected to see makeup or perfume bottles on the dresser, her intimates in its drawers. But the top of the furniture piece was empty and so were the drawers. There was a small closet in the room, but none of her clothes were there. No shoes. Nothing. Crash had tried to rationalize everything all day at work. Maybe she'd just moved into a new place. Maybe there was a reasonable explanation for all of it. There *had* to be.

Panic didn't set in until he'd gotten to *Sackett's* after work. Helena always worked Thursday nights. But there'd been no sign of her. After a couple of hours battling his thoughts and downing whiskey, he finally asked another of the girls if she knew where Helena was. The younger woman had told him she'd quit. That was all she knew. The disappointment had been crushing. Crash had eyed her for months and he'd finally gotten a chance. They'd spent the night together and he'd thought it was amazing. He'd wanted to see her again.

Crash had driven by the duplex on Vermilion Street twice a day for a month. Her car wasn't there. No one answered the door. When he drove home from work the next week, he saw a realtor's sign in the yard announcing it was available to rent. Just like that, Helena was gone from his life. It was over before it ever had a chance to start. And it killed him. It left him to wonder if he'd done something wrong. Had he missed something that night?

It was dark and a storm was coming in when Crash reached the house where he grew up. The house was hollow and cold when he strode in, soaked from the chilly autumn rain.

Crash'd had the power reconnected last week and when he flipped the light switch in the kitchen, the warm light was an improvement. The kitchen had new cabinets, gently used appliances, and fresh paint and new light fixtures. The kitchen and dining room shared space. He'd taken the old broken table and chairs to the dump, and he planned to check out some thrift shops to see what he could find this weekend for the bare dining room.

But he just couldn't get Margot's offer, or Helena, out of his head. He shrugged off his jacket, left his boots at the door. He had a few microwave meals in the freezer, and he got one of those ready, watching it rotate in the appliance mindlessly.

Since Helena was a therapist now, maybe Crash really did need a fucking therapist. She was at least part of the reason why. Should he take Margot up on her offer? Shouldn't he at least confront the woman he'd spent a single night with and ask what the fuck happened that next day? He deserved to know why she left him and ripped his heart out, didn't he?

Crash turned on the small space heater next to the threadbare couch that had been in the living room since he was a boy. A flatscreen TV was mounted over the fireplace, but he watched the news without really taking anything in. He ate the convenient meal he'd prepared but he didn't taste it. All he could do was weigh the decision in his head. Did he have Margot make the appointment for him? Or did he let it go just like Helena had five years ago? What if he got an answer to his questions and it made it worse? What if it only brought more pain?

With a deep sigh, he realized he couldn't carry on like this.

Sometime around midnight, Crash pulled his phone from his pocket. Before he could change his mind, he pulled the business card Margot gave him from the pocket of his leather jacket. *Helena Benjamin.* Crash sent Margot a text, hitting send before he could talk himself out of it.

I'll take that appointment. Next week. I want the first spot available.

Chapter Three
Helena

The display on her phone showed it was one in the afternoon and time for her first appointment after lunch. The appointment was for Charlie Ford. Margot had just asked her about seeing him on Friday and it was now Monday. That went a lot faster than she'd anticipated. A biker agreeing to therapy? When her office phone rang, it startled her.

Answering, with a quick "Hello," she heard Gemma at the front desk.

"Charlie Ford is here," Gemma said.

"Please send him back." Margot had mentioned his brother had died back in the summer and that he was still struggling with it. Flipping to a new page of her legal pad, Helena was ready for her new patient and their first meeting.

Until he walked in. Charlie Ford was a new patient, but he wasn't new to her. She had known his ruggedly handsome face. She knew what the rest of him looked like too, and shadowy memories of that night flashed in her mind.

Helena knew after what had happened with Baby Face that she'd have to leave Mercy. She could have just let him drive her home that night without inviting him into her bed. No, she'd done that out of pure selfishness. She resented the fact that she had to leave to save herself and it'd robbed her of a chance with Crash. That night, she decided she was owed something for all she'd been through without stopping to think of the impact it might have on someone who was blameless in the entire mess. Her heart raced as his gaze met hers. In an instant, she realized he recognized her too. Now, she was facing the consequences of her selfishness.

Why hadn't Margot mentioned his club name?

"Hello, Helena," he said quietly.

Crash was just as gorgeous as ever, maybe even more now. Tall and muscular, her office seemed smaller with him in it. Her heart flew, making her catch her breath. His blond hair was a little longer than he'd used to wear it, just reaching his broad shoulders. His eyes were still the bright blue of a summer sky. But there was a hardness in those eyes as his gaze moved over her. Any softness from his face was gone, now all hard planes and angles. His mouth was a grim line as he took a seat in one of the chairs on the other side of her desk. "Thank you for talking to me today."

She didn't miss the sarcasm in his voice.

"Hello, Crash," she told him, struggling to keep her emotions in check. After that one night they'd had together, she'd disappeared on him with no explanation. She'd left the bar, left town without a word to anyone. She'd told herself for the thousandth time she had to. But the cold anger she read on Crash's face was completely justified. She didn't blame him. He had no way of knowing why she'd run from Mercy like the devil was on her heels. Because, truthfully, he had been.

Worse, Helena had to explain that because of that night they shared, she couldn't ethically see him as a therapist. His brother was dead and he needed help, and she couldn't offer that because of her own selfish, stupid actions. It took her down a peg, making her remember the desperate girl who'd always looked for someone else to save her.

"This is a little awkward," Helena said after they stared at each other for a beat.

"No shit." Crash folded his heavily muscled

arms across the wide expanse of his chest, holding her gaze.

"I'm very sorry," Helena said quietly. "If I'd known it was you, I could have spared you a trip here. I apologize."

His brows lifted at that, amusement bleeding into his expression as if he were enjoying her discomfort.

"Margot told me she had a friend who was in the Hounds who lost his brother back in the summer and that she thought he might benefit him to talk to a therapist." Truth was best. "I only knew you as Crash, not your real name."

"Crash *is* my real name," he said coldly. "And you don't know anything about me. You only gave me a few hours and I don't remember doing much talking." Oh, he was angry. But then she realized that while she hadn't known who he was when the appointment was set, he would have recognized her name. It was the reason he was here. This wasn't for treatment. He was here because he was pissed and wanted her to know it.

Now, she just needed to be a big girl and take it, hear him out.

"You're right." It still made her feel like an enormous pile of shit. "I shouldn't have just left like that. There were a lot of things going on in my life at the time, things I ran from. But none of it justified my doing that to you. You didn't deserve it. And I truly am sorry, Crash."

Surprise flashed in those baby-blue eyes but was gone in an instant. He was listening to what she was saying but it was clear he wasn't just easily going to forgive her. Why did she think it would just be that simple?

"That's it?" Crash's voice was tinged with anger, the hurt in his gaze making it so much worse. "Is it that easy? Sorry about five years ago. Let's talk about what's bothering you?" Shaking his head, he scrubbed a hand over the short blond beard he wore now. "You're a big fucking part of what's bothering me."

The guilt he was forcing her to confront made it difficult to stay within her professional persona. *It was just one night.* She almost said it. But that didn't sound right. If she hadn't been running scared, it would have been more than one night. She would have wanted more even though he was a biker, and another biker had nearly destroyed her. Just having him there now, glaring at her from across the desk, stirred up old feelings she had no business examining.

Why did she think it was okay to just spend the night with him and toss him away like that? Sure, men did it to women all the time. Men like him, *bikers*, were notorious for taking what women offered and tossing it away without giving a fuck. But that wasn't who she thought Crash was back then. It really wasn't who she was either.

"I understand that. I can't change my actions, but I can apologize and take accountability. I'm ashamed of what I did." She was. "I just hope in time you'll accept my apology. It wasn't my intention to hurt you in any way. And with the recent loss of your brother, it was the last thing you needed to deal with right now."

Angry red darkened his face and neck. That told her he wasn't anywhere near accepting her apology. It made the next thing she had to say terrifying.

"Because of that night," she said slowly. "I can't ethically see you as a therapist, Crash. I'm very sorry. It's... completely my fault. If I can't work with you from a detached, professional point of view, I can't give you the help you need." Taking a deep breath because he just sat motionless in that chair, she rushed on to say, "There are two other wonderful therapists here and --"

Slamming a heavy hand on her desk, Crash stared her down. "I didn't want to talk to a fucking therapist at all!" he yelled. "I just wanted to see what you had to say to me now. Maybe get an answer on why you fucking cut out like you did that night."

Tears stung the backs of her eyes. The persona she put on for her patients was torn to shreds. One thing she truly appreciated about being a therapist was her position in any given conversation. It wasn't so much being in a position of power as it was being the person listening, offering to help, offering the lifeline. She'd been scrutinized and given so much unwanted advice in her life for being young, naïve, and lost by people who were passive-aggressive, manipulative or just plain mean. Helena had wanted to be a therapist to be the opposite of those people. She wanted to actually help others, offer the help she wished she'd received when she needed it.

She'd made so many poor or abrupt decisions in the past because she only had herself for counsel and not much life experience. But she'd tried to do better.

It had been the hardest thing she'd ever done, but she'd gone back to school, completing her bachelor's and master's degrees in five years. Once she had two or three years of supervised clinical experience, what she was working toward in Mercy now, she'd be a licensed therapist. Becoming a therapist had shown her what she could achieve. She'd thought the past was long behind her. If she hadn't, she wouldn't have returned to Mercy. But here, in her second week on the job, another of her past mistakes was yelling at her in her office.

"This isn't the time or place for that," she said, trying to use her professional tone and missing it by a mile. "You just said you weren't interested in talking to a therapist and I can't talk to you in that capacity because of our history. So maybe at some point, we could have a beer and talk about everything that happened. Would that work?"

Helena had to de-escalate the situation. Otherwise, with all the shouting and slamming, she was afraid someone might call the police. Margot had believed he needed help because of his brother's loss. Helena had hurt him too and she didn't want to do him further harm.

Crash still stared at her in cold fury. "Yeah? You think we can go have a beer and talk about it? I can't even trust you to show up." Rising from the chair in a quick, fluid motion, Crash strode for the door. With his hand on the doorknob, he stopped. "I'm sorry I came."

He didn't slam his way out of her office like she expected. But his parting words caused the crack in her heart to deepen. There had been an hour allotted for his appointment, and he'd swept through her like a hurricane, leaving her devastated in his wake all in ten minutes. Scrambling to lock her door, she didn't want to talk to anyone right now. She let the tears come.

* * *

Crash

He felt Beast's gaze on him as he marched back onto the construction site, carrying his toolbox and eager to get back to work. Crash needed his mind occupied so he wouldn't think about *her* and the whole mess that had just gone on in her office for his so-called therapy appointment.

"How'd it go?" Beast called over the din of machinery all around them.

Crash shook his head. He just wanted to get back to work on the fucking new bank they were building. Hadn't Beast told him they were already a week behind? "Waste of time," he grumbled. "It was a stupid-ass idea. I shouldn't have agreed to it." He was still pissed his brother even knew about it. Fucking Margot.

Beast's dark eyes showed a hint of surprise. After a minute he shrugged because they had a job to do. Since Crash had been gone less than an hour, there really wasn't anything he needed to be brought up to speed on. It was a crisp December day. The faster he got to work, the quicker he'd warm up.

Wiping the sweat from his brow, Crash's muscles strained as he lifted another stack of concrete blocks into place. The sun didn't do a lot to cut through the cold, but he barely felt it. His mind was somewhere else, replaying that damn appointment with Helena repeatedly. The truth was he hadn't gone there to get his head fixed. Did he look like the therapy type? Crash wanted answers. Instead, he walked out more wound up than when he went in.

Beast called out to him, reminding him to keep pace. "You gettin' sleepy over there, Crash, or is that just your old man knees givin' out?" His boss grinned, but Crash didn't acknowledge him. His head wasn't in it today and it wasn't likely to fucking change.

Leaning against the half-built wall, hands tightening around the rough cinder block, Crash stared at the ground. The steady thrum of construction filled the air all around him and it was a straightforward job. Building a bank, brick by brick. But he couldn't get Helena out of his head. The way those big green eyes widened when she realized exactly who her patient was.

What had he expected? An apology? An explanation? The apology he got but she only hinted at an explanation, and without it her fucking apology meant nothing. All he got was her trying to play therapist while dodging the real conversation. And yeah, part of him enjoyed watching her squirm in her posh little office, fumbling for words when she realized he wasn't just another case file. No, he was a guy she'd walked out on. At one point, he had her on the verge of tears, and it'd felt good -- like maybe she finally understood just what she'd done to him.

But satisfaction didn't last long.

Slapping mortar onto the next row of blocks with his trowel, Crash's muscles were working on autopilot. What had he really wanted from her, anyway? He wasn't sure he knew the answer to that. He wasn't the same guy he was five years ago, and yet the second he saw her, it was like no time had passed at all. All those feelings -- the ones he thought were dead and buried -- came rushing back, clouding his mind. The feelings he'd had for her were still very much there, tangled up with anger and hurt.

Helena didn't owe him a damn thing. She'd been the one to leave. But it didn't keep him from wanting something. He couldn't decide if he wanted to punish her or pull her closer. Maybe it was a little of both. With a deep sigh, he shoved the next block into place with more force than necessary. The entire situation was a mess. Therapy was the last thing he needed -- someone picking apart his brain. What he needed were answers, something to settle the storm still raging inside him. Helena? She was part of that storm, and he couldn't let that go.

"If you're done daydreaming," Beast's voice pulled him out of his thoughts, "we've got a schedule to keep."

"Yeah, I'm good," Crash muttered, picking up the pace again. There was a lot for him to sort through. Right now, he needed to focus on his job.

* * *

Kimmie grinned at Crash from the other side of the bar. "Hey, darlin'. What can we do for you this evening?"

Inside Big Billy's, the Cottonmouths' notorious hangout, the atmosphere felt oppressive, thick with tension and stale cigarette smoke. The bar was dimly lit, the flickering neon signs above casting an eerie, sickly glow over the cracked vinyl booths and scuffed wooden floors. The bar counter stretched along one wall, worn from years of rough use. The dark wood was scratched and gouged, and the stools along it were patched with duct tape, their edges fraying. A line of whiskey bottles gleamed in the sparse light, their labels faded and peeling.

A pool table sat off to one side, the faded green felt peppered with cigarette burns and a few old, dark stains that had probably seen more than spilled beer. A jukebox in the corner cycled through a mix of old rock and outlaw country, its speakers crackling and barely holding onto a tune. The patrons -- mostly Cottonmouths and their regulars -- eyed newcomers with suspicion, their gazes sharp and assessing, like wolves deciding if you were worth the trouble. There were maybe two there who would recognize him, but neither made a move. If they wanted an ass beating, he was down for it tonight.

The air reeked of cheap booze and burnt rubber, a hint of motor oil hanging in the background. Fights were a regular occurrence, and the evidence was clear: a couple of patched-up walls, a broken mirror behind the bar, and a battered "NO FIGHTS" sign barely hanging on a nail near the restroom. Everything about the place screamed hostile territory, from the dark red light casting shadows over tattooed faces, to the clinking of glasses that sounded more like a threat than a celebration.

Crash hated being in the Cottonmouth hangout but for what he wanted, he didn't really have a choice. He hated leaving his colors out in his car, shrugging off his MC just to be here. But the Hounds didn't deal in pussy, and he needed relief. *Tonight.*

What the fuck would they say to him? That he was betraying his MC? He'd *love* to have that talk with any of them. Where the fuck was the loyalty when the Mafia fucks got his brother? Nailed him to a fucking cross? Either way, he stayed alert, his back against the wall, wary of every glance sent his way. He wasn't a Cottonmouth, and he sure as hell wasn't welcome.

"I'll take a bourbon," Crash told the pretty green-eyed waitress. As he slid three hundred-dollar bills across the counter to her, he said, "And my usual."

Excitement lit up her face as she counted the bills, folded them over and tucked them into her bra. "Give me fifteen to get set up, okay?"

Crash nodded. It'd give him time to down his drink. He hadn't been able to shut his mind down all day. After he'd replayed and analyzed the shit out of his therapy appointment, it occurred to him that maybe he *did* need therapy.

If he took Helena out of the equation, yeah, Margot was right. He'd been struggling since the Mafia fuckers crucified his baby brother. He hadn't known about Perry's death until the fight was over, and it was too late to exact revenge on any of them. Bianchi was killed by the twins, most of his men either killed with him or taken to jail. And none of the Mafia had returned to Mercy since that night at *Sackett's*.

It didn't do Crash a damn bit of good. None.

He was still a Hound but life with his brothers wasn't the same. It took a while, but he understood why they had moved the crosses and the bodies of their fallen prospects until after the ambush at the bar. Still, a sense of betrayal burned him every time he thought about it. Why hadn't his brothers told him before the ambush? Had they been afraid he would upend their plans in his sorrow and rage? Had they just not cared enough to even think of it? Sure, they were sorry *after* the fact. Razor and the rest had talked to him for an hour the next day as they sat beaten and bloodied in the clubhouse. But Crash had mostly listened while they talked at him. When he hadn't gone back to being good ole Crash, it raised concerns among his brothers. They'd tried to talk to him, but they had no way of knowing how much damage their decision had done. Perry had been heading out to his post near Cowboy Pete's the last time Crash saw him the day before *Sackett's*. Doing the math, he realized that's when they must have gotten hold of his birth brother because he'd wound up dead on a cross by that night.

Downing the whiskey in health gulps, Crash felt it burn its way down to his stomach, welcoming it. As he waited, he spotted a kid who reminded him of Perry at the end of the bar, telling tall tales with a couple of other young bucks who were probably Cottonmouth prospects. Perry used to be animated like that when he talked, big hand gestures and wild-eyed expressions.

Crash recalled the last time he'd talked to Perry. All he could remember was his brother's excitement at everything going on. He was sure they'd find Chance and kick Mafia ass the next day at the ambush that was planned. Crash hadn't been as nice to him as he could have been. He'd told him to just focus on his post and report anything he saw that was out of place. He hadn't even wanted Perry anywhere near the damn fight at *Sackett's*. Perry was strong like he was, but his little brother was tall and slight. Perry had never been much of a fighter, but he was fast as lightning on a drag strip.

Crash had gone to bed early. He hadn't heard from Perry, hadn't worried about it. His little brother had been dead and gone, and Crash hadn't known.

"Hey!" Kimmie stood before him, her red hair covered up by a sleek black wig. In all black from the barely-there tank top to the painted-on jeans and boots, she looked more like a goth girl than like Helena. Fuck, she'd do. "Are you ready?"

"I'll take another one of these." He held up his empty glass.

Nodding, Kimmie called at another girl behind the bar, barking at her to refill his glass and which bourbon to use. Once he had his refill in hand, he followed Kimmie to the back where the girls who worked for Big Billy took the men who paid them for special favors. They kept those small bedrooms a bit nicer than the bar out front. Crash downed his second drink, placing the glass on the bedside table as he sat on the edge of the bed and pulled off his boots.

Kimmie hastily pulled off her own boots, somehow made it out of those tight jeans in a way that wasn't comical. When she went down on her knees, he spread his thighs. Expertly, she opened his jeans, and he took them down for her. When she took control of his dick with her hands, got her mouth on him, his eyes slid closed.

All he could see was Helena. Today, he saw her again as she'd sat across from him. Those striking green eyes that once seemed to pierce right through him, framed by thick, dark lashes. Her long black hair, which he remembered in shimmering waves around her face, lying flat with a few stray strands escaping the loose braid draped over her shoulder. Her face had been as beautiful as ever with those high cheekbones and full, inviting lips, holding a softness he hadn't forgotten. She'd always looked like a dark angel to him, delicate features offset by a quiet strength.

As Kimmie worked him into her mouth, he remembered the weariness that'd clung to Helena in that office, settling into the faint lines around her eyes and mouth. She looked like she hadn't slept in a week, the shadows under her eyes betraying a heaviness he couldn't ignore. Helena's beauty was tinged with fatigue, as if the weight of the years and the battles she'd fought had taken their toll. The brightness he remembered had dimmed; her fiery gaze muted. She still looked like his dark angel, but this version was worn down, rougher around the edges. And damn if that didn't make her more captivating, despite the ache of anger and regret he still felt.

Crash was close but he didn't want to come in Kimmie's mouth. Taking her head in his hands, he pulled her off him. If he just slit his eyes open a little, he could almost pretend she *was* Helena. Motioning for her to get on the bed, he put her on all fours and ripped off her thong, pushing her head down so her ass was just where he wanted it. Grabbing the condom she'd left on the edge of the bed, he tore into the package, rolled it on quickly. Sinking into Kimmie, his hands grabbed her hips roughly. Helena never left his mind as he fucked Kimmie hard and fast.

Maybe he *did* need to talk to someone. Crash didn't feel any better. Bottled up anger at his brothers -- at *her* -- just kept building more pressure. The resentment choked him to the point that sometimes he just had to walk out of club functions, even the fun ones. More and more he knew Margot was right, though he'd never tell her that. He *was* struggling. Helena just made things more complicated.

Yeah, he knew he shouldn't have gone to that appointment. He'd gone just to confront her, to watch her scramble to try and explain to him why she fucked him over. But honestly, Helena *was* a therapist. Maybe in her new career she could help him out.

Except she couldn't because they'd shared one night together. And then she'd walked out on him.

Kimmie's breathy cries and moans were background noise as Crash worked himself inside her, chasing release. The memories from meeting with Helena in her office earlier played over and over in his mind. Had she been afraid of him? Yes. Had she still wanted him?

The signs were subtle, but there. The way her hands shook on the desk in front of her, how her breath hitched when he slammed his hand down on her desk. Her eyes, those green eyes that haunted his dreams, had flicked to his mouth more than once. Oh yeah, she was still interested. That was the part that twisted him up the most, knowing she wasn't as over him as she acted, even if she didn't want to admit it.

Crash growled loudly as he came, thrusting hard into the woman he fucked a few more times as he rode out his release. As he watched her drop onto the bed, he fought to get his breath back under control. He needed to get *himself* back under control. Pulling up his jeans, he realized he needed to talk to someone about his inability to get over the past, the loss of his brother. He wanted to talk to Helena about what'd happened that night while pushing down the small hope that maybe there was a future for them, a second chance. Two birds, one stone.

The question: what was he going to do about it?

Chapter Four

Helena

Helena closed the door to her office when she arrived that Friday, leaning against it, her hands trembling as she let out a shaky breath. She'd stopped to gas up her car at the small station across the street from the building where she worked. Margot had invited her to attend the first meeting for Mercy's annual children's Christmas party committee after work. Getting gas before work instead of after as she normally did would just make things easier.

Until it wasn't. Helena nearly dropped the gas nozzle trying to return it to its holster when she heard the roar of a motorcycle coming up fast. And it had been exactly who she'd expected -- Crash. Although this was in an area where there were two good-sized MCs with many members, of course it had to be him. Five years hadn't dulled the effect he had on her, not even close. The moment their eyes met across the gas station lot, it was like her heart forgot how to beat.

Pressing a hand to her chest, she willed herself to breathe steadily. But her mind raced with too many thoughts. How could she have been so blind? She'd agreed to meet one of Margot's friends, knowing he was a biker but thinking it would be just another patient. Professional. Straightforward. But the second Crash had walked in, her composure crumbled. His eyes, still burning with that mix of anger and something else, had ripped completely through her carefully constructed facade.

The worst part? Helena couldn't blame him for being angry. She'd had it coming. She'd walked out on him that night. No goodbye, no explanation, nothing. Leaving seemed like the right move back then. Helena knew she couldn't stay because of the threat she was facing. So, she'd settled for just one night of amazing, mind-blowing sex. What man would say no to that? And then she disappeared.

Helena had been running from many things: her past, an escalating, violent situationship, and her fear of getting too close to anyone.

Now, seeing Crash again, regret clawed at her chest. It was the way he looked at her. It was more than just anger. Hurt waited beneath the surface, the unspoken question hanging between them. *Why*? Why had she left? She could still feel the weight of his gaze, the tension crackling in the air between them. To top it all off, the part she hated to admit, was that she still felt something for him. That pull, that undeniable connection, was still there, no matter how hard she'd tried to bury it.

Helena rubbed her temples, closing her eyes as she fought to calm the storm inside her head. She was a therapist now, a professional. Helena had worked hard to rebuild her life, to find a way forward from the bleak place where she'd dwelled for so long. Maybe Mercy hadn't been the best choice of location considering she'd grown up in Oak Grove next door and all the troubles that haunted her were centered around that town. But she'd wanted to be close to home even if she hadn't felt safe actually being there.

At least one of those stressors from her past was now gone. When she moved back to Mercy, she heard that Baby Face had been killed last year. While she'd never celebrate anyone's death, that bit of news did a lot to make her feel safer in her new life.

Now the past, whether she liked it or not, was coming back to haunt her in the form of one holy hallelujah of a hot biker that she still couldn't resist.

Helena couldn't deny she still very much had feelings for Crash. That he now needed someone to talk to only made the guilt worse. How the hell was she supposed to help Crash? She couldn't help him professionally, something that was also her fault, when she couldn't even untangle her own feelings.

Fuck.

Somehow, she made it through her morning appointments, ran out to grab fast food for lunch, and came back to make it through her afternoon appointments. And there were many. Helena was grateful for the work, especially now when she needed to keep her mind occupied. But by five, when she was supposed to be leaving, she was running on fumes because she still wasn't sleeping, and there were two patients sitting in the waiting room. There was no way she could make it in time for the meeting with Margot at six. With no other options, she sent a text to Margot explaining her situation. If anyone would understand it was Margot, who'd sent a lot of folks her way.

Including Crash. The handsome biker she'd shared a night with long ago wasn't very far from her thoughts, ever. Guilt killed her enthusiasm for anything else now. Helena hated feeling that way, knowing that the man really could use help, and she couldn't provide it because on top of the loss of his brother, she'd fucked him over too.

Margot texted back, telling her that she'd fill her in on the plans for this year's charity event and not to worry. That was a good thing since it was almost seven before Helena was able to leave the office and head back home. She'd planned to grab groceries -- just a few items -- but it was late, and she was so tired. Probably more emotionally exhausted than anything. Helena drove straight home to her apartment, deciding a quick supper, a movie, and a soak in the tub before bed might lift her spirits.

Later, she'd realize the big muddy shoeprint on her welcome mat was the first red flag. It was a lot bigger than her shoe. In the back of her mind, she'd decided maybe someone from the apartment complex had showed up when she wasn't at home. She usually didn't order anything online, so she wasn't expecting any deliveries. With a shrug, she let herself into her apartment, blowing out a sigh of relief for the safety of its walls. Somehow, she'd made it through her second week on the job. And it would have been exhausting all on its own, even without the drama of having to confront Crash and her own bad behavior after all this time.

It had been a while since lunch, so she started with dinner. She had leftovers from the takeout she'd ordered the evening before. Yeah, it was fried chicken and mashed potatoes, which weren't the healthiest choices. But back when she worked at *Sackett's*, that greasy fried food was her reward for hustling that week and getting good tips. Now it was comfort food, and she needed that.

Within minutes, she had her plate warmed up and sank down onto her couch, turning on her TV to find a movie. Anything to take her mind off things.

When she thought about it later, she realized there shouldn't have been an aftertaste to her leftovers. Well, it wasn't as fresh on the second day. Maybe it was just because she was so tired? It did little more than make her pause because her stomach was rumbling away, and the scary movie pulled her into the action of its story. Helena ate on autopilot as she watched the film, feeling oddly more relaxed as minutes ticked by.

By the time she finished her meal, she was halfway into the movie about a haunted old house and a plague of vampires that struck the town. There were a few jump scares which normally had her jumping in her seat. But Helena was too tired today, her body relaxing. She welcomed it, putting the container on the coffee table and stretching out on her couch to finish the film. She drifted off into a deep sleep a few minutes later.

* * *

Crash

Since Helena never left her office until just after seven, Crash waited a couple of hours before he drove back over to her apartment complex in his Charger. It was a hell of a time to realize between his bike and his car that put out over 700 horsepower, he didn't have a quiet mode of transportation. He just had to hope, since it was Friday, that everyone would be too tired or distracted from the work week to notice anything out of the ordinary tonight at the apartment complex.

Parking in the small lot of Helena's apartment building, he spotted her car in the same space she always used. It was a shadowy part of the lot, and it didn't strike him as safe but hopefully, it wouldn't be a problem for long. Glancing up, he saw the lights of her apartment were on. *Perfect.*

Picking locks was something he'd perfected living with his stepfather's abuse as a kid. Once the fucker killed their mother, he'd taken their house keys whenever he found them. Did the bastard think when he locked them out of their own home they'd just disappear somewhere? Where the fuck did he think they'd go? What really pissed him off was his brother coming home from school, waiting in the cold for

Crash to get home to pick the lock. Every day, Crash waited for the fucker to do something else to keep them out, to start using a padlock. It must have been too much effort because it never happened.

When Crash had let himself into Helena's apartment earlier, he'd found her spare key with a Scooby-Doo keyring in a bowl on the kitchen counter. Crash took a deep breath before letting himself into her apartment this time. He hadn't known all that much about her aside from the fact that he still wanted her, maybe even needed her on a level he couldn't explain. Maybe she'd eaten the leftovers in her fridge he'd laced with a sedative. If she had, she was out, and she'd be easy for him to move.

If she hadn't eaten those leftovers, Crash letting himself into her apartment could have some very loud consequences.

Standing in the dim light of Helena's apartment, his heart felt like it would pound its way out of his chest. The soft glow from the lamp by the couch cast long shadows on the walls. His Helena lay there, asleep on the couch, her breathing slow and even. Right now, she was completely unaware of what he'd done. The empty takeout container was still on the coffee table, the remnants of the mashed potatoes he'd drugged left on the plate.

Just how far was he willing to take this?

Crash didn't want it to be like this. He wasn't a complete fucking psycho like his stepfather; it wasn't who he was. But every time he stopped and thought about how she'd left him five years ago, just walked out of his life when he thought it was the beginning of something together, it twisted something deep inside him. All the confusion, anger, and hurt came flooding back. And considering how their conversation in her office had gone earlier in the week, well, he didn't know how else to make her listen to him. She'd told him she couldn't treat him because of the night she spent in his arms that he'd never gotten over but offered to talk later. Sure, he'd stormed out of her office that day. But then he'd given her a few opportunities to talk to him out in town and she'd run like a coward.

Helena hadn't given him a choice back then. Now, he wasn't giving her one. She *was* going to listen to him.

He gazed at her sleeping form, her black hair spilling over the arm of the couch. Her beautiful face was peaceful with her hands tucked under her chin like a child. It was almost like none of his madness had touched her at all. Yeah, Crash couldn't deny all the feelings for her were still there. They'd never gone away, no matter how hard he tried to bury them deep. Now here he was, about to kidnap her, and the enormous weight of what he was doing made his stomach churn.

Taking a knee by the couch, Crash watched her breathe. For a second, he hesitated. Should he be doing this? Maybe this wasn't the way to get the answers he wanted. But what else could he do? She hadn't talked to him in her office, not really. He'd made sure she saw him out in town, hoping she'd approach him, say *something*. Instead, she'd cut and run in fear. He understood that, especially considering he'd lost his temper during their "appointment."

But that wasn't what he needed. Crash didn't want her fear. He wanted her to talk to him. He wanted her to tell him why she'd left him that night, disappeared without a fucking trace. Brushing his fingers over the softness of her cheek, Crash blew out a breath.

He was in too deep already, unable to entirely block out a tiny voice in the back of his mind screaming that he'd been too hasty, hadn't thought it all through. He couldn't turn back now. They needed to talk, and if this was the only way she was really going to talk to him, then that's the way it was going to be.

Quick as he could, he went through her bedroom, grabbing a tote and collecting personal items for her -- a hairbrush, her toothbrush, a pair of pajamas, and a few other clothing items. With that hanging off his arm, he headed back to the living room.

Crash patted the spare key in his jacket pocket, staring down at her one last time. Carefully, he lifted her from the couch, her small form limp in his arms, knowing she'd probably never know how much it hurt him to do this, the conflict he battled even as he carried her to the door. He was able to carry her to his car, get her situated in the back seat with no trouble. Tossing her bag into the back, he started the engine and pulled out of the lot.

Crash drove them to the house that held all the ghosts of his past.

They were both about to face them. Together.

* * *

Stopping at the clubhouse for a couple of things he needed, Crash parked his Charger at the edge of the lot and sprinted for the front door. He should have thought things through a little better. He should have had his shit ready. No one was in the main room, so he made a beeline for his. He went through it like a SWAT team, grabbing clothes for the next couple of days. When he headed back for the door, the main entry room was no longer empty. Outcast was there, looked to be heading out himself, keys in hand. He stopped when he heard Crash's steps.

"Thought I heard someone," Outcast said. "You headed off for the weekend?"

He'd been leaving every weekend for weeks. His brothers knew this even though he never told them where he was going. He just needed to keep his wits right now. That was all. No one knew of his connection to Helena that he knew of. Unless it was Outcast. He'd been there that night in *Sackett's*, realized that Crash had left the bar with Helena. But in his brother's eyes, it had been a one-night stand. That was it. In their world, that wasn't an uncommon occurrence.

Crash nodded, his heart thundering in his chest. "Yeah. You?"

Shrugging a casual shoulder, Outcast said, "Heading off to *Sackett's* while I can." What did that mean? Outcast must have read the confusion on his face. "Old man Phillips is retiring. He's putting *Sackett's* up for sale. The last day is Christmas Eve."

That stopped Crash in his tracks. It's where Helena had worked as a server, where he'd met her. After a moment, Crash nodded. His mind everywhere. "Hopefully someone else will buy it. It's a decent place."

"Yeah. Have a good one," Outcast said, heading for the door.

Crash was on his heels, relieved to see his friend's bike wasn't anywhere near his Charger where Helena was fast asleep in the back. When he was behind the wheel of his car once more, Crash turned quickly to see she hadn't moved while he was gone. She sighed softly in her sleep, and with that he was ready to go. Driving through Mercy to get to the interstate, the digital display on the stereo told him it was almost ten. Thirty minutes on the interstate and he'd reach the house in Oak Grove.

Chapter Five

Helena

Helena stirred, her eyelids heavy, her head swimming in a fog she couldn't quite shake. The world felt distant, muffled, like she was floating somewhere between dreaming and waking. Her body felt heavy, and as she tried to move, a wave of dizziness and nausea forced her back down. Something was wrong -- very wrong.

The surface beneath her was hard and unfamiliar, the fabric rough. This wasn't *her* couch. Blinking, she tried to clear the haze from her vision. Dim light filtered in through a window she didn't recognize, a streetlight or the moon maybe, casting long shadows across the room. Panic seeped in at the edges of her consciousness as her mind tried to piece together where she was. This wasn't her apartment. She was sure of that.

Helena's pulse quickened. Her breathing came fast and shallow as she struggled to push herself up, her limbs still sluggish from the effects of something in her system. She hadn't been drinking and wasn't currently on any medications. The last thing she'd remembered was eating dinner and watching a movie… and then nothing. Her heart raced in her chest. Had she been ill or had a stroke? Had someone drugged her?

Frantic, her gaze darted around the room, taking in the old, faded wallpaper peeling at the edges, the thick layer of dust on the windowsill, the dark wooden floor beneath the couch where she lay. Everything looked abandoned in the room she was in, like no one had lived here in years. With a view of the kitchen beyond, she saw those walls looked freshly painted. A tray of paint rollers sat next to two buckets of paint on the floor, and there was a huge toolbox behind that. Wherever she was, someone was working on the house.

She just didn't know in her confused state why *she* was there.

Her fingers dug into the softness of the blanket that had been thrown over her, and the reality of her situation began to settle in. She was in a strange place, alone -- and someone had brought her here. But why? Panic surged, and she bolted upright, dizziness be damned. But before she could scramble off the couch, a shadow moved in the corner of the room.

"Easy," a voice rumbled, deep and familiar. Too familiar.

Helena's breath caught in her throat, her body going rigid. She blinked, trying to focus through the blur, and then, like a cold wave breaking over her, it hit her. *Crash*.

He stepped out from the shadows like an image from a dream, his figure unmistakable. Tall, broad, the same blue eyes that had stared into hers so many times before. His face was hard, unreadable, as he watched her from across the room. Why did he still have to be so gorgeous?

"What..." Her voice was rough, her throat dry as sandpaper. "What did you do? Why am I here?"

Crash's jaw tightened, but he didn't answer right away. His silence only made her panic flare hotter. Struggling, she tried to get up. But her legs wobbled beneath her, too weak from the drug or whatever he'd given her.

"I didn't think you'd be awake just yet," he muttered, stepping closer but stopping short, as if unsure how to approach her.

Helena's mind scrambled as her heart raced in her chest. He *had* taken her. The man she'd walked away from all those years ago, the one she'd thought she could leave in the past, had drugged her and brought her here. To what? An old house? Somewhere isolated, far from help? Fear constricted her throat.

"Why... why are you doing this?" she whispered, her voice trembling.

Crash looked away for a moment, his hand running through the long locks of his blond hair. For the briefest second, she saw something -- conflict, regret -- but it vanished as quickly as it had appeared. When his gaze returned to hers, his eyes were hard, full of determination. "We need to talk," he said quietly.

Was he serious right now?

"I'm willing to talk, Crash," Helena said slowly. "I even offered to meet you somewhere to talk about it if I remember right."

"And if I remember right," Crash said, "I told you I couldn't trust you to show up. I've seen you in town several times this week, Helena. You had plenty of opportunities to talk to me on any of those occasions. You ran the other way."

She hadn't run but she got his meaning and yeah, she'd worked hard at avoiding conversation with him. Having managed to get into a sitting position, her gaze met his as he took a seat in the armchair next to the couch. She understood Crash wanted to talk to her about that night five years ago and she knew from Margot that he'd lost his brother. When she'd talked to him earlier in the week, she'd convinced herself he wasn't there to talk to a therapist. He'd shown up to confront her about what had happened between them.

But maybe, and she was forcing thoughts

through the fog the drugs he must have used left in her mind, she'd read the situation wrong. How desperate was he to have someone's attention if he would go so far as to kidnap her? What if he were no better than Baby Face?

The truth was that Helena knew Crash from when she worked at *Sackett's* as a server. For weeks, they had talked and flirted. He came across as a little scary at first, a prospect for the infamous Hounds of Hell. Crash was gorgeous, rugged, and knew his way around a pool table. What wasn't to like? After some time went by, well, he was still scary but nice to her. He represented strength, someone who could maybe protect her. When he'd sought to comfort her the last time she saw Baby Face, she'd surrendered herself to his strength, wanting -- no, *needing* the shelter he could offer.

And while she didn't regret that night with him, she had to stop and realize she hadn't really known Crash all that well. He could have changed in the last five years. She had changed, hadn't she?

Helena had no idea where she was. Crash, still as gorgeous to her as he'd always been, sat staring at her from the nearby chair. His fingers drummed on the arm of the chair; his gaze wild as it roamed over her. He was clearly agitated, and she couldn't reasonably say she knew what to expect. She had to be careful. If he just wanted to talk, Helena would listen. Maybe if she gave him what he wanted, she could convince him to take her back.

"Okay," she said slowly. "If you want to talk, let's talk. I'm here."

"Yeah, you are." Again, he scrubbed a hand through his thick blond hair. "It didn't have to go this way, you know? Why couldn't we have talked without my having to resort to this shit?"

Taking a deep breath, Helena decided that maybe this would go better if she could be honest with him. Within reason. She didn't know him that well and had no idea what he was capable of. He'd already plucked her out of her own life to get her attention. She had to be careful because she didn't know what else he could do if he felt threatened or slighted.

"Margot told you I was coming," Crash continued. "You knew I was coming."

"Margot told me *Charlie Ford* was coming. I only knew you as Crash. I never knew your real name." Helena forced herself to hold his gaze. "I didn't know it was going to be you. I'm sorry."

Nodding, Crash seemed to be processing that. "Then I get there and you're not answering my questions about that night," Crash went on. "And telling me how you can't even be my therapist because I went home with you."

Guilt weighed down on her. He was right about all of it. "I wasn't ready for you to walk through the door, Crash." It was a lame excuse but it was the truth. "I didn't know what to say. I just…"

"You thought you got away with it." His gaze was intense on her, anger darkening his face. "Didn't you?"

Careful now. "I wasn't trying to get away with anything," Helena said. "There were things going on in my life at the time, things that scared me. Yes, my decision to leave was abrupt. My actions hurt you, which wasn't my intention, and I regret that. But I hadn't promised you anything, Crash. There was no discussion. Remember?"

"Abrupt?" Anger flared in his eyes. "And you must have grabbed all your shit while I was asleep and ran for it. I went by your place twice a day for a month after that. No sign of you."

Helena sighed. "I was planning to leave Mercy. I didn't realize I was going to go that night but that's what ended up happening."

"So that night with me was so *awful* you just cut and ran?"

Was that what he thought? "No. My reasons for getting out of Mercy had nothing to do with you, Crash." Taking a deep breath, she decided to be honest. "I don't regret that night with you at all. Is that what you want to hear? I don't."

There was no quick answer to that. When he didn't say anything, she rushed on.

"All of those weeks we talked at *Sackett's*," she said. "For me, that was real. I don't expect you to believe that but it's the truth."

"And that's why I heard from you after that, right?" Crash asked, the sarcasm unmistakable.

The anger in his face had her hesitating. If she pissed him off, what was she going to do? She wasn't big enough to fight him. With no idea where she was, she had very limited options if the conversation took a wrong turn. "What would I have said? How could I have reached you? It wasn't like I had your number."

"And I'm so sorry that I had to tell you that I couldn't see you because of our personal connection." Helena spoke slowly. "Ethically, I just can't be your therapist because of that night." When his expression hardened, she sped up. "It's just to help any patient, I have to be able to approach my work with the patient from an unbiased, professional place. Talking to you after what happened between us, that could do more harm than good. For your mental well-being and mine."

"After leaving like you did, you expect me to think you care about my mental well-being?" Bitterness crept into his tone. "Sure doesn't feel like that."

"I *do* care." She needed Crash to believe her. "But that had to be said as soon as I realized you were my patient. It's just for everyone's benefit."

Shaking his head, a glare formed on Crash's face. "Not everyone's benefit. *Yours.*"

"Crash, I understand why you feel the way you do," Helena said. "And now, all that doesn't matter. I'm here. I'll talk to you about anything you want. I promise. All of this, the loss of your brother. And then when you feel better, you can take me back to my place. No one will know. I won't say anything."

He studied her for a long moment, his expression hard to read. She knew he was hurt, angry. That she was tied up in all of it was her own fault. She'd own that. But she needed to make him understand that the situation with them being in the house they were in was temporary. He needed to realize he had to return her, to make things right.

"It's just that easy for you, isn't it?" Crash was still angry. "We'll talk until I say we're done."

Crash rose from his chair, heading into the kitchen. Helena watched him pull a bottle of beer from the refrigerator. When he caught her watching him, he rocked the bottle back and forth. "Want one?"

Helena shook her head. She was groggy enough. If she drank a beer on top of it, she could go back to sleep for a few hours. No, she didn't want that.

"Can I go to the bathroom?" she asked as politely as she could.

With a curt nod, Crash walked back into the living room. Getting off the couch was a struggle in the shape she was in. She flinched when his strong fingers wrapped around her upper arm and hauled her up. He kept his grip on her arm, guiding her to a small bathroom down a narrow hallway. She was grateful for his help because she wasn't sure she would have made it to relieve herself without it.

* * *

Crash

He brought Helena back to the couch after her trip to the bathroom. Crash sat in the old armchair next to the couch, the springs creaking beneath him as he leaned forward, elbows on his knees, hands clasped tightly together. Turning on the TV, he flipped through channels as he nursed his beer. He hadn't expected Helena to drift back to sleep, but she had. The sleeping pill he'd crushed and put in her food was maybe too strong. All he'd wanted was to make sure she was sleeping soundly so she wouldn't wake up before he got her back to the house in Oak Grove.

Helena was still so goddamn beautiful. Five years hadn't changed much for her. Her black hair was just as glorious as it always was, a shining onyx pool on the pillow her head rested on. The dark fan of her lashes showed the contrast of sinful black on an angel's white skin. Yeah, she still had some makeup on, particularly at her eyes and cheeks. Her lips were still as tempting as ever, even when she spoke words that pissed him off.

The blanket covering her hid the rest of her from him, but he knew what was under there. Now she wore dress suits or slacks with blouses and sweaters that made her look like a young schoolteacher. Hell, she looked good in everything. Her breasts were full, tempting twin mounds that were bigger than a handful. Her ass was still glorious, but firmer now, like she worked out. Her legs were long and graceful.

That one night with her hadn't been enough. Not nearly enough. As much as he tried to convince himself that getting his fill of that luscious little body was all this was to him, at heart he knew it was an outright lie. If he just wanted to tap that again, he didn't have to show up at an appointment to confront her for leaving him high and dry after one spectacular night with her. Crash constantly told himself that it was really because his heart was all tangled up, but his mind shot it down every time. Why couldn't he convince himself that she was one of many?

It didn't ring true.

Was it betrayal? Maybe. Crash had lost so much already in his life. His father early on to an accident. His mother at the hands of a brutal stepfather she'd hoped would help her sons have a better childhood. Perry had been the only family he had left, and the fucking Mafia had taken him. He still harbored resentment toward his brothers because they should have told him when they found Perry. But fucking no, they'd moved them to the barn behind *Sackett's* because they didn't want to lose their chance to lure Bianchi and his men to *Sackett's*, to get rid of them for good. Was Perry collateral damage to the Hounds? Did they care at all that he was his birth brother?

The old house was still, save for the faint sounds of Helena sighing in her sleep on the couch. He could still feel her fear. The way she tried to mask it whenever she caught him looking had his heart breaking. He knew better. He knew when he'd taken her that she'd be afraid of him and on the surface, he'd been happy about that. She *should* be afraid of him, begging for his forgiveness.

Crash dragged a hand over his face. This wasn't how he'd imagined it going down, not really. He hadn't planned it out, hadn't thought beyond the need to make her listen, to keep her from slipping through his fingers again. Drugging her food had been drastic -- he knew that. But every time he tried to convince himself it was worth it, it was the right thing to do, a flicker of doubt crept in.

Helena *was* afraid of him now, and maybe he deserved that. He'd crossed a line, pulled her into a place he never thought he'd revisit, much less inhabit every fucking weekend since Perry's death. The old house held so many ghosts, so many memories he'd tried to leave behind. He hadn't been back here since he and Perry had inherited it. Somehow, for a reason he wasn't really in touch with, Crash had dragged her here, to the heart of his pain, to the one place he thought he could finally get some answers. He needed her to see him -- really see him -- and she needed to understand why he couldn't let her walk away again.

Who the fuck was he kidding? She'd handled it so well. Helena had been barely nineteen when they'd shared that stormy night together. In some ways, she'd still been a girl back then. Now, she was a young woman who was a little more confident in herself and fuck, that was sexy. Yeah, she'd been scared and confused when she awoke. It didn't take her long to get her bearings. Helena not only talked to him like a reasonable person, but she'd started to analyze him. While it pissed him off -- he hadn't brought her there to screw with his mind, had he? -- he admired her bravery. She promised she'd talk to him about everything. Then when he felt better, he could take her back home. She wouldn't say anything.

Right.

But now, watching her from where he sat, he couldn't shake the guilt weighing him down. Helena was here against her will, and he'd seen it in her eyes. She wasn't just nervous; she was terrified. And as much as he wanted to believe she had it coming, she deserved it, he knew that wasn't entirely true. The fear he saw there was his doing, *his* fault.

Still, he doubted her sincerity. Five years was a long time. Why should he believe anything she said now? She could spin it however she wanted, talk about timing or fate or some other nonsense, but he couldn't let himself trust it. He had to be in control of how this went.

Leaning back, Crash stared at the cracked ceiling as he thought about how this "arrangement" might go. She'd stay here, at least until they *really* had it out. Maybe then, he'd finally get the truth from her. Maybe, once she understood him, he could let her go. But until then, they were both stuck here, in the house that had shaped him, broken him. For now, she was his captive audience, and he was determined to make her see who he'd become -- the man he was now, with or without her. If she hated him for it, so be it. He'd take whatever she threw at him. He just hoped he could live with his actions when all was said and done.

Crash blew out a sigh. What the fuck had he been thinking? He'd taken her, kidnapped her, and he was unsatisfied with the result. *Really*? Of course she was going to tell him what he wanted to hear. She would play along just to get out of there, to get away from him. What had he expected? That if he just plucked her out of her apartment, she'd see reason? She'd realize she made a mistake in leaving him without another word or thought all those years ago?

Crash drank the rest of his beer quickly. Once he

drained it, he went for another one. Agitation kept his mind spinning, kept him from being able to sit still. When he couldn't bear to be in that chair another minute, he went back into the kitchen. There was one last wall in there to paint so he worked on that, slowly but with an unsteady hand. His hands shook and no matter how hard he tried to find some peace he just couldn't do it. The simple activity was meant to keep his mind occupied, to keep him calm.

Inside, he was falling apart. Yeah, he knew he'd been wrong. But he couldn't take it back now. He'd deal with the consequences, no matter where they led.

It was almost six in the evening when he decided to wrap up the painting for the day and went to prepare dinner. Every time he glanced into the living room to see if she was still asleep, she was. She'd barely fucking moved. Dinner was simple, burgers with frozen fries he dumped into the drawer of his air fryer. With dinner ready, he looked into the living room for the hundredth time and found Helena stirring. Walking to the couch, he helped her into a sitting position, unhappy that she still looked sedated. "Need to go to the bathroom?"

At her nod, he helped her up, walked her to the bathroom. When she emerged, he helped her back to the couch. Putting together plates for each of them, Crash handed her one when he joined her on the couch to eat dinner. He left only once to grab a beer for him, a glass of water for her.

The news was on, and he watched it, knowing that even if someone figured out she wasn't where she was supposed to be, that it wouldn't be on the news yet. They ate in silence; she never said a word. It made him happy to see her eat because she hadn't eaten since the night before in her apartment -- and he'd drugged that.

"Did you give any thought to what I said?" Helena asked as she set her plate on the coffee table before them. She took a drink of water, eyed him warily.

"Which part?"

Clearing her throat, she seemed to be thinking about what she'd say. Guilt battled with anger as he waited.

"The part where we talk about all the things you need to talk about," she said slowly. "And once you're feeling better, you can take me home."

Already, she was scheming on how to get out of this. To get away from him. She'd offer anything, say anything. But Crash couldn't trust her. What didn't she get about that?

"The problem with that is trust," Crash explained. "I can't trust you. That's going to take some time to earn back. You understand?"

She nodded, but disappointment was clear on her face. "I understand, Crash. I'll earn your trust back."

That got Crash's attention. "How do you think you're going to do that?"

Helena swallowed hard, looking nervous as hell. He felt vindicated. He also felt like a pile of shit, waiting for her answer.

"By listening to everything you want to tell me," she said. "By trying to help you as I should have in my office."

"But you couldn't," Crash reminded her. "Because of your ethics."

She forced herself to hold his gaze. He could feel her frustration.

"That doesn't matter now," Helena said. "We're

not in my office. This isn't an appointment. We can talk about whatever you want to talk about."

"So you're not my therapist?" he asked.

"I'll be whatever you need me to be," Helena said.

She shouldn't have said that. That little offer worked its way through his mind, and it went to the worst places. Yeah, maybe Margot was right, and he needed a fucking therapist. But if Helena wanted to talk about what he *really* wanted...

She must have realized how he might have taken that statement, but she didn't run screaming for the hills. Not yet.

"You'll do anything?" Crash asked, watching her expressions.

After a moment, her gaze returned to his. "Yes."

Chapter Six

Helena

Crash's gaze was intense. Helena took a deep breath. She honestly didn't know what to do. Yes, he'd taken her from her apartment. She'd hurt him and he was struggling with that. He wanted answers.

But Helena didn't understand. She would have thought she wouldn't be so memorable to a biker. And she wasn't the only thing eating at him, she knew that. But she had to think about her own safety until she could get back to her apartment, her life. If sleeping with him would help her get back to her life faster, couldn't she do that?

Helena had spent one night with him before and the sex had been mind-blowing. It had been her choice. Sitting in her car, in her driveway that night, he hadn't asked to come in with her or demanded sex. Crash had asked if it was okay to wait in her car in the pouring rain for someone to pick him up.

No, she'd been selfish. Helena had flirted with him for weeks, as drawn to him as he seemed to be to her. Yeah, he was a prospect for the Hounds, which terrified her given that her previous boyfriend, if she could even call him that, had been a Cottonmouth. But Crash had a completely different manner about him. Crash was soft with her even though his demeanor scared the shit out of many other folks. Her heart beat a little faster whenever he came into the bar. When he smiled at her, she just could have melted on the spot.

But not all of her thoughts were of pure romance. Crash was sexy with the way those sky-blue eyes had darkened and his gaze had moved over her body. Early on when she worked at the bar, she'd wear jeans and plain T-shirts. But Helena found herself doing a bit more as time went by. She threw in short skirts here and there, and low-cut tops. She was rewarded with more smoldering glances and flirty winks from her favorite biker. She'd drawn unwanted attention from other bar patrons too, but it had been worth it.

By the time they ended up in her car that night, she should have just appreciated his kindness and left it there. But Helena had wanted him. Came on to him. And that night, it had been totally worth it. Sex with Crash to this day was burned into her brain as one of the most exciting nights of her entire life. In that small room with the storm raging outside, Crash had taken her apart, had her begging him for release. And he had given her that, over and over.

Crash hadn't been the only one who wasn't the same again after that night. The worst part had been leaving him there, sleeping in a bed she'd never return to. It had punched a hole in her heart that was still there. She still dreamed about him sometimes. Crash kept telling her over and over that he couldn't trust her. If sex would rebuild that trust and get her back to the sanity of her own life, Helena was willing. She was just afraid that more of Crash might make the hole in her heart even bigger -- might prove to be a fatal wound.

He was definitely interested. Placing his own plate on the coffee table, his gaze was intense on her, already stoking flames in her body that she thought she'd never experience again.

"Prove it," he said, challenge lighting up his eyes.

Helena's hands were shaking as it was, but okay. She could do this. Carefully, she scooted closer to him on the couch. Just the smell of him was enough to send sparks of excitement running through her bloodstream.

As much as her mind tried to banish Crash and that one hot night, her body remembered him. She wanted more. One hand landed on his thigh, hard and heated beneath the tight denim of his jeans. The other clutched at the blue flannel shirt he wore, opened down the front to reveal the T-shirt that appeared to be straining to contain his broad shoulders and chest, all those muscles. The challenge was still there in his gaze as she moved even closer, feeling the heat of him.

Don't back down now, coward. Leaning closer, Helena pressed her lips to his. A tentative kiss, light and teasing. The soft brush of his whiskers, the silk of his lips, was enticing. Kissing him again, she lingered this time, her lips dancing against his. It was just enough to get a slight taste of him, and that taste was something she remembered. Something she wanted again. She used her grip on that flannel to pull him closer and she deepened the kiss, her tongue teasing the seam of his lips. Crash wasn't being uncooperative, but he wasn't doing anything to help her either. Still, she'd be lying if she said that she wasn't enjoying the hell out of being able to explore him. It was amazing.

When he opened his mouth to her, she plunged her tongue in for a deeper taste. Pleasure rippled through her entire body as her tongue slid along his. Now he was kissing her back, his breath coming fast like hers was. Her hand slid up his chest, up into the silky locks of his hair. Helena moved closer. Crash was warm, restrained heat, and he tasted so good. His arms had been crossed over his muscular chest to that point. When he dropped his arms, letting her move closer, he broke the kiss long enough to whisper against her lips. "That all you got?"

He wanted more?

Feeling emboldened, she threw a leg over his lap,

straddling him. The movement made her aware of all the wetness causing her panties to cling to her beneath the slacks she'd worn to work yesterday. She would have been embarrassed about that if she hadn't wanted him so much. Both hands slid up into his hair as she kissed the breath from him, enjoying the opportunity to do what she wanted. When his hands slid over her thighs, slowly moving up, she moaned into his mouth. When he shifted his position beneath her to move his ass closer to the edge of the couch, Helena ground against the heated length of his cock, straining the front of his jeans.

She couldn't help herself. She slid a hand down to his cock, closing around it as much as she could through the denim. He felt so good. Helena remembered how he felt inside her, how she wasn't able to think of anything else while he rocked her world that night.

Helena felt lightheaded, the kiss so intense she wasn't sure she remembered to breathe. Taking advantage of the opportunity, Crash's heated mouth moved across her face to her jaw and then blazed a trail to her neck, the rough brush of his beard and the slick heat of his lips an intoxicating combination that had her body bursting into flames. She moved hers wantonly as she worked him with her hand. Still, Crash wasn't taking over. He wasn't doing more than slightly participating.

Well, he'd wanted more...

Backing away from him, Helena got on her knees on the floor, positioning herself between his massive thighs. Those blue eyes were dark and filled with excitement as her hands moved to undo the buckle of his belt, to work the button at the top of his jeans. Once she had him unzipped, Crash grabbed the waist of his jeans and hurriedly pushed them down those gorgeous muscular thighs sprinkled with golden hair. He wasn't wearing underwear. On one thigh was a tattoo of a race car with the number seventeen that she hadn't noticed before.

It had been a while since she'd given anyone a blow job and Crash's cock was gorgeous. She held him up for herself, applying careful pressure to the base. With the other she played with his balls, trying to figure out what he liked while teasing the smooth head of him with her lips and tongue. At first, he tried to act unaffected but she grinned before she pulled the head of him into her mouth because there were signs that gave him away. His thighs tightened around her ribs and his fingers clutched at the couch beneath him. Just a little at first. But when she did something he liked, the motions of his fingers were more pronounced.

The taste and feel of him in her mouth was a heady experience. The huge, handsome biker tried to fight her but he didn't get far. She worked him into her mouth, getting him good and wet as she went. When she slid him to the back of her throat, he sucked in a breath. He liked that, did he? While still playing with his balls, a little rougher since he hadn't indicated otherwise, she slid him as far back in her throat as she could manage, again and again. Now his fingers were clawing at the couch, the muscles of his thighs tight. Taking a break to tease the head of him with her tongue, she glanced up at him from beneath her lashes, and the sight that greeted her pushed her own excitement higher.

Crash's mouth was open, his eyes fixed on her mouth as it worked around his cock. His breath came fast as he watched and she decided she'd up the ante. She used pressure on his balls and worked him back into her throat again. Helena was determined to draw more of a reaction from him, doubling down on her efforts. The first sound she pulled from him was a deep growl, feral almost. His hands slid into her hair, clutching there. The slight sting of pain only egged her on. Helena swallowed him, traced every inch of him with her tongue. Wrapping her lips around her teeth, she closed around him tightly, all the while discovering what he liked and what truly drove him insane. He pulled at her hair hard when she found one of his kinks. And as she discovered those weaknesses, she did more and more, trying to bring him off.

"Fuck," he finally muttered from between clenched teeth. He fought her still, but that only made her more determined. Using his desires against him, not letting up, she brought him right up to the edge. Crash made a sound that sounded like a small sob when she hit the right motion, hitting the back of her throat with each pass. Now his hands took control of her head, moving her at the speed he wanted, fucking her face. Helena just tried to hold on, tears spilling from her eyes. It took several more minutes but he came, spurting his release into her throat while she did her damnedest to swallow it down, to take all of it.

When Crash finally released her head, she was gasping for breath, the taste of him flooding her mouth. She got all of it down, slowly turning to reach for her glass of water. Crash captured her face in his hands before she could, pulling her to him for a purely dirty kiss. She knew he could taste himself on her tongue and she surrendered to that kiss, letting him get his fill.

"Fuck," he whispered when he finally released her. She was proud of having destroyed him, grinning as she watched him over the rim of her water glass.

She'd done *that* to the big bad biker. It had been glorious.

Scrubbing a hand through his hair, he reached for his jeans and hauled them back up his slim hips, studying her all the while. "You're good at that, darlin'." His voice was rough. "But don't think that I'm finished with you tonight. Not by a long shot."

Her heart squeezed in her chest. He was happy. That was a much more comfortable place for her to be right now. Trying to catch her own breath, she stayed where she was, gently resting her head on one of his hard thighs. She was content for the moment. If he wanted to do more, she was okay with that. She wanted him. She was still afraid of his intentions, but she didn't think he would hurt her. She just needed to convince him to take her back to her place. Back to a situation where they could proceed like normal people. Maybe they'd even get that chance they didn't get before because of her hasty exit.

Still groggy from the drugs he'd used, she allowed her eyes to close. He slid his hand back into her hair, but it was gentle this time, slipping easily through the strands, his touch soothing. Maybe he'd been a man who had too much to deal with in a short period of time. He could be helped. She'd help him. Maybe everything would be okay. With his hand in her hair and the din of the TV in the background, Helena relaxed.

* * *

Crash

When she'd accepted his challenge, he hadn't expected her to level him like *that*. The term "suck-starting a Harley" took on new meaning as he petted her, her head resting on his thigh. As she gazed up at him with those big green eyes, Crash felt his heart squeeze in his chest as he fought to catch his breath. Bliss ran through his veins as he enjoyed that simple moment. It was what he wanted, right?

Guilt gnawed at him. He wanted Helena. But not this way. Not doing whatever she thought he wanted to run away from him again. Crash was a mess from staying up much of the night, watching her sleep. Then he'd painted the kitchen all afternoon. It gave him an idea considering she'd been in the same clothes she wore to work the day before. "Feel like a shower?" he asked, his voice rough.

Helena's nod was eager. A little too eager. *Fuck.*

He took a couple more minutes before he could haul himself off the couch but he managed, watching her scramble back just enough to allow him up. In her expensive slacks, blouse, and cardigan, it was a jarring view. Naked girls, girls in lingerie or skimpy tank tops? *That* he was used to. But the beautiful woman on the floor of his living room didn't remind him of any of the women he'd ever been with. Didn't seem like she belonged. *Too good for the likes of you.*

Holding out a hand, he helped her up from the floor, leading her to the one bathroom in the house. At least it wasn't a tiny cramped space. Pulling a couple of fluffy towels from the small closet just outside the bathroom, he rushed back in to turn on the heat, to get the shower going. He shrugged out of his flannel shirt before grabbing the hem of his T-shirt.

Helena's eyes were wide in alarm.

"What's wrong?" Crash asked, watching her make herself smaller as she moved away from the shower.

When he'd asked if she wanted a shower, had she thought he meant taking a shower alone? What was this?

"You... you can go first," Helena told him. "I'll stay right here."

The pleading way she said she'd stay made him feel like an even bigger bastard. "With what just happened in the living room, you don't want to share?"

Why did it look like her fear was escalating? After a moment, she shook her head, dropping her gaze.

Crash had no idea what that was about. With a deep sigh, a combination of disappointment and concern, he proceeded with stripping off his T-shirt, his jeans. Maybe she'd decide she liked what she saw and join him. There was an old frosted-glass enclosure around the tub. Only the steam on the glass would block her from seeing anything.

And she was watching. As he lathered up, washed his hair, she wedged herself in the corner of the bathroom in front of the door, arms wrapped around her body in a strange way. His mind went over options of why she was skittish now. Helena had just blown him. Thinking back to their night together before, yeah, it had been dark but he remembered they'd been pretty naked in her bed. It hadn't seemed like she had body issues then. Had something happened in the five years since he saw her last?

Wrapping it up, he left the shower running. Climbing out of the shower wet and bare as the day he was born, he reached for a towel and began to dry himself while she kept watching. Snatching up his discarded clothes, he motioned her away from the door. "I'll be just outside," he said.

Frustrated with how his body was stirring again, he left her to shower.

* * *

Helena

When Crash strolled out of the bathroom, Helena looked longingly at the still running shower. She hadn't had one since yesterday and had just the clothes she was wearing. And her makeup... What was she going to do? Crash would probably know as soon as he saw her clean face. She never carried her makeup with her unless she knew she was staying overnight somewhere.

Just in case the hot water wouldn't last long, she stripped off and jumped in. The almost-hot water felt good running over her body. Between the lingering effects of the sedative he'd used and the fact that she'd been so out of it she hadn't moved much in sleep, her muscles were sore. Fear had something to do with it too. Everything ached and the heat of the water, the caress of the steam, felt amazing.

The shampoo he'd used was nothing to write home about but there was an unused bottle of conditioner in there. She used it, but had to wonder if he got that beforehand because he knew he was going to snatch her from her place and bring her here. Anxiety flooded her as she used it on her hair. What was she going to do? Sure, she could play along. But they needed to talk. What were his intentions? Every time she mentioned listening to him and him returning her to her apartment, he'd just shut down or turned it back on her.

And when he saw the fucking scar on her face, and she was one of many who had one, he'd know her story. Then what? Would he throw her out like garbage?

Not wanting to take too much time, she finished

Jamie Targaet   Crash/Razor Duet

quickly and climbed out to grab the other towel he'd left for her. Once she'd wrapped herself in it, she shut off the water, just in case he was listening. Yeah, there were a few random scars Baby Face had left on her body. But the one on her jaw? Everyone in the MCs knew that one. That simple little slice was his calling card, the mark he left on all of his "sluts."

Crash was now a card-carrying Hound, sworn enemy of the Cottonmouths, the club Baby Face had belonged to. He was dead but it would be a long time before anyone forgot all the biker's terrible deeds. At best, Crash would view her with disgust. At worst, he could harm her. He'd already taken her from her place to talk about everything. Once she had no further value, or she repelled him, what was stopping him from making her disappear?

Just as she was about to scoop her clothes off the closed toilet lid where she'd left them, the door to the bathroom opened. Helena froze, dropping her head so the wet mess of her hair would cover that side of her face. She could feel his gaze on her, standing there wrapped in a towel with her towel-dried hair a tangled mess around her head. As he moved closer, she could feel his warmth.

"Do you need something?" he asked, putting his hands on her hips, her back to him.

"A comb?" she asked quietly.

Walking around her to the sink, he pulled a wide-toothed comb from the medicine cabinet above it, handing it to her. "Will that work?"

Helena nodded. "It won't take long," she said, hoping he'd take the hint and give her a minute to deal with it.

"Don't take too long." There was just a note of warning in his voice as he walked back out. She couldn't help but ogle his ass as he left because he didn't have a stitch on. And she knew he wouldn't give her a lot of time.

Getting to work, she combed through the wet mass of her hair, working through the tangles as best she could without the products and comb she normally used. On the one hand, her hair could mask the scar long enough to maybe get her through tonight. On the other hand, it was a temporary fix. Without a way to conceal that vicious little gift Baby Face had left, Crash was going to see it sooner rather than later. When her hair was as good as it was going to get, she slowly walked out of the bathroom, heading to the left, the direction he'd gone. The bedroom where he waited for her was next door to the bathroom and warm when she walked just inside the door. Crash was stretched out on his back on the bed, staring up at the ceiling. His gaze wasn't on her, but she sensed that he knew exactly where she was.

"Are you coming to bed?" Crash asked, sounding impatient.

Anxiety froze her to the spot. She wanted to join him in bed, her body craving the pleasure he'd given her on the single night they'd spent together. She also wanted to run screaming from the house even though she knew she'd never make it out the door. And she had no idea where she was. It was almost winter, less than three weeks until Christmas, and she was in a towel so her prospects for escape were slim to non-existent.

All the while, Crash was gloriously naked on the bed, and she was staring. He was perfection, all long muscular limbs with gorgeous tattoos wrapping around his upper body like they were drawn to his beauty too. But his impatience was growing. What was she going to do? With a deep sigh, Crash rolled onto his side facing her, propping his head on a hand. *Fuck.* Now he looked like some nude calendar model. His blue-eyed gaze roamed over her, and she could almost hear the gears turning in his head. Impatience, frustration, mistrust.

Hiding behind the wet locks of her hair, she took a couple of steps closer. She knew what he expected, and he was definitely recovered from the blow job she'd given him. "Can you turn out the lights?" It was worth a try. If he'd just grant her that small mercy, she could make it through tonight. Maybe tomorrow she could figure out what to do. How to hide the scar. How to convince him to let her go.

"Why?"

That one word stopped her again. Her mind scrambled for an answer.

"I don't look the same as I did five years ago," Helena explained. "I'm tired and… I'm doing my best given my current circumstances."

Daring to glance up at him, she found he was staring at her hard. Blowing out another sigh, he rolled onto his back, reaching to turn out the lamp behind him. The bedroom was now shrouded in shadows, and it offered her protection, helped her quell some of the panic.

"Shut the bedroom door," he said, still lying on his back on the bed. "It will help keep it warm in here."

Helena did as he instructed, slowly making her way over to the bed and sitting on its edge with her back to him. Now what did she do? A striptease with the towel? Did she just whip it off and lay herself out like a sacrifice? The sad part was that she wasn't exactly unwilling.

Some of the tension she felt from him had

dissipated. She was aware of him lying on the bed behind her, but she had not a clue as to what she should do.

The bed shifted behind her as he moved closer. Crash felt so much bigger than her as he sat up behind her, wrapping her in his arms from behind. The heat of him was heavenly, helped ease her shaking body -- and it wasn't just winter's chill that had her trembling like a leaf in his arms. His lips, the brush of his beard at her ear, had her shivering. "I know it's been a long day. It's okay," he whispered. "I've got you."

Gentle kisses rained down her neck, across to her shoulder. She breathed a sigh of relief that he wasn't hovering below her scarred jaw, but the other. He let his hands roam her breasts and hips, moving slowly even as they worked their way under her towel. His fingers felt so nice as their rough pads smoothed her warm, damp flesh. Her body remembered his touch, going up in flames at the covetous strokes of his hands, the possessive kisses he'd dropped over her skin. Helena hadn't had sex since that night with Crash. She craved that level of pleasure again. She wanted to know if that connection between them was real or if it had just been a matter of her needing to get away from Oak Grove and her past, painting her memories of everyone and everything apart from Baby Face as idyllic.

She allowed him to pull the towel away from her, and he scooped her up and moved her to the center of the bed, his eyes glittering in the faint light from the window. On her back, her hair offered no cover for her jaw. She hoped he couldn't see it in the dark as his mouth claimed hers for a searing kiss. His lingering kisses burned away her worries, his flesh against hers a perfect echo of that one night they'd had together.

Helena wrapped herself around him, his kisses leaving her breathless. Crash's hands moved over her in a frenzy, seeking out all the places where she needed him most.

When those strong, rough fingers slid on the wetness between her thighs, his moan into her mouth was obscene. Her core clenched from the sensuality of that sound, from the masterful way his fingers moved over her clit. Above her, Crash broke the kiss, gasping for breath. "I promise I'll take my time with you later, Helena," he whispered against her lips. "I just need you now. So much…" His thighs pushed between hers, spreading hers wide.

Helena braced for his cock, but his pause had her opening her eyes, gazing up at him in question.

"Tell me you want me," he whispered. He'd taken himself in hand, the hot, swollen cock head sliding through the folds of her pussy on the silky wetness there, pushing every thought out of her mind. "Tell me."

"I want you," Helena said, meaning it. She was so worked up that she needed him, *craved* him. "Please."

She felt surrounded by him, protected as he pushed inside. Crash was all she could see, the scent of him rich as he stroked down to her ass, holding her there while he impaled her on his cock. It felt so good to touch the hard muscle of his back, her fingers finding rough scars here and there. Her thighs were tight around his slim hips as he powered into her, pushing her up the mattress beneath him until she had no other thought left in her head.

In the cozy warmth of the dark bedroom, their bodies worked together. It was a sensual dance with the chorus of their moans and cries as background music. No one in her life had ever handled her with such care in the bedroom only to burn her down and scatter the ashes once they got started. The way his cock filled her pussy, hitting all the places that took her breath away. He pounded into her, doubling down when her body started clenching around him. She was close, hanging onto Crash for dear life as his thrusts sped up, grew in strength. Her nails sank into his flesh, her eyes squeezed shut.

Helena screamed as she came while Crash held her there, caged to the top of the bed as he sped up, drowning her in the pleasure that swamped her. Stars burst behind her eyelids as Crash chased his own end. His hold on her tightened, his cock punching into her, pushing her back up on that wave while she gasped for breath beneath him. The second time she came, release rode her hard, shook her like a rag doll. Their cries mingled as the world spun away, Helena hanging onto him like a lifeline in a storm.

When the storm passed, Crash eased himself over her. His weight was a heavy, warm blanket as opposed to just collapsing onto her. It was comfortable, intimate. His head lay on her bare chest, his ear pressed to her heart. It felt so natural to hold him, slide her fingers into soft, blond locks of his hair. It was heaven there, safe and warm with the handsome biker. For now, tonight, she could pretend they were lovers, exploring their relationship, instead of a broken man who'd kidnapped a woman he knew to demand answers.

Crash just didn't realize yet that she was broken too.

Chapter Seven

Helena

When she woke up it was still dark. Crash lay next to her on the bed, his back to her. The bedding barely covered him because she was wound up in most of it. She didn't have her phone, nor had she seen him with a phone. There wasn't a TV in the bedroom either, no clock. What time was it?

Where was she?

As carefully as she could, she made it out of bed, shivering in the cool night air. Finding her clothes, she pulled them on and went to the bathroom. The lights were still on in the living room, so she decided to quietly go in there and take a look around.

The more she saw of the house, the more she realized it had long been neglected. The room was dimly lit by the soft glow of a single lamp, casting faint shadows around the space. The sagging couch where she had lain had seen better days and so had the old gray blanket she'd been covered with. The cushions were stained, the upholstery worn from years of use. An ancient TV sat on a wooden stand covered in dust. The newer flatscreen TV was the only modern thing in the room, mounted on the wall above the brick fireplace.

Scattered around the room were recent signs of home improvement. Buckets of paint, one with its lid slightly ajar, sat by the wall just outside the kitchen. A paint tray with a roller rested on it, as if abandoned mid-task. Next to that, a toolbox sat opened, wrenches, screwdrivers, and assorted nails spilling out onto the stained shag carpeting. A few sheets of drywall leaned against the wall near the hallway.

The only things on the fireplace mantel were a

handful of photographs, faded in their frames. Memories of a happier time? Two were of a young couple. The man had a small boy on his hip, the woman held a baby. When Helena took a closer look, she recognized the boy as Crash. Was the photo of him with his parents and younger sibling? Another photo showed the couple dressed up. The man, who she guessed was Crash's father, wore a dark suit, the woman a white dress with lacy sleeves, her wedding dress, with the bouquet of flowers in her hand. The last photo showed two small boys, Crash being the older one, digging through Easter baskets.

Okay, maybe this was the house where Crash had grown up. It still didn't answer her question. Where were they?

There was a bookshelf standing awkwardly in front of the living room window. The frame looked sturdy, but it wasn't finished. A pile of screws and pieces of wood were left on the floor next to it, giving it a strange, transitional feel. It wasn't completely in the past and it hadn't yet reached the future. The state of limbo seemed to reflect who Crash was right now. He was still haunted by the past, but he was trying to get better for the future.

The curtains hiding the front windows in the living room were so ancient she was almost afraid to touch them, but she pushed one aside. The streetlight showed her a couple of run-down houses across the street. One had its front windows boarded up. But there were two cars in the driveway and a light in another window, so someone lived there. She didn't see a street sign.

Think. Helena reviewed the last two days in her mind. When she'd last checked the time, it had been just after eight. She'd been watching a horror movie while she ate dinner.

Backing away from the window, she searched the living room then moved to the kitchen. It dawned on her when she spotted her Scooby-Doo key chain on the counter that somehow he'd got into her apartment and laced her food with a sedative. She woke up Saturday... early morning? The truth was, she didn't know where the hell she was and how many hours had passed. Maybe they were still in Virginia, maybe they were hours away. The question was what was she going to do now?

Crash had been non-committal about returning her to her apartment and life every time she asked. Hell, he wasn't even really talking to her and when he did, he made accusations. She got it. She'd hurt him. But now she'd given him a blow job to prove herself, and sex after that, maybe he'd talk to her. Maybe they could resolve everything. She could reason with him, and they could get back to their lives.

But honestly, she had no guarantee how all this would go. Truth be told, Helena wanted to help him, and she was still as drawn to him as she'd ever been. But what if he just meant to take her? Was this supposed to be her life now? Helena had never really known Crash that well back in the day when they were circling each other in *Sackett's*. She had no idea what could have changed in his life since then aside from the loss of his brother.

Normal people didn't resort to kidnapping when they wanted to talk to someone about the past and they were still raw about it. Helena needed to remember that first and foremost. It was now Sunday, she thought. If she missed her appointments Monday, someone would begin to ask questions. Margot certainly would. If Helena could just get him to take her back, everything could be worked out. They'd talk, maybe build on what they'd already rekindled. They could move forward from there.

But that nagging little worry that he meant to keep her wherever she was now just wasn't going away.

The other thing she could do, while he was asleep, was to try to find a way out of there. He had to have brought her there in a car or truck as opposed to his bike. She just needed to find the keys and she could be out of there, on her way back to her life. Yeah, it would be awkward when they returned. But she could talk to Margot. Surely something could be done. Helena didn't want to press charges against Crash. She didn't want to hurt him any more than she already had. She just wanted him to communicate with her.

Helena searched the kitchen thoroughly, looking for car keys. A glance out the window in the kitchen door showed a car out in the driveway. It was perfect. Where were the fucking keys?

She found a bag of items from her own apartment on her quest. It looked like he just grabbed a handful of her underwear, a couple pairs of jeans, a few tops and shoved them in there. While she very much wanted to change into fresh clothes right now, her safety came first. She needed the keys to the car. Where would he keep them?

Her stomach dropped a little to think that maybe he kept them on him. In his jeans? Could she even risk going back to the bedroom and search there, through his clothes? Did she really have a choice? *Only if I can't find them anywhere else.*

When she'd fully searched the living room, kitchen, bathroom, she found two other rooms aside from the bedroom where he slept. Both appeared to be additional bedrooms, both with old furniture, boxes, and bags crammed into them. After looking at each, she seriously doubted she'd find the keys in either room. That just left one last option, the bedroom where Crash slept.

Her instincts screamed at her to just go back in there, strip off and get back in bed before Crash noticed she was gone. She'd only been there for a day or so. Maybe if she could just be patient, they could have a talk and maybe she could help him out, offer some strategies for dealing with his grief, and he'd take her back. She could hang out for one more day, right? So she walked back in, quietly as she could, to see that Crash hadn't moved. He was still lying on his side, his back to her and the door. *Just get back in bed.*

But what she did, once her eyes were adjusted again to the dark of that bedroom, was to drop to her knees on the thick carpeting and crawl around looking for his discarded clothes. She remembered him grabbing them off the bathroom floor once he'd showered but what had he done with them after that? She had no idea. It didn't take her long to figure out they weren't on the bedroom floor. Getting up on her knees, she stretched to see if by any chance they were on a dresser or chest of drawers. No. Was there a hamper?

Get back in bed, dumbass.

Helena had no idea how much time had passed but she needed to make a decision. If she'd just walked out of the house, she could have been a mile up the road by now. She could have reached a gas station maybe or somewhere with access to a phone. But, no. She was still crawling around Crash's bedroom floor looking for the keys to his car. It was insane. She knew she should just get back in the bed and that would be that. Live to fight another day.

But *would* she live? Once he saw the scar on her jaw, would he see her as the disgusting sloppy seconds of the enemy? Would he decide she wasn't good enough to live? She'd seen it firsthand. Women with that mark would get taken by other Cottonmouths who decided that the mark meant they were as good as club sluts, to be used however they liked. Would a member of the Hounds treat her any better? How did she know Crash wouldn't just lose his shit when he discovered that mark?

Baby Face marking her face up hadn't been the only aftereffect of her hellish relationship with him. Helena had scars in other places, little nicks he'd made in her flesh with his knives. The fact that he'd liked to cut women up during sex might have been a turn-on to some women, but it had terrified her. By the time she'd figured out that his pretty face hid a dark heart, he'd marked her face and sliced into her flesh during rough sex -- which was all he had. Baby Face had no concept of making love or playful sex; everything with him was rough and violent. The other scars, she could explain away and the only other person she'd had sex with since was Crash. But her jaw?

What would he do? Anxiety had her heart flying in her chest as she considered her actions. *Get back in bed before he catches you.*

It also occurred to her that she could look for something to cover the scar with while he was still asleep. But what would he have? Crash wouldn't have makeup, and it didn't appear he'd grabbed any from her place. Did he have Band-Aids? If he did, how would she explain that? What would she have cut her face on? Wouldn't it just draw attention to what she didn't want him to see?

It was hard pushing thoughts through her panic. Her breath came too fast, her vision fading out around the edges. She had to decide something or else she was going to pass out.

Scrambling across the floor, she made it back into the bathroom. Maybe there was something there she could use to hide her jaw. A topical cream? Anything. She pushed the door gently closed with a shaking hand and flipped on the light. Carefully as she could, she went through the medicine cabinet over the sink. There were bandages, shaving cream, and a bottle of pink anti-itch cream. Was she going to claim she had mosquito bites at the start of winter? Could she claim she broke out in hives, dab it on other areas so it wouldn't be obvious? Maybe.

But she had to do something really fucking fast before --

When Helena stepped back from the sink with the bottle of pink lotion in her hand, she yelped from the pain of stepping on something hard on the floor. With a hand over her mouth, she glanced down to see something shiny and silver under her bare foot. Keys! Snatching them up, Helena's heart raced in hope to realize it was a set of car keys with a key fob that looked relatively new. If these were the keys to his car, she could make it out. She could escape!

Stopping in her tracks, the keys clutched in her hands, Helena took a deep breath as she set the bottle down. This was the point of no return. If she decided to take those keys and run, she needed to commit to it and never look back. She knew if that was what she chose, she needed to go *now*.

Why did she feel conflicted about trying to escape Crash and his home? Sure, he'd had no right to bring her here and hold her captive. But if she were completely honest with herself, was she that scared of Crash and the possibility of him hurting her? While there was a possibility of him doing her physical harm, somehow, she just didn't think he would. On a certain level, she trusted him with herself. If she hadn't, she wouldn't have voluntarily slept with him, given him a blow job.

Then why wasn't he answering her when she asked if they could make a deal about taking her home?

If she ran now and managed to get away, how would that go? Anything she thought she had with Crash was over. And that should have been okay. She'd been alone since she'd left Mercy. Wouldn't she be okay just going back home and pretending the last two days never happened?

Or you can put the keys back where you found them and get back in bed. Right fucking now.

A scream ripped from Helena when the bathroom door was roughly pushed open, pushing her behind it. Helena held her hands up defensively, the keys clutched in her right hand.

Crash's expression went from sleepy to livid in about five seconds. Without a care that he didn't have a stitch on, he snatched the keys from her hand before grabbing a handful of her hair with his other hand, dragging her head back sharply, pulling a cry from her. He got in her face, his eyes reflecting a gamut of emotion from anger to something she thought might be hurt.

"Running out on me again, huh?" His tone was bitter.

"No, I just found… your keys and --"

"Don't lie to me!" Crash shouted.

And she was. Yeah, she'd found the keys on the

bathroom floor, but that wasn't the whole truth. She'd been searching all over the house, his bedroom floor, for the means to escape. He had her dead to rights.

"I'm sorry," she muttered as he roughly steered her out of the bathroom and into one of the two rooms she'd discovered earlier, filled to the brim with items he just wanted out of the way.

"You're gonna be," Crash growled, shoving her into the room until she sprawled across bags on the floor. Lucky for her, they were soft. "Stay here. Rot. I don't give a fuck!"

The door slammed, leaving her in the dark. Panic had her scrambling to her feet, as best she could with all the mess around her and reaching for the doorknob. When she turned it, she found the door was locked. There wasn't an unlocking mechanism on her side of the door.

Helena shivered, wrapping her arms around herself in the dark room. It was chilly and dark in the room he'd locked her in. Guilt made her realize she'd set off his defenses; his actions were an armor against something raw and wounded in him. Crash was a man trapped in cycles of grief and anger, someone desperate to reclaim control. She'd just have to wait him out.

* * *

Crash

Turning on the bedside lamp, Crash sat on the edge of bed with his head in his hands. His mind scrambled to piece things together. His heart was crashing in his chest.

He'd dared her to prove he could trust her and to his delight, she had, a couple of times. It messed with his head because sex with her had been so good. It reminded him of why he hadn't gotten her out of his head all these years. Pleasure with her was so easy, so right. He'd gone to sleep with her nestled against his chest, secure in his arms. It felt like he could begin to heal at least some of the wounds of the past. Crash hadn't had any set-in-stone plans for the next morning, but he thought maybe they could talk over breakfast, work together on where to go from there.

Until he'd woken up to find her gone and heard noises in his bathroom. He'd listened outside the closed door for long minutes. There were no sounds to indicate she was in the tub or shower, nothing to show she was on the toilet. When he heard the familiar jingle of keys, he knew exactly what was happening. Helena was trying to escape him for the second time.

Instead of stopping to consider the best course of action, Crash quietly manipulated the lock on the door. He'd done it many times in his life. He'd shoved open the door, catching her red-handed with his car keys in her hand. There she was, fully dressed, pleading with him, telling him she was sorry. But he knew she didn't mean it. She didn't care about him. Oh, she'd said she had and he'd believed her. For five fucking years, he'd believed her. It had all been a lie.

Crash couldn't even look at her. Grabbing her by her hair, he'd yanked her ass out of the bathroom and shoved her into the room he used to share with Perry. In hindsight, he really wished he'd shoved her into the guest room that his family had always used as a junk storage room. The bitch didn't deserve to be in the room where he and Perry'd stayed. She didn't deserve anything.

The enormity of what he'd done hit Crash hard. Helena didn't really want him. She probably never had. Over the last few months, his entire fucking life had come down around him. The brother he couldn't protect, the woman who'd fooled him with her easy charm and a smile. Now Perry was dead and Helena? He'd taken her but she wasn't his and he was going to have to deal with the fallout of that stupid ass-decision. She was here against her will. No way she wouldn't press charges against him.

Crash wasn't afraid of prison. Hell, his so-called Hound brothers wouldn't care if he ended up there. They hadn't had Perry's back. Why should they have his?

What the fuck was he going to do?

There was no way he was going back to sleep, so Crash sat there for a long time.

* * *

Helena

Despite the fact that she was a therapist, Helena sat on the floor, nestled among the trash bags that felt more like clothing, and cried. How had her life come to this? To get out of the hole her life used to be, she'd left the area and gone back to school. She'd deliberately blanked out a lot of her old memories of where she'd lived and had messed up so badly. She hadn't been back there in years.

It has taken a while for her to recover from the scars Baby Face had left on her, seen and unseen. But slowly, she got better. She'd worked hard to get an education and go through all the steps to become a therapist. By the time she'd achieved her goal, five years had passed. Baby Face was now dead. She hadn't thought returning to Mercy, the town next door to Oak Grove where she'd grown up, would be that much of a challenge. It was close to her old home but in a different county, making her feel like she was out in the world.

It wasn't that she'd forgotten about Crash in all that time. She hadn't. He could and probably would make the case that the single night they'd spent together meant a lot more to him than to her. But if that were true, why had she used it as justification for turning down every guy in school who'd asked her out? Sure, she could have also chalked it up to the abuse she'd suffered at the hands of Baby Face, but he wasn't that important to her in the grand scheme of things. He had been a cheap thug she'd had the misfortune of falling in with for a short while.

Crash was different. He had left a different type of scar on her heart. How many times had she considered setting herself up on a dating app? Thoughts of him always stopped her cold.

Helena tried to tell herself that they'd been good decisions. That it was her therapist side talking. But it was a lie. She'd had no idea what to do with Crash. She'd panicked when he showed up at her office under a name she didn't recognize and followed her around town, daring her to talk to him. Now, he'd full on kidnapped her, taken her somewhere his family had once lived. She'd slept with him because she'd wanted him and there were no regrets there. But fucking seemed to be the only thing she felt confident in doing with him. How sad was that? And that could well be over when he saw the scar on her face.

Both windows in the small bedroom were boarded, shrouding the room in gloom. But as her eyes adjusted to the darkness, she spotted a light switch and tried it. The dim light from a single bulb hanging from the ceiling cast shadows across the disarray, making the room feel smaller than it was. It felt like she was locked in a tomb of forgotten things, suffocating and heavy with neglect. The air was stale, thick with the scent of old fabric and dust that clung to every surface. Piles of boxes and bags were haphazardly stacked against the walls, some teetering dangerously as though one wrong move could send the entire mess crashing down.

Old coats, dresses, and shirts spilled from some of the bags, in dull and lifeless colors, the fabric looking stiff from years of abandonment. A toppled stack of cardboard boxes took up one corner, some labeled in faded marker with things like "Perry's books" and "Mom's stuff." The boxes had clearly been shoved in here to be forgotten, their contents deemed unimportant. Against the far wall, an old dresser sat, its drawers half open and overflowing with miscellaneous items -- crumpled papers, broken trinkets, and more discarded clothes. Dust covered every surface around her. Cobwebs clung to the corners where the ceiling met the walls. An ancient lamp leaned awkwardly in another corner, its base dented, lampshade missing.

Helena's heart raced as she surveyed the chaos, the weight of all these unwanted things pressing in on her. The door behind her was locked, trapping her not just physically, but emotionally, in a place that represented everything that had been discarded, ignored, and pushed aside. Just like she was in this moment. How long had the room had been like this? It was just filled with the remnants of lives left behind, long ago. Now, she felt like she was a part of it, hidden away in Crash's past. And she had no idea how to escape.

Taking a deep breath, Helena tried to get a grip on herself. It hadn't been dawn when he'd shoved her in there. She just needed to give Crash a little while to think about things. Before long, he'd open that door, and she needed to be ready. Yes, she'd lost the trust she'd earned earlier. But earning trust through sex might not have been the best approach. The two of them needed to talk about a lot of things: what'd happened between them before, what had happened tonight.

Anger and grief were consuming Crash. It was written all over him. Her training made her realize he was likely acting out of confusion and pain. It didn't feel like Crash was out to hurt her. He just didn't know how to handle everything that had been dumped on him. He didn't trust her, so she couldn't treat him as a normal patient. It didn't matter anyway because the entire situation was personal, and she was part of the wound he was trying to heal.

Helena *had* to get him to talk to her. If she could get his focus off her and get him to open up, even just a little, maybe she could help him face what he was going through. Grief often manifested as anger, isolation, and mistrust, which seemed to be where he was right now. The trick was getting him to listen, to see that she wasn't his enemy. Wasn't she still that woman he'd flirted with at *Sackett's*? If she could make him understand she wasn't running this time, that she was trying to help him, maybe together they could work through it so he could heal.

Knowing she'd never get back to sleep, Helena looked around at all the items. The clothes and other household odds and ends didn't interest her at all. But one box caught her eye. There were old notebooks in it, the dates written on their pages some twenty years ago. Random printed pages were shoved inside, the name at the top of each read "Perry Ford."

Was Perry Crash's brother? Where did Charlie

Ford's biker name, Crash, come from, anyway? She'd never asked.

A few minutes passed and Helena moved on from the cheap notebooks to the fancier notebooks at the bottom. One was a nice leather journal with pages that had gentle wear. Unlike the school notebooks, the journal had been valued. She half expected to find its pages blank, but they weren't. Inside were several journal entries from 2004 written by Perry. Helena probably shouldn't have read them. Journals were private and if Crash caught her, it might really piss him off considering his brother passed earlier this year. Finding a bigger book, an old encyclopedia, Helena did her best to hide the journal. She told herself that she would only read the journal to learn something -- anything -- about Crash and his family. Maybe she'd find something in there to help Crash deal with some of the things plaguing him.

After a couple of hours passed, she heard Crash walking from the bedroom they were in earlier. His steps moved away from the door of her room, not toward it. Maybe he went to the living room or the kitchen. She was so lost in the journal she read she wasn't concerned about his whereabouts.

From Perry's journal entries, she figured out that Perry was a freshman in high school in 2004 and Charlie, before he was Crash, was a senior. She smiled. Okay, he was older than she was, but she could live with that, right?

The smile didn't last long. Helena read one journal entry after another, the story of Crash and his brother's lives at that point in time grew more horrifying with each page. The boys' mother had died before the entries in the journal. They were then left with a monster of a stepfather who apparently had made their lives hell.

Helena's heart sank just thinking about them. What had happened to their mother and father? Perry's mentions of their mother were kind, and he often mentioned how much he missed her. How had she come to marry such a monster? When she'd died, her underage sons had been left to the mercy of a violent stepfather addicted to drugs.

By the time she finished the journal, her bladder was screaming at her. Just as she was about to knock on her side of the door to beg to go to the bathroom, the door unlocked. With shaking hands, she shoved the books under the bed. Her gaze landed on Crash and he still looked angry.

Helena was ready. She didn't know his intentions and had no idea how he'd react when he saw Baby Face's mark on her. But she'd learned a little bit about him and felt better prepared for whatever direction their conversation might take.

Chapter Eight

Crash

It was late morning when Crash finally got over himself enough to go to the door of the bedroom that had been his and Perry's. Betrayal and guilt blended into a subtle poison that ran through his veins as he unlocked the door to confront the woman he'd locked inside.

Helena was on her knees on the floor, looking small among the bags and boxes of shit that had accumulated in the unused room over the years. Slowly she rose near the foot of Perry's bed, meeting his gaze and looking like a woman headed for the gallows. As frustrated as he was with everything, Crash knew he was in the wrong here.

What was the matter with him? Helena had been someone he'd wanted before he was even a Hound. Maybe she didn't feel the same way about him. There could also be a dozen other reasons why she ran from Mercy like her ass was on fire. Didn't mean it was him. No matter how hard he'd tried, Crash had never been able to convince himself that *he* had been the reason she'd left, that he'd done anything wrong. It just didn't feel right when being with her that night long ago and last night had felt so fucking good. When Margot had made him the appointment with Helena for therapy, all he had to was tell his Ryder's old lady that he didn't need therapy. That would have ended it. Crash didn't have to take the extra step and go just to confront a woman who might not have even remembered him.

But she'd remembered him all right and not in a good way. Then Helena told him she couldn't treat him because of their personal interaction. It just brought everything back to the surface in a rush, making his blood boil. But if he were being honest with himself, he knew what his actions really meant. He'd basically kidnapped her to vainly demand answers about why she was running from him. Crash was punishing her for not doing what he wanted. And he wasn't proud of his handiwork. There were deep shadows beneath her eyes, tension pulling her body rigid. She probably hadn't slept a wink from the looks of her.

"Need to go to the bathroom?" he asked. It was a ridiculous question, given the situation.

Nodding, she moved closer, and he led her out the door, keeping her in his peripheral vision to make sure she didn't fall as she made her way around everything that had been stuffed into the room. Crash lingered in the hallway as she walked into the bathroom and shut the door. When she came back out, her expression was hard to read but she stopped, awaiting further instructions. He could have cut the tension with a knife. It made it hard for him to even breathe.

"We need to talk," he said. Crash led her back to the living room, taking a seat on the couch. Patting the cushion next to him, he waited for her to join him. And without a word, she did, sitting at his right. "Want to tell me where you were planning on going at three this morning?"

Helena hung her head, her dark hair a wavy black curtain that she hid behind. For a long moment, he wasn't sure she was going to answer. "I wasn't entirely sure I was going anywhere."

"You were dressed," he pointed out. "You thought about it."

She still wasn't looking at him. "I did think about it."

"Even knowing you were betraying my trust," he said. "Again."

That had her gaze meeting his. "Again? You know, you act as if we were in a relationship or had some sort of agreement that night. We didn't, Crash. But last night I was hoping to earn your trust. To show you I care. I'm also scared. You would be too if someone drugged you, dragged you out of your apartment, and took you away somewhere. I don't even know where we are." Her words stung but he'd earned that. She was right. She hadn't made him any promises that night and she hadn't asked to be here now. But Crash wasn't backing down. He wanted to get to the heart of things. With her anyway. It was too important to him.

Feeling like he couldn't breathe, Crash rose from the couch, began pacing the floor. "Let's talk about that night. Since you brought it up. What was that about? I didn't expect anything that night. I would have stayed in the car. I offered to. You remember that."

"I do." Helena angled her body on the couch to face him, propping her jaw on her right hand as she watched him pace.

"Why? Why did you just take off like that?" Crash knew how sad and pathetic he sounded. He didn't care. That night had been something he'd wanted so badly for a long time.

"I'll answer that question," she said. "I promise. But that's not the only thing that's wrong, is it? It's not even the primary thing. You lost your brother. Do you want to talk about *that*?"

That stopped him. "My brother isn't anyone's fucking business," he warned. "I know Margot used that to reel you in but --"

"Reel me in?" Helena's gaze locked with his.

"Margot doesn't know that you and I ever crossed paths. She just saw a friend she thought could use someone to talk to. She mentioned your brother died in the summer and that you were struggling. That I was someone you'd had a one-night stand with is incidental. And as I mentioned earlier, I didn't know who Charlie Ford was."

"I'm not struggling," he argued. "Is that what they think? Fuck them. Including Margot. If they cared so damn much, maybe Perry wouldn't be gone in the first place."

Helena's expression shifted. "What happened to Perry?"

Crash hated how she did that. How could she look up at him with those big green eyes and act like she gave a shit? His heart clenched in his chest. What if she did care? Isn't that what he longed for all along?

"Who do you mean by 'them'?" Helena asked, her expression open, kind. "What happened, Crash?"

"What do you care?" Crash asked, his tone surly. But her expression didn't change. She wasn't looking around nervously or speaking fast. Her words were careful, her gaze on him as she waited. Still, he felt the urge to keep her from changing the subject. "You're not here so I can talk about my brother. You're here to talk about you and why you disappeared."

Her demeanor didn't shift. "I'll tell you anything you want to know," she said slowly. "If you tell me about your brother Perry."

Scrubbing a hand down his face, he started pacing again, glaring at her though his anger wasn't entirely directed at her. "Margot had no business talking to you or any fucking therapist on my behalf. I hope she fucking knows that."

"She cares about you," Helena told him. "That

much is obvious."

Crash stopped. "Why would she ask *you* to talk to me I wonder? How are you two connected?"

"Margot has sent a lot of folks my way," Helena explained, sighing. "It was my first week on the job and I almost had a full schedule. It was the craziest damn thing. Come to find out, our office works pretty closely with the sheriff's department, usually helping crime victims. Margot's pretty great."

Crash nodded, putting his hands on his hips. "She tell you she's dating a Hound?"

"As a matter of fact, she did." Helena smiled. "She told me that the friend she wanted me to talk to was a Hound too. But like I said, I didn't know the name Charlie Ford."

"You didn't stop and think for a second that it could be me?"

"Sure, I did," Helena told him. "There was a *chance* it could be you. But what were the odds? Five years ago, you weren't in the club yet. You were a prospect. You could have given up the life by now or be in another chapter if you stayed. It was possible but unlikely."

"Not really," Crash said. "If you knew me at all, you would have known I'd never leave the Hounds."

"I don't know you all that well," she admitted, "so I wouldn't have known that. Are the Hounds the ones you were talking about? When you said if *they'd* cared, maybe Perry wouldn't be gone? What happened?"

She wasn't backing off and frustration pushed his anxiety higher. His jaw tightened and his muscles tensed. "I don't want to fucking talk about it!"

"I think you do." Helena stayed patient though the way her hands clasped tightly in her lap told him she was a little nervous. Her knuckles were white. "This is a good place to do it. Did you grow up here?"

Crash's chest felt tight, his fists clenched at his sides. Helena had figured out this was his childhood home. She was a lot smarter and more perceptive than he'd realized. He hadn't thought about it until that moment -- talking about what happened to his brother, to Perry, in the very house they grew up in. Where their young lives began with promise and ended in pain and chaos. It left him feeling raw and vulnerable, like fucking Larry could reach him from the grave and choke him out. Beat him one last time and tell him everything that came out of his mouth about their stepfather and lives was a lie.

How many times had Crash tried to reason with the bastard, explain to him that they could all live there and get along? Larry had always laughed and punched him harder. He'd told Crash that no one would ever fucking believe him if he tried to say Larry abused them, or locked them out of their own home, or took their money and food. Larry would tell him that he and Perry weren't worth anything and it would have been better if they'd died like their parents. He'd also told Crash that if they ever tried to tell anyone that Larry killed their mother, he'd kill *them*. The room seemed to shift around him, and his breath came fast, like it did when he was scared. When the edges of his vision started to black out around the edges, he knew he had to stop. Put the brakes on.

Helena's arm around him brought him back, her soft touch warm, gentle. It reminded him of his mother, how she was the only one who could reach him sometimes when things seemed to be at their worst. Crash let her guide him back to the couch, taking a seat on it as he tried to slow his breathing.

Helena again sat at his right, her green eyes filled with concern.

"Take deep, slow breaths. Okay?" With one arm still around him, she placed her other hand over his heart. "Breathe slowly. Your heart will slow down once your breathing is under control. It's flying right now."

Every ounce of his anger was buried under panic and confusion. What was happening to him? Was he having a heart attack?

"Crash," she whispered. "You're not alone. I'm here with you. I'm right here with you. Take your time."

Crash couldn't even utter a response. All he could do in that moment was try to breathe with her, to keep his focus on *her*. When he closed his eyes, he saw images from the past that shattered him. Larry's enraged face. His mother lying broken on the bathroom floor that day when they got home from school, her skin already cold and gray. Perry's haunted eyes when Crash found him hiding in the bushes behind his own house, freezing because it was winter, and Larry had locked them out.

After a few minutes, sitting there with Helena on the couch, the panic that gripped him started to ease. His chest hurt and he still felt a little disoriented, but she stayed there with him, arms wrapped around him. She was a lot smaller than him, but her strength didn't waver. She was steady, comforting, her voice soothing. "Are you okay?" she asked, her voice gentle.

Crash nodded, taking a deep breath.

"Where did you get the name Crash?" Helena asked. "I don't think you ever told me that story. Is it your MC name?"

He grinned at the unexpected question. "It is, but the club isn't where I got it. We made some friends before we ever fell in with the Hounds. They were into drag racing. Every weekend at Rupp Park, we'd be there trying to Frankenstein our car together, trying to win."

Helena's smile was gorgeous as she gazed up at him. "You're a mechanic?"

Crash shook his head. "Not so much. I'd tell you that I was a better driver."

Her brows knit. "But your nickname is Crash."

Now he laughed. "Exactly. That's why we were always trying to piece the fucking cars back together."

Crash had never heard her laugh before. It was a warm, happy sound that had his heart shifting in his chest. "Number 17?" she asked.

Wait. What? "How did you know that?"

Helena patted his thigh. "Your tattoo."

He'd forgotten she'd gotten a closer look at the tattoo on his thigh last night when she had those beautiful lips wrapped around his cock. It had been his first ink though not his best tattoo. Back then, he'd just wanted to fit in and find a place where he and Perry would be safe.

It seemed like a good place to start if he was going to tell her their story. Helena's kind gaze on him had him thinking maybe talking to someone was a good idea. With her here, it felt safe. He wanted to. Taking a deep breath, Crash decided to try.

"As soon as I turned eighteen," Crash said slowly, "I took Perry and we moved in with a friend of mine that I worked with. He lived in an old house his father left him. It was a real shack, but it had plenty of room and we helped him renovate it to earn our keep."

"But this house is where you grew up?" Helena asked.

He nodded. "From the time I was three until the

day we left. Our parents were young when they had us, but we had a decent life in the beginning."

She didn't say anything, just gave him the time he needed to think about how he wanted to phrase his story. Their history. It was Perry's too, and he needed to push his words through the searing guilt and pain of that loss. Helena's attention was solely on him, her gaze open and kind.

"Our dad worked for a construction company and died in an accident on a site when we were little," he explained. "It was a bad time. I was in school, but Perry was too young, and Mom had to find a way to care for him and find a job. She made it work. She found work at a day care, and they let her bring Perry, for a price. I took the bus from there to school in the morning and back there after. It worked out. For a few years, we were okay, you know."

Helena's smile faded, almost like she knew things were about to take a dark turn.

"I think Perry had just started second grade when Mom met Larry." He didn't even try to keep his hate of the man out of the tone of his voice. "I knew she was lonely, but if she went on any dates, we didn't know much about it. She never brought men home. It was always just her with us. If Larry hadn't been a selfish, alcoholic motherfucker, it might have worked. I don't remember any happy times with that asshole. Not one."

Dropping her hand from his chest to his hand, she laced her fingers with his. A quiet show of support.

"They fought a lot," Crash continued, "Right from the start. As soon as he had a few drinks in him and started on us, she'd get me and Perry in our room, tell us to stay put no matter what. The next morning, she'd be scrambling around in the kitchen getting ready for work, getting us ready for school. There'd be fresh bruises and marks on her. She hid them as best she could, sure. But if you paid close attention, you could see them. Hell, we noticed them, and we were kids."

Helena swallowed hard. Her hand tightened around his. "What did they fight about?"

Crash shrugged. "His drinking. His whoring. The fact that he couldn't hold down a job and we went without a lot because now she was struggling to take care of us and his ass. Liquor wasn't cheap and cigarettes weren't either. Mom didn't smoke or drink. She'd done a little weed with Dad when he was still alive, but that's about it. I loved her. Me and Perry both did. But it got to the point that we wanted to be anywhere but home. Because the minute you walked in the door, you knew it was going to start any time over the stupidest shit. Every damn day."

"Sounds like the three of you were living a nightmare," Helena said when he paused.

"Putting it mildly," he replied. "There was a period of time when I hit my teen years that I was fucking angry at her. Yeah, I loved her. I hated watching what that fucker put her through. But she was the one who'd bought his bullshit. She was the one who brought him into our fucking house."

"As you got older, you saw the situation for what it truly was," Helena said. "That you were angry about it was natural. Did he ever hit you or your brother?"

"Oh, hell yeah." Crash snorted. "A lot of times he was between jobs. He'd be home when we got off the bus. Most of the time, he was just waiting on us. He'd thought up some reason he was pissed at us and he'd come stumbling to the door, drunk and angry. He'd grab one of us by the shirt, slam us against the wall.

He'd get in your face and just the smell of all the shit he'd been drinking would damn near make you fucking sick... There at the end, I was just so fucking angry with her."

"At the end?"

"The son-of-a-bitch killed her," Crash said, hating the way his voice shook while he watched her eyes widen. "No one will ever be able to convince me otherwise. Never. When the cops arrived that day, Larry told them she hadn't been feeling well for a couple of weeks. That she'd been having seizures. I never saw her have a fucking seizure."

"But that left you and Perry alone with... him," she said. "How old were you?"

"Not old enough to strike out on our own," he said. "Not old enough to defend ourselves. I'd just turned fourteen. He kept the rest of our family away. He got deeper into drugs and brought so many fucking women in here..." Shaking his head, he thought of so many things he wished he'd done back then. Hindsight had twenty-twenty vision, true. But if he'd just been braver, stronger... Could he have made their lives better? Could he have discouraged Perry from wanting to be a prospect in the Hounds? Perry might still be alive if he had. "I took as much off Perry as I could but..."

She studied him for a few seconds while he fought to get himself under control. It felt like a wave was about to crash over him, the memories, the beatings. It was why he'd avoided the house until after Perry died, not wanting to be in it though it belonged to him now. Even when Crash tried hard, he couldn't recall what his father looked like or even many memories of him unless he looked at one of the photos Perry kept on the mantel. There were a few happy times with his mother that came from before her marriage to fucking Larry. Perry had been three years younger than him. He probably wouldn't even have had those memories.

"Do you know how strong both of you were to have survived that?" Helena asked.

"Strong? We didn't have a choice." Crash shook his head. "It wasn't just us having to live here in the same house as that bastard after our mother was gone. It was our house. Not his. And the fucker would go through our stuff and take our house keys when he found them, hoping to just lock us out. As soon as I was old enough, I got a job. He didn't work, so there was rarely any food or money for clothes. That's where my money went. But he'd look for that too. He'd take any money he found to buy his fucking drugs. When he was high, he wasn't as bad. When he couldn't afford the fix, he was hungry, and he didn't make anything. It wasn't like he ever bought food even to feed himself. We had to hide everything we had."

She hadn't expected that last part of his story. Helena's eyes were glossy with tears, and he was grateful because he couldn't shed them, not even for Perry.

"As soon as you could, you got Perry out of here." It wasn't a question. She didn't release him to swipe at her tears. "The two of you moved in with friends?"

"We did," Crash said. "Perry was terrified the first few days. I guess he was afraid that fucker would find us, drag us back to this house. I knew he wouldn't. He *wanted* us gone. It worked out in his favor. Within a year or so, Perry was old enough to work. Somehow, we both made it through high school and made our way. We stuck together, even joined the Hounds together."

Crash knew she wouldn't miss the emotion in his voice at the end. Her fingers squeezed his. A warm tear fell on the back of his hand.

"It was a few years before we crossed paths with the Hounds," Crash said. "They've been part of Mercy since before my time, but it wasn't anything I was ever interested in until I was around thirty or so. Me and Perry eventually got apartments, had jobs and lives. I ended up working in construction. Perry followed me there. Street racing was still a big thing around here, though I wasn't as involved as I'd been fresh out of high school. The friend that took us in, Denny, still participated. He had a kid named Richie who was all about it. He was fearless, like me, but he was also a good driver. The Cottonmouths had a couple of members who helped organize the races. Won most of them, too, at least until Richie started getting good. Winning races."

Something shifted in Helena's expression. Fear or dread? She listened, her full attention on him.

"When Richie started winning, little things started to go wrong," Crash explained. "Everything could be checked and double checked on Richie's car and still, minor issues would pop up. Loose lug nuts, brake problems. It scared Denny enough he confronted the other teams about it because he knew someone had been fucking with his kid's car. And after he looked each one of them in the eye, he knew -- he fucking *knew* -- it was the Cottonmouths. Problem is, those motherfuckers don't take kindly to threats, no matter how they're presented."

"They hit back, didn't they?" Helena asked in a quiet voice, her eyes wide.

"They sure as fuck did." Crash blew out a breath.

"Richie had just turned nineteen when he died in that car. The brake line was cut. Denny was devastated. The fucking Cottonmouths said they'd take him out too if he ever showed his fucking face at Rupp Park again."

When she didn't say anything, just listened with an expression that was a cross between surprise and growing fear, Crash went on. "Denny took it to a local garage, got Hero to take a look at it. He's a member of the Hounds. And he backed up what Denny was saying. The Hounds and the Cottonmouths have bad blood between them. Always have. Denny's kid getting killed for being a better racer didn't sit well with Razor. The Hounds took up our side." Crash chuckled remembering just how bad it was. "Without going into detail, let's just say the Cottonmouths haven't raced since."

After a moment, Helena nodded. "That's how you got to know them?"

"It was." Crash remembered that summer and how fascinated he'd been with the Hounds of Hell. "The more time I spent with them, the more I realized they weren't just a motorcycle club. They were the stable family I wanted."

After losing their father at a young age, Crash was left shouldering a weight that should have never fallen on a kid's shoulders. His mother's second husband had filled the void with violence, molding his and Perry's young lives into a never-ending cycle of fear and survival. Their mother's death had ended the concept of family as they knew it, snuffing out the last flicker of warmth and care in their lives.

The Hounds offered a different type of family that was hard but fiercely loyal to each other. Their unbending code offered a level of protection and solidarity Crash craved but never thought he'd have.

His Hound brothers didn't just stand by each other, they fought for each other and their loved ones. They bled for each other, no questions asked. In the club, he wasn't "the kid whose stepfather beat the shit out of him." No, he was Crash, a brother, a prospect working his way up in a family that was ready to take him in. Even before he earned his cut, Crash found strength in the bonds they offered. The club had its own version of loyalty and justice, something he respected and understood. Every rule, every act of initiation was a test of his commitment and resilience... something he'd had to prove his entire fucking life. With the Hounds, finally, he found a place where his strength and tenacity were valued.

"And Perry?" she asked, keeping her voice low and steady. "Did he finally become a Hound too? What happened to him?"

"He was a prospect," Crash said, feeling the bitter sting of betrayal as he thought about what had happened to his brother at the end of summer. The Hounds, his chosen family, had withheld the most devastating news of his life. They'd kept him in the dark about his brother's brutal murder, staging Perry's body like a pawn in a bloody game of chess they played with the Mafia.

The fact that they'd found Perry nailed to a cross behind their clubhouse, along with Chance and a third cross marked with Sadie's name, and then hid the scene until after their ambush was a betrayal so deep it felt like a knife that kept twisting in his gut.

It wasn't just a lack of communication. No, it was a deliberate choice. It was a harsh reminder that while the Hounds accepted him as a brother, his loyalty might never be enough to shield him from the club's darker side. Despite his brothers' explanations and even talking to the club president, Razor himself, he questioned everything he thought he knew about his place in the club. Was it naïve to think he could fully trust them when it mattered most?

There he was with Helena, holding him close. The thought of telling her what'd happened to Perry threatened to break him. It was almost like he was afraid to tell that tale in the house where they grew up. The site of so much pain in their lives.

Maybe Crash had kept it bottled up for too long. Maybe he would feel better telling someone how he felt. Explain that it wasn't just anger at his brothers for what had happened to the little brother he'd sworn to protect. Crash was angry at himself for failing to be there for Perry. If he told that tale in these four walls, just maybe Larry or his parents would reach beyond the grave to end him. Sometimes he thought he wanted that.

Deep down, he felt it was what he deserved.

Chapter Nine

Helena

"He was a prospect," was all Crash said when she asked what'd happened to Perry. Then he seemed lost in thought. Whatever had happened to his brother must have been traumatic. From the way he sat next to her, his heart flying, his breathing rapid, to the way he stared off into space, no longer seeing their current reality. She already knew something horrible had happened. Margot knew what'd happened, or else she wouldn't have asked if Helena could talk to him. Maybe it was because she was a deputy or maybe it was because of her Hound boyfriend.

As Helena waited for him to find a way to continue his story, it wasn't lost on her that the reason he'd found the Hounds was because of the Cottonmouths. They couldn't take his friend's son beating them at the drag strip, so they conspired to kill him. A young man with his whole life ahead of him. The Cottonmouths being the rivals of the Hounds of Hell MC was one thing. The fact that they'd killed his friend's son made it far more serious. Personal. And there was no doubt in her mind that the story was true.

It caused her own fear and anxiety to climb. With the hatred he must have harbored toward the other MC, how was he going to take it that she was just another of Baby Face's discarded playthings? She even had the scar. Would he be disgusted by her? Would he physically harm her? The only reason he hadn't noticed it now was because she was strategically placing herself and he was lost in his memories.

Helena sighed. No, she didn't think he'd harm her. It just wasn't who he was. What he *could* do was much worse. Crash could turn his back on her and see her as someone unworthy of his trust, and that would hurt a lot more. She'd always been attracted to him. Now in their current situation, the more she found out about him, the more she realized who he really was, how he was many things she'd always longed for in a man. Crash had brought her here to find out why she'd run. That meant he cared beyond the night of passionate sex they'd shared. His feelings were involved, and as tough as his exterior was, he wasn't afraid to show her that side. Not at all.

The weight of her past threatened to poison her present along with the fragile bond they had begun to build here in his childhood home. Crash's loyalty to the Hounds ran as deep as his hatred for the Cottonmouths. Baby Face, with his twisted cruelty, had been the worst of the rival MC and she was afraid the scar the bastard had left on her face would just serve as a painful reminder of everything Crash had lost.

Fear twisted within her. Her conflict between the need to be honest with him and the desire to protect herself from the judgment she'd already braced for made it hard to stay and listen even though there was nowhere else she'd rather be right now. For a therapist, she was a fucking head case at the moment.

"Earlier this year, a woman came to town," Crash finally continued. "All beat up. Her car died at Cowboy Pete's there in Mercy, and Elsie Damron, who works there, called the garage in town that Hero and the twins run. They towed it in, but the woman begged them not to fix it. She was running from an abusive boyfriend. She decided to hide in Mercy. She got close to one of the twins, Axel. She became his old lady. But eventually, her ex caught up with her. Turns out he was Mafia."

Helena remembered seeing some of the stories in

the news before she returned to Mercy. She'd wondered while reading those stories what on earth the Mafia was doing in such a small town.

"Her ex sent his men into town looking for her. First, they killed a woman who looked like her and shot up Ryder while they were at it. He almost died." Crash blew out a breath. "Her ex showed up himself. He killed two people at Cowboy Pete's trying to find out where she was. One was Elsie; the other was Clyde Donner."

"Any relation to Margot?" she had to ask.

"Yeah, her father."

Helena was stunned. Margot's own father had been killed but there she'd been in her office, asking for Helena to help Crash. Her new friend was braver than she'd thought.

"Her ex then threatened an old couple who'd given her a job," Crash went on. "So, she showed up to meet the ex and the fuckers almost made it out of town with her. The cops got there first, but the Hounds were right behind them. Axel fought him and the ex got arrested. If the cops hadn't fucked it up, he'd have been dead, and it would have ended there. It should have ended there."

But it hadn't. He must have thought if only it had, Perry might still be alive. *Damn it.*

"For a few weeks, it was quiet. Life in Mercy got back to normal," Crash said. "Then the Feds showed up, wanting to talk to Sadie -- Axel's old lady and the Mafia fucker's ex-girlfriend. They were building a case against him that probably went way beyond what he'd done to her. That's what Razor said anyway. His Mafia family got wind of it and decided they needed to keep her and anyone else from talking. They started terrorizing Mercy. They burned down Emily Frost's bakery. She's Snow's old lady. They hit the garage, busted up a bunch of their clients' vehicles waiting for repairs. One of the prospects we had assigned to the garage that night chased after them and disappeared."

Helena felt his hand start to shake in hers as she held it. The fact that Crash was telling her the story was alarming. She didn't know a lot about MCs, but she did know they usually weren't supposed to discuss club business with those outside the club. Maybe he was so upset he just didn't remember that rule.

"The club made a plan that night. If we didn't hit them back, they'd just keep coming at Mercy. Our town. Our *turf*. We couldn't allow that. So, we planned an ambush at *Sackett's*," Crash explained. "Made it look like a fundraiser to rebuild Emily's bakery, put pictures of her and Sadie on there to get their attention. We knew they wouldn't miss a chance to come and stir up trouble there. If they suspected something was up, they'd look like fucking cowards if they *didn't* show. It was a sure thing, right? And they showed up. The fucking Cottonmouths were there too, wanting in on it because the fucking Mafia was squeezing them on guns. I still can't believe Razor allowed that."

Helena didn't miss the bitterness in his voice as he talked about the ambush. They'd actually confronted the Mafia at the bar where she used to work? The pain she felt coming off him as he told the story felt like he was peeling back layers of a wound that was still raw, bleeding right in front her.

"It was an ugly fight," Crash said. "Most of it was outside but not all. The place was pretty busted up once we were done. Some of the Mafia guys hightailed it out of there when they saw they weren't winning. We kicked ass. And it was over pretty much in an hour. The cops showed up. Margot was there. I never saw the main guy, but it turns out he followed the girls, including Sadie, his ex, out to the old barn out behind the bar. Do you remember it?"

Helena nodded. If she remembered correctly, Emery Phillips told her that the barn had been in use up until the '50s when the farmer sold his father the land.

"When the fight was over, I ended up back there. Behind the bar. There were lights out there. Something just… drew me in that direction." Crash pulled in a deep breath. His words came slowly, painfully, each word a blade slicing deeper. "I'd been a little upset because I hadn't seen Perry that day. At all. All of us had been assigned somewhere in Mercy. We were trying to be ready in case the Mafia goons hit somewhere else before the ambush. I didn't know where Perry ended up and I didn't even think about it. When I got to *Sackett's* before the fight, I even asked a few of them. 'Where's Perry? You seen him?'"

Helena's heart sank. He was about to tell her Perry's fate. Her anxiety was growing. "What happened?"

"No one told me anything," he said. "So, I'm out there watching cops heading toward the barn and there's people in there with flashlights and everything. I just knew somehow I needed to go out there. When I reached the door, and they tried to get me out of there? That's when I knew. I knew something fucked up had happened. I made it inside and saw the dread on their faces. Axel and Ryder. Margot, Sadie… It was dark in there, so I got my phone out, turned on the flashlight. There were Mafia guys in the hay, some dead. That was the blood I smelled. But there were three wooden crosses, crude shit, laying there on the floor off to the side. One was empty, had Sadie's name carved into it.

The others weren't empty. The two men actually fucking nailed on them were dead. They'd been dead for several hours at least. One of them was Chance, the prospect who chased them out of town when they hit the garage. The other..."

And Helena knew then.

Perry. His birth brother.

She became aware she was staring at him with her mouth open but... His brothers, birth and MC, had been crucified. Tears stung her eyes as she sat there, stunned at his story. The violence of organized crime didn't surprise her in the least. In her short time as a therapist, she'd actually had a patient who had left the life after having been part of a crime family. But why Perry?

"It's worse," Crash said. "They weren't just left out there in the barn behind *Sackett's*. No. They had been found the night before, all three crosses shoved into the ground with Chance and Perry on display on either side of Sadie's cross, right behind our fucking clubhouse. Razor and the rest of them running the club found that display the night *before*. And they took it down, hid that shit, until we could get past *Sackett's*. They didn't fucking *tell* me."

His tears came then and Helena's heart broke. He shook as much as his voice did. "My baby brother, who I swore to protect always, and they just moved him and Chance like they were fucking inconvenient and didn't say shit to me or Chance's family. Do you have any idea how bad that shit is? The Hounds are a fucking family and that included Perry, even though he was just a prospect. That he was my *birth brother* should have been enough. He was under the club's protection. He..."

He stopped talking, as if he couldn't speak for a

moment.

"Crash, I'm so sorry," she whispered.

"They all talked to me about it," he went on bitterly, making air quotes around "talked to me." "Razor talked to me. He told me that if they'd said anything when they found them, we would have lost our chance at the Mafia. We might never get a better opportunity to get them the fuck out of Mercy is what he said. So, he's telling me that my brother was sacrificed for the greater good of Mercy and so the Hounds could get their fucking revenge? My fucking little brother deserved more than that. He was *more* than that."

"Yes, he was," was all she could say. "He was worth much more than that. I'm so sorry that's how it all happened." It wasn't hard to pull him to her, to hold him there while he fought back tears. Helena was slightly ashamed of herself now, worried about her past with Baby Face and the scar he'd left on her. What was a scar compared to that?

Helena was shaken to her core, trying to piece together the broken fragments Crash had laid bare. The betrayal cut him deeply; his faith in the Hounds -- the family he'd finally found after so much loss -- had been shattered by their deception. It was clear to her that the scars from his past, losing his parents and surviving an abusive home, already ran deep. But this? The brutal discovery in the barn, his own brother crucified, felt like the wound that finally broke him, severing any last tie to the trust he once had in others.

Crash had carried the weight of so much trauma for so long -- fighting, surviving but not healing. She just wished she could absorb the intensity of his anger, heartbreak, and struggle to stay whole, to keep him from spiraling. Somehow, he had managed to keep his job, staying with the Hounds so far. All while it was eating him alive.

As she held him on the couch, Helena felt the deep ache of wanting to help him, wanting to be his strength, even though she'd hurt him too. If she wanted him to see he could count on someone, on *her*, she had to tread carefully. Could she even reach him now through all this pain? After all he'd endured, what if no one, not even she, could bring back the man she once wanted to be with?

Glancing beyond Crash to the living room windows, one of the curtains was pulled back enough to show her the streetlight shining now that the sun had gone down. Snowflakes fell, so thick it was hard to make out much else, as it turned the world white.

* * *

At some point during the night, Crash woke up, stretching on the couch where he'd ended up with Helena draped over him. She didn't know how long they'd been sleeping but it was cold and her limbs were stiff. Crash gently shifted her onto the couch so he could get up and move to the fireplace.

"Sorry," he muttered, walking into the kitchen. The door in there opened and Helena felt a cool rush of wind from the bitter cold outside. When Crash had returned, he'd brought an assortment of wood pieces. "I'll get a fire going."

Curling up on the couch, she realized she'd been wearing the same clothes for days. "I'm going to take a shower."

Crash didn't react at all, working on a building a fire while she went for the bag of items he'd taken from her apartment, and jumped into the shower. When she came back out, she had on her favorite pair of pajamas -- that was something good -- and returned to the couch. The fire's blaze was comforting, and Crash was busy in the kitchen. She didn't know what he was making but her stomach growled in approval.

When he returned to the living room, exhaustion already weighed heavily on her. The weekend had been a lot, from being taken from her apartment and the misunderstandings and the long talk they'd had before falling asleep on the couch. Finding the remote, she turned on the TV, selecting the local news. It was the same TV station she always watched for local news. It confirmed the hints that she was somewhere near Mercy.

The longer she sat there waiting, the more her nerves stretched. They had discussed the brutal death of Crash's brother, but as he reminded her, that wasn't the reason she was there. He wanted answers from her about what happened between them. He hadn't yet noticed her scar and considering the hate he seemed to have for the Cottonmouths, she still believed she might be in danger from him.

But he'd been so honest with her, so authentic in wanting to tell her about his brother, maybe in the hopes that it would feel better. She hoped telling her had brought him some relief even though it had cracked her heart open. She was lost in thought when he walked back into the room, carrying a plate and a glass of water. She accepted the plate, thanking him. It was a simple meal of a baked chicken thigh with a couple of vegetable sides. It all smelled wonderful, so it wasn't a hardship to eat.

Crash joined her with his own plate and for a few minutes, they just ate and watched the news, enjoying the cheery warmth of the fire. It was a comfortable silence and for that, she was grateful. He was sitting on her left, making it harder to see the side of her face bearing the scar.

"Do you feel better?" she asked, hoping that listening to his story had brought him some small measure of relief. "After we talked?"

Crash nodded after a moment. "It doesn't really change anything, but yeah. I guess."

"I'm here if you want to talk about it more," she told him, her heart still aching for him.

She felt his gaze on her as they ate. "You know, I know how hurt you are that they didn't tell you that night when they found your brother," she continued. "Crash, they knew what Perry meant to you. Maybe… that's why they made the choice they did. MCs are made up of men who protect what's theirs. Mercy is part of what you all, the Hounds, protect, right?"

When her gaze met his, he nodded. "It is."

"There wasn't a lot of time to make the decision they did," Helena went on. "Maybe they thought carrying on with the ambush that they could hold it together. They could make it right somehow. Maybe… it was the only way they could honor him in that moment."

Helena ate some of the chicken, waited for him to process what she'd just said. Or to respond. When he didn't say anything, she added, "They lost Perry too. He meant something to them. They were preparing to face the Mafia, to protect the town. To protect you too. All of us. So, no one would have to look over their shoulder ever again."

Crash didn't say anything, just ate his meal in silence. They watched the late news until it went off just before midnight. She could feel the intensity of his emotions from where she sat a foot away on the couch. He watched the TV but wasn't *watching* it, his mind lost in thought. She hoped that with everything said tonight, Crash could begin to heal and make peace with the scars of the past.

At midnight Crash took his plate to the kitchen and headed to the bathroom. Helena heard the shower running, as she carried her own plate to the kitchen. The sink was full. It didn't take long to load the dishwasher. She didn't run it until he was out of the shower. With that done, she realized he'd gone to bed. After turning off the lights and checking that the doors were locked, she went back to the bedroom they'd shared the night before.

The lights were out. Had he done that for her? As her eyes adjusted to the darkness, soft light from the streetlamp outside streamed in through the gap in the curtains; she saw that Crash stretched out on his back on the bed. His arms were folded under his head, his eyes open.

"Are you okay?" she asked.

It was almost Monday. Helena had no idea how any of this would go in her future. Getting back to her apartment and job didn't seem as pressing now. Right now, her focus was on the broken man on the bed. Helena wanted to get his mind off all of it for a little while.

When Crash didn't answer, she closed the bedroom door behind her and walked toward the bed. When his gaze moved to her, she put a knee on the edge of the bed. Maybe she could take his mind off all the pain and catharsis.

He didn't speak, didn't move. He also wasn't stopping her.

With quick movements, she pushed down the pajama bottoms she wore. Crash shifted on the bed, his body angling toward her. Okay then. When she pushed down her panties, she could have sworn she saw his hips pump. Taking that as encouragement, Helena climbed on the bed, up to him. Pulling down the covers, she found him naked under there, his flesh warm and damp from his shower. When she straddled him, her core tightened. She loved how he felt inside her, and her intentions had his cock hard and ready, resting along his abdomen. Perfect.

Planting her hands on his chest, she began sliding her swollen pussy lips up and down his cock, getting him wet. It only pushed her excitement higher. Pulling his hands free from behind his head, he slid them down to the hem of her pajama top. Well, if it was a show he wanted... Grabbing the hem, Helena pulled it up and off, revealing her breasts to him. When he palmed them in his big rough hands, the craving in her pussy grew stronger. Now she undulated over him while her nipples were rock-hard peaks against his palms. It felt so good. He felt so good, and she wanted more, not just to make him feel better but because she couldn't remember a time when she didn't want the man. Crash was all hard angles and long, powerful limbs.

It was just too easy to lift his cock and slide down on him, taking him deep inside her. Crash's low moan was an indecent sound in the dark bedroom. Her heart raced as she stopped moving, savoring the way he filled her pussy. His cock was perfect, almost too big. And it made her ache in all the right places.

Crash's hands slid to her hips, encouraging her to move. With her hips in his powerful grip, he fucked up into her while pushing her down. It was an easy motion at first. Once they got going, his thrusts were hard, and it felt like he was punching the air from her lungs. His mouth gaped open as their bodies worked together in need. The chorus of grunts and moans provided the perfect soundtrack for their fucking. As her pussy clamped around his cock with each pass, slick on the juices her excitement produced, Helena's nails raked his muscular chest. Throwing her head back and closing her eyes, she moved faster on his cock, chasing orgasm. And it was chasing her down, threatening to take her sanity with it.

"That's it, baby," Crash's deep voice egged her on. "Fuck me... Come for me... Come all over my cock."

And she did. Helena cried out, her entire body a live wire as pulses of pure pleasure raced through her veins, through every inch of her. She thrashed in his hold, screamed as he dragged out her release, angling his movements to stimulate her clit with each repetition. Crash held her there all the while. His thrusts came harder, faster. He pulled her down on his cock with each thrust, his lower body hammering into her on a wild ride. She knew he was chasing his own release now, but the room was spinning for her. She panted, her muscles clenching as she fought to keep up with him. Spasms still rippled through her pussy as the last vestiges of orgasm rocked her body. It was a moment of nirvana that she could have happily stayed in, even as her strength was waning.

Crash's growl ripped open the silence around them as he came, his final frenzied movements on the edge of pain. Helena rode him, fought to hang on, fought to make sure he got as good as he gave and just hoping that she didn't pass out before he reached his end.

Helena couldn't have said she remembered rolling to his side or when their bodies parted. All she knew was that she ended up with her head on his damp chest, listening to the quick cadence of his heart as she fought to get her breathing back under control. It felt amazing being held by him, a cocoon of warmth in the chilly room. There with him, she couldn't think of anything else she needed. Crash's fingers gently sifted through her hair.

"Sweetheart," he whispered. "Are we covered here?"

Helena smiled. He just now thought of that. "We are. I have an IUD. Still has three years on it."

Crash hummed, holding her in the darkness. She was somewhere between dreaming and sleep when he said, "Thank you" before pressing a kiss into her hair.

Chapter Ten

Margot

It was lunch on Monday before she made it to the building next to the sheriff's department where Helena worked. Truth be told, she should probably be bringing the woman flowers or lunch for all the people she'd seen during her first week as Mercy's newest therapist. Since Margot had heard nothing, she wanted to at least check in and ask how Crash's appointment had gone even though ethically, Helena couldn't provide any details. She also wanted to ask Helena if she could make it to a meeting for the kid's Christmas party today after work. Helena could also have some insight to offer that might help some of the kids who might not have a happy holiday season.

When she knocked at Helena's office door, she didn't get an answer. Maybe she'd stepped out to get lunch. Surely the practice receptionist would know, so Margot stopped by the woman's desk. Gemma was busy eating a sandwich she had apparently brought from home. "Hey, did Helena step out for lunch?" Margot asked, smiling.

Gemma dabbed at her mouth with a napkin, her brows knitting. "No. She didn't come in today. It's weird. She didn't call in. Nothing. I mean I've tried calling her but only got her voice mail."

Shit. Hope I didn't overdo it on sending her people last week. "That's strange. So, no one has heard from her?"

Gemma shook her head. "Not that I know of. I mean maybe it's the snow. A few clients have cancelled their appointments today because of it. But I could have sworn that Helena told me she lived right here in town. Want me to try her again?"

"Yes, please." Helena had told her she *did* live here in town.

Picking up her desk phone, Gemma dialed a number and waited with the receiver to her ear. After several rings, Margot heard the familiar drone of a voice. Gemma left a brief message, asking Helena to check in when she could.

"Who's been seeing her clients?" Margot asked.

"I was able to work one in with another therapist who had a cancellation," Gemma said. "But the others? I told them I'd get back to them when we got her new schedule. She only had three appointments this morning, but this afternoon is loaded. Or was. Two had cancelled because of the weather. I was considering calling the rest in case she doesn't show."

Damn. Margot didn't know Helena that well, but she sure didn't seem like someone who would shirk her responsibilities. Something felt off.

"Check in with your boss," Margot told her. "But yeah, you may want to consider trying to catch the rest of her appointments, so they don't waste a trip."

"Thank you," Gemma told her, looking worried now.

Margot hustled out of the office, decided to drive by Helena's apartment and see if she was sick or something. Hadn't she mentioned that she'd lived at the apartments near the high school? It was just a five-minute drive in her squad card, even with the snow coming down and the slush on the road. She pulled into the lot, spotting Margot's SUV in the front row of spaces. Her vehicle was there but it was covered by a couple of inches of undisturbed snow. Maybe she was really sick?

Margot didn't know which apartment Helena lived in and that was a problem. She tried calling

Helena herself but got a message that her voice mail box was now full. *Shit.* With no other options, she walked around to the front of the building to the office. An older woman was behind the counter there. Pulling off her glasses, the woman regarded Margot curiously.

"Can I help you?" she asked.

"Yes," Margot told her. "I need to make a welfare check on someone who lives here in your apartment buildings. Helena Benjamin."

With a nod, the woman put her glasses back on and moved to her computer on the far end of the counter, searching. Margot watched the reflection of the changing screens on the woman's glasses as she waited. After a moment, the woman said, "Looks like she lives in 4A."

Margot nodded. "Thank you so much for your help."

Walking back around on the recently shoveled sidewalk, she found A building. Finding 4A was easy after that. But she didn't hear any noise coming from within the apartment and no one answered when she knocked. Weird. Checking under the welcome mat, she didn't find a key. She did notice a man's boot print there. Odd. Did Helena have company? A boyfriend? She'd told Margot she was single and hadn't been wearing a ring on her hand. Checking at the top of the door sill, she didn't find a spare key. Margot tried calling Helena's phone again. Within seconds, a cheerful song started playing within the apartment. Her *phone* was there. But without a warrant and reasonable evidence that Helena was in danger, there wasn't anything she could do.

Out of options for the moment, Margot headed back to her squad car. She was still on duty, but she made a mental note to check in later. When she climbed back into her car, she checked her phone. Maybe Helena had called or texted her back. Margot kept her phone on silent out of necessity, so she checked, but she had nothing from Margot. There was just a text from Ryder. Instantly, Margot smiled.

Ryder: *How's your day going, beautiful?*

Margot: *Typical Monday so far.*

Ryder: *You have that meeting after work, right? The kids' Christmas party?*

Margot: *I do. Why?*

Ryder: *Razor has called a meeting at the clubhouse after work. In case you beat me home, just wanted you to know where I was.*

It worked out. Sending another reply that they could have leftovers for dinner, and she'd see him then, Margot got back to her job. But wondering where Helena was and why she wasn't answering anyone never quite left her thoughts. Margot even drove by the apartment lot a couple more times and sure enough, Helena's SUV was still there. It hadn't moved. Its snow cover was still in place.

At the end of her shift, Margot sent a text to Jade and Emily to let them know she would be late for the meeting. She had something she needed to finish up first. She could catch up on Christmas party stuff later even though it was only two weeks until Christmas. Instead, she headed straight for the Hounds' clubhouse. She also hadn't heard from Crash how the appointment with Helena had gone. Maybe he knew something she didn't. It seemed a long shot. But several Hounds were usually there for meetings. Maybe someone saw or knew something about Helena's whereabouts since the MC considered Mercy their territory and themselves unofficial guardians of it.

Trying to be a good "old lady" who was also an officer of the law, Margot knocked loudly, waiting in the cold, blustery wind. It took a moment, but then she heard heavy footsteps coming toward the door. Beast, the tall, shaggy biker who had shoulders just about as wide as the doorframe, answered the door.

"We've got a meeting going, Margot," Beast said, crossing his beefy arms across his chest. "Can you wait?"

Margot grinned up at Beast. "I'll only be a minute."

Beast didn't try to stop her as she darted around him and headed straight for the meeting room. Yeah, she knew her way around the Hounds' headquarters now. And she was right. There were several Hounds there today. Axel and Ryder, Razor, Hero, and Snow. There was a scattering of others there too who she recognized even though she didn't know most of their names.

When Ryder's blue-eyed gaze met hers, he looked surprised. Rising from the table, he asked, "Margot, what's up?"

With a wave of her hand, she cut him off. "I'm just here for a second. I'm probably overreacting but I'm looking for someone. Helena Benjamin, the new therapist in town. Anyone seen her recently?"

The bikers looked from one to the other, exchanging confused looks. Maybe she'd need to elaborate. "She's mid-twenties, really pretty, jet-black hair, green eyes. She used to work at *Sackett's* back in the day as a waitress."

"What's this about, Margot?" Razor asked, the club president's expression one of amusement blending with confusion.

"She didn't show up for work today and they

hadn't heard from her. Her SUV is at her apartment building and her phone is in her apartment, but she isn't. I just thought I'd ask if anyone had seen her or heard from her," Margot explained. "She works for the practice in the building next door to the sheriff's office."

Beast, who had followed her in, filled the doorway of the meeting room as he stopped there, leaning against the doorframe. "She *that* therapist? The one you sent Crash to?"

Margot nodded. A quick glance around the room made her realize that Crash wasn't there. The Hounds around the table shot each other curious glances. "Yes. Do you know anything about that?"

"I know he came back from that appointment acting weird," Beast said. "He said he'd be gone for an hour, but it was more like thirty minutes. He came back to work and his head wasn't in the game. He was all quiet and moody. The rest of the week he wasn't a lot better."

Margot was confused. "Where's Crash now?"

Razor's gaze met hers, a salt and pepper brow lifted. "That's interesting, isn't it? Anyone heard from him today?"

"Last time I saw him was Friday night," Outcast said. She *thought* that was his name anyway. The biker had shorter dark hair and distinctive sea-blue eyes. He was handsome in an unconventional sort of way, covered in the most beautiful, ornate tattoos. "He was heading out like he always does at the end of the week."

"You see him here at the clubhouse?" Razor asked.

Outcast nodded.

"No one was with him?" Margot asked.

"No." Outcast studied her for a long minute, his gaze speculative.

Razor shrugged. "Aside from a therapy session that apparently didn't go too well, I don't see how they could be connected."

"Well," Outcast spoke up. "There *is* a connection. At least there was some time ago."

Margot and Ryder exchanged a look. *What was this?*

"Spill it," Razor said.

"She used to work at *Sackett's*," Outcast explained, "back when Crash and I were prospects and headed over there every evening after work. They flirted. *A lot.* One night we had some Cottonmouths show up while we were playing pool. It was fucking Baby Face and his goons, and they must have said something to her. She went out the back, upset."

"I remember that," Snow chimed in. "He was heading for Baby Face, all large and in charge. Me and the twins handled them."

Ryder nodded.

"Crash chased after her, said he gave her a ride home," Crash said. "Not sure if they hooked up or not that night. Apparently, she left town the next day and didn't tell anyone. Crash didn't say a lot about her after that. But he took it hard, her leaving."

Helena and Crash. *Damn.* And she'd set them up for a therapy session. Crash had to have known who she was when he agreed to the appointment. Margot had given him Helena's card. But had Helena known it was *him*? Margot had told her his real name. She couldn't remember if she'd mentioned his club name.

"Okay," Margot said, her mind already presenting options. "This really helps. Thank you all."

With that, she strode out of the meeting room,

but Ryder was on her heels. His hand on her shoulder brought her to a stop before she reached the front door.

"Baby, what are you up to?" Ryder asked, looking confused and concerned in equal measure.

Margot huffed. "I'm just going to see if I can find him. No one knows where Helena is and it's just her second week back in Mercy. Now I find out she has a connection to Crash and he's not where he's supposed to be either."

"Maybe everything is okay and you're overreacting. A little," Ryder said. "Maybe she skipped town again."

Margot shook her head. She wasn't overreacting and Helena hadn't. Margot always trusted her gut, and something wasn't right.

"It's okay," Margot told him. "No one's breaking any laws here and I'm off duty. I just want to make sure everyone is all right."

Ryder sighed, knowing he wasn't going to change her mind. "You're not going to the Christmas party meeting?"

"No, I'll catch up on everything later," Margot said. "I love you."

"Love you too," Ryder muttered.

With a quick peck on his cheek, Margot dashed out the way she came. She'd see if she could find Crash next. It seemed a stretch that he would have anything to do with the fact that Helena was missing. Maybe they'd hooked up five years ago. So what? People did that all the time. But at least it gave her ideas for how to proceed.

* * *

Crash

It was cold the next morning, but it was warm in

the bed he shared with Helena. Was it Tuesday? He had no idea. At that moment, it didn't even matter. They were on their right sides, Crash spooned behind Helena. It was bright outside, probably from the snow. He stretched but he was unwilling to relinquish his position behind her, her skin against his.

It was a rare moment of contentment. Hell, he couldn't remember the last time he'd felt anything close to contentment or hope. They'd talked for a long time last night and Crash had to admit that he did feel surprisingly lighter today, like a weight he'd been carrying for many years was finally shifting. When was the last time he felt anything close to relief from the pain that had been his constant companion for so long?

Communication, especially when it came to anything personal, was just not something Crash excelled at. Maybe he was programmed that way from a young age. After their father died, he and Perry spent a lot of time trying to understand what was happening and how to survive. Their mother cared about their feelings but had little time to be there for them with the extreme demands of the second man she'd married. When Larry took her away too, Crash began to shut down. What good were emotions when no one cared or made you feel you weren't allowed to have them? He locked his emotions away, buried them deep.

Having them dug up and pulled out into the light for examination had been uncomfortable, painful even. But that's what had happened when he and Helena talked last night. Talking about Perry and the trauma of that night, facing the betrayal that he wasn't sure he'd ever get past -- it was like an impossible knot, slowly beginning to loosen. The extreme tension that he'd disregarded for years and had seeped into every part of his life slowly released.

It wasn't why he'd taken Helena from her own home, but she was still there, listening. She didn't push him at any time or judge him. What she did was make him feel less alone in his grief. It was more than him losing his brother. It was the loss of his father, mother, and ultimately his home. Each was a brick in the wall he put up, intended to keep out future hurt, to protect what was left of his heart.

Crash had first brought Helena into it because she was the woman he'd wanted for a while and she left without a word. He told her, no *demanded*, answers for that. But he knew had no right to demand them. He had no claim on her, no matter how badly he wanted one. Fate put her in his path again and he'd behaved badly. It had him feeling like a pile of shit because she understood his anger, guilt, and the constant questions he'd been battling since Perry's death. Helena suggested that maybe his MC brothers, flawed as each one of them was, didn't mean to leave him out in the cold. And for the first time, he wasn't carrying the burden of most of his past all by himself.

It was like finding his footing after a long, damaging storm. He knew someone was out there -- not just anyone, but Helena -- that cared enough to stand by his side through his darkest moments. Her support gave him hope, fostering a slow-growing renewed strength. Maybe now he could move forward, not just with his grief but with his entire fucking life. Not bearing all that weight alone changed everything.

Helena shifted in her sleep, burrowing back against him with a contented hum. He tightened his arms around her, enjoying the ability to hold her while he could. Deep in his heart, he knew that despite the way they'd worked through his issues, she could be playing along until the opportunity presented itself for her to flee from him, to run away. In her head, she was his captive. What was he going to do with that situation? They had to have that talk too, because he had no right to do what he'd done. None. His hurt feelings didn't justify drugging her and bringing her back to his house caveman style.

Crash knew he had to face the music. If she turned him in, that was just the way it had to be. If he lost her for good, never to see her again, well, he deserved that too. It was stupid to hope that somehow his story ended with her forgiving him, much less giving him a chance. But it was a hope he harbored anyhow.

"What are you thinking about?" she asked, pulling him out of his thoughts.

"You." It was the truth. "I was just thinking about you and what you did for me... and what I've done to you."

She stiffened for just a second in his hold but then tension quickly eased immediately after. Crash was already feeling the weight of his confession blending with his new emerging fear. He'd been so blinded by his need to know the truth and his anger at the world that he didn't consider the consequences of his actions -- that he might lose her after all. He'd crossed a line to get where they were. He could hardly ignore that he'd taken her from her apartment against her will and made her a captive to his hurt and confusion.

"I hurt you too," she whispered, not moving in his hold.

The vulnerability of his situation put his nerves on edge. It also made him realize, realistic or not, his feelings for her weren't superficial. Crash felt deeply for her and his feelings had only grown after her care and generosity. He felt no small measure of guilt for projecting his hurt and insecurity onto her over the past. Yeah, he expected everything to go a little differently. But he went too far in how he chose to deal with it.

Crash pressed a kiss into her hair, buried his face in the sleek locks. "It wasn't your fault," he said. "I don't even know if I had anything to do with your leaving. And whether I did or not, I had no right to do what I did, Helena."

"I understand now what happened," she said. "You were trying to process everything you were dealing with."

"No excuse." It wasn't.

She sniffled, a quiet sound. When she did it again, it stopped him. Was she crying? "Hey, no. Don't do that. I'm sorry." He couldn't handle her tears. He'd done enough already. Her tears could break him.

"You don't understand," she whispered, tears in her voice. "You're… not the only one guilty here. There is something I haven't told you, Crash. And it's the reason you brought me here. To find out *why* I left."

It was. But the anger he harbored that demanded answers was diminished now. Now, after everything he'd put her through, she wanted to confess something to him? What fucking secret that she was sitting on could do him any harm now? Was there a husband? Another man? Fuck them. He'd fight them if that was the case.

Pressing a kiss to her shoulder, Crash sighed. "What do you need to tell me?"

Crash held her, waited. She didn't move from his grasp, but she trembled now. Why was she afraid? He didn't like it. He wanted her warm and sleepy in his arms. She had nothing to be afraid of. He'd make damn sure of that.

"You can tell me." Crash wanted to sound encouraging. "There's nothing to be afraid of."

"There is," Helena said, her voice breaking. "You don't understand... I..."

"Make me understand," Crash said, rising up in bed, so he could see her face. It broke his heart to see the tears streaking her face. "Tell me. I'll listen. I promise."

She glanced up at him, her gaze searching his with something like desperation. He read fear in her green eyes, but there was a sliver of hope there too. Slowly, she moved, shifting to lie on her back. Wrapping a hand around the back of his neck, she pulled him to her for a kiss. It was sweet, slow, and full of promise. Crash tasted her tears, felt her slight form pressing into his in need.

"Love me first," Helena whispered. "Just one more time. Please."

As if he could refuse her. Crash returned her kisses, matching her need. Lowering himself over her, Crash enjoyed her kisses, the way her body wound around his. She didn't seem interested in foreplay as her hands roamed down his body. He hissed when her small hand wrapped around his aching cock. He didn't fight her when she positioned the head of him where she needed him, at the slick opening of her pussy. Crash's thighs pushed her own wider as he gently slid into her body, enjoying the way her hot, wet passage stretched around his cock. Helena was so tight and wet around him it took his breath. It had him already fighting not to come and they'd just started.

It wasn't sex. It was lovemaking. It was slow and sensual, a beautiful sharing of bodies and hearts. Crash knew in that moment he'd never want another woman more than Helena. His need for her was raw, as essential to him as breathing. With every push into her body, he tasted her lips. Each time she squeezed his cock, clawed at his back or moaned for him, she made herself his. Just his. Just as she always should have been. Helena had left him, yes, but she was here now. And Crash meant to fight anyone he had to -- including her -- to keep her.

Crash knew the minute she was about to come. Her body tightened around him, under him, her breathing quickened. Crash moved in the ways he knew she liked, sliding a hand between their bodies to tease her clit, to help her along. As he teased that little bundle of nerves, Helena's movements became frenzied. As he pushed her over the edge, she grabbed him, screamed. Crash wanted all of it, every single moment burned into his memory. He never wanted to forget this moment. Ever.

Helena came hard and the way her pussy clamped around him triggered his release. Crash drove into her like a madman, growling when he reached his end, and his vision whited out. Pleasure swamped him, took his breath away. He was panting like he'd run for miles when his body was done and it was all he could do not to collapse on top of her, bury her in the mattress. But he didn't go far. Crash dropped onto the bed at her side, pulling the covers over her to protect her from the cold of the room.

Helena lay there on her back, her eyes closed and a smile on her face. She was so beautiful, looked so at peace. He couldn't resist tracing the side of her face with a careful finger while the scent of sex floated on the air around them. Her profile was perfect, her skin so clear, free of makeup. There was no imperfection at all except for a tiny scar just above her right jaw. A tiny silver curve that he traced, finding it looked strangely familiar.

When someone pounded on the front door, Crash's body went on full alert, even though he was so fucking drained physically and emotionally. Helena's eyes flew open in alarm. Who the fuck was at the door? What was happening?

Chapter Eleven

Helena

When someone knocked sharply on the front door, Helena didn't know whether to be relieved or heartbroken. Crash had only just discovered the scar on her jaw, tracing it with his finger. Crash jumped off the bed, grabbing his jeans off the floor and hastily pulling them on as he went to the bedroom window, peering out to see who was at his door. "Fuck!" he growled. Without sparing Helena a glance, he dashed out of the bedroom, running for the living room.

Helena shook as she scrambled out of bed, grabbing the pajamas she had barely worn last night and pulling them on. She probably should have stayed in the bedroom and waited. For all she knew, it could be a neighbor or service person. But instinct had her quietly making her way down the hall, stopping when she reached the end of the hall. From there, she could sneak peeks around the corner into the living room. Crash opened the door a beat later.

"Hey," a familiar female voice said at the door. "Crash, how are you?"

"I'm fine, Margot," Crash said, his voice rough. "What... what are you doing all the way over here?"

Margot was here. Were they still in Mercy after all?

"Just checking on you," Margot explained. "Ryder and the guys missed you yesterday. At the meeting for the toy drive? Anyway, I just thought I'd check in. Especially since I'm the one who sent you for therapy. And hey, at least it stopped snowing. It made for an easier trip for me."

Crash blew out a breath. Helena peered around the corner to see him standing, his body taut, on the defensive. "You drove all the way out here to make sure I was okay?"

"I did," Margot went on. "But I was also hoping you might know where Helena is. We also missed her yesterday. Mind if I come in? Damn it's cold."

Oh shit.

Before Helena could duck away from the corner, Margot saw her. Her dark eyes widened as she stepped around Crash into the living room. She wasn't wearing her deputy's uniform, just jeans, a flannel shirt, and a heavy winter coat. Caught now, Helena slowly walked into the living room, afraid if she didn't there might be consequences for Crash. Especially if Margot had guessed correctly that Helena wasn't here of her own free will. Well, it hadn't started that way.

"There she is," Margot said, smiling at her. "Looks like I was overreacting. You two were visiting and were probably wanting to stay off the roads because of all the snow. Am I right?"

Crash shoved his hands into his jean pockets, and Helena admired the way his movements showed off all those powerful muscles. But there was worry in his eyes as his gaze met hers, watching her carefully. She was free to say pretty much anything she wanted to Margot in the way of explaining why she was here, and he couldn't stop her. Was he afraid she'd claim he kidnapped her? From a certain point of view, he had.

Or was he afraid she'd leave him again?

"I was a little worried about the weather," Helena told her. "I should also have checked in with the office too. I had appointments with clients. It was very irresponsible of me."

One thing she'd learned about Margot in the time she'd been working with her was that the woman was amazingly observant and perceptive. She couldn't really say she was surprised that Margot had tracked her down and she was grateful. Helena realized now that Crash would never hurt her. But if something had really been going down, it was nice to know someone noticed she was gone. But she could also tell that Margot didn't exactly buy what she was selling.

"Yeah, Gemma said some of your appointments were canceled because of the weather. She was going to contact the others. I know she'll be relieved that you're okay." Margot's gaze moved from her to Crash and back. "I got some kickass snow tires on the truck this year. Some hot biker may have gotten me a discount. Want a ride back to town?"

Helena's heart cracked in her chest because part of her didn't want to leave Crash like this, even though he was in a much better place than he had been prior to last night. The other part of her knew she needed to get back to her life and try to keep her job. So many emotions reflected in his eyes as he watched her along with Margot, waiting for her answer.

"That would be great," Helena said, knowing it was the right thing to do. "Let me go get dressed."

"I'll be right here," Margot told her, staying in the living room with Crash.

Helena heard their voices as she scrambled around to find the same clothes she'd been wearing, her shoes. Aside from the few things she'd found in that bag and the keys to her apartment, that was it. Jamming her pajamas back in there, she returned to the living room with the efficiency of a SWAT team. She was ready to go, but a piece of her heart would be staying in that house. With him.

The same hurt she felt was reflected in his eyes but when Margot led her to the door, he stepped back. His gaze never left her. "Thank you for driving her back, Margot. I'll be back over there in a little while."

"Sounds good," was all her friend said. Margot followed her into the white snowy landscape outside with the sun reflecting off it. It was bright and cold. There was a little warmth in the cabin of Margot's truck and it warmed fast when she started the engine. Her friend didn't say anything until they'd pulled out of the driveway. Helena watched Crash standing there in the doorway as Margot drove her away.

"Are you okay?" Margot asked when they reached the end of a familiar-looking street.

"Where are we?" Helena asked.

That earned her a look from Margot. "Oak Grove."

Helena blew out a sigh. "Okay. I grew up here. I thought this looked familiar."

"Crash and Perry grew up here too. You didn't know each other?"

"No," Helena said. "I can tell he's older than me, so..."

Margot nodded. "Are you sure you're okay? I can be here as a friend, but I could also be here as a deputy if need be."

Margot saw a lot. Helena knew that if she wanted to press charges, she could. Crash had taken her from her home and brought her to Oak Grove. And it had been a tense three days. But all she felt was sadness as they got on the interstate that would take them back to Mercy. Would Crash be okay? Would he ever speak to her again after this? Had he recognized the scar on her jaw and what would he think of her if he did? Would he hate her? What would happen?

But she owed Margot her gratitude. Her friend had handled everything perfectly, from her reason for checking up on them to accepting their answers. It was entirely Helena's choice, and Crash wouldn't intercede. It just made her decision to go home with Margot feel that much worse.

"Thank you, Margot." Helena swiped at a tear. "For everything. I'm okay. I don't want to press charges or anything. It's a long story."

"I'll bet." Margot kept her eyes on the road as she drove. "Outcast thought maybe you two were a thing back in the day. I figured it out from there."

Helena didn't know how to answer that. Maybe it was better that she didn't try to explain. She didn't think Margot would mind.

"My appointments for today?" Helena asked, trying to change the subject. "I should probably call in as soon as I get home and hope I still have a job."

"Well, some of your appointments didn't want to get out in the snow," Margot explained. "I think Gemma was calling them to reschedule. It's all covered."

It didn't take long to reach her apartment complex, and it felt like it took forever. Helena was so lost in her thoughts the entire way she had no concept of time. When Margot pulled up in the truck, she regarded Margot seriously. "If you need anything, even just someone to talk to, you can call me any time. Okay?"

"Thank you," Helena said, climbing out of the truck with her bag. Her legs were shaking, her body sore in many places. Emotionally, she was a wreck.

"Hey," Margot called as she started up the sidewalk, powering down her truck's window. "The next meeting for the kids' party is tomorrow. Think you still want to help?"

"Can I?" Helena turned to ask. "I've missed the first two."

"So have I." Margot laughed. "It's six tomorrow evening."

"I'd love to," Helena said. She knew she'd need to keep her mind occupied, or she'd go crazy. Besides, Margot, Jade, and Emily were all with Hounds. Maybe she'd hear something about how Crash was doing.

Helena just hoped that everything with Crash wasn't over now.

* * *

Crash

"You ready?" Beast's voice pulled him out of his thoughts, which was where he'd pretty much been living for the last week or so.

Crash nodded, climbing into the cabin of his friend's truck. They'd been able to finish at their latest construction site early today and Beast told Razor that they'd drive around and pick up some of the donated Christmas toys for the charity party on Friday. Of course they would be working a block away from the sheriff's office this week and the office building where Helena worked.

"You talked to her lately?"

The question was so unexpected that Crash thought he must have misunderstood. "What?"

"Helena? That her name?" Beast cut him a glance as he drove. "Have you talked to her?"

Fuck. Crash shook his head. His Hound brothers were as bad as a bunch of gossiping old women when damn near anything came up. It had always irritated him but now having it directed at him personally pissed him off. Besides, it wasn't anyone's business if he'd talked to Helena.

But he hadn't. He didn't like the way things ended. Pissed as he was at Margot for taking her away from him, he did appreciate how she played it. Instead of making assumptions and taking his ass in with handcuffs, Margot put the ball in Helena's court. Let her choose how it would go. Crash knew she'd leave with Margot. She almost had to. But the way things were now didn't sit well with him. Did Helena hate him? Was she afraid of him? What had she been hiding? What was that little secret she said she had?

"No one's business if I've talked to her or not," Crash told him.

"All right," Beast said, stopping the truck in front of *Three Guys Garage*. "Just thought I'd ask. Just so you know, everybody's trying to figure out what happened that weekend."

"And everybody can fuck right off." Before that weekend, he might have taken his happy ass and left, gone nomad. But he didn't think so poorly of his MC brothers these days. The pain of Perry's loss and how it happened still hurt. It always would. But he was healing, and he owed Helena for that. The way she'd listened and cared…

What drove him insane now was wondering if all of it had been real that weekend. Or had it been in his head? It felt like Helena had had feelings for him. When they made love, it had brought him back to life. He wanted so badly to rush over to where she worked or her apartment and just talk it out. Was there any chance for them? Was she afraid? What had she wanted to tell him that morning?

"Yeah, they can," Beast said in that way of his that led Crash to know he was working up to some bigger talking point. "Player was in there, talking about how she used to hang out with the Cottonmouths before she started working at *Sackett's*. Said she was tied up with Baby Face for a time."

Crash froze, the realization hitting him hard. The scar on her jaw, the fact that she wanted to tell him something and she'd been so scared just mentioning it. Was that what she'd been trying to tell him?

"Player, huh?" Crash ground his teeth. "What else did they have to say about her?"

Beast parked the truck, putting his hands up defensively. "It was just Player running his mouth. Outcast threatened to kick his ass if he didn't shut up."

Crash was going to kick Player's ass instead.

But the revelation had his mind spinning. That was the reason Helena had been so upset that day at *Sackett's*, why she'd walked out of the bar entirely. Was it why she'd left? Baby Face had been one sadistic son-of-a-bitch and if his eye had fallen on Helena, and apparently it had, it could explain why she left town altogether that night. Baby Face was the sort of coward that cut up women, turned them out. Rumor had it he'd killed one or two. Hell, Hero was lucky he'd been able to snatch Jade away from him after her grandmother Mina died. That son of a Cottonmouth had been fucking evil, and everyone knew it. His own father had put the fucker down in the Hound clubhouse. Crash remembered that day.

It was starting to make sense. Baby Face was dead. The next year, Helena came back to Mercy.

Holy fuck. Crash felt like the world's biggest pile of shit for putting her through what he did. And through it all, she loved him. *Helped him*. If Baby Face had messed with her, ran her out of town, and Crash was pretty sure he was right, then he needed to get his head out of his ass. Crash had been waiting to see if she would contact him. Considering he pretty much had kidnapped her, he felt it was only appropriate to let her make that decision.

Knowing what he did now? He was the one who needed to make a move. He needed to make this right and claim what was *his*.

* * *

Helena

"I'm so glad you're here." Emily Frost smiled when Helena and Margot walked into the vacant office space on Main Street. The pretty blonde woman was dressed as an elf. "We usually hold the party at my bakery each year but…"

"We're building her a new bakery soon," Margot explained. "But hey, I'm glad we were able to rent this space for the party."

"Right?" Emily shook her head. "I just underestimated how much prep work we would need here."

The place was alive with activity as it was. Jade and Emery Phillips had just pulled up when they did with a truck bed full of folding chairs and tables. The two tables already in place were loaded with a ton of baked goods. A group of high school kids had spread blankets on the concrete floor and were talking and laughing as they wrapped a small mountain of presents.

"We're here with the tree!" Liza Austin looked flustered but then she always did, cheeks red from the brisk December day. "Henry's putting the finishing touches on the new wreath. He's going to drive it over when he's done."

"Perfect," Emily said.

"What would you like us to do?" Margot asked and Helena nodded. With so much to do, she wanted a task.

"Help Jade and Emery with setting up the tables

and chairs?"

"We can do that." Following Margot outside, they greeted Jade and Emery, who had once been Helena's boss at *Sackett's*. They had a pretty good operation going, first getting all the tables and chairs in so they could get them set up.

It went by quickly. They'd just started setting up the chairs when the rumble of motorcycles drew close. The Hounds had arrived. Apparently, Snow, Emily's man, was playing Santa Claus. Liza paused in setting up the Christmas tree to go get his costume, and to help him get ready. When the handsome, white-haired biker strolled in, he wasn't alone. Hero was behind him, winking at Jade. The twins, Axel and Ryder, were right behind them. When she glanced up next, she thought her heart would stop. Crash walked in; his gaze was fixed on *her*.

Helena smiled at him, continued setting up the chairs. She hoped it wasn't too obvious her hands were shaking because seeing him again after so many days of him consuming her thoughts was just about to tear her apart. But she had to realize that he was there to help the Hounds, his MC brothers, who she hoped he felt better toward these days. She hoped if nothing else came from that weekend, he had bled out some of the anger and betrayal he'd been harboring toward them. That would make it all worth it.

Then again, Helena wasn't *that* altruistic. Selfishly, she wondered if he still thought about her. If he missed her anywhere near as much as she'd missed him.

"Hey," Crash purred close to her ear when she went for another couple of chairs to set up.

Helena almost dropped both. "Hi," she said. Her heart was racing in her chest as she straightened, meeting his gaze.

"Can we talk?" he asked, sounding so sincere despite his tough, biker exterior.

Margot walked toward them, jerking her head to the side as if to say "go."

"Okay," Helena told him, following him from the main room where all the activity was happening. The first two rooms off to the side had people working in them. The room at the back was empty and quiet. For a moment they stood facing each other with neither sure what to say.

"I was hoping you'd be here," Crash said quietly.

"I was hoping to see you too," she admitted. He'd been all she could think of since she left that house.

Was that hope in those sky-blue eyes? "I wanted to tell you that I'm so sorry for how I acted, Helena. You offered to talk to me, to help me, and I still went way over the line. You may never forgive me for taking you the way I did. I've got no excuse for that except that... I didn't just need someone to talk to. I needed you. The minute I saw you again I just... I lost my mind. Seeing you again was the only good thing that's happened to me in a long, long time."

Her heart melted at his words. Before she could say anything, he pressed a finger to her lips. "Let me finish. You were... all I ever wanted all those years ago, Helena. I never got over that one night with you. I know that's not right, or normal, or mentally sound -- whatever you want to fucking call it. I can live with that. I just hope in time you can forgive me. I mean that."

He meant it. Every word. The blended pain and hope flashed in his eyes as he moved closer to her. "Despite all of that, you saved me. You made me realize that my brothers weren't the enemy. They weren't even who I was so angry with. I was angry at myself. I swore to always keep Perry safe and when I didn't, I turned all that anger on myself. I hated myself. I'm going to be squaring with that for a long fucking time. But I'm healing. It will be all right. In time."

A tear slid from the corner of her eye, from the beauty of his words, his confession. "You will be," she whispered.

"I really wish I hadn't let Margot drive off with you," Crash went on. "There was more to talk about. Something you wanted to tell me."

There it was. His words sent a spike of fear into her heart. Her jaw dropped open; her hands began to shake. Crash captured them in his.

"I recognized that scar," he said. "You can't see it right now and I get why you don't want anyone to know, Helena. But you have to realize something. Baby Face was a sadistic son-of-a-bitch. All of us in the MCs knew that. He'd cut up girls way worse than that. He beat them. Hell, he apparently killed a couple of girls in his time. I'm just so sorry he hurt you."

Helena couldn't stop her tears. A raw, ugly sob tore from her throat and Crash was there to catch her, sweeping her into his arms. She had been terrified of how he'd react if he found out, that he'd hate her. She'd been so young when she met Baby Face. Only seventeen. She was naïve and he was all too willing to exploit a young girl who fell for his charms. Helena let Crash hold her as relief broke her apart.

"That scar is part of you," Crash whispered into her hair. "But it doesn't define you. The only thing I'll think when I see it from now on is how glad I am that you survived that asshole and became the beautiful woman you are."

Helena hung onto him, trying not to let those words burn into her soul. It sounded like he meant they'd be together in the future. That he wanted to be.

"Once I realized what it was and why you were acting that way about it, it was pretty easy to piece together," he went on. "You left town that night he upset you so bad at the bar. The night I went home with you. And you didn't come back until he was dead. But you'll never have to run again, I swear. I'll fucking kill anyone who so much as makes you fucking unhappy."

When she eased back to look him in the eye, Helena's heart clenched in her chest at the pure sincerity she saw. "You still want me?" She swiped at her tears with her fingers.

"It's more than that," Crash said. "I'm in love with you, Helena. I just… Is there any way you could give me a chance? Let me try to be the man you need? If not, I understand but…"

"Yes," she said through tears, over the drumbeat of her heart. "Yes!"

He smiled. "Merry Christmas to me."

Crash pulled her back into his arms, claiming her mouth with a kiss that left her breathless. He poured all the love and desire he felt for her into that kiss, holding her tight as if he'd never let her go. And she didn't want him to. There in that quiet space with all the chaos of the Christmas party going on just beyond that room, they held each other, the kiss sealing a promise of a happy holiday and hopefully many more meaningful days to come. Together.

They were so lost in each other that neither saw Margot peek into the room with a smile before she pulled the door close to give them some privacy.

Razor (Hounds of Hell MC 6)
A Hounds of Hell MC Romance
Jamie Targaet

She's a spark I never saw coming, in a fight I can't afford to lose.

Deva -- *No Mercy Ink* is my sanctuary, the shop I built with my brother Jackson. But after a string of attacks leaves him in the hospital, I'm left to defend everything we've worked for. That's when Razor storms into my life -- intimidating, loyal, and maddeningly protective. He's everything I've avoided in a man, yet I can't deny the pull between us. But as danger closes in, it's clear Victor Grayson and his crew will stop at nothing to destroy us. Razor swears he'll keep me safe, but how can I trust him with my heart when my survival demands I protect myself?

Razor -- Leading the Hounds of Hell means protecting my family at any cost. When Deva's world collides with mine, she's more than just a mission -- she's a fire I can't extinguish. Fierce, stubborn, and utterly captivating, she's determined to fight for her shop, even if it puts her in Grayson's crosshairs. But this isn't just about the club or Mercy anymore -- it's about her. The deeper I fall, the higher the stakes. To win this war, I'll have to face my past, defend my future, and prove to Deva that she's not just worth fighting for -- she's worth everything.

Chapter One

Deva

Zipping the front of her coat against the bitter cold wind of January, Deva Crane climbed out of her SUV. After slinging her backpack over one shoulder, she walked from where she parked behind the building. She and her brother Jackson had been lucky to have rented a space in the strip mall when they did. Theirs was a corner shop in a gritty, historic part of Mercy. Dark, graffiti-style art covered the outer wall of the building, perfect for their vibe. Decades of imagery and symbols decorated that wall conveying rebellion, strength, and transformation.

Deva and her brother, called Outcast by his biker brothers, had opened the shop three years ago. She was damned proud of what they'd built. The shop's bold neon sign read *"No Mercy Ink"* in fiery red and cool white. She liked the way the sign caught people's eyes on gray, rainy days, and the ominous light cast on the street outside at night. It had been her brother's idea to tint the windows, and it was a good one. The lighting made the intricate tattoo designs they displayed there stand out, giving passersby a taste of the artistry within while maintaining privacy. A small wrought-iron bench sat out front under the old metal awning with a bucket that served as an ashtray, finishing the exterior -- an invitation to rest, get lost in thought, smoke a cigarette…

Deva unlocked the shop to get started with her day. As she flipped on the light, she smiled. Inside the shop was a weird mix of her style and her brother's, like an odd cross between an art gallery and an old biker bar. The walls were painted in dark, muted tones of indigo and slate gray. There were metal accents and hints of exposed brick lending an authentically rough vibe to their studio. Framed tattoo flash, custom designs, and photos of some of their best works hung on the walls.

The waiting area in the front had metal stools and a weathered leather sofa bought from thrift stores. She kept their high-end aftercare products and branded merch in a glass display case there. *No Mercy Ink* was stamped on everything from leather jackets to T-shirts and trucker hats.

Their tattoo stations were further in, separated by worn steel dividers, offering their clients a little more privacy. There were three stations. One was hers, one was Jackson's, and a third that she hoped to fill one day with another hired artist. They just needed to get their profit margin a little higher to finally pull that off. Each station had a tattoo chair, a tool cabinet, and an adjustable lighting rig. The workstations were well organized with tattoo machines, bottles of ink, and sterilized needles. The presentation was important to her because it showed their pride in their craft. Jackson usually kept his area bare bones, all except for a photo of a phoenix tattoo that he kept there. It was odd because she was pretty sure it wasn't his work. Her station had warmer lighting and a few plants, reflecting her creative style.

Her goal had been to work on paying bills this morning, since she had no appointments scheduled today. Business off the street didn't pick up until lunchtime or after. But suddenly the door sensor triggered the low rumbling sound of a chopper engine that Jackson assured her would be so cool. At first, she'd begrudgingly tolerated it. Over time, she came to love the rumble of the sensor. Still, Deva had to wonder who was there.

It was a familiar-looking young woman Deva couldn't quite place, with long, red curls and big eyes who stood in the waiting area, looking more unnerved than excited. Her dark winter coat reached her knees and had a faux fur-lined hood that she eased back. A tattoo virgin? Deva smiled when the woman's gaze found her.

"Hi, there," Deva said. "Can I help you?"

A flush of color brightened the young woman's face -- no one blushed quite like a natural redhead -- and she nodded. "Yes, I was hoping to make an appointment to speak with Deva."

"That's me. And I've got a few minutes. We just opened. Come on back." Deva motioned for the woman to follow her, heading for her own station. Motioning to the tattoo chair, she said, "Have a seat."

The woman's green-eyed gaze took in everything before she sat down, perching on the edge of the chair. The visitor's emotions were palpable, her posture hesitant. Deva waited patiently, giving her the time and space to speak when she was ready. Whatever it was the young woman was dealing with, it was obviously still haunting her.

"My boyfriend recommended you," she explained. "Axel?"

That got Deva's attention. Axel was one of the twin enforcers of Mercy's chapter of the Hounds of Hell. The same MC her brother belonged to.

"I know him," Deva said. "My brother is Outcast. We co-own this shop and we're both artists here."

A little of the tension in her pretty face eased at that. "Outcast is… very nice."

Deva laughed. "No, he's not. He's a quiet, broody asshole, but I love him."

The redhead smiled. "He is quiet and…" Shaking

her head, she held out a hand. "I'm Sadie Downing."

"Sadie. Well, I'm honored that Axel sent you to me," Deva said. "What can I help you with?"

"I'd like to get a tattoo. To, um, cover something up. It's..." Sadie paused, drawing in a deep breath, then rose from the chair instead, her movements deliberate. Shrugging off her heavy coat, she draped it over the divider and swept her long red curls over her left shoulder. With hesitant hands, she tugged her shirt off one shoulder, revealing just enough for Deva to glimpse the markings. What little she could see was enough to make her stomach twist.

With Sadie glancing over her shoulder, Deva asked, "May I?"

At Sadie's nod, Deva gently shifted the shirt and bra strap to reveal the full extent of the damage. The words "Bobby's Bitch" were crudely carved into her skin, a brutal mark of ownership. The sight infuriated Deva. The jagged, uneven lines spoke volumes -- rage, entitlement, and pain. It was a violation, both physical and emotional, leaving scars that went far deeper than the skin. Just the thought of the agony Sadie must have endured made Deva's stomach churn.

Deva adjusted Sadie's strap and blouse back into place with care. Sinking into the chair, Sadie swiped at the tears spilling down her cheeks. Deva reached for the box of tissues on the counter, handing her one. It took every ounce of control Deva had not to cry alongside her.

"I'm... sorry," Sadie said, her voice trembling as she dabbed at her eyes with the tissue. "Axel thought maybe there was a way to cover it up. It's not that he's bothered by it -- he's actually been so kind. It's just..." Her voice trailed off, unable to finish, the weight of her pain and vulnerability hanging heavy in the air.

"You want to reclaim that part of you," Deva said simply.

"Yes." Sadie nodded. "I'm sure that's so bad that there's probably not a lot you can do but…"

"There's plenty we can do to cover that," Deva assured her. "I get a lot of requests to cover old wounds and scars these days. It's a specialty of mine."

Sadie's eyes widened, flashing hope. "You can?"

Deva nodded and reached beneath the counter to retrieve a photo album. She flipped it open to a specific section, her fingers brushing over the pages with care. Positioning the album on her lap, she turned it so Sadie could see the images through the protective clear plastic sheets.

"Most of these are cover-ups for cutting scars." Deva gestured to the first two pages, which showcased intricately tattooed inner forearms. The designs were bold yet delicate, turning painful memories into something personal, meaningful. "But not all," Deva added, flipping through the rest of the pages. The other photos featured stunning tattoos covering hips, thighs, and backs -- art meant to reclaim and transform.

Sadie leaned in, her eyes scanning the intricate designs. Deva watched her closely, seeing the spark of hope flicker across her face as she took in the possibilities. Some of Deva's best work was in those pages, helping people turn something they felt self-conscious about into something beautiful. She could see Sadie beginning to believe that for herself.

"I'll be honest with you," Deva said gently. "Tattooing over scar tissue can be a bit more painful, and the tattoos don't last as long -- usually around five years or so before they need a touch-up. But the good news is they're easy to refresh." She paused, offering an encouraging smile. "Do you have any tattoos currently?"

Sadie shook her head.

"There's some pain involved," Deva said. "But nothing even close to what I'm sure you endured for that."

Sadie's chin lifted a notch. "I can handle it. I just want it covered up. How long will it take?"

"That really depends on what you choose," Deva explained. "Smaller tattoos might only take about an hour, but larger, more intricate designs can require several sessions. For this one, I'd recommend spreading it out over a few sessions since scar tissue is more delicate. It's also a bit tricky to predict how the colors will take."

Sadie tilted her head slightly. "So, mine would probably need multiple sessions?"

"Exactly," Deva confirmed. "I'll use lighter pressure and keep the sessions shorter to make sure your skin handles it well. Do you have any ideas in mind for a design?"

Sadie hesitated for a moment before smiling shyly. "Well, nothing too specific. I work at the greenhouse here in town, and I absolutely love gardening. Maybe something along those lines?"

Deva grinned. Plants and flowers were some of her favorite subjects to tattoo. "That's a wonderful idea," she said. Retrieving the album Sadie had been browsing, Deva slid it back under the counter. From the same spot, she pulled out another binder, this one with a green cover that felt fitting for the theme. Inside was a collection of plant and flower tattoos that Deva created over the last five years. There were some stunners in there and she was hoping that Sadie would like what she saw. Her ego got a real boost at the way Sadie's face lit up, looking at various examples of her art.

"You did all of these?" Sadie asked. "They're so beautiful."

Deva nodded, proud. She was happy to sit there and watch the expressions play across Sadie's face as she looked over the photos. Sadie stopped on one photo of a tattoo of lilies gracing a woman's upper arm. Deva remembered the tattoo and the client. It was wonderful to have a client willing to come as many times as it took to get the best work possible. She was hoping Sadie might present a similar opportunity.

"I love this one." Sadie put her finger on the string of lilies, delicately tattooed on the woman's skin. "Would it be possible to create one that looked like this to cover... that?"

"Absolutely," Deva said. "We could do a bouquet of lilies or --"

"No, I don't want cut flowers. I want them to look as they do when they're growing in the soil. Alive."

"Even better." Deva understood the symbolism.

Sadie smiled, her gaze meeting Deva's. "That's perfect then. How do we start? What does it cost? Do I pay up front or..."

Deva held up a hand. "Nothing today. I work by the hour, and I'll have an estimate ready for your first appointment. When would you like to start?"

Excitement was easy to read on the other woman's face. "Well, anytime that works for you. I work at Liza Austin's greenhouse. I'm also in town every Wednesday night for self-defense class."

"Wait, there are self-defense classes? In Mercy?" Deva asked, her interest immediately piqued. This was news to her.

Sadie nodded, a small smile tugging at her lips.

"Yep, Margot Donner runs them on Wednesday nights. You should join sometime. If you're interested, of course. I've learned so much from her."

"The deputy?"

"That's her," Sadie said.

Deva knew who Margot was. Self-defense classes? That sounded fun. "I'll definitely think about it. So, Wednesday evenings are out for your tattoo?"

Sadie's laugh was a pleasant sound. "They are. But anything else, I can work with."

Deva reached for the well-worn appointment book resting on her desk -- a physical journal she preferred over digital options. It was old-fashioned, but it worked for her. Flipping it open, she scanned the week, noting her scheduled appointments. Looking up, she asked, "Do you prefer mornings or afternoons?"

"Either one," Sadie said.

They set her first appointment for Friday morning. Writing the date and time on an appointment card, Deva handed it to her. "Our number and email are on there. If you have any questions, call, email, text. We do them all."

Sadie left the shop with a grateful smile, looking visibly lighter now. Her parting warmth lingered, and Deva found herself genuinely looking forward to working with the woman.

With the photo albums tucked back in place, Deva turned her focus to the more mundane side of running the shop. First was tackling the bills and checking where they stood financially for the month. But, as was her habit, she started with their social media channels. She composed a few posts -- one promoting their merchandise sale to clear out lingering Christmas inventory, and another showcasing some of their standout tattoo designs to draw in new clients.

Finally, Deva logged into their local business account to check for new reviews. One immediately caught her eye. As she read, her stomach sank. Deva read it, stunned. Then she read it again, disbelief washing over her.

I was just there before Christmas. I will NEVER go again. The place is dirty, the staff was rude. I had an infection after getting my small-azz tattoo which means they don't even clean their instruments. DO NOT GO THERE FOR YOUR TATTOOS.

The accusation was not only a lie but a direct attack on everything she and Jackson worked so hard to build.

The fuck? Deva jotted down the username, Andria66631, determined to dig a little deeper. She started with a quick search for the name, but nothing turned up -- no other reviews, no social media accounts, no trace of the person anywhere. It was like they didn't exist. Frustrated but curious, she combed through every platform she had access to, coming up empty-handed each time.

Who was this person? And where had they supposedly gotten a small tattoo the week before Christmas?

Still baffled, Deva decided to respond to the review, hoping to clear up what had to be a misunderstanding. Maybe they'd confused *No Mercy Ink* with another shop? Though, as far as she knew, her studio was the only tattoo shop in Mercy. Typing carefully, she wrote:

"Hey there, we're sorry to hear you had a bad experience with your tattoo but think you might have meant another shop. No Mercy Ink is located in Mercy, and we'd love to have you visit anytime!"

She hit send, feeling better after responding.

Enough to steady her nerves so she could get through the rest of her tasks. Diving into the pile of bills and spreadsheets, she made decent progress balancing the books, though the review lingered in the back of her mind.

At lunchtime, the door opened, and her brother strolled in. Deva had always thought her brother Jackson looked like he belonged in another time, a darker era where men settled things with their fists or not at all. His cheekbones could cut glass, and those pale, ice-blue eyes of his had a way of seeing straight through people. There was a quiet storm in his expression, a brooding intensity that never went away, even when he was trying to be lighthearted with her. His dark hair, always perfectly slicked back, only added to the illusion of a man who knew how to control every aspect of himself -- except maybe his temper. Lean but solid, his build was all tension and potential energy. To Deva, Jackson was equal parts protector and enigma, the brother who always had her back but kept his own wounds buried deep. Even when he was quiet, which was most of the time, his presence filled a room, commanding respect without asking for it.

His leather jacket was zipped up tight, and he carried a paper bag from the diner. Without a word, he dropped it on her counter.

Deva smiled. "Thanks for bringing lunch. We're going to need it. We've got a busy afternoon."

"Yeah, we do," Jackson said. "How have things been here?"

"Quiet. Axel's girlfriend stopped by earlier. I'll be working with her for a few weeks."

"Sadie?" Her brother nodded. "That's good."

"We also got a strange review," Deva said,

pulling up the list of online feedback for their shop. At the top was the suspicious review she responded to earlier. She watched as Jackson's expression shifted, confusion darkening his sharp features as he scanned both the complaint and her reply.

"Who the hell is that?" Jackson asked. "Do you know them?"

Deva shook her head, frustration simmering. "I couldn't find anything useful about the person who posted it. The name doesn't show up anywhere, and it looks like it's from a woman. But we didn't have any female clients the week before Christmas. Did we?"

Jackson shook his head firmly. "No. Wait -- looks like they replied to you."

Deva clicked on the notification, her scowl deepening as she read the response. The words glared back at her from the screen: *"Oh, it was most definitely your so-called tattoo shop. Y'all should close. You SUCK!"*

"Unbelievable." Deva's irritation flared. This wasn't just a review -- it was a targeted attack.

"Don't engage with these people," Jackson said, his tone casual but firm. "Seriously. It's not worth your time."

"It *is* worth it if people are going to spread lies about our shop," she shot back, her voice rising with frustration. "Our online reputation matters."

Jackson shifted uncomfortably, clearly wanting to steer the conversation away from the topic. "We doing okay on bills this month?" he asked, his voice a little too casual.

Deva exhaled sharply. "We're holding our own," she replied, her tone pure resignation. It wasn't the reassuring answer she wanted to give, but at least they were keeping their heads above water -- for now.

"I've got an appointment in an hour," he said.

"I'm going to set up."

Deva nodded, still pissed off. The reviewer's claims gnawed at her, especially since she knew they were lies.

* * *

Razor

Razor glanced up from his phone when the bells on the gun shop's front door jangled. He smiled to see Jade walking in, her winter coat bigger than she was. His daughter's cheeks were flushed from the biting January air and her dark hair cascaded in glossy waves, perfectly framing her delicate features.

There were moments, like this one, when just watching her stole his breath. She was the image of her mother, Vanessa, and that resemblance brought both joy and a pang of regret. Razor saw glimpses of himself in Jade too, but Vanessa's presence in her was unmistakable -- a bittersweet reminder of the woman he'd lost. At least, in Jade, he still had a piece of her. For that, he'd always be grateful.

Razor should have taken Vanessa and his daughter from Mina Dock when he'd had the chance. Instead, he threw that opportunity away, choosing to climb the ranks of the Hounds of Hell. Now, he stood as president of the MC and had a relationship with his daughter. Jade was a gift he knew he didn't fucking deserve. That fragile bond had only come into his life after Mina's death. If he could go back, he'd fight harder for them, no matter the cost. Maybe he wouldn't be president today. Still, the thought lingered, heavy and unshakable: he might have been a happier man.

"What are you so deep in thought about?" Jade asked with a smile when she reached the counter where he sat.

Razor shook his head. "Not much of a deep thinker. What are you doing out of work?"

"It's a teacher workday," Jade said. "So, I thought I'd come by and say hi to my dad since assistants don't have to be there."

"Glad you did." Razor meant it. "Not a lot going on here."

Jade glanced around the small shop that used to be a small house. It'd taken some work to transform it into a clean, functional shop but with help from the Hounds, he pulled it off. The old living room served as the main display area with tall, reinforced glass cabinets lining the walls. They showcased the firearms he sold, arranged by type and purpose.

Razor converted the kitchen into a private office and general storage area. It wasn't accessible to customers but was fully stocked with ammunition boxes, paperwork, and a relatively well-organized inventory. Snow set up a high-tech security system. Razor liked to watch the camera displays from inside and outside the shop sometimes. The old dining room was set up with a high countertop. He'd added a few stools for customers to have a seat to discuss custom work with him or ask for advice.

Jade smiled as her gaze wandered the shop. "I guess it's slow everywhere right after the holidays."

"It always is this time of year," Razor said with a shrug. "If you're smart, you save up during the busy months. You know the slow stretch is coming."

"Smart," Jade agreed, her smile widening with admiration.

Razor nodded. "It's also a bummer to have our main watering hole closed up." Emery Phillips had retired at Christmas and put his bar, *Sackett's*, up for sale. Old man Phillips was up in his seventies, and Razor couldn't blame him for hanging it up. The Mafia ambush the Hounds staged there in the fall had partially trashed the place. Thinking about it now, he guessed maybe that's why Emery allowed them to have the ambush there. Also, probably for Jade -- Emery had been her grandmother's boyfriend the last decade of her life and had stepped in as a second father to her when Razor wasn't around. He didn't know if Emery had made the repairs or planned to. The Hounds offered to help but Razor had heard nothing from him.

"Someone bought *Sackett's*," Jade said. "This week in fact. They're not local but they're hoping to have it back up and running soon."

"Where did you hear that?"

"Emery."

"How are things at the school?" he asked. "You work with those… ah…"

"Special needs kids?" Jade asked, her expression softening. "Yeah. Some days it's tough, but I love it. I got into education because I wanted to make a difference, and I feel like I'm actually doing that. Staying here in Mercy was the right choice. Towns like this don't have much funding for kids who need extra help, let alone enough trained people to support them. And honestly, it gave me the chance to finally get to know you after all these years. I'm glad for that."

"So am I," Razor said, his chest tightening with pride as he looked at her. He spent years hating Mina Dock for keeping him away while Jade was growing up, but he couldn't deny the results. Mina raised a strong, compassionate woman. And for that, he respected her. "Your mom would be proud of you, Jade. She really would."

Jade's smile faded as she studied him. "She died when I was little. I barely remember her. I know what Grams said about her, but... what can *you* tell me?"

The question struck like an old wound reopened, catching Razor off guard and dragging up pain he thought he buried long ago. He couldn't remember the last time anyone asked him about Vanessa, and for a moment, he wasn't sure how to respond.

"You look a lot like her," he said, a small smile pulling at his lips. "She was a little shorter than you, but you've got her smile and her eyes." Vanessa's face, clear and vivid in his mind's eye even now, softened his voice. "She was a hell of a dancer. I used to love watching her out there with her girlfriends, tearing up the floor at the clubs. She'd always try to drag me out there with her, and I gave it a shot once or twice. Let's just say all I managed to do was look like a dumbass with two left feet."

Jade laughed, the sound warm and familiar. "Where did you meet her?"

"At a party the Hounds threw," Razor began, his voice tinged with nostalgia. "I'd seen her before -- hard not to. She was so beautiful. She lit up the room." In his mind, he could see Vanessa standing at the bar, wearing short shorts, boots, and a low-cut top. Her personal style showcased her sexy little body along with her bold, magnetic personality. She'd worn more makeup than Jade ever would, but it suited her.

That was when it struck him -- Jade wasn't like her mother that way. She had his temperament: reserved, measured, careful. Traits that would serve her well in life. Not that he worried much about her with Hero at her side; she was in good hands. Hero was one of his best enforcers, and he loved Jade deeply, almost as much as Razor himself did. "You know," Razor said, "I think I met her at *Sackett's* now that I think about it."

Jade simply listened with a soft but introspective gaze. Razor's thoughts drifted to what her life must have been like. Her mother had been gone by the time she was three; her father had been kept at arm's length. He could resent Mina all he wanted, but Jade grew into a remarkable woman. He was the one who hadn't fought hard enough for the woman he loved or the daughter he should have been there to raise.

"She had a big laugh," Razor went on. "She would help anybody she could. Vanessa was a good person, Jade. Too good for this ugly world."

Jade's eyes glistened. "Grams used to say something like that about her," she said. "She didn't sugarcoat anything, though. She said Mom struggled with drinking and drugs. She told me Mom had horrible taste in men."

Razor let out a dry chuckle. "Yeah, she did. Your mom could drink, no doubt about it. But she wasn't much of a drug user, really -- unless you count weed. Alcohol? That was her downfall. And the fucking Cottonmouths? They played a big part in that."

Jade tilted her head, her brows knitting together. "Okay, see, there's a question I've always had," she said in a cautious tone. "Was she just... all about hanging out with bikers? That's what Grams said. But, you know, I remember Mom going back to school when I was little. She seemed so excited about it, like she was ready to do something with her life."

Jade's perceptiveness never ceased to amaze Razor. She got that sharp intuition from him. She wasn't the type to take anything at face value, even from the people she loved most. Growing up with Mina Dock couldn't have been easy, and Razor felt the weight of finding the right way to explain things without making excuses.

"I didn't know your mom until she was in her early twenties," he said. "From what she told me, she fell for the wrong guy right out of high school. A biker, like me. But he wasn't looking for anything serious, just a good time. He was a Cottonmouth and ended up moving out of state to another chapter. She tried like hell to go with him, but… he left her here. That's when the drinking started getting bad. That's how she ended up… well, with Eli Crizer for a while."

"The Cottonmouths' president?" Jade asked, her brows lifting in recognition.

"That's him," Razor said with a weary sigh. "When that fell apart, she started showing up at our parties with a girlfriend. That's how we got together. And to be honest, I wasn't any better than the guy who left her. She came to me one day, scared out of her mind, saying she was pregnant. She wouldn't even consider getting rid of it. But me? I was about to become a patched member of the Hounds, and I didn't want the responsibility of a baby -- or an old lady. I just wasn't ready. So, I told Vanessa… I wasn't sure the baby was mine and made it her problem."

The look in his daughter's eyes as her gaze moved over him threatened to break him. But she had to know the truth. He'd always promised himself that if he ever had the chance to talk to Jade, get to know her, he'd be completely honest. It was the least he could do after bailing on her and Vanessa when they needed him the most.

"I've never regretted anything more in my entire life," he finished, fighting back tears himself. "We weren't together long when she found out she was pregnant, but she meant a lot to me. Vanessa was the only woman I ever actually cared about. When Mina found out she was pregnant, I decided that was it. I couldn't fight her. She wouldn't let me near Vanessa. And once your mother was gone, it felt like you were permanently out of my reach."

When Jade's hand slid across the counter to cover his, he smiled. "Mom loved you too. When I went through Gram's things, I found a picture of you and Mom from back then. I'd never seen it before, but Mom looked so happy in that moment."

"I'd like to see that sometime." Razor let her lace her fingers with his. "I only have one picture of her myself and I've hung onto it all these years."

"I have pictures of Mom," she said. "You can have any of them you like."

Razor nodded, trying to get his emotions under control.

"Hey, I didn't come by to bum you out," Jade said. "But I guess there's just one more thing I always wanted to ask you."

"Ask away," Razor said, meeting her gaze squarely.

"Did you ever find anyone else?" Jade asked. "Did you ever have an old lady?" She must have been able to read the answer in his eyes because her face looked ready to crumble from the weight of her emotions. "No one? Why?"

"Just never met anyone else like your mom," he said. "And I can't change the past. But I'm getting to know you. And it's more than I deserve but I'll take it. I'm glad you've given me a chance, Jade. I love you."

"I love you too, Dad," Jade said. "Still getting used to the part where my father's the president of a biker gang and all, but…"

Razor chuckled with her. Yeah, that had to have

taken some getting used to.

"Just do me a favor?" Jade asked. "Like you said, nothing can change the past. But if you find someone and she makes you happy, do it. Don't for a minute think if you find someone, you're losing anything with me. I'll be happy for you. I just want you to know that."

Razor didn't deserve what he had with his only child now. And she still found ways to amaze him. Ducking out from behind the counter, he walked around to hug his daughter. Pressing a kiss into her hair, he whispered, "Thank you."

After he agreed to have dinner with her and Hero soon, Jade walked back out of the gun shop, leaving him with a lot to think about. Especially her selflessness in the last point she made. The truth was, Razor had never loved anyone beyond Vanessa. He'd gotten laid, had had a handful of casual relationships. None for very long and no, he'd never kept an old lady.

Razor had never looked for love. He didn't deserve that. Not after what he did.

Chapter Two

Deva

When Deva arrived at *No Mercy Ink* the next day, a man she wasn't expecting waited by the front door. He was an older man with silver hair, dark eyes, and a mustache. Dressed in dark slacks, a white shirt, and a coach-style jacket, he looked all business, and not like a client. The clipboard he held firmly in one hand confirmed as much. When he shifted it to his other hand, she noticed the embroidered letters "VDH" on the jacket. *Fuck*. Her stomach sank. The Virginia Department of Health. Was this about the suspicious online review she'd found and replied to yesterday?

Deva drew in a steadying breath, deciding to keep her response measured. "Can I help you?" she asked evenly.

"Yes," the man replied, his gaze meeting hers. "I'm Jordan Nester, with the Virginia Department of Health. Do you own this shop?"

"Yes, I'm Deva Crane," she said, offering a polite nod. "My brother and I co-own *No Mercy Ink*."

"Good morning, Ms. Crane," Nester said, his tone professional yet firm. "I'm here in response to some concerns that were reported about your shop. I'd like to take a look around to make sure everything is up to code." He glanced down at the clipboard in his hand, scanning his notes before focusing on her again. "Specifically, I'll need to review your cleanliness and sterilization procedures, especially in your workstation areas and with any reusable equipment. We've received a report claiming some of the tools here might not be properly sterilized, and I need to verify that your practices meet health department standards."

It *was* about that fucking review.

"Second, we need to assess the waste disposal system, particularly for any sharp objects and contaminated materials. The complaint mentions potential improper disposal, so I'll just confirm everything's being safely contained and disposed of according to guidelines. Finally, I'd like to check the ventilation system. There's been a concern about ventilation around the chemical storage area, anything containing strong inks or solvents. I'll confirm you've got proper air circulation, especially where fumes might build up."

"Okay," Deva told him, nervous because she'd never had a health inspector come to the shop before and had no idea what to expect. Pulling her keys from the pocket of her coat, she opened the shop door and let them in. After turning on the light and adjusting the thermostat, she turned back to her guest. "How do we begin?"

Deva was relieved they didn't have their first appointment until eleven. Hopefully, two hours would be enough time for the inspector to complete his evaluation.

Still, the process was nerve-wracking. She started by showing him their sterilization station, walking him through how they cleaned reusable equipment and tools. Their autoclave was old but got the job done sterilizing daily items. She was grateful she was prepared when he requested maintenance records, knowing everything was documented and current despite Jackson's usual indifference.

Next, Deva explained their waste disposal system, allowing him to inspect everything from sharps containers to their secured storage area. She had made sure it was off-limits to clients. They inspected the ventilation, including fans and windows, in work and storage areas. She answered every question thoroughly to prove their commitment to hygiene standards.

By the end of the whirlwind morning, the inspector stood jotting notes on his clipboard while Deva nervously chewed her lip. The silence stretched, each second feeling like an eternity. Finally, he handed her a yellow copy of the completed form. But as she reached for it, he didn't let go, his gaze meeting hers with quiet intensity.

"It's a clean bill of health," he said. "If I can get your email, I'll send you a copy there too to keep for your records."

Out of habit, Deva pulled one of her business cards from the holder at her station and handed it to him.

"I didn't find any violations today. That's good news, but I want to be transparent with you. When we receive multiple complaints like this, and they don't match the actual conditions in the shop, it sometimes means that someone may be targeting your business intentionally."

That appeared to be the case. But who was doing it and why? "So, what should we do about it?"

"You're doing the right things," he said. "Keep doing that. Document inventory, cleaning schedules, repairs, and any equipment inspections. Make sure everything is in order because it will help if this happens again. And if it does, feel free to contact us and let us know of any patterns you're noticing. Things like odd visits from competitors or people with something to gain in causing your business to fail. Just know, we take false reporting very seriously."

Deva shook her head. "We don't even have competition here in Mercy. I don't know who would benefit from us going out of business."

The man's gray eyebrows rose. "Well actually, there is a new tattoo shop opening on the other end of town. Not far from the sheriff's department."

"What?" Since when?

"I saw the signs go up before Christmas," he said. "I'm due to inspect it next week before their grand opening."

"Now I'm wondering if our forthcoming competition had something to do with this," Deva said, making a mental note to drive by there after they closed.

The inspector shrugged. She knew he couldn't respond. "If you think of any questions later, please let us know." He handed her his business card and made his way out of the store.

"Hey," Sadie's voice pulled her from her thoughts. "I wanted to let you know I'm here. Are you okay?"

Deva hadn't noticed Sadie walk into the shop. Smiling, she met the gaze of her first client of the day. "Yes, sorry. Go ahead and have a seat and we'll get started."

The redhead followed Deva's instructions, settling into the chair with a nervous but determined expression. At Deva's guidance, she lay on her stomach, allowing them to adjust the loose-fitting sweater she wore. Deva carefully exposed the cruel carving etched into the skin behind her right shoulder.

"How old is your scar, Sadie?" Deva asked, her tone calm and professional.

Sadie exhaled slowly, her shoulders relaxing just a little. "I've been in Mercy for almost a year now, and it happened a few months before I came here. So, around eighteen months? Maybe a little longer."

"Okay, thank you," Deva said reassuringly, grabbing the supplies she needed. She set out gloves, ink cups, needles, and other essentials. They reviewed the process and design one more time to make sure Sadie was completely comfortable before Deva took her seat.

After sterilizing the area, she was just about to start when the door sensor's signature chopper-like rumble announced someone had entered the shop. Deva glanced up, unsurprised to see her brother Jackson striding in -- but he wasn't alone.

She recognized the man who followed her brother into the front of their shop as the president of Mercy's chapter of the Hounds of Hell. Razor was older and ruggedly handsome with a presence that commanded respect. Deva didn't mean to stare but the man was hot as hell. His lean, muscular build spoke to years of physical work and barroom fights. His shoulder-length, wavy gray hair framed his face, making him look both distinguished and untamed. Either way, it made her want to know how those silky strands would feel in her hands, skimming along her thighs.

Razor's hazel eyes were a witch's brew of deep green and gold, with just a little amber that seemed to catch the light. When his gaze found Deva, his eyes softened, the hard edge of his usual expression melting into something warmer. Razor's eyes seemed to hold secrets, scars, and undeniable strength. Yet, when he looked at Deva, there was a promise -- a quiet, unspoken truth that made her pulse quicken and her heart stutter.

His thick mustache twitched as he smirked, perfectly balanced with the salty, stubbly beard he always wore. When his gaze shifted back to Jackson, she kept staring. Her eyes traced his lean form, from the worn jeans to the black leather boots that matched his heavy jacket. Deva had never spoken to him, but she wanted to. She knew from her brother that Razor was not one to fuck with. Taking in his weathered face and confident stance, she couldn't help but wonder what it would be like to fuck him.

Not wanting to neglect her client, Deva refocused her attention on Sadie, beginning the outline of the tattoo. As always, she found it easy to lose herself in the precision of her work, each stroke of the needle a meditative escape. Razor's low conversation with Jackson hummed in the background, but she stayed focused on her task. Even when she felt Razor leave the shop, she refused to glance up. True to her word, she kept Sadie's session brief, mindful of the sensitivity of her scar tissue. She couldn't help but admire how stoic Sadie remained through the entire process, especially for her first tattoo -- and one so emotionally charged.

After completing the session, Deva scheduled Sadie's next appointment for the following week. Cleaning up afterward gave her something to focus on while Jackson finished a small snake tattoo for the young woman in his chair. With no more appointments for the day -- a typical January lull -- she realized they had some extra time today before closing time.

"Jackson, I need to tell you what happened earlier," Deva said, watching him clean up his station.

Jackson paused, his sharp blue eyes narrowing in curiosity as Deva launched into the story about the health inspector's visit, spurred by false complaints. She recounted the chain of events, including the fake online review -- something she was sure he hadn't fully absorbed when she'd mentioned it the first time.

As she detailed everything, Jackson's expression shifted from mild curiosity to focused attention. When she mentioned the new tattoo shop opening in Mercy, his reaction mirrored her own initial shock.

"What?" Jackson's eyes flashed with confusion. "Another shop? Here?"

Deva nodded. "Yeah, the inspector said it's near the sheriff's department. That was the first time I'd heard of it."

"No shit." Jackson scrubbed a hand through his jet-black hair, frustration tightening his features. "So, we get some bogus review, then the health department shows up in the same week? Yeah, that's no fucking coincidence."

"Exactly," she agreed, folding her arms. "By the way, I noticed Razor stopped by earlier." Her tone turned pointed, skirting the edge of frustration. The MC's unspoken rule about not discussing club matters with outsiders -- even a member's sister -- always grated on her nerves.

"Yeah?" Jackson prompted, his expression unreadable.

"Is there any way the Hounds could dig into who we're dealing with?" Deva asked, meeting his gaze directly. "I mean, this is our shop -- *your* shop. Shouldn't it be protected by the Hounds?"

"It is," Jackson assured her, his voice steady but firm. "And yeah, I'll see what we can find out."

"Thanks," she said, her tone appreciative. Then, after a moment of hesitation, she added, "I'm thinking about driving by to see if I can spot this new place when we close up."

Jackson's gaze lingered on her for a moment, his expression turning thoughtful. "Be careful," he said, his voice carrying a quiet but unmistakable warning.

* * *

Razor

He was nearly done with his burger and fries at the corner booth of the diner when he spotted her for the second time that day. Outcast's younger sister caught his attention like a neon sign in the dark. Barely five feet tall, her vibrant purple hair gleamed under the harsh fluorescent lights, making her impossible to miss. Razor couldn't help but smile as he watched her stride to the counter, shoulders back, head high, confidence radiating from her petite frame.

Dressed entirely in black, her puffy winter coat covered her upper half. It didn't do much to conceal the short leather mini skirt, fishnet stockings, and sleek boots beneath. Those legs -- the kind that could make a man's thoughts stray into dangerous territory -- gave him pause.

Razor wasn't a saint and never pretended to be. He'd sought pleasure when he wanted it, a way to keep his life uncomplicated and free from the weight of an old lady. Commitment had crossed his mind a few times over the years, but no one had ever measured up. Not to Vanessa. And as tempting as the little enchantress at the counter was, he knew better. Pushing fifty and entertaining ideas about the sister of one of his Hounds? That wasn't just a bad look, it was a disaster waiting to happen. And yet...

He had been about to gather his wrappers and make for the exit when a movement drew his attention. Looking up, he froze. There she was, standing beside his booth, purple hair tucked behind one ear, luminous eyes fixed on him.

"Want some company?" she asked, smiling and full of sass. Her lips, painted a deep rose color, had him wondering what they'd taste like.

"Sure," Razor replied. It probably wasn't the best idea, but they were just talking.

She set her tray down on the table with a casual air, tossing her purse onto the bench seat across from him. As she unzipped her coat, Razor's gaze was momentarily snagged by the deep purple blouse she'd been wearing earlier at the tattoo shop. The wrap-style top hugged her figure in ways that made it nearly impossible not to notice her curves.

As she slid into the booth and got comfortable, Razor couldn't help but appreciate the view. She moved with unintentional grace. For a moment, he had to remind himself to focus on something other than the enticing sight in front of him.

"I'm Deva," she said. "Jackson's younger sister. You're Razor?"

He nodded, watching her peel the paper from the plastic straw and push it into her drink cup. She unwrapped her burger in no particular hurry.

"Thanks for this. It hasn't been the best day," she said. "It's nice to have some company for dinner."

Razor loved a confident woman, content to sit with her as she grabbed the ketchup bottle from down the table and literally drowned her French fries in it. Shaking his head, he asked, "You want some fries with that ketchup?"

The sexy little smirk the question earned him only made his growing interest worse. "Don't judge. Ketchup is one of my few vices."

"What are your other vices?" Razor felt compelled to ask.

"Ink," she said. "Chocolate, diet soda, shoes."

"Shady shit," he said, teasing.

She nodded and took a hearty bite of her burger,

attacking it with enthusiasm. He rarely saw anyone eat like that outside the Hounds. Maybe she was just that hungry, but there was something undeniably endearing about her lack of pretense. It was real, unfiltered, and cute as hell.

"Why was your day so bad?" he asked, since she introduced the topic.

Deva finished her bite and dabbed at her mouth with a napkin. "This actually started yesterday. Someone left a really nasty review online, and I just happened to catch it. I replied, tried to be polite, but their response to my reply was even worse than the original review."

"Do you know who the client was?" Razor asked, his tone serious.

Deva shook her head, her voice steady but laced with frustration. "No idea. The username didn't ring a bell. That's the thing -- they claimed they came in the week before Christmas, got a small tattoo, and it got infected because our shop is dirty, our staff is rude, and we don't clean our instruments. Total bullshit. The only clients we had that week were regulars working on big pieces or sleeves. None of it adds up."

"Damn," Razor said, his hazel eyes narrowing. "I'm sorry you're dealing with that."

"I can handle a crappy review. Honestly, that's part of the business," Deva said, her voice steady but edged with frustration. "The real problem was the health department showing up this morning to investigate complaints. Yeah, they went that far. Apparently, someone reported that we don't sterilize our equipment and a bunch of other lies. It took over two hours of my morning, and it was stressful as hell. We passed, though. The inspector even said we're doing everything right. He did warn me to keep documenting everything just in case these were false claims, like something a competitor might cook up."

She paused, her eyes narrowing. "I told him I didn't think it was the competition because, until today, I thought we were the only tattoo shop in Mercy. That's when he dropped the bomb -- another shop is opening in a few weeks. I wasn't expecting that."

Razor leaned back slightly, processing her words. The idea of another tattoo shop in town caught him off guard. Normally, he had a pulse on everything happening in Mercy, and this was news to him.

"Sounds like you've had one hell of a day, darlin'," he said, his voice low and warm, the nickname rolling off his tongue naturally.

"I told Jackson, and I think he's still processing everything. I guess…" When Razor smirked at her use of Outcast's birth name, she put her burger down. "What?"

"We call your brother Outcast," he said. "It throws me off a little when you call him Jackson."

That sly grin returned. "I'm not calling him Outcast. I really don't care why he has that name and I'm not calling him that."

"Any particular reason?" Razor followed up.

"Are you asking to make conversation or do you really want to know?" Deva asked.

"I think I want to know." Razor watched her wrap her lips around the straw of her drink, finding her movements way more mesmerizing than he should.

"I'm his sister," Deva explained. "Jackson may be Outcast to all of you. To me, he's my dorky older brother who thinks he looks cool. Yeah, he's quiet and broody and plays the part. But he's horrible at karaoke, can't cook to save his life, and he collects Pez dispensers. Did you know that?"

Razor had to laugh at that. Outcast sure as hell did fit the part but like the rest of them, he was an ordinary guy. Hell, would she be laughing at him, the club's president, if she knew he could cook and was a pretty solid baker?

"I asked Jackson if there was any way the Hounds could dig around and find out who's behind this mysterious new shop and when they plan to open," Deva said, her tone carrying just a hint of exasperation. "But, as usual, he just grunted at me all noncommittal, like he always does."

She paused, her gaze locking with Razor's, a spark of determination in her eyes. "But since I'm sitting here with the president of the Hounds himself, I figured I'd cut out the middleman. So, let me humbly ask -- any chance you guys could help us out? Maybe find out who we're dealing with?"

"I'll bet he did grunt noncommittally. He's not allowed to talk about the club to anyone not in it."

"I know." Deva's gaze locked with his. "First rule of Hounds of Hell is don't talk about Hounds of Hell, right?"

"Something like that," Razor said. "But yes, we'll find out who is moving in here. Do you know anything else about them?"

"I know they're supposed to be close to the sheriff's office," she said, gnawing on a fry. "I'm planning to drive by there when I'm done here and see what I can find out."

"Why don't you let me handle that for you?" Razor suggested, his tone calm but firm. "Just to play it safe."

Deva rolled her eyes, clearly unimpressed.

"Jackson already told me to be careful. I'm just planning to drive by, not case the joint."

Razor couldn't help but admire her fire. It was one of the first things he'd noticed about her, and at times, it reminded him of Vanessa. But where Vanessa's confidence had often been more of a mask -- a fake-it-until-you-make-it kind of courage -- Deva's strength was real, steady, and unshakable. Vanessa's quiet determination might have grown into something equally formidable, but death had taken her too soon.

Deva, on the other hand, carried strength with an effortless confidence Razor respected, wrapped in a petite frame with striking purple hair, captivating curves, and a whole lot of sass. She'd carved out such a strong sense of herself, running her own business alongside her brother. Deva also didn't mince words. She was as blunt and straightforward as any man Razor had ever met, and he couldn't help but appreciate that about her. She had a fire that made her unforgettable.

"Humor me," he said, his voice softer but still resolute. "The sun's down, and you're planning to go alone without knowing what you might walk into. If they're the ones targeting your shop, chances are they already know what you look like. Let me handle it for you. I'd rather check it out and keep it from turning into a bigger problem."

"I'd be finding my Glock if there is a problem," Deva said. Something told him she knew her way around the gun too.

"Which Glock do you have?" he asked. "I run a gun shop here in town. *Old Guard Guns.*"

Her dark brows rose. "Okay, I wondered who ran that. I drive by it just about every day on my way home. You're on Elm, right?"

Razor nodded. "That's the one."

"Mine's a G19. It's smaller. I like the way it handles. And yeah, before you ask, I've got a concealed carry permit. I even did the class because Jackson wouldn't shut up about it." Deva smiled. "But it's good to know where I can get ammo."

"Come by and get some," Razor said, his gaze locking with hers. Little Deva could come by and get almost anything she wanted.

Her response was that devilish grin. "Do I get any sort of Hound discount since my brother is one of you guys?"

"We can do that." Razor shifted in his seat, his jeans tightening as the conversation worked him up.

"Fine," she relented, picking up her burger. "Go check out the competition. But you will come back and tell me everything, right?"

"Yes, ma'am." Razor couldn't help but smile. She had a commanding way about her, and he liked it. He didn't take orders from just anyone, but the way she made demands was equal parts bold and endearing. "How do you want me to deliver my findings? A full report or a PowerPoint?"

"Don't you dare tell Jackson to tell me." She pointed a fry at him. "Just stop by the shop when you get a chance. In person is better -- I'll have questions."

He nodded, amused by her insistence. "Deal." He'd head over to scout the new shop as soon as she was done with her meal.

"You know," she said, her tone light, "it's funny. Ever since we opened *No Mercy Ink*, I see the Hounds around town, but I rarely get the chance to actually talk to any of you. Jackson's the one doing their tattoos, so I don't get much face time. But today, things feel... different."

"Because you're sitting here with me?" Razor asked.

"That, and I met a woman yesterday who's with one of the twins." Mischief lit up those big, expressive brown eyes. "What is it you call them? Old ladies?"

Razor shook his head at the teasing glint in her gaze. "You got a problem with that?"

"It's none of my business," she replied, her tone airy. "I'm not in your big, bad biker club."

"And if you were?" he pressed, curious to hear what sass she'd throw at him next.

Deva shook her head, tucking a strand of vibrant purple hair behind her ear as she stared him down. "No way some biker dude is calling me his old lady. Even if I am fucking old. Ain't happenin'."

Why wasn't he surprised? "Which old lady did you meet?" he asked, curious.

Deva licked her lips, plucking a couple of fries from the paper pouch before leaning back thoughtfully. And damn it, was there anything this woman did that wasn't completely adorable? "Can't remember her name, even though we spoke earlier. I was focused on calming her down," she admitted. "She's a couple of inches taller than me, has big green eyes, and long red curly hair. Totally gorgeous."

"Sounds like Sadie," Razor said.

"Sadie! That's it," Deva exclaimed, snapping her fingers. "Yeah, she is having work on a tattoo. She's very sweet."

"Take good care of her, darlin'. That little lady has been through a lot in the last couple of years," Razor said, his tone somber.

"That's putting it lightly," Deva replied, a flicker of anger flashing in her eyes.

Razor raised a brow, surprised. "She told you?"

Deva shook her head. "No, she didn't say a lot. But the tattoo she's commissioning me for is to cover one of the worst scars I've ever seen in my life. A man who could do that to a woman is a true sadistic asshole. He deserves to be dragged out into the street and shot."

Razor's jaw tightened, her words hitting a nerve. She wasn't wrong. Not even a little. He didn't know what scar she was talking about, but he could imagine how bad it was given everything he knew about what the fucker did to Sadie, to many folks in Mercy.

"He was dealt with," Razor told her.

"By the Hounds?"

Razor nodded.

"Good," she said unapologetically, her tone firm.

As she finished her meal, their conversation drifted to the chaos of Christmas at their respective shops and the inevitable lull January always brought. The bitter cold of this winter wasn't helping matters either. Low temperatures and post-holiday debt had a way of keeping customers at bay every year. The trick, as they both knew, was simply surviving it.

When Deva finished eating, Razor took both their trays and dumped the trash without hesitation. Then he walked her to her SUV, parked right out front under the streetlight.

"You're going by there right now?" she asked, her gaze locking onto his. The way her big, expressive eyes caught the light made it hard to focus on anything else.

"I am," Razor replied, towering over her by the door of her vehicle. "Now get in. It's freezing out here."

"You promise to tell me everything you find out?" she asked, unlocking her door and pulling it open, her gaze probing his like she was gauging the sincerity of his promise.

"I will," he said.

For a moment, she just stared at him, her eyes searching his face. Finally, she seemed to decide she could trust him. Without another word, she climbed into the driver's seat and closed the door. Razor stayed put until Deva started her SUV and headed home.

It wasn't until she disappeared down the road that Razor realized he was smiling. Their impromptu dinner had been the most fun he'd had in a woman's company in longer than he cared to admit -- and there wasn't even anything sexual about it. At least, not yet.

But he did plan to keep his promise. Razor cruised on his bike, the low rumble of the engine vibrating through him as he rode toward the sheriff's department. The hospital loomed across the road, its sterile, orderly facade a stark contrast to the gritty undercurrent of what he was looking for. Clusters of medical buildings surrounded it, and he knew he wouldn't find what he was looking for there. The light from many streetlights glinted off the chrome of his handlebars. His sharp gaze was fixed ahead, scanning for signs of the enemy tattoo shop Deva had told him about.

It didn't take long for him to find it.

On the far edge of a small strip mall just down the road from the sheriff's station, nestled between a payday loan office and a vape shop, was *Sinister Skin Studios*. The name screamed trouble, scrawled in sharp, jagged lettering across a black awning that seemed to absorb the light rather than reflect it. The shop's facade was dark and foreboding, with tinted windows that hid whatever was going on inside. It was similar to *No Mercy Ink* in their set up, but they had more of a creepy atmosphere as opposed to the cool, trendy vibe presented by Deva's shop. The door bore a logo -- a skeletal hand holding a tattoo machine, dripping red ink like blood -- and a neon "Opening Soon" sign buzzed faintly in the corner of one of the windows. Next to that was an intricate symbol in silver that looked like three snakes, locked around each other.

Outside, a couple of bikes were parked alongside a tricked-out black SUV with vanity plates that read "INK4LFE." A few men loitered by the entrance, their postures relaxed but their eyes sharp, scanning the parking lot like they were guarding something more than just a tattoo parlor. They didn't look like artists or customers to Razor, they looked like muscle. What was this happy horseshit?

Slowing his bike, Razor pulled into the gas station across the street, pretending to check his mirrors as he took in the details. He parked, sitting there for a moment. There were a few people who appeared to be working at the competitor shop, and faint strains of heavy metal music spilled out every time the door opened. A bigger woman with bright green hair exited the shop, her arms covered in ink, as a tall man in a leather vest held the door for her. He wasn't wearing any colors Razor recognized, but the guy had the distinct swagger of someone who thought they were untouchable.

Razor's jaw tightened as he climbed off the bike, walking into the gas station for cigarettes. Something about the new shop felt off. It wasn't just another tattoo shop trying to outdo the competition. There was a vibe here -- something calculated, something darker. Razor's instincts had kept him alive for decades, and right now, they were screaming at him that *Sinister Skin Studios* was more than it seemed. Shoving his pack of cigarettes into his pocket, he slowly made his way back out to his bike and climbed on. Looping back toward the strip mall, Razor made a mental note of every detail. The faces, the vehicles, the way the men outside subtly shifted when he started his bike. Yeah, this wasn't just about tattoos. There was more going on here, and he intended to find out exactly what. For now, he'd seen enough to report back to Deva.

Razor knew one thing for sure -- this wasn't the last time he'd come calling.

Chapter Three

Deva

The next morning was bitterly cold, the kind of chill that seemed to seep into her bones no matter how many layers she wore. Deva and Jackson had no appointments on the books for the day. She could have driven down to *No Mercy Ink* and sat around, just in case someone wandered in. Maybe she'd go later.

But her thoughts kept circling back to the new tattoo shop opening in town. What had Razor learned? When he offered to check it out for her, she'd initially brushed it off as more macho, overprotective bullshit. She got enough of that from Jackson. But when Razor pointed out that the owners of the new shop might already know who she was -- especially if they'd been digging into *No Mercy Ink* -- his offer started to make sense. Still, the suspense ate at her.

Deva rushed through breakfast, then pulled on a black sweater with a deep V-neck and slid into a pair of skin-tight jeans. She took extra care with her makeup, swiping on mascara and lipstick, her purple hair styled into loose waves. Razor was brutally hot, and if the sinful gazes he cut her were any indication, he liked her too. Her brother's judgy voice echoed in her head, but she shoved it aside. Deva had turned thirty this summer. A grown woman who didn't need Jackson's permission to fuck anyone, least of all Razor.

Grabbing her high-heeled boots, she tugged them on and dashed out to warm up her SUV before running back inside to grab her coat and purse. Phone charged, keys in hand, she slid behind the wheel, determined. *Old Guard Guns* was on the way to her shop, so she had the perfect excuse. Nothing suspicious about stopping by to say hi and ask what

Razor learned about the competition. And if business at his shop was slow as hers right now, maybe they'd have time to talk about other things too.

She reached the converted house-turned-gun-shop in ten minutes. There were no vehicles in the parking lot except for a single bike tucked around the back. *Perfect.* A slow grin spread across her face. She liked the idea of having Razor to herself right now.

The bells above the door jingled loudly as she stepped inside, the sharp sound smacking the glass when she closed it. The smell of oil and faint gunpowder greeted her, and then Razor appeared from the back room. The gorgeous president of her brother's biker club strolled toward the counter, his hazel eyes lighting up the second he saw her. He smiled, slow and warm, and for a moment, the freezing cold outside didn't seem so bad.

"Good morning, Deva," Razor said, shoving his hands in the front pockets of his jeans.

"Morning," she said, glancing around the shop he kept and impressed by the organization. "I thought I'd check in and see if you had anything to tell me about the new tattoo shop."

Razor's gaze locked with hers. "And here I thought you just wanted to see me." His tone was teasing.

"Never said I didn't," Deva said, walking up to the counter. "But first things first. Did you see anything?"

"Business before pleasure?"

A spark of desire coursed through her at his words, igniting something warm and thrilling deep inside. Pleasure, huh? At least they were on the same wavelength. Deva sauntered to the front door, her movements slow and deliberate. She turned the deadbolt with a satisfying click, flipping the "We're Open!" sign to "We're Closed." She moved slowly, leaving plenty of time for him to stop her. Shrugging out of her coat, she just tossed it over the nearest display case.

When she turned back, her pulse quickened. Razor stepped out from behind the counter, his tall frame radiating casual confidence. Those stunning hazel eyes of his moved over her, gleaming with unmistakable interest, and the air between them seemed to crackle with possibility.

"What did you have in mind, little lady?" Razor asked, grinning at her as she invaded his personal space. Razor smelled good, like leather and deep woods. He looked even better. How did a girl get on this ride? Pressing her body into his, her hands slid up his chest, pulling the hair tie out of those gun-metal gray locks so she could run it through her fingers as she'd been daydreaming of doing since yesterday. When his arms closed around her, his hands moving slowly over her back and hips, it only made her want him more.

Easing back, Deva glanced up at him, only then realizing just how much taller Razor was than her. But not so tall she couldn't stretch up and kiss his mouth and finally see if the man was truly hot as he looked. His lips were soft, his salt and pepper stubble lightly brushing her skin as she kissed him. When he didn't stop her, she deepened the kiss, wrapping her arms around his neck to get her hands in his silky hair and she wasn't disappointed. Razor pressed his body into hers, kissing her back with the finesse that only a mature man possessed. *Damn.*

"Do you have somewhere more private we can take this?"

"Yeah, I do," Razor said, his hazel eyes flashing with mischief. Before she could react, he dropped his shoulder and scooped her up, tossing her over it like she weighed nothing.

The world tilted and spun, and Deva let out a startled squeal that quickly turned into delighted laughter. Razor carried her with effortless strength, striding from the front room of the gun shop to the back, every step sending her heart racing in exhilaration. Then he just kept going. Deva wouldn't have objected if he wanted to throw her across a desk or wanted her against a wall. But when she saw the small, neat bedroom he carried her into, she was surprised. Deva giggled when her back hit the mattress on the twin bed with its pale blue comforter. Razor followed her down and she grabbed his head, claiming his mouth in a searing kiss for her preemptive strike. Their lips danced together, making her head spin with his hands running all over her body. Older men had experience, knew how to kiss. Razor had apparently mastered the art of kissing long ago.

"You bring all the girls here?" she asked, breathless and smiling before she continued the kiss.

Razor smirked at her as he pushed off his cut and grabbed the back of his T-shirt and pulled it off over his head. "You're just dynamite, aren't you, darlin'? Fucking you would probably blow a man's world apart."

How was she supposed to answer that when he hovered over her with his gorgeous torso on display, all rippling muscle covered in a collection of tattoos? And she would be closely inspecting those. *Later*.

She'd planned ahead. Deva had known what she wanted when she woke up this morning. The warm winter sweater easily pulled off, revealing the lacy purple bra beneath that just barely harnessed her ample breasts. The best part? Watching the man's eyes light up in unholy interest as she unzipped her jeans and pushed them down to reveal lacy panties that matched the bra. Razor helped her with the boots but encouraged her to keep the fuzzy black socks on. The room was cool, the faint chill in the air teasing against her skin... but that wouldn't last long. They were about to heat things up in a way that would make the cold an afterthought.

Impatient, she unhooked her bra before pushing Razor onto his back and straddling him. She loved the way her breasts filled his hands, how the calloused surface felt against her skin. Her nipples tightened to aching points against his palms, and when he gave her a squeeze, pure desire coursed through her veins. The heated flesh between her thighs quivered and wept. *This is going to be so good.*

Deva took control, sliding down his body and taking his jeans and black boxers with her as she went. She didn't bother with totally removing them, just shoving them down enough to get her hands and mouth on him. He was ready, his cock hard and impressive, twitching against his belly. When she got her hands on him, his groan a porno-worthy sound, he watched her movements with lusty interest. She got her mouth on him, and he was big, but she loved the challenge. Deva started by getting him wet, teasing him with lips and nips of her teeth while the primal taste of him filled her mouth.

"Fuck," he muttered as his hands tried to control her motions. The slight sting of pain when his grip on her hair tightened was sweet as she worked him further back, down her throat.

Deva grinned around him, trying to burn him

down and push him to the edge. Razor fought her, his hips moving with her, his back arching as pleasure swamped him. Finally, he reached his limit, sitting up and pulling her up with him to kiss her, panting into her mouth.

"Your mouth is heaven," he whispered against her lips. "But we'll finish that later. I want more right now..."

The way he said *more* had her pussy clenching, more wetness seeping into her already soaked panties. When his strong fingers slid into the lacy little garment while he deepened their kiss, Deva's moan echoed loudly through the room. Damn, he was good. The way he teased her clit with a single finger was magic, an experienced touch. His fingers slid around her pussy lips easily on the slick of her excitement.

All she could do was stare when he slid those fingers into his mouth, savoring her taste with greed in his eyes. "Normally, I love a bit of foreplay but I'm in a bad way. Can't wait."

That fucking worked for her. Dropping onto her back, she opened her legs wide in welcome. Razor slotted himself between them as if he was made to be there. She pulled her panties to the side for him and his wide cock slid into her easily enough. He took his time, diving deeper into her with each thrust. Her thighs wrapped around his, and she gasped as he finally slid home. Razor more than filled her and she loved the secret spaces inside her that he hit so easily. Deva rolled her hips, encouraging him to fuck her already. She couldn't wait to see what he could do with that magnificent cock.

Deva was far from disappointed. Razor went wild above her, fucking her with just enough force to drive her insane but not enough to make her come. Yet.

Deva hung on for dear life as his thrusts pushed her up the bed, punching the air from her lungs. Her cries blended with his savage grunts as they moved as one, writhing on the bed in the feverish pursuit of pleasure. Razor brought her off the first time by working her clit so delicately while his cock's movements were brutal. Deva's screams echoed off the walls as the orgasm shook her, left her breathless.

Her world upended when Razor pulled himself free of her body and flipped her onto her stomach like she was light as a feather. He buried her in the mattress as he dropped his weight onto her and speared back inside her, pounding into her with a vengeance. Struggling to breathe, to keep up, Deva clawed at the mattress. The new pressure points he played inside her had release riding her as hard as he was. She shifted beneath him, willing to do anything for relief. Razor pushed her thighs wider with his own, doubling down and fucking her with abandon.

His hot breath pelted her ear even as his hips kept driving into her. "You can do better than that, can't you?" The sultry timbre of his voice went to her head like good whisky, leaving her just as disoriented as the liquor would. Before she could think of a retort -- did he expect her to be able to form sentences? -- his weight lifted and he grabbed her hips roughly, pulling them up and back toward him. When she went to lift her head, he pushed it back down onto the mattress and held it firmly there.

"Let's see what else you like," the lusty devil behind her taunted.

Razor fucked her hard, his other hand slapping her ass with abandon. The man was fucking talented, heating up her ass as he pumped into her hard and fast. Deva cried out, yelled encouragement. Hell, she wasn't entirely sure what she said. She just didn't want it to fucking end. There was no rhyme or reason to the slaps on her ass that had to be fire-engine red from his attention. Her pussy clenched around his driving cock with each slap, weeping. Her ass was on fire, and it only heightened the lust that held her hostage. Deva wanted more; she wanted him to ride her like they were going somewhere.

He brought Deva off again, leaving her panting and breathlessly laughing because of how fucking good it was. Thinking he would chase his own end, she braced for it, tightening herself around his cock and moving with him as best she could. Older men had experience, true. But Razor was also ruthless. He rode her wildly until her cries filled the room and the last orgasm left her shaking and dizzy. When he finally went over the edge, he pulled free of her body. His growl was a primal sound she felt to her core. She felt the warm, wet drops of his release on her skin as she collapsed, face down on the bed.

Deva smiled, the only thing she had enough energy left to do. It was a good thing she'd gotten a new IUD before Thanksgiving. Razor rolled to his back, taking her with him, and she ended up sprawled across him, her head resting on his broad chest. Now that she wasn't distracted by lust, she could take her time looking at the tattoos adorning his chest and arms, and he had quite a few. He bounced her on his chest as she realized he was laughing. Pulling herself up to look into his eyes, she smiled. "What?"

"I wondered how long it would take you to start critiquing my tattoos," he said, eyes twinkling.

Despite trying to think of something clever to say, she just shook her head and proceeded to look over them. Her fingers gently traced the ink across his chest. Her touch was light, skimming over his tattoos like she was reading a story written on his skin. The Hounds of Hell tattoo was over his heart, and she recognized her brother's work, the lines sharp and precise.

"That's Jackson's work," she murmured, her lips curving into a small smile.

Razor chuckled, his hand coming up to rest over hers, his calloused fingers warm. "Outcast."

Deva rolled her eyes. "He'll always be Jackson to me. He did this before we opened the shop, didn't he? His style is unmistakable. The shading, the depth -- it's his."

"Well, he didn't do the first version of it," Razor explained. "But he made it a lot better."

Her hand pulled free of his, her fingers moved lower, exploring the other tattoos on his chest and arms, her expression shifting as she studied each one. Razor's ink was more than decoration. It presented a map of his life, etched in moments of triumph, pain, and loyalty. A wolf howling at the moon on his shoulder, fierce and solitary. A banner wrapped around a pair of crossed pistons on his bicep. And under his collarbone, a name scripted in delicate lettering: Jaeden. That one had meaning for him.

"You're a sentimental one, aren't you?" Deva teased in a soft tone.

Razor smirked, his blue eyes twinkling. "Don't tell anyone. I've got a reputation to keep."

Deva's smile faded as her fingers hovered over the name under his collarbone. "Jaeden," she said quietly. "Your daughter?"

"Yeah," Razor said, his voice rougher now. "Lucky guess, or did you already know?"

"I heard," she said. "And not from Jackson. It

was a big deal when Razor's daughter came back to town for her grandmother's funeral. The gossips were all over it."

"Lord," Razor said, exhaling. "Do you know Jade? You go to school with her?"

"No." Deva took the hint. Did their age difference bother him? "I moved here in my early twenties. Jackson, you know, was here before that."

Razor got quiet then. She felt his fingers tracing small circles over her shoulder.

"Does the age difference bother you?" she asked, grinning at him. "If it does, we probably shouldn't have fucked."

His smile returned. *That's better.* "You're not a shy little thing, are you?"

"What gave it away?" she teased. "Yeah, I'm told I'm too much for some people."

"Not for me," Razor said. "And age is just a number as far as I'm concerned. Just hope it doesn't become a problem for you."

"Why would it?" Deva understood his concern. "Guys my age have their heads so far up their ass it's pathetic. They don't have anything to offer me."

"I was like that once myself," he told her. He watched her fingers gently trace the tattoo of his daughter's name. "Jade's mother found out she was pregnant with her and told me about it. I ran like a scalded dog. I didn't want any part of it. I was making a name for myself in the club, trying to earn a patch. That, at the time, seemed more important."

The pain that flashed in his eyes as he spoke was raw. Her heart went out to him as she listened.

"It wasn't until after I got that patch that I started rethinking things," he explained. "By then Jade was two and Va -- her mother wasn't running with the MC anymore. She cleaned up her act, got a job. I think she went back to school. I tried to find a way for us to talk but Mina... I didn't get anywhere, and she got killed in a car accident the next year. I was grateful Jade wasn't in the car. But Mina had custody then and kept her under lock and key. She kept me away all those years. It wasn't until the old woman died and Jade came back for the funeral that... I got a chance to get to know my own daughter."

"Trying to scare me away?" Deva asked.

"Just thought you should know what you're getting involved with."

The heartfelt way he told the story had tears stinging the backs of her eyes. The pain from a mistake he could never take back haunted his words.

"The tattoo isn't recent," Deva pointed out. "You got it some time ago."

Razor nodded. "Got it on her fifth birthday. Didn't matter that her grandmother wanted me gone. She was mine. Always will be."

Deva looked up at him. "Your tattoos... they're all about the things that matter most to you, aren't they? Your club, your family, even the engine on your arm -- it's all pieces of who you are."

Razor nodded, his expression unreadable. "They're reminders. Of what I've done. What I've lost. What I've got to fight for."

Deva's fingers trailed over a long scar that cut through one of the designs, marring the ink but not its meaning. "Looks like you've been through a hell of a lot."

"Yeah," Razor said simply. He caught her hand again, holding it in his, his thumb brushing over her knuckles. "But I'm still here. Still fighting."

For a moment, they lay there in comfortable

silence, her fingers still tracing his ink, learning the language of his past. It wasn't just the tattoos she admired -- it was the man beneath them, every scar and story that shaped him into the man she knew now.

"Is it a bad time to ask what you found out about our competition yesterday?" Deva wanted to change the subject, to let him off the hook for the moment.

"They're setting it up." His body grew tense beneath her. "I'd like to tell you it's just good old-fashioned competition, but something about that place gives me a bad feeling."

Of all the things she thought she might hear, that wasn't one of them. "How bad?"

"*Sinister Skin Studios* doesn't look like some hole-in-the-wall shop." He paused, running a hand through her hair. "They're setting up in that strip mall by the sheriff's department. Dark windows, loud music, and a vibe that's not quite welcoming. They've got muscle hanging outside -- guarding the place."

Deva tried to wrap her mind around his description. "Guarding? But it's a tattoo shop. You think there's more going on than tattoos?"

Razor nodded. "Yeah, I do. I saw bikes parked out front, an SUV with vanity plates, and a few guys giving me the stink eye when I rode by. It felt like they're daring someone to start something."

Crossing her arms, Deva shook her head. "Do you think they're targeting us?"

Razor let out a humorless chuckle. "I don't think it, darlin'. That place isn't set up to blend in, it's there to intimidate and make a statement. Whoever's behind it has resources and connections. They've got plans, and I'm willing to bet those plans involve shutting you and Outcast down."

That wasn't what she wanted to hear. Their shop

had been open a while in Mercy, did good business. Even if they ended up dealing with a competitor, they could make it work. The two shops could coexist. Couldn't they? Why would it be necessary for them to come after her and Jackson? "What do we do?"

"We're not going to panic." Razor's voice was low and steady. "I'll call a club meeting, see if anyone's heard anything about these assholes. We need to come up with a plan to protect you and the shop until we know more. You and your brother need to keep your heads down, play it smart. Don't give them any excuses to come after you."

All the momentary desire and excitement of their new relationship evaporated pretty fast with his explanation of what he'd found when he went to check out the new tattoo shop. For the first time since she read that fucking review, a sliver of fear crept in, filling her with dread of what could happen next. What would she do if these people shut down their shop? Best case scenario, she'd be looking for a new job to pay off a whole lot of debt. Worst case scenario? No, she was overreacting. Surely no one meant her or her brother any physical harm, right?

Whoa. What? "Do you think they pose a physical threat to us? The shop?"

"I wouldn't be surprised." His tone was firm, leaving no room for argument. "I just don't know their motivation yet. We'll find out. You just focus on keeping the shop running and doing what you do best. The shop is under our protection. I'll handle it."

Deva exhaled slowly, nodding. "Thanks, Razor."

"Don't thank me yet," he said, giving her a pointed look. "Hey, I didn't mean to ruin your day, darlin'," Razor said slowly, moving closer. "I'm also not trying to scare you. I'm just asking you to be vigilant and careful until we figure this out. I'd love to see that smile back on your face."

The remark got the response he wanted, making her smile. "Is that your way of saying you'd like to see me again, Razor? "

"It is," he said with no hesitation.

* * *

Razor

Razor couldn't get Deva out of his head for the rest of the day. It had been years since any woman lingered in his thoughts after he got what he wanted, but Deva was different. The little tattoo artist had been around Mercy for a few years, but Razor hadn't really noticed her before. Now that he had, she was turning his uneventful personal life completely upside down... and he wasn't complaining. Deva was pure dynamite, wrapped in a gorgeous, compact, and fiercely sassy package. The heat they shared earlier left him reeling. Since she walked out of his shop, focusing on anything else had been damn near impossible.

He considered dropping by *No Mercy Ink* once he closed to see if she wanted to have dinner with him again, but pride stopped him. As much as he would like a replay of this morning, he was content to let her set the pace. At least until he could determine if it was just an infatuation or there was something more serious forming. Razor could be patient. He had all the time in the world. Besides, guessing what she'd do next was proving to be fun.

* * *

He'd just gotten to the gun shop the next morning when his phone chimed. Razor hoped it was Deva but the number on the screen showed it was Outcast, her brother.

"What's up?" Razor answered as he shrugged out of his coat and hung it up in his office.

"We've got a problem," Outcast said with tension in his voice. "Someone broke into the shop overnight. Busted up the place pretty fucking badly."

"Whoa. Hold on," Razor said. "Which shop?"

"*No Mercy*." Outcast sounded flabbergasted. "They fucking busted us up."

Fuck. Whoever these pricks were, they definitely had bad intentions toward *No Mercy Ink* and maybe even its owners. Given what he'd seen when he drove by the new shop preparing to open, Razor's instincts told him that something was wrong there.

"Was the security system engaged?" Razor asked. Snow had installed the new system in *No Mercy Ink* last summer along with all the other Hound-owned businesses when the Mafia burned down Emily's bakery and vandalized *Three Guys Garage* and the cars in its lot waiting for repairs. "How did they get around that?"

The pause told him the situation was bad. "I'm heading that way," Razor told him, ending the call.

Putting his coat back on, he locked up the shop he hadn't opened yet and jumped back on his bike. The rumble of Razor's Harley echoed down the street as he approached *No Mercy Ink*. Even from a distance, something felt off. The normally welcoming glow of the shop's neon sign was gone, and the street in front of it was unusually still.

Razor's jaw clenched as he pulled up and killed the engine. The shop loomed ahead, its shattered windows catching the dim streetlights. Bright red spray paint, chaotic graffiti, ruined the store's black-and-white facade.

"Jesus," he muttered under his breath. Swinging

off his bike, he walked carefully. Broken glass scattered across the sidewalk. The front door hung on by one hinge, its lock clearly busted.

Scanning the scene, Razor's instincts honed from years in the MC kicked into high gear. The air smelled of paint and destruction, heavy with the tang of anger and defiance.

"Razor!" Outcast's voice rang out, raw with frustration and fury. The younger man emerged from inside the shop, his ice-blue eyes blazing. His knuckles were bloodied, and his breathing was heavy, like he'd been restraining himself from tearing someone apart.

"What the hell happened here?" Razor asked, his voice calm but edged with steel. He stepped inside, his gaze sweeping over the wreckage.

The interior of *No Mercy Ink* was unrecognizable. The sleek, modern setup Razor had admired just days ago was in ruins. Tables were overturned, chairs smashed, and expensive equipment lay scattered, some broken beyond repair. Ink bottles had been deliberately spilled, their contents staining the floors and walls in chaotic streaks. Artwork from the walls was ripped down, crumpled, and thrown into piles of destruction. Sketchbooks were shredded, their pages strewn like confetti.

"Got a call from one of our regulars," Outcast said, his voice tight with rage. "They drove by and saw the windows busted. By the time I got here" -- he gestured to the devastation --"it was like this."

"Anyone see who did it?" Razor asked, his eyes narrowing as he inspected the damage.

"No," Outcast growled, pacing like a caged animal. "They fucking disarmed our security system. We got nothing on them. But this…" He pointed to a corner of the room at a spray-painted symbol Razor recognized from the night he drove by the new shop preparing to open. It was the unmistakable logo of *Sinister Skin Studios*, three snakes looped around each other, scrawled across the wall.

Razor's blood boiled at the sight. His hands curled into fists, the veins on his arms bulging. "They're sending a message," he said, his voice dangerously low.

Deva appeared then, stepping from the back room, her face pale but set with determination. Her eyes were glassy with unshed tears, but her expression was fierce. She carried a notebook in her hand, likely making notes of all the damage for their insurance company despite the overwhelming mess.

When her gaze met Razor's, a flicker of relief crossed her face. "I was hoping you'd come," she admitted, her voice quiet but steady. "We called you first."

Razor crossed the room to her, his broad frame radiating strength and reassurance. "You called the cops?" he asked.

She nodded. "A deputy came, took pictures, and half-ass investigated. But you and I both know that's not going anywhere."

"Which deputy?" Razor asked.

"I didn't catch his name," Deva told him, looking like she was trying so hard to hold it together. "Talk, dorky, large, and in charge."

"Fucking Dawson." It had to be him. Razor nodded. "We'll see if we can get Margot on this. She's our best shot of getting help from the sheriff's department."

"What are we supposed to do?" Outcast demanded, his frustration boiling over. "What is their fucking problem?"

Razor's expression hardened, his voice like steel. "We need to find out. They think they can pull this shit, but they just poked the wrong bear."

He glanced around the shop again, his gaze lingering on Deva. Despite the destruction, she stood tall, her chin raised, ready to fight for what was hers. Razor felt a surge of admiration… and protectiveness. He'd do whatever it took to make sure *No Mercy Ink* and the people who'd built it weren't brought down by cowards hiding behind spray paint and broken glass. He was unable to tamp down the wave of protectiveness flooding him, and he knew he would do anything to keep her safe. Outcast cut him an odd look. The younger man was likely wondering what was going on between the two of them. Hell, he might be opposed to him and Deva being together if it grew into something more. But as far as Razor was concerned, it wasn't his business.

"First," Razor said, looking between Outcast and Deva, "we secure the shop. I know you need your insurance people to come have a look. Don't start cleaning up until Margot has been here. Then we start sending our own message."

Outcast nodded. Deva raised her chin in defiance.

She might have said more but then her phone chimed. Deva fished it out of her pocket. "It's the insurance company." Dashing off, she took the call.

"Got good insurance? Razor asked.

Outcast nodded. "Yeah. We'll probably need some help if we can get it. Otherwise, they'll try to stick us with one of their contractors who'll charge an arm and a leg to get us back up and running."

That had Razor grinning. Before too long, the Hounds of Hell would be called the Hounds of Home

Improvement. The MC had been working on rebuilding Emily's bakery since last summer. Now they'd be rebuilding *No Mercy Ink*. It would take time away from club interests because most of them had day jobs. Lately any spare time they had was spent on fixing shit their enemies had torn up rather than earning money for the club by way of running guns. He needed to call a meeting. *Soon.*

"You've got it," Razor said. Casting one long look in the direction Deva went, Razor fished his phone out of his pocket to give Margot a call.

Chapter Four

Deva

Deva stood just outside what was left of *No Mercy Ink*. The chilly January morning made her feel cold. But it wasn't just the weather. *No*. She felt numb, paralyzed by the unprovoked attack on their shop. The crunching sound of glass underfoot behind her made her flinch, but it was only Razor stepping closer. She hadn't realized that he was still there, staying near the gaping hole where the front door was barely hanging on.

Margot Donner's cruiser pulled up quietly, the rumble of its engine cut off as it rolled to a stop. The deputy parked precisely between the white painted lines marking the parking space.

Deva knew who Margot was, but they'd never talked. Now the other woman was a deputy in Mercy. The concern on Margot's face as she climbed out of the car had Deva's tears threatening to start. She was glad Razor had called her. Maybe Margot assessing the damage would yield better results than the arrogant deputy who'd been there earlier and didn't seem to give a shit.

"Deva?" Margot's voice was calm but firm, snapping her out of the momentary shock. "Are you okay?"

Was she okay? Deva couldn't even begin to answer that. Her shop -- her sanctuary -- looked like a war zone. Graffiti was slashed across the walls, the windows were shattered, and shards of glass glittered in the sunlight. It felt like someone had gutted *her*, not just the shop.

"I -- I don't know," Deva said, her voice barely above a whisper. She stepped aside as Margot approached and Razor stayed close behind her.

Margot surveyed the damage with sharp, experienced eyes. She didn't say anything right away, just pulled a notepad and pen from her coat pocket. "When did you find this?"

"This morning," Deva replied, her arms tightening around herself. "One of our regulars called Outcast... my brother, you know, to let him know someone broke in."

Margot nodded, jotting it down. "Everything was okay when you closed and locked up last night?"

Deva nodded. "Yes."

"Was anything taken?"

"No," Deva said, glancing at the chaos inside. "Not that I've noticed anyway. It doesn't look like they were after money or equipment. Just... destruction."

"Has anything been moved or cleaned up?" Margot asked.

"No. We called the sheriff's department first thing. They sent Dawson over."

Margot shook her head. "I'm sorry," was all she said. She looked like she wanted to say more but professionally couldn't continue.

Margot stepped carefully into the ruined space, Razor following her in. Deva stayed outside, struggling to make herself walk through the door again. The shop just didn't feel like hers anymore. It felt... violated. That violation felt personal.

A moment later, Margot motioned her in, dusting glass off the latex gloves she'd pulled on. "Your security cameras. Where are they?"

Deva motioned to the corner of the building. "There's one above the door and another at the back. But..."

"But what?" Margot asked.

"They worked around them," she said, her voice trembling with frustration. "Jackson checked the footage. It's useless. All we got were shadows of someone walking up to the front door and then it went black. They somehow managed to just turn them off."

Margot's jaw tightened. "So, this was organized." She scribbled something else in her notebook. Margot cut Razor a look and he nodded.

"I've already called Snow," he said. Deva wasn't used to others taking on her jobs but she trusted Razor to ask the right questions.

Margot's attention was back on Deva, pointing to the front door. "This door was where they forced their way in."

"Yeah," Deva confirmed, nodding toward the busted frame. "They knocked the hell out of it."

Margot walked over, examining the broken doorframe. "I'll dust it for prints. If they were wearing gloves, we probably won't find anything."

Deva's heart sank further. "What does that mean? You can't do anything?"

Margot's tone softened, but her expression remained focused. "Not necessarily. Vandalism is a crime. Just because they covered their tracks doesn't mean they didn't slip up somewhere. I'll go over everything. Then I'll write up a report and look into any other incidents like this."

Deva nodded numbly.

Margot glanced at Razor. "You mentioned a rival shop. What's the name?"

"*Sinister Skin Studios*," Razor said, his voice like gravel. Walking over to the divider between Deva's station and Jackson's, he pointed to a symbol that looked like three snakes interlocked, crudely drawn in spray paint. "They're not hiding. This same symbol is in the window of their shop. So, either this was them, or someone wants us to think it is."

Margot frowned, scribbling the name down. "I'll look into them. If they're connected to this, we'll find out."

Deva felt tears prick her eyes, but she swallowed them back. Crying wouldn't fix anything. She couldn't let them see her fall apart. Not here. Not right now.

Margot's voice pulled her back to the moment. "Deva, I know this is hard, but I need a statement from you. Same for Outcast. I'll also take photos and check for anything they might've left behind."

Deva nodded, forcing herself to focus. "What if they come back?" she asked quietly.

"It's not likely they'll hit the same place twice, especially now with law enforcement involved. But I'd recommend upgrading your locks, having Snow add more cameras, and hardening your security system. I'll give you some tips too."

Deva wanted to think they wouldn't strike again. Grateful as she was for the advice, she still felt hollow. As Margot started her work, Razor came to stand beside her. He didn't say anything, just rested a hand lightly on her shoulder. His quiet strength steadied her, even as the sight of her destroyed shop made her want to scream.

She took a deep breath, her voice trembling as she whispered, "We built this place from nothing. It isn't just a business. It's our home."

Razor's hand tightened just slightly. "And you'll build it back."

She wanted to believe him. Desperately. But as she stared at the shattered remains of *No Mercy Ink*, all she could feel was the weight of everything she'd lost. Jackson had said he was riding across town to talk to their insurance agent, but Deva knew better. She knew he had to get out of the building, that he couldn't breathe. She understood. Keeping herself together was the hardest part, as her mind kept racing with the countless tasks ahead. The thought of getting anywhere close to functioning like a normal shop again felt overwhelming.

And *Sinister Skin Studios*? Why were they hitting them so hard? Unless there was some ugly business Jackson got into that she didn't know about, what was the motivation? It seemed like a lot for just being pre-existing competition. "Unless my brother pissed the wrong person off, I just don't get why they're doing this."

Her breath caught in her throat as she took in the devastation. The acrid smell of spray paint and smashed wood hung heavy in the air, mingling with the metallic tang of her own fury. Shattered glass covered the floor, and the overturned chairs and broken equipment were strewn about like trash. Graffiti bled over all of it, mocking them. It was a brutal sight -- a personal attack that felt like a punch to the gut.

Her hands trembled as she looked around, her boots crunching over shards of glass. She barely felt the sting when a sharp piece nicked her palm as she righted a fallen chair. It was the silence that gutted her most. The shop, usually alive with the hum of machines and conversation, was now eerily quiet. Her sketchbooks were ripped to shreds and scattered across the floor. Those were years of designs, personal pieces, and commissions she hadn't yet inked. She picked up a torn page, her fingers tightening around it as her throat constricted. The delicate line works she'd once been proud of now were smeared with dirt and paint.

"Why?" she whispered, her voice breaking, as if speaking aloud might answer the question. Still, Deva wasn't willing to let whoever did this win by breaking her spirit.

Razor's voice broke through her haze. "Deva," he said gently, but his voice carried an edge of fury. "They won't get away with it. We'll make damn sure they regret it."

Deva turned to him as she fought to steady herself. "I won't let them take this from us," she said, her voice firmer now, despite the tears threatening to spill. "We'll rebuild it, no matter how long it takes."

Razor nodded. "You won't be doing it alone."

Deva swallowed hard, standing a little taller, even as her heart ached. She looked around at the mess, her determination slowly taking root beneath the pain. She would clean every piece of glass, repaint every wall, and put her shop back together, stronger than ever. Whoever thought they could break her didn't know who the fuck they were dealing with.

* * *

Razor

Razor sat at the head of the long, scarred wooden table in the Hounds' meeting room, his steely eyes scanning the gathered men. The air was thick with tension as the brothers waited for him to speak. Every patch-holder was present, from Axel and Ryder to Snow and Hero. Even Outcast, his jaw tight with barely contained fury, leaned forward in his chair between Crash and Beast, ready to explode into action. Snow cut Razor a look. He was the only one who had any idea of why the meeting had been called.

Razor stayed calm given the simmering unease

among his men. "Outcast's shop was hit last night. *No Mercy Ink* got torn apart -- windows smashed, walls spray-painted, equipment trashed. Whoever did this wanted to send a message, and they made damn sure we got it."

A ripple of murmurs swept through the room. Outcast's fists clenched on the table, his knuckles white. Snow muttered a curse under his breath, and Player leaned back in his chair, his gaze dark and calculating.

Razor held up a hand, silencing the room instantly. "We're going to figure out who did this and fucking deal with them. We're going to find out fast and hit them hard. Just be careful. The law's watching us closely, especially after the mess at *Sackett's* last summer. Margot's helping us all she can, but we can't afford to draw more heat."

Ryder smirked at the mention of his old lady.

Outcast couldn't hold back. "I don't care about the fucking heat, Razor! That shop's everything to Deva. To me. They just fucking trashed our place."

Razor's eyes locked on Outcast, his voice razor-sharp. "And we'll deal with it. But not with blind rage. You want revenge? You follow my lead."

Outcast bit back whatever retort he had, nodding once.

Razor leaned forward, kept his tone steady even though he was plenty furious himself. "I want surveillance on *Sinister Skin Studios*."

Crash wasn't the only one who looked confused around the table. "Who?"

"*Sinister Skin Studios*," Razor said slower this time. "It's a new tattoo shop in town that's about to open. Curious, because this is the first I'm fucking hearing of it. Anyone else?" He could tell by the looks on his men's faces that it was new to them too. "They're setting up shop in that strip mall across the road from the hospital."

Razor studied his men, the dim light of the meeting room casting shadows over them. The room was quiet, the tension tangible as the Hounds waited for him to say more. Outcast looked angrier by the second, his elbows on the table. Axel, Ryder, and Snow exchanged sharp glances.

"When I rode by *Sinister Skin Studios*, I got a good look," Razor began. "The place is meant to look like your average hole-in-the-wall tattoo shop, but it's too clean, too polished. Big neon lights out front flashing like a damn nightclub, the kind of place that screams for attention. Something about their setup doesn't feel right. It's more for intimidation than security, like they're trying to keep people out, not just keep the place safe."

Razor paused, looking at each of them around the table. "It's not open yet, but soon. Didn't see much foot traffic. But some of the people I did see were muscle, security. Didn't look much like artists to me. What kind of tattoo parlor needs muscle?"

Outcast frowned, shook his head.

"And there's something else." A detail Razor hadn't explained to Deva because she wouldn't understand the significance of it. "Around the back, they've got a loading dock. Looked like it was built for something a lot bigger than what they're doing. A tattoo shop doesn't need that kind of setup."

Axel raised a brow. "You think they're moving something besides ink?"

"Wouldn't surprise me," Razor replied.

Snow's voice pitched low. "What's the move, Razor? Besides me figuring out how they fucking got around my security system and beefing that up?"

Razor's expression hardened. "We don't make a move until we know what we're dealing with. We keep our eyes and ears open." To Outcast, he said, "Whatever they're playing at, we're going to make them fucking regret it."

The room fell silent, the weight of Razor's words settling over the brothers. The determination in their eyes matched his. "Keep your heads down, but keep watching. Snow, you and Hero tail their crew. I want to know who they're meeting, where they're going, and who's funding them. Axel, Ryder -- monitor their shop. I want to know about any deliveries or new faces."

He turned to Outcast. "You stick close to Deva. Her safety's priority one. I don't care if she tells you she's fine. You don't let her out of your sight."

Outcast's jaw tightened, but he nodded. "Got it."

Razor was also putting himself on that detail. He just didn't have to advertise it.

"Beast," Razor continued, turning to the huge, shaggy biker, "reach out to our contacts in Oak Grove and any of the surrounding counties where you have contacts. Let's see if this crew has been stirring up trouble anywhere else.

"If any of you see or hear anything suspicious, you bring it to me before you act. This isn't just about *No Mercy Ink* -- it's about Mercy, our turf. And I'll be damned if I let anyone think they can waltz in here and start tearing down shit. We'll find out what they're hiding, and when the time's right, we'll take them down. Together."

His words sank in, the expressions of his men hardened with resolve. Razor's eyes lingered on Outcast for a moment longer as he stood, signaling the end of the meeting.

"Let's get to work," Razor said.

Chairs scraped back, and the Hounds drifted out with their assignments. Only Outcast lingered, his gaze meeting Razor's. "They're gonna pay for this," he said, his voice low but fierce.

"They will," Razor replied. "But we do it *my* way."

Outcast nodded, and Razor clapped him on the shoulder before heading out, already planning their next move.

* * *

Deva

Deva sat on her couch and cried, finally able to let out some of the crushing fury and sadness that had welled up in her. They'd talked to the police and an insurance adjuster. They'd canceled their tattoo appointments for the rest of the week, including poor Sadie's. All they could tell them was that they'd be in touch to reschedule their appointments as soon as they were back up and running. When would that be? Who the fuck knew?

At least all but one of them were designs in progress that were started at *No Mercy Ink*. Deva wasn't too worried about them going elsewhere to finish them. Still, it was a top priority to get new equipment, new ink. To get back up and running as soon as possible. They could worry about the appearance of the shop later, even though it broke her heart to know what the fuckers did to it.

Jackson had introduced her to a handsome biker from the Hounds who looked young for someone with solid white hair. Snow reviewed all the surveillance footage with them. He spent the rest of the day trying to figure out how the bastards managed to disable their cameras. Deva assumed at first that they had done it to conceal their identity. As it turned out, like Razor said, they weren't really trying to hide at all.

Razor… Despite his own shop, he'd stayed with her at *No Mercy Ink*. Yeah, she knew he was the president of the MC but until today, she hadn't seen that side of him. The man was a force. Standing near the doorway with broad shoulders squared, he seemed to absorb the chaos and somehow defy it. His jaw was set, the tension there matching the simmering storm in his dark hazel eyes. The Hound patch on his leather cut stood out under the overhead light, catching her attention as he barked orders. Directing Snow once he arrived to get on the cameras and the other young men, some of them prospects, who arrived up to help clean things up.

He kept his voice low but commanding, and the men around him moved without question, falling into place like soldiers following their general. Deva hadn't spent much time with Razor yet. To this point, he'd been so charming with her, using that easy smirk she loved to his advantage. But what she saw earlier was something else. Razor was a man who exuded authority and an unyielding determination to protect what was his. And somehow, in that moment, she realized she was included in that. The thought hit her hard, leaving her breathless.

Swiping at her tears with cold fingers, Deva sat there numbly, unable to think of what she should do next. Normally, her life was very ordered. There were leftovers from the dinner she'd made last night, but getting off the couch to warm them up seemed like a Herculean feat. So did showering and selecting what she'd wear the next day. What was the point? She wasn't going to be running her shop. She was going in to clean up the mess there and try to piece it all back together. Maybe she'd stay home and bed rot. Hiding under her bed covers for a week sounded pretty good about now.

The unexpected knock at her door made Deva jump from where she sat curled up on the couch. A glance at her watch revealed it was after eight. She hadn't realized how late it had gotten. Shaking her head, she frowned. Who would be showing up at her door at this hour on a Thursday? She moved to the large window by her living room door and spotted the shadow of a man on her doorstep. The Hounds of Hell patch on his heavy leather jacket, an image that struck fear in many, made her smile. Scrambling to unlock the door, she found Razor standing there in the cold, an enormous pizza box in his hands.

When his gaze landed on her, his expression softened. "Have you eaten?" he asked.

It was freezing and Deva motioned him in. Locking the door behind him, she led him into the kitchen, and the pizza box he placed on her small kitchen table took up most of it. She hadn't felt hungry until the smells of the rapidly cooling pizza had her stomach rumbling with interest. Razor's gaze was fixed solely on her as she pre-heated the oven.

Deva knew she was a wreck, but the sight of him standing there filled her with relief. Razor crossed the room without a word, his eyes kind as he reached her. Wrapping his strong arms around her, he held her close in the quiet of her kitchen, letting her cry more tears. No words were needed; his steady embrace said everything. Her arms snaked into the warmth of his jacket, the heat of his body carrying the scent of his cologne, that fragrance that was just naturally him.

Deva felt safe and sheltered in that moment. It was his way of trying to absorb some of the blows for her.

With no idea of how long they'd been standing there, Deva muttered, "Sorry." She didn't want to relinquish her place in his arms, but the man had done so much for her today. He deserved a break and some pizza. Slowly, with her brain in a fog, she pulled out her wooden pizza peel and used it to slide the pizza into her oven. She got plates and cutlery out for them while it warmed. Razor shrugged off his heavy jacket and hung it on one of the pegs just outside the kitchen before taking a seat at her table.

"Would you like a beer?" Deva asked.

"That would be great, darlin'," he said, his gaze on her as she shuffled around the kitchen.

Deva kept a brand of beer she liked in the fridge, grabbing a bottle and twisting off the lid for him. His grin widened as he read the label of the beer he held.

"What?" she had to ask.

Razor took a long drink, seeming to savor it. "It's nice to see a woman who knows good beer," he mused.

She couldn't help but smile at that. "Why? Who has bad taste?"

"My daughter Jade," Razor said. "Keeps a fridge full of her fancy IPA beers. Most of them are God awful."

Deva laughed. "They're supposed to have a higher alcohol content though."

"Not high enough to justify how shitty they taste." He was dead serious. "Hero keeps good beer in a cooler under their porch when we go over there to eat. It's gotten to be a not-so-private joke."

Deva shook her head, picturing a bunch of big, bad bikers whining over IPA beers. Still, she made a mental note of it. "So, you and Jade see each other often?"

"Yeah, we do," Razor said as she joined him at the table. "How are you holding up, Deva?"

A few reassuring things to say floated through her mind, but she couldn't bring herself to say any of them. Finally, she just went with the truth. "I'm a fucking wreck."

He nodded, drinking from his beer. "We're not going to let anything else happen to you or the shop. You understand?"

Deva nodded. "I keep thinking about what Margot said. What if she's wrong? What if they do come back?"

"We'll be waiting," Razor told her, his hazel-eyed gaze intent on her. "I guaran-damn-tee that."

His answer didn't make her feel better. "The Hounds can't be there every minute of the day."

"It's not going to be like that," Razor said.

"I wonder what they're doing besides tattoos?"

"Me too."

The aroma of pizza filled the kitchen as Deva pulled their dinner from the oven. Grabbing plates from the table, she served them, aware of Razor's steady gaze following her every move. They ate in silence for a while, but it wasn't awkward -- just a comfortable quiet that gave her room to breathe. The first bite reminded her she hadn't eaten all day, and the beer dulled the sharp edges of her emotions. By the time they finished, the sadness lingered but the exhaustion that crept in had softened her rage into a weary kind of acceptance.

As she gathered their dishes to rinse them off, Razor moved behind her. His warm presence wrapped around her like a blanket as his arms encircled her waist. Deva leaned into him, craving the solid reassurance of his strength. His kiss brushed lightly against her hair, a tender, chaste gesture that spoke more of comfort than seduction. It was nice -- quiet support without expectation, a reminder that she wasn't alone in her struggles. But she almost wanted him to start something. To make her fucking forget a genuinely awful fucking day.

"What are we doing here, Razor?" Deva asked cautiously. She felt the tension ripple through Razor's body at her question, and her stomach sank a little. His deep sigh didn't help, and the silence that followed only made the air between them feel heavier.

"Did I read the situation wrong?" she pressed, the words escaping before she could stop them.

"Darlin'," he said softly, his tone calm, "given the day you've had, let's save this discussion for another time. We've got all the time in the world to figure out what we're doing here."

Deva turned to face him, her brows drawing together as she nudged him out of her personal space. "What if I want to talk about it? Yeah, it's been a fucked-up day. But sometimes it's better to see the whole picture -- to hit rock fucking bottom all at once."

The wary flicker in his gorgeous hazel eyes was both disappointing and a warning. The subtle thrill of fear that look sent rippling through her was enough to brace her against the "I'm-not-looking-for-anything-serious" speech she was almost certain was coming. She loved that edge of danger about him -- it was part of why she'd been so bold in the first place.

"Rock bottom, huh?" Razor shook his head, a faint smirk softening his expression.

Deva shrugged, attempting a nonchalant air but missing the mark entirely. "I like to plan ahead. To at least have a rough idea of where I'm going."

"I'll be honest with you," Razor said slowly, his tone steady. "I'm not looking for anything right now. It's been a long time since I even thought about having someone in my life. And even then, I didn't let her in."

His words hit her like a punch, the realization sharp and immediate -- he meant Vanessa, Jade's mother. The thought twisted in her gut. If she pursued something with him, would she always be competing with the memory of another woman?

Deva hesitated; her anger flared. "You're a good fuck, Razor. But that's not so hard to find these days. If that's all we are…"

"Excuse me?" Razor's voice dropped an octave, the warning clear in its sharp edge.

"You heard me," Deva shot back, crossing her arms over her chest in defiance. "I know you'll still help with the shop because of Jackson. But let me be honest with *you* -- I'm not looking for another fuck buddy. Especially not right now. I've wasted enough time on those."

His poker face was good -- almost perfect. The faint flicker in his hazel eyes, a quick flash of disbelief that betrayed how her words hit home. For a second, she thought she'd gone too far, that he'd turn and storm out of her house, slamming the door behind him.

"What are you really looking for?" His tone was deceptively patient. "With the exception of your visit to my gun shop, you seem to be mostly in that beautiful head of yours. Think you might need to get out of there for a while?"

Deva didn't want to answer that question because that would be acknowledging that he was right. But it was the truth. If his idea of getting out of her head was more of what he'd given her at his gun shop, yeah. She'd play along.

"Okay," she said, adrenaline and rising desire rushing through her veins.

He closed the distance between them in two determined strides, the intensity in his gaze setting her nerves on fire. Before she could say another word, Razor's hand shot up, tangling in her hair with a firm, almost punishing grip. The roughness pulled a startled cry from her lips, the tension between them electrifying and impossible to ignore.

"You need to tap out," he whispered in her ear, "say red. Got it?"

Oh, hell. This is how he wants to play? Deva was just about shaking in anticipation. "Got it."

"Hard limits?"

"I love a little breath play," she explained. "I don't like pain."

Deva saw the need shaking down her body reflected in his gorgeous hazel eyes along with a flash of triumph. It wiped away the last vestiges of a truly shitty day. At least for the moment.

"Maybe you need to be shown what you need," Razor growled. He marched out of the kitchen still gripping her hair in a way that forced her to keep up or have it ripped from her scalp. When they reached the living room, he let her go long enough to shove her against a wall, hard enough to knock some of the wind out of her. One of his big hands wrapped around her throat. His grip wasn't tight enough to cut off her air completely, but it didn't allow much. Her hands flew up, trying without really trying to pry his hand away. It only took seconds before she felt dazed and light-headed under Razor's intense stare.

"You gave me that pussy so sweetly yesterday, didn't you?" Razor growled. "And it's mine until I decide I've had enough. Got it?"

Deva's eyes watered and the thrill of his threat made the lack of oxygen worse. Jackson's words about Razor being someone she wouldn't want to fuck with echoed in her mind. No, she really did want to fuck with him. When she kept pretending to pull his hand off, wanting to provoke him, he got in her face.

"Keep going and I'll squeeze harder," he warned. "Now be a good girl and take off your jeans and panties for me."

He's good. Rising excitement had pulses of need running all through her and for a fleeting moment, she had to wonder what was wrong with her. She had just provoked a fucking biker. Her hands shook as she lowered them to the front of her jeans to undo them. When he didn't release his hold on her to do as he commanded, she did the best she could. She pushed down her jeans and panties, able to get them to her knees but no further.

Razor lifted his boot and roughly shoved her garments down to her ankles. Deva wasn't sure what to do next and it wasn't easy pushing thoughts through the oxygen deprivation. He didn't leave her long to wonder as he stepped over the clothes bunched at her ankles. She gasped when his hand dropped from her neck. While she struggled to get air back into her system, he roughly grabbed her hips and hoisted her thighs up and around his waist, keeping her back against the wall. His fingers dove into her exposed folds and found them soaked, sliding easily on the wetness he found there.

When he looked up, his gaze meeting hers, his smile was all dominance. "That's what I thought," he murmured. "You can run that mouth all you want. But your little body's fucking begging for me."

Razor's lips claimed hers in a ruthless kiss that

left her head spinning. While he dazzled her with his lips, she felt the movement of his hand beneath her, frantically working his belt, the opening of his own jeans. In the span of a heartbeat, she felt the head of his cock poised at her entrance. Deva shuddered in his hold. Her body ached for him.

When he plunged into her, a cry escaped her lips. Razor stretched her open, holding her against the wall and making her take him. Deva was so worked up from his ruthlessness that he slid home inside her easily. When he couldn't go any further, he broke the kiss. Deep lust flashed in his eyes as his hand returned to her throat. Now he was inside her, filling her in a way no other man had. He restricted her air so that all she knew was the feel of him buried in her body. Then he tightened his grip a little more.

Razor started fucking her against the wall in wild abandon, his thrusts hard. Deva could only make the tiniest sounds as his cock drove in and out of her, hard and fast, claiming her in the most primal way. Her heart raced in her chest while fear and desire clouded her mind. Razor made her fight to breathe, made her ride his cock. His rough growls were the only sound in the quiet of her living room. Her vision threatened to fade to black every few seconds as he took her with sharp snaps of his hips all while his hand deprived her of air.

"Okay?" he whispered in her ear. "If so, pull my hair hard."

He didn't have to tell her twice. Deva grabbed a handful of his hair, giving it a sharp yank because she could.

"You're taking me so good, darlin'," Razor's voice was low and rough. "Can't wait to see what you look like… choking on my cock."

His words pushed her over the edge the first time, cries stifled in her throat by the strong grip of his fingers. Deva choked on those cries as he fucked her through it. And he didn't slow down as she came. He didn't ease up to allow her to recover. Razor kept going and the second time she came, she thought she really might lose consciousness. But then he dropped his hand, powering into her hard as he chased his own end. His thrusts gained in speed and strength, setting a punishing pace. Deva hung on for dear life until he yanked himself free of her. The jets of his release were hot against the soft flesh of her tummy as he worked himself with his hand. His guttural cries and the fierce pounding of her heart were the only sounds she was aware of.

Setting her carefully on her feet, Razor stepped away, tucking himself back into his jeans with haste. Deva couldn't read his expression and she sure as shit couldn't move as she watched him walk over to pluck his jacket from where he hung it.

Deva's legs gave out and she slid down the wall onto the floor. She didn't have the energy or wherewithal to try and cover herself as she watched him. She thought he meant to just walk out of the room without saying anything, but he paused while pulling his jacket on by her front door.

"Goodnight, darlin'," he said, meeting her gaze squarely. "I'll see you tomorrow."

Chapter Five

Razor

What are we doing here, Razor?

Razor could still hear Deva's voice in his head, asking the one question he hadn't been ready to answer. Any other woman would have gotten a curt response. But this wasn't just any other woman. Yeah, they'd been talking, and sure, they'd hooked up. Razor made no promises, and he wasn't the kind of man who suddenly changed his ways.

So why the hell was she still on his mind? He'd replayed that unexpected turn in their conversation countless times since leaving her house last night. The night ended on an explosive note, one he hadn't planned. But he couldn't stop fucking thinking about how responsive she'd been to his rough handling. The mix of desire and fear in those big, expressive brown eyes undid him as much as it fueled him. He meant to teach her a lesson, but now he wondered if she'd been the one teaching him something instead.

Had the break-in been the reason he hadn't put Deva in her place? As much as he tried to tell himself that was it, he knew that shit wasn't the truth. Why then? What the hell was going on with him? The entire day went like that, and only two customers showed up at the gun shop. With an hour to go, he followed up with his crew on *Sinister Skin Studios*. He checked in with Axel, Ryder, and Snow, but none of them had anything new to offer. But Hero, living up to his club name, came through for him.

Razor leaned against the counter; phone pressed to his ear. The scent of gun oil and glass cleaner from dusting the display cases filled the air, grounding him as Hero's voice came through the line, tense and urgent.

"Razor," Hero said without preamble, "I've got something. Just got off the phone with one of my contacts in Richmond."

Razor straightened. He could tell by the edge in Hero's tone that this wasn't going to be good. "What'd you find?"

"*Sinister Skin Studios* isn't what it's labeled on the can," Hero continued. "Turns out it's tied to Victor Grayson."

The name hit Razor like a punch to the gut. He gripped the edge of the counter until his knuckles turned white. "Grayson? The same Grayson who's been trying to take over Mercy for the last decade?"

"The very same," Hero confirmed. "He's been quiet for the last couple of years, but it looks like the new tattoo parlor is part of a bigger plan. My contact says *Sinister Skin* is just a front. Grayson's using it to get his foot in the door here."

Razor's mind raced. Grayson was notorious for playing dirty -- blackmail, bribery, and when those didn't work, threats that hit closer to home. Worse, the man was a trafficker and had made a good part of his fortune selling young women, and some young men. No, he wasn't just a threat to Deva and Outcast. If Grayson set his sights on Mercy, the whole town and all its people were in the crosshairs. And that he wouldn't allow.

"What's he got to gain by messing with a tattoo parlor?" Razor asked.

"Control," Hero said. "He moves in slow, builds his influence one piece at a time. The tattoo shop gives him a visible foothold. If it works, the next thing you know, he's buying up properties left and right. And anyone who doesn't play ball..." Hero let the thought trail off, but they both knew how it ended.

Razor ran a hand down his face, his jaw clenching. "What else did your guy say? Is Grayson working with anyone local?"

"That's where it gets worse," Hero replied grimly. "He's got someone on the inside feeding him information. Someone tied to law enforcement."

Razor's stomach dropped. He didn't need Hero to spell it out -- he already had a hunch who it might be. "Dawson," he growled.

Deputy Dakota Dawson had always rubbed Razor the wrong way. Margot didn't like him which hinted that he was right in his assessment of the man. Then he remembered that he'd been first on the scene when *No Mercy Ink* got hit. Deva said he wasn't there long, hadn't really seemed to care. It raised a red flag.

"Could be," Hero said. "But I haven't confirmed it yet. Grayson's playing this one close to the vest."

Razor's free hand curled into a fist. He wanted to put it through the nearest wall. Deva and Outcast had worked their asses off to build *No Mercy Ink*. He wasn't about to let some slick-talking criminal dismantle it for his own gain. And whoever Grayson's informant was, yeah, he'd deal with him too. Maybe Margot could help them figure that one out. As concerned as he was when Ryder first started going around with Margot, just now he was very grateful to have that connection.

"Keep digging," Razor ordered. "If Grayson thinks he can set up shop in our town, he's sorely mistaken. And if Dawson's dirty, I want proof before we do anything about it."

"Want me to talk to Margot?" Hero asked.

"No, I'll take care of that one."

"You got it," Hero said, his voice firm. "I'll let you know as soon as I hear more."

Razor ended the call and stared at the phone in his hand for a moment, his thoughts a whirlwind of plans and worst-case scenarios. He wasn't just fighting to protect a business. He was fighting to protect Mercy -- and everything the Hounds of Hell stood for.

And he was fighting to protect Deva. With half an hour to go, he decided to call it day for his shop. He closed up and headed for town.

Razor slowed his bike as he approached *Three Guys Garage*. The sight of Margot's squad car parked out front made him veer into the lot. He needed to talk to Ryder's old lady. With what he'd learned about Victor Grayson, and likely Dawson, he couldn't let the opportunity slip. Killing the engine, Razor swung off his bike, heading toward the open bay doors. Inside, Hero stood over an engine block, wiping grease from his hands. Axel and Ryder worked on another car, exchanging a few quiet words. Margot stood near the counter, scribbling notes on a clipboard. She looked up as Razor approached, her brow arching slightly. "Razor. How are you?"

Razor glanced around, making sure no one else could overhear. "Need to have a word with you."

Margot tilted her head but set down the clipboard. "All right. Let's talk in the office."

They walked back to the office the three owners shared, where the din of tools and engines faded into the background. Razor closed the door and crossed his arms over his chest. "What I'm about to tell you stays between us. I'm serious, Margot. This is club business, and nine point nine times out of ten, that means just the Hounds."

Margot nodded, her gaze sharpening. "Understood. What's going on?"

"*Sinister Skin Studios*," Razor began, keeping his

voice low. "You know anything new about that?"

The deputy's gaze at him was speculative. "Nothing new. Why?"

"Turns out they're not just another tattoo shop. They're tied to Victor Grayson."

Margot's eyes widened, then narrowed in suspicion. "Grayson? The same guy who's been trying to shoehorn himself into Mercy? Well, that's bad news."

"Damn right, it is," Razor said. "This isn't just about Deva and Outcast's shop. Grayson's using *Sinister Skin* as a way to plant his flag in Mercy. I've got reason to believe he's got someone feeding him intel -- someone in law enforcement."

Margot's lips pressed into a thin line. "You think it's Dawson."

"I don't like accusing people without proof," Razor admitted, "but it fits. He was the first one on the scene after *No Mercy Ink* got trashed. You know anything more than that?"

"Since we're strictly off record," she said, "yeah, I know a couple of things. After what Deva said, I did a little follow up. Dawson treated it like a drive-by. According to his log, he couldn't have been in their shop longer than thirty minutes. He rushed it." Margot's shoulders sagged slightly, and she rubbed the back of her neck. "When I looked closer, I found his report on the B&E. It was vague, rushed. He didn't even follow up with Outcast or Deva, which is standard procedure."

"That's not all," Razor added. "Grayson's MO is to use leverage -- blackmail, bribery, whatever it takes. If Dawson's in his pocket, that's trouble for all of us."

Margot met his gaze, her dark eyes reflecting a mix of frustration and worry. "I've been suspicious of

Dawson for a while. Ever since I took this job, he's just half-assed everything. And lately he's been... off. Not just with *No Mercy Ink*. Other cases, too. He's been cutting corners, acting jumpy. I just didn't want to believe it."

"Well, believe it," Razor said firmly. "We can't afford to let this slide. If Dawson's dirty, it's not just the club at risk -- it's Mercy."

Margot nodded slowly.

"Keep your eyes open," Razor said. "I don't expect you to put your neck on the line, but if you see anything -- *anything* -- that points to Dawson being tied to Grayson, let me know. This stays quiet until we have something solid."

"You have my word," Margot promised. She paused, her expression softening slightly. "And Razor? Be careful. If Grayson's involved, this could get dangerous fast. I've seen a lot of gruesome crimes in my time. More than a few are loosely connected to Grayson. But there's never any proof."

Razor smirked, but it didn't reach his eyes. "Danger's nothing new, Margot. Thanks for the heads-up about Dawson."

With that, Razor turned and headed back to his bike, his mind already racing with plans for his next move. If Grayson thought he could worm his way into Mercy, he was in for a rude awakening. The Hounds of Hell didn't back down. Ever. *No Mercy Ink* belonged to Outcast and Deva. Outcast was a Hound, his brother. *His*. And Deva? A voice in the back of his mind whispered that she was going to be his too.

* * *

Deva

Deva stood in the middle of *No Mercy Ink*, feeling

a little better about the state of her shop given the work the group of them had put in all day to bring some semblance of order to it. It was a slow, grueling process -- picking up shattered glass, scrubbing away spray paint, and trying to salvage what they could. The air was thick with the acrid scent of cleaning supplies, mingling with the lingering smell of fresh paint.

Jackson was on his hands and knees in one corner, methodically scraping away the streaks of red and black spray paint from the tiled floor. Beast worked at fixing the damaged counter, his large hands deft with the tools. Crash, who worked at Beast's construction company, was in the back, sorting through what remained of the tattoo machines. Everyone threw themselves into the task with grim determination. Deva was grateful for their help.

And then there was Razor. The Hound that she was trying not to fall for showed up around five. He moved with an easy, commanding presence, pitching in wherever he could. Though he wasn't doing anything particularly heroic -- just carting away broken furniture and tossing ruined materials into trash bags -- his presence grounded her. Deva stole a glance at him, her stomach twisting in an infuriating mix of attraction and frustration. His gruff charm hadn't wavered since he arrived. His reaction to her attempts to get clarity on what, if anything, was between them, exploded last night. It left her wanting more. It also left her feeling unsettled.

Deva hated that her pulse quickened whenever he got close, that his rough voice sent a shiver down her spine even when he was barking out directions to the others. Razor's presence was magnetic, even when he wasn't trying. After a while, Razor straightened up from helping Beast and caught Deva's eye. His expression softened slightly, and for a moment, she saw something in his gaze -- apology, maybe? Regret? Whatever it was, it passed quickly, replaced by his usual composed demeanor. He walked over to her, brushing his hands on his jeans.

"Deva," he said, his tone quieter than usual. "You and Outcast have a minute? Let's talk in your office."

Her curiosity piqued, she nodded and called for Jackson, who reluctantly abandoned his task. They followed Razor into their small back office. The space felt cramped with the three of them in it, and Razor's presence somehow managed to make the room feel even smaller. He leaned against the desk, arms crossed.

"I wanted to catch you both up on what's going on," he said. "Just like we thought, *Sinister Skin Studios* isn't just another shop. It's a front for something bigger, and I'm not about to let it slide."

Razor explained the connection to Victor Grayson, the corporate developer with criminal ties, and his suspicions about Deputy Dawson. He explained that each of the officers had an assignment with the other Hounds, like Beast and Crash, assigned to provide backups and coordinate patrols.

Deva listened intently, trying to process everything he said, to grasp the gravity of the situation. Anger bubbled beneath her calm exterior. Everyone had a role to play -- except her. Razor barely looked in her direction when he discussed them.

Her brother knew her well enough to know something was wrong. He looked from her to Razor and back, and he wasn't stupid. He'd already figured out something was going on between her and Razor.

When Razor finished talking, Jackson seemed over it. "I'll let you two finish up," he said impatiently, reading the tension in the room. "I need to get back to work."

Razor nodded to him and watched him leave. If he was surprised, he didn't show it.

Deva waited until Jackson left, closing the door behind him, before crossing her arms and leveling Razor with a hard look. "What about me?" she asked, her voice laced with frustration. "What's my assignment?"

Razor sighed, his broad shoulders slumping slightly as he uncrossed his arms. "Deva, you're not a Hound. And I'm sure as fuck not putting you in harm's way."

Her jaw tightened. "I'm not asking you to, but this is *my* shop, Razor. I won't just sit back and let everyone else fight for me. I've been searching the Internet and social media for anything I can find on these assholes. I was up until two this morning. For *some* reason, I just couldn't sleep."

Razor ignored her pointed reference to last night. But she could tell it wasn't without effort. "If you want to look for shit on them on the Internet, I'm fine with that. I just need you to do this without putting yourself in danger. You find something, you bring it to me. You don't run off on your own to deal with shit. Is that understood?"

Deva bit the inside of her cheek, torn between her lingering irritation and the undeniable logic in his words. Still, the idea of being given an "assignment" that wasn't that important just to appease her didn't sit well. "Fine," she muttered, though her tone made it clear she wasn't entirely satisfied.

Razor stepped closer, his expression kind. "Look, I get it. You want to fight for what's yours. But trust me on this, okay?"

Her breath hitched at his proximity, the genuine concern in his voice catching her off guard. She hated how easily he got under her skin, but she couldn't deny the flicker of warmth his words sparked in her chest. "As a *friend*?"

To his credit, Razor didn't back down or start shutting down. His gaze remained locked with hers. "Take it any way you like."

"I will," she said angrily, tipping up her chin and trying to mask the hurt with sass and false bravado. "I don't know what I was thinking." With a hair flip, she marched out of the office and went right back to their cleanup operation. Yeah, maybe she'd been excited about their hook-up, even the way he manhandled her last night, and seeing where things could go with the brutally hot president of the Hounds. But if that was the way he was going to play it -- throwing it back in her face each time she straight-up asked him for a status -- then he could go fuck right off. She didn't care who he was.

After going back to work at her station, she felt Razor walk into the main area but she didn't look up, didn't acknowledge his presence. Oh, she felt his attention on her all right. But fuck him. The Hounds would still help them with trying to put the shop together again because Jackson was a member of their precious MC. The club would help them deal with *Sinister Skin Studios*. But if their president thought he was getting anything else off her he had another think coming.

Eventually, Razor left, and the prospects wandered out not long after that. Deva watched him go, her emotions a tangled mess of admiration, frustration, and something she wasn't ready to name just yet. She shook her head, steeling herself for whatever came next. Beast and Crash left just after he did. It *was* getting late.

When Jackson popped up next to her, she jumped in her chair. "Hey," he said impatiently.

"What?" she snapped.

"Let's call it a night," her brother said. "We've made good progress but we're not going to be worth a damn if we don't get any rest."

"You can head out," she told him. Yeah, it was late, and she was tired, but anger kept her afloat.

"No," Jackson told her. "You're not going to be left alone in the shop. Razor's orders."

Deva stopped, glaring at him. "Really? Well, I'm not a fucking Hound so that doesn't apply to me, now does it?"

"Where is this coming from?" His brows inched up as surprise showed on his face. "Did Razor piss you off or something?"

"Absolutely fucking not." Yeah, she *was* mad as hell, but she'd be damned before she'd admit to it.

"Something going on between you two?" he followed up with.

"Of course not," she shot back. "We're *friends*."

Taken aback, Jackson stayed where he was. "Whatever. But you're not staying here alone. You want to be here by yourself if those assholes come back?"

Deva glared him down. She was thirty -- a grown ass woman. She knew she was taking a risk. Couldn't she decide for herself when it was time to fucking leave?

"You can leave whenever you want," Deva said. "I'll leave when I'm good and damn ready."

Mumbling curse words under his breath, Jackson marched away, roughly yanking his jacket from the back of a chair and pulling it on as he headed straight for the door.

When she was once again alone in *No Mercy Ink*, even in its state of disrepair, she could breathe a sigh of relief. Alone was her preference when there was a lot on her mind. And honestly, she felt like her life was falling apart at the seams. Her shop had been fucking trashed by some corrupt developer who wanted to get his hooks into Mercy. She, Jackson, and their shop were merely collateral damage. They meant nothing really in this man's plans. He was willing to destroy their livelihood for his own selfish gain.

Razor? She'd hooked up with him, and thought they'd made a connection. But he tapped that twice and didn't seem particularly interested in more. The thought hit hard on a more personal level. It ground home that point that she was just a throwaway person. No one in the grand scheme of things.

Minutes ticked by as she finished trying to get the spray paint off her nice leather tattoo chair. And it was coming off slowly. She was grateful they hadn't used a knife and ripped through it like they had Jackson's. A few more minutes and she'd be ready to leave for home, call it a day.

When someone started pounding on the door, her heart jumped in her chest as terror gripped her. Was it them? Had the fuckers from *Sinister Skin* returned to do more damage and here she was all alone? Deva hoped with everything in her that Jackson locked the damn door. If he didn't, her only chance was to try and make it out at the back of the shop. The pounding continued, loud and demanding. A voice shouted her name beyond those front door and it sounded familiar. But it wasn't her brother.

Furious at the scare he gave her, Deva stomped

up to the front of the shop. Peering through the glass front door confirmed her suspicions. Fucking Razor stood just outside her door, glaring at her and looking as angry as she was right now.

"We're closed right now!" she shouted at him, crossing her arms across her chest.

"Open the fucking door!" Razor yelled, with fists clenched at his sides. He looked pissed enough to break it down and she knew he could.

"Fuck off!" Deva didn't want to hear anything he had to say. And she sure as hell didn't plan on letting him in.

It was cold as shit outside and yet, Razor's face flushed with anger. The big, bad president of the Hounds of Hell wasn't used to getting no for an answer, huh? Deva decided that he better fucking get used to it. Because she was fucking done with him.

They stood there staring at each other for a long minute when finally, Razor turned on his heel and marched off into the darkness. Part of her didn't want him to go. She really did have a thing for him even though she wished she didn't. The other part knew she'd earned a victory, and she'd take it. With everything that happened this week, it was nice to win at something.

After she got the chair cleaned the way she wanted it, she got her things together so she could head home. Checking her watch showed her it was after nine and she really was tired on so many levels. Gathering her things, Deva turned everything off, made sure everything was locked up. Her car warmed up quickly as she drove out of town and headed home. Her heart squeezed in her chest as she passed *Old Guard Guns*, even though it was dark and closed and she was still super pissed at Razor. Trying to get those thoughts out of her head, she kept going until she reached her house.

Fatigue was wearing on her hard. She wasn't even hungry. She just wanted to go to bed. No sooner had she used her key to open her front door when someone marched up behind her, fast as lightning, and shoved her through her own front door. Fear had her heart thumping wildly in her chest as she turned to see who was attacking her, slamming her front door shut with brute strength.

Even in the darkness of her living room, Razor was gorgeous. His breath came fast as hers did as they stared each other down in the shadows. Thinking the entire situation was ridiculous, Deva dropped her purse and bag on the couch, reaching to turn on the lamp next to it. Razor looked even more pissed off in the light.

"What?" she snapped.

"I told Outcast you weren't to be left alone in the shop," Razor said, emphasizing each word.

"I told him I'd leave when I was good and damn ready," Deva said. "And that's exactly what I did."

"Are you fucking stupid?" Razor scrubbed a hand over the stubble he always wore. "What if it hadn't been me beating down your door? What if it had been *Sinister Skin*, huh? You ever stop and think about that?"

Oh, she had. But no way was she backing down. "I'm not the one who disregarded your order," Deva stated flatly. "You should take that up with my brother."

"Excuse me?" Razor's eyes glittered dangerously in the low light, and she knew she was playing with fire here.

But the man needed to understand something.

Jackson and Deva had been on their own most of their lives. Their father hadn't been in the picture; their mother was an alcoholic who had left them behind. They'd survived so much -- from shady foster homes to streets ruled by assholes every bit as dangerous as him if not worse. Somehow, they'd survived. *She'd* survived.

"I'm not one of your Hounds, Razor," she said flatly. "If Jackson wants to jump whenever you snap your fingers, that's his choice. But there's nothing between me and you. No promises were made. We just hooked up. So, if you're done, I'm tired. I'd just like to go to bed."

"That's the best idea you've had all day." Something in Razor's tone should have registered as a warning. Maybe it was because she was so tired. Maybe it was because she'd liked last night -- a lot. But the man still stood his ground, eyeing her like someone raised a red flag and he was a full-size fucking Brahma bull.

Deva put up her hands defensively, her heart racing. Adrenaline and an edge of fear had fatigue falling away. What was it about the man that could get her motor running and take her from zero to sixty with a glance and a few well-chosen words? Razor stalked her, forcing her to step away from him as he closed in. She let him. Pissed as she was, she wanted him. And it wasn't lost on her that she was backing up in the direction of her own bedroom. The thought made her both scared and excited, her panties wet in seconds. Part of her brain screamed that the man could actually fucking hurt her. He'd left her devastated on the floor last night. Maybe she *did* want him to hurt her. A little. Sparks of excitement started racing through her blood as her back met her own bedroom door. More sex like last night? Yes, please.

Razor closed in on her, his gaze darting to the doorknob. The spicy scent of him permeated her senses, made the primal lust jarring her body out of its fatigue even worse. Blindly, her left hand fumbled for the doorknob and all she had to do was open the door, dive in, and shut it in his face. She just needed to be quick. But he immediately realized what she was up to, and his gaze narrowed. "Don't even think about it."

"Or what?" Deva challenged him. "What are you going to do about it?"

"You really want to know?" he asked, a smile playing around his lips.

"Yeah," Deva teased, "I would… old man."

Razor's smile faded. "If we're going to do that, I might have to put you over my knee, little girl."

"Have to catch me first," Deva yelled as she turned the doorknob and darted into her bedroom. She wasn't quite quick enough. Razor's arm hooked around her, hard as a steel bar, and roughly pulled her back against his body.

Deva fought him, not seriously, but they tumbled onto the floor with Razor hovering over her. Catching him off guard, Deva flipped them -- probably it was closer to the truth that he allowed it -- so that she was on top, straddling him. When Razor rolled his hips beneath her, letting her feel the heated ridge of his cock, she groaned at how good he felt against the aching, wet flesh between her thighs. She wanted that. *Now.*

Her hands undid his belt, ripped open his jeans. Razor helped her push them down to his knees, freeing the hard length of him. Deva moved back so she could get her mouth on him. Her lips wrapped around the head of him, her tongue swirled all around the smooth helmet at its end.

"Fuck," Razor said, moaning. "That mouth is good for more than just sass... Damn, girl."

All the while, she frantically opened her own jeans, shoving them and her panties off. It wasn't as sexy as she would have liked but the performance didn't mean as much as the goal. Once she rid herself of everything below her waist except the black fuzzy socks she wore, she climbed back up his body. Razor was working himself, wet and hard in his hand, holding himself up for her. Deva positioned herself over it, slid down his length.

When she was where she needed to be, his big hands grabbed her hips, and he wasn't delicate about it. Deva planted her hands on his chest and began riding him. Or maybe Razor moved her up and down his dick. She wasn't sure which was true or if they both were. She loved how he felt filling her up, how he stretched her open. Her slick walls tried to grab him in vain each time he thrust up into her. Her heart raced as they moved together, the chorus of their cries and moans seeming so loud on the floor of her bedroom.

"You look... so fucking good," Razor muttered, his gaze glued to her. "Love the way you take me, darlin'."

Fuck talking. Deva kept moving on him as sparks of excitement raced through her veins. Her nipples tightened to rock-hard points as she found just the right movement that stimulated her front wall. Her pussy clenched around him, her movements faster, harder. Razor realized she was close and helped her out until she came. Her eyes squeezed shut and stars burst behind her eyelids as she rode it out, the orgasm shaking her apart as her cries filled the room.

Deva wasn't even aware Razor rolled her under

him. He was above her now, riding her hard. He trapped her hips between him and the carpeted floor. He made her take him, thrust after thrust, and as she came back around, she started moving with him. His pace was relentless, but she wanted it all. She wanted to ache tomorrow morning, to not be able to walk straight. Razor's cock was so good, and she wrapped herself around him and enjoyed the ride.

Above her Razor dropped kisses over her face and hair. For the president of the Hounds, it was endearing and a lewd contrast against the way he was literally fucking her into the carpet. When he got close, Deva's hands slid under his shirt, raking her nails down his back. His thrusts came fast, stealing her breath and claiming her in the most elemental way, and she wanted more.

Razor growled when he reached his end, a savage sound there in the light from her bedroom window. Above her he was lost to sensation, hers, and her heart skipped a beat just watching him as he pumped himself into her body with abandon.

She didn't know how much time had passed when she came back to reality, tangled with Razor on the floor. There in the shadows of the bedroom, he looked gorgeous. She smoothed a lock of his hair back from his face, tracing the line of his cheek. He brushed a kiss over her forehead.

"What are you thinking about?" she asked.

Razor chuckled. "Just wondering if we're covered here."

Deva grinned. "We are." When he claimed her lips for a sweet kiss, she didn't protest. "You're not going to run off again tonight, are you?"

"That bothered you, huh?"

Yes. "It would have been nice if you'd help me

off the floor," she whispered. "I might not be able to walk tomorrow at the rate we're going. Jackson already asked if there was something going on with us."

"What did you tell him?" Razor asked.

"That we're friends," she said, her tone sounding sad to her own ears.

Razor sat up and her heart lurched in her chest. He was leaving? Just because she said that?

But in the span of a heartbeat, he helped her off the floor, carrying her to the bed. When he pulled the covers back, she climbed in with shaking legs. She watched him strip down -- well, she couldn't take her eyes off him. When he climbed in the bed with her, Deva's heart skipped a beat. Easing into his arms, Deva got cozy, and they drifted off to sleep.

Chapter Six

Razor

Razor's phone vibrated on the nightstand, waking him up. Half asleep, he grabbed it, trying not to wake Deva. She was still out next to him, her purple hair splayed over the pillow. The sight of her finally resting after the anxiety of the break-in gave him a moment's hesitation before he swiped the screen to answer. It was Snow and it was just after three in the morning.

"Yeah?" he asked, voice rough from just waking up.

"I've got something you need to see." His tech guy's voice on the other end was clipped and serious. "I've been monitoring *Sinister Skin*'s cameras like you wanted, and I've picked up a pattern. Same vehicles, late-night visits -- four of 'em tonight. These aren't tattoo customers, Razor. I ran plates. I found ties to some shady fucking real estate outfits."

Razor swung his legs off the bed, dragging a hand down his face as he stood. "You sure?"

"Positive. You're gonna want to look at this, Prez. I'm sending you the footage now."

Razor grabbed his jeans off the floor and pulled them on, heading for the living room to take the call away from Deva. The floorboards creaked under his feet, and the room was cool and dark. Once he downloaded the files Snow sent over, Razor watched the grainy surveillance clips -- SUVs and sleek sedans pulling into the lot behind *Sinister Skin* Studio. Expensive vehicles. Their drivers lingered in the shadows to meet unseen contacts. Snow was right, it was shady as hell.

"Shit," Razor muttered under his breath. "You

see any faces?"

"Not yet, but I'll keep running it down," Snow replied. "Wanted to give you the heads-up."

"Good work," Razor said, disconnecting the call. Leaning heavily on the back of Deva's worn couch for a moment, he stared off into space as the weight of it sank in. Something was going on and he had a feeling it went way beyond *No Mercy Ink*. Maybe even Mercy itself. But first things first. The last thing he wanted was for this mess to start by blowing up Deva and Outcast. Keeping them safe was the top priority.

Running a hand through his hair, Razor forced himself to focus. He really needed to head to the clubhouse, review the full footage on a larger screen, and decide how to handle it from there. Reluctantly, he returned to the bedroom, watching Deva's peaceful form for a beat longer than necessary before getting dressed.

* * *

Deva

When she woke up, she was alone. The steam of her anger was already gathering -- until she saw the note left on the pillow Razor had slept on last night. It was written on one of the girly pink pages from her grocery list pad, and that had her smiling.

Deva, Snow had something for me to look at on SSS, so I left a little early. I'll tell you all about it later today. R

Deva shook her head as she re-read it. She was learning Razor could be all business and it was something she needed to get used to if they became a thing. She went about her morning routine. Just as she was about to leave her house and head for the shop, her phone rang. It was Sadie returning her call. Her newest client was the only one she hadn't heard from in reaching out to reschedule tattoo appointments.

With a sigh of relief, Deva smiled, hoping it came across in her voice when she answered the phone. She'd only done one session with Sadie on her tattoo, and that didn't sit well with Deva even though there wasn't a lot they could do until their shop was back in order. Emotional tattoos were Deva's specialty and demanded a sensitive, caring touch. It had taken a lot for the young woman to come for the consultation considering her violent past with her ex and the humiliating reminder he'd literally carved into her back. She didn't want Sadie to be discouraged from continuing for her own well-being.

"Hi, it's Sadie," the other woman said. "I'm returning your call."

"Thank you." Deva placed her bags back on the couch. "I know I called before to tell you that we hoped to be back up and running soon. But your tattoo is a special case. I was wondering if we could still continue working on it, even before we have the shop put back in order. If you'd be willing."

There wasn't much of a pause. "That would be great. How would we do that?"

"Well, the shop is still a work in progress, and we wouldn't have a lot of privacy," Deva explained. "But we could work on it here at my house, or I could drive out to you."

"Hang on," Sadie said before speaking to someone in the background where she was. "That works," Sadie said, returning to their conversation. "Liza said she wouldn't mind if we did it here at the nursery. It would probably be more convenient for you since it's here in town."

"That would work out nicely," Deva said. "Thank Liza for me. And just let me know when."

Deva was guessing that the muted voice she heard in the background was Liza Austin. She couldn't make out what the woman said, but Sadie came back and said, "It's probably a long shot but we don't have a lot going on this morning if you just happened to be free. If not, I completely understand."

Deva didn't have to think about it long. Maybe a break from restoring the shop for even a little while would be a good idea. Considering how she spent a good portion of the night, she was physically tired, but a creative endeavor might be just the thing to get her moving. "I can do that. I'll call my brother and let him know where I am. But yeah. I'll see you in twenty minutes?"

"Sounds perfect," Sadie said. "Thank you!"

She tried to call Jackson, but he didn't answer, and his voicemail box was full. He was probably riding to the shop right then and wasn't able to check his phone. Deciding she'd call him and explain where she was once she reached the nursery, she ran back to her room to get her personal tattoo machine and some ink she kept on hand. Deva made sure the shop used the same quality ink she always preferred, and she had all the colors she needed for Sadie's tattoo in her own stash. Once she had everything, she placed it in her bag and dashed out to her car.

* * *

Razor

Razor sat in his dim office at the clubhouse, the glow of the laptop screen casting sharp shadows around the room. Snow had sent over hours of surveillance footage from *Sinister Skin Studios*, and Razor combed through all of it, frame by frame. The pattern was undeniable -- late-night visitors pulling up late at night, the kind of cars that didn't belong in Mercy, much less at a supposed tattoo shop. Razor paused, narrowing his gaze on one clip. A man in a tailored coat stepped out of a black Escalade, his face just visible enough for recognition. Razor swore under his breath. The guy was Victor Grayson -- real estate developer, power player, and all-around bastard with enough money to buy half of Virginia.

Dawson, or whoever in the sheriff's department was working with Grayson, had to be helping them keep things off the radar. Razor was almost sure it was Dawson. How long had this been going on?

Razor leaned back in his chair, exhaling slowly, the pieces starting to fall into place. This wasn't about competition. It was about control. Grayson and his people were up to something bigger, and they'd set their sights on Mercy. Before he could dig deeper, his phone buzzed on the table, vibrating against the wood. He snatched it up, seeing Hero's name flashing on the screen.

"Yeah, Hero," Razor said, his tone sharp, already on edge. "What's up?"

"Razor..." Hero's voice was tight, rushed, and full of worry. "It's Outcast. I found him on the side of the road out past *Sackett's*."

Razor shot out of his chair. "What do you mean you found him? What the fuck happened?"

"Someone beat the shit out of him, Razor. Blood everywhere. His bike's wrecked -- looks like someone ran it over. Doesn't much look like a fucking accident."

Razor's knuckles turned white as he gripped the edge of his desk. "Is he alive?"

"Yeah," Hero confirmed. "Barely breathing, but he's alive. I called an ambulance -- it just got here. I'm riding with him to the ER. I'll call the twins and have them come pick up what's left of his bike and mine."

"Fuck," Razor growled, pacing the small office. "What about Deva? Is she with him?"

"She's not here," Hero said, his voice strained. "That's all I know. Razor, I've gotta go. They're loading him up now."

The line went dead, leaving Razor standing in silence, the phone still clutched in his hand. His heart thundered in his chest as panic clawed at the edges of his mind. Outcast was hurt -- bad -- but the glaring absence of any mention of Deva lit a firestorm of fear in him. That they found Outcast out by *Sackett's* was no surprise. It was the way he drove into town every day. Deva lived on the other side of town, her route taking her past his gun shop. Did she make it to the shop or did the fuckers intercept her too? Thoughts of what might be happening to her right now made him feel sick, filled him with rage.

"Shit, shit, shit!" Razor slammed the phone down and grabbed his keys. He tore out of the clubhouse, leaving everything behind as he jumped onto his bike. The engine roared to life, but his thoughts drowned out the sound.

Where the hell was Deva? If these bastards had laid hands on her... He didn't finish the thought. *Couldn't.* Razor pushed the throttle to the limit, weaving through traffic like a demon as he raced toward *No Mercy Ink*. When he arrived, the shop was locked up, dark inside. No sign of Deva or anyone else. He punched the wall next to the door, frustration and fear boiling over.

He had no choice now -- he needed to get to the hospital. If Outcast was talking, Razor would find out what the hell happened. Ask if he knew where Deva was. If not... he didn't want to consider the alternative.

The ride to the ER felt like an eternity in the cold January air. Every second stretched out, a cruel reminder that Deva could be in the hands of Victor Grayson's men. His mind spun with dark scenarios as he pulled into the hospital parking lot, screeching to a stop near the entrance. Razor stormed into the ER, his heart slamming in his chest, his posture tense. Old Yale Thomas glanced at him warily as he approached the desk.

"Outcast," he said sharply. "Where's the guy they just brought in?"

The older man flinched but quickly checked his records, the computer screen reflected in his wire-rimmed glasses. "Room four. He's --"

Razor didn't wait for more details, his boots pounding against the tiled floor as he made his way down the hallway. When he saw Hero standing outside the room, Razor's breath hitched. Hero's jacket and shirt were covered in blood. There was even a streak of blood in Hero's blond hair.

"Hero," Razor barked. "What the fuck happened?"

Hero glanced up, his face grim. "They worked him over good, Razor. No witnesses, no camera footage. EMTs said his injuries line up with being run off the road and beaten afterward."

His fists clenched at his sides. They ran Outcast off the road before they started beating him? That sounded like Grayson, all right. But now it was different. Really fucking different. This wasn't the Hounds rushing in to protect a civilian who lived in Mercy, their turf. Outcast was a Hound, and a major fucking line had been crossed. Razor wouldn't let this go. Someone would be paying for *this*.

"And Deva?" Razor demanded, his voice a

growl.

Hero shook his head. "Nothing. I've been trying to call her, but no answer."

That was all Razor needed to hear. His mind went straight to the darkest corners. He clenched his fists, every muscle in his body taut with barely restrained fury.

"I'm going to fucking end them," he said through gritted teeth, his voice low and dangerous. "If they so much as touched her -- if she's hurt -- I'll burn everything they've ever built to the fucking ground."

Hero placed a hand on his shoulder, steadying him. "We'll find her, Razor. We don't know that they have her."

As Razor stepped into the stark, sterile room of the ER, the sight of Outcast hit him like a fist to the gut. His brother lay motionless on the hospital bed, surrounded by the low hum of medical monitors. The faint antiseptic tang in the air made his stomach turn. Outcast, usually so full of life and sarcastic wit, looked pale and fragile under the harsh fluorescent lighting.

Outcast's face bore the brunt of the attack -- bruises already deepening into ugly shades of purple and black. His lower lip was split and a nasty gash at his cheekbone was hastily stitched. There was dried blood flaking around the edges. His left eye was swollen shut, the skin around it puffed and angry. His muscular arms, inked with intricate tattoos that told his story, were marred by abrasions and deep scrapes. His knuckles were raw and bloodied. He'd put up one hell of a fight before being overpowered. His breaths were shallow and uneven beneath the hospital gown, his broad torso bandaged tightly -- likely concealing cracked ribs or worse.

The sheet covering him stopped at his waist,

revealing one leg in a cast. His right ankle was wrapped in gauze, swollen and discolored, suggesting he'd been thrown or struck with violent force. The brutality of the attack he endured was breathtaking.

Even in his battered state, Outcast's jaw was set, a stubborn defiance etched into his features. Razor couldn't help but feel a mix of fury and guilt. This shouldn't have happened -- not to Outcast. Not one of *his*.

Outcast's lips moved, his voice low and gravelly. The words barely formed as he muttered something Razor couldn't make out. The sound was a mix of frustration and fatigue, trailing off into the quiet of the hospital room. Razor leaned in slightly, trying to catch the thread of it, but Outcast's voice was like a frayed wire -- disjointed and faint. It seemed important, but Outcast's strength was failing him, leaving Razor to piece together the weight of his brother's unsaid words.

"What did he say?" Hero asked.

"Sounded like... Anna or Anya?" Razor wasn't sure but it sounded like a name.

The chime of Hero's phone got Razor's attention. He watched and listened as Hero talked to the caller. Somehow Razor knew it wasn't Deva. When Hero motioned him over, Razor was right there, his body primed for battle.

"It's Axel," Hero said. "The twins just showed up for the bikes. The sheriff's department is still there."

"Give me the phone," Razor ordered. That the police were on the scene wasn't a surprise. He just wanted to know *who* showed up. "Axel? You with the bike?"

"Yeah," Axel said on the other end of the line. "Not sure he'll let me touch it right now. We've got

Hero's bike in the truck."

"Who? Is it Dawson?"

"Yeah," Axel said after a moment.

"Look at it for me. Do you see anything painted on it?"

The line went quiet, and he heard Ryder with Axel as they looked over the bike. "Yeah," Axel said in a quiet voice. "It's the same fucking symbol that we saw at *No Mercy Ink*."

Razor was livid. The fuckers weren't even trying to hide what they were doing. It pissed him off on a few levels. They clearly had no fear of the Hounds nor anyone for that matter. "Take photos of the scene. As much as you can get. Once he's done with whatever the fuck he's doing, take the bike back to the garage and secure it."

"On it," Axel said, sounding unsettled.

"And if either of you hear *anything* from Deva, let me know ASAfuckingP. Is that clear?"

"Deva? She's at the nursery with Sadie," Axel explained. "I haven't talked to Sadie since before we found Outcast. Deva doesn't know about her brother yet."

"She's at the nursery with Sadie?" Razor demanded. "You're sure of it?"

"I didn't actually go over there and see for myself, but yeah, Sadie got off the phone with me because Deva had just arrived. She's working on Sadie's tattoo at the nursery."

Relief washed through him like a river in flood. Deva was safe? That made things feel a little better. But she'd be devastated soon when she learned what happened. And with Outcast laid up, his sister was in even more danger. Razor couldn't have that. She'd be with one of the Hounds twenty-four-seven until Razor found a way to put a stop to Grayson's plans.

Handing the phone back to Hero, Razor marched out and headed for his bike. But his thoughts were already racing ahead. If *Sinister Skin Studios* or Victor Grayson thought they were going to take what mattered to *him*, take from the MC, they were about to learn what true hell looked like.

* * *

Deva

Outcast is in the hospital…

Deva didn't remember what had been said before those words and she didn't hear anything after them. Axel offered to drive her to the hospital where Razor was waiting with her brother, and she didn't even remember climbing into his Jeep or even the ride over. She was barely aware of the hum of fluorescent lights and the soft beeping of machines filling the hospital hallway. She rushed along one corridor after another, looking for her brother's room.

Razor stood just outside Outcast's room, his back to the wall and arms crossed. His jaw was tight, every muscle in his body coiled with barely restrained anger. The sound of her boots and Axel's drew his attention to them as they walked up the hallway.

Deva moved quickly, trying to dart into her brother's room. Razor caught her easily, stopping her just outside the door. That was when the tears came on.

"What happened?" she asked the second she reached him. "Oh, God, Razor. Is he going to be okay? Is he --"

"Listen." Razor cut her off, leaning down to get on eye level with her as he kept a firm grip on her arms. "He looks like hell, but the doctors seem to think he'll recover. So take a deep breath."

"You promise?" Deva didn't even try to stop the tears running down her face now. "He's going to be okay?"

"Darlin'," he whispered, pulling her into his arms and holding her close, comforting her. And it did temporarily silence the barrage of fears flying through her head right now. He also didn't seem to care about any onlookers. "He's going to make it." After a long moment, Razor eased back enough to gaze into her eyes. "Breathe."

On top of everything they were dealing with at the shop, now her brother was in the hospital, and she knew in her gut what had happened. "It was them, wasn't it?" She barely got the question out.

Razor nodded, his jaw tightening. "We can talk about all of that later. Let's go in and see your brother. He isn't awake yet and he's in real bad shape. But he needs to know you're here."

When Deva stepped into the quiet hospital room, the sight of Jackson -- her unshakable big brother -- brought her to an abrupt halt, her breath catching in her throat. Jackson, who always seemed untouchable, now looked small and broken beneath the stark white sheets. It felt wrong -- *impossible* -- to see him like this. His face was a swollen mess of bruises, deep purples and angry reds blooming across his cheekbones and jawline. A gash ran from his temple to his brow, held together by fresh, angry stitches. One eye was swollen shut, and the other, though half-open, showed no sign of the sharp ice blue that usually cut through anyone who dared look at him wrong. Instead, his features were slack in uneasy sleep, softened by the painkillers coursing through his system.

Deva's gaze fell to the machines beside him, the

steady beeping a cruel reminder that Jackson had been left barely breathing on the side of the road. That's what Axel told her on the way over. His breathing, though steady, was too shallow, each rise and fall of his chest almost imperceptible beneath the thin hospital gown. Her heart clenched. This wasn't Jackson -- *her Jackson*. He was the strongest person she knew, her shield, the guy who could level someone with a single cold glare or a cutting word. Seeing him like this, so still and battered, shattered her composure.

Her boots felt like lead as she moved closer to the bed. "Oh, Jack." The whisper cracked in her throat. Her hand trembled as she reached out, brushing his bruised fingers with her own, afraid of causing him more pain. He didn't stir, and somehow, that made it worse. Deva had grown up watching him fight off anyone or anything that dared threaten them. He was the one constant in her life, unmovable like a mountain -- and now, he appeared so fragile it nearly broke her.

Tears burned her eyes, but she blinked them back, refusing to let them fall. Jackson wouldn't want her crying. He'd want her to be strong. But God, seeing him this way lit a fire of helpless anger in her chest, burning alongside the raw fear she refused to name. Whoever did this had meant business. The very real threat these people posed sent a chill of foreboding through her.

Her fingers tightened around his even though he couldn't feel it. "You're gonna get through this," she said, her voice barely audible. *"We're* going to get through this. And when you do, we'll make sure they regret every goddamn bruise they put on you."

She didn't know if Jackson could hear her, but she hoped he did. Hoped he knew that no matter how bad this looked, she wasn't giving up on him -- *on them.* The quiet rage inside her grew with every beat of the heart monitor, a cold determination solidifying in her bones.

Razor's hand landed on her shoulder. His voice, steady but firm, cut through her frustration. "We'll deal with them. But we need to be careful. I've got Snow pulling surveillance footage from *Sinister Skin*, and it's bad."

Razor's gaze met Deva's. "Snow's been noticing late-night visitors at their shop. Men in suits -- developers with ties to Grayson's real estate group. We were right. They're not just here to run a tattoo shop. They're setting up something bigger. And they're not afraid to play dirty to get us out of their way."

Deva's chin lifted stubbornly. "And Jackson? You think this was from Grayson's people?"

Razor nodded grimly. "It lines up. They're sending a message, and now they're making it personal."

The sound of quick, purposeful footsteps approached. Margot rounded the corner, her sharp brown eyes taking in the scene. Dressed in her deputy uniform, she was authoritative, but her expression held a note of worry.

"Razor," she said, her tone brisk as she closed the door to Jackson's room behind her. "I was hoping I'd find you here."

Razor's brows furrowed. "What've you got?"

Margot glanced at Deva before focusing on Razor. "I dug deeper into Dawson after you mentioned your suspicions." She paused, lowering her voice. "Turns out Dawson's cousin is Victor Grayson. He's a silent partner in *Sinister Skin Studios*."

Deva's head snapped toward her. "Cousins?"

Margot nodded grimly. "Yeah."

"They're cousins and your department hired Dawson?" Deva had to ask.

"Dawson was hired before me," Margot explained. "But Grayson doesn't have a record. He's got his fingers in a lot of shady dealings, and we're aware of that, but nothing has ever been linked back to him. He's very careful.

"And it gets worse," Margot continued. "I can't prove it yet, but I think Grayson's blackmailing Dawson. He's got something on him -- misconduct at his old precinct from the looks of it -- to keep him in line. You want to talk about hiring Dawson? I don't understand why they hired him knowing *that*. Now he's compromised. And that's why Dawson's been dragging his feet and turning a blind eye to anything involving *Sinister Skin*."

Razor swore under his breath, his hands curling into fists at his sides. "That bastard's got his hooks deep."

Margot nodded. "I didn't want to say anything until I had solid proof, but once I heard about this..." Margot tipped her head in Jackson's direction. "Dawson's compromised, and if Grayson's behind this, he'll go to great lengths to get what he wants."

Deva let out a shaky breath. "What do we do?"

Razor's gaze was pure steel as he looked between Margot and Deva. "We're going to hit them back. Hard."

"Razor --" Margot began, a note of warning in her voice.

"Margot, we're not going to sit back and let the law handle it," Razor cut her off, his tone firm. "The fucking law is *in on it*. They won't stop at Deva's shop. They'll target other citizens in Mercy. And I'll be damned if I let these bastards run roughshod in our town."

Deva nodded. "Whatever you need me to do, I'm in."

Razor gazed down at her; his hazel eyes gleaming with something unreadable. "You just focus on keeping *No Mercy Ink* open and Outcast steady."

"I'm not sitting this out," she said stubbornly.

"I know," Razor said, his voice gentler but no less resolute.

Margot sighed, clearly trying to decide whether to push further. "I'll keep an eye on Dawson, see if I can use what I found to squeeze him for more."

"Does Sheriff Sawyer know?" Razor asked.

"I'm going to try and talk to the sheriff later tonight," Margot explained. "He thinks a lot of Dawson so I'm not sure how this is going to go."

"Thank you."

Margot made her way out. Deva and Razor stood by Jackson's bedside, the weight of the situation pressing down on them. Finally, Razor's gaze landed on Outcast, his jaw tightening. "They want a fucking fight? They've got one."

Deva nodded, her voice quiet but fierce. "Damn right they do."

Chapter Seven

Deva

Razor crossed his arms as they walked out of the hospital later that evening, his hazel eyes fixed on Deva with a determination that brooked no argument. "You're not going back to your place, not tonight," he said, his tone firm but not unkind. "Outcast was attacked on his way to the shop. Until we deal with these assholes and put a stop to their bullshit, you're staying with *me*."

Deva narrowed her eyes, folding her arms to mirror his stance. "I can take care of myself, Razor."

His lips twitched at the fire in her tone, but his expression remained serious. "I know you're strong, Deva. But this isn't about pride. Whoever did this didn't just take a swipe at Outcast. They meant to fucking end him. And I'm not giving them the chance to do the same or worse to you."

She wanted to argue. Hell, every fiber of her independent spirit screamed at her to push back, to tell him she'd handle it her way. But then she thought about Outcast -- brutalized, beaten to the edge of his limits -- and the air left her lungs in a rush.

"I spoke to one of the doctors who examined him when they brought him in," she said, glancing toward Razor. "They said he's stable, but... He has bruised ribs, several hairline fractures on his face, arms, and legs, and a concussion. He told me it's a miracle he didn't have internal bleeding."

Razor's jaw tightened. "Did they say anything about how long he'll be in here?"

"They're keeping him for a few days for observation," Deva replied. "They're worried about the head injury, and they want to make sure there's no swelling."

Razor nodded, his hazel eyes darkening with quiet fury. "Whoever did this is going to regret it. And that's why you're coming with me."

"Fine," she relented, her voice quieter now. "But only because I need to get some sleep, not because I'm agreeing with you."

Razor gave her a small, satisfied nod, as though he'd expected this answer all along. Without another word, he placed his hand on the small of her back and guided her out of the automatic hospital doors. She agreed to follow him to his place. The ride in her SUV was long, the weight of the evening pressing down on her. Her brother was a broken mess in the hospital, their tattoo shop was a long way from being back to normal, and she realized that Razor was right. The same fuckers who had torn her life apart would do the same to her body if they got their hands on her.

As Deva stepped out of her SUV, her gaze swept over Razor's house. It wasn't what she'd expect from the president of the Hounds of Hell. Nestled at the edge of town, it was a modest single-story brick home with a wide front porch framed by sturdy wooden beams. It was weathered in places but well-maintained, giving the house a quiet charm. A low iron railing bordered the porch, and a single porch light glowed softly, casting a warm circle of light onto the wooden steps.

The yard was neat, with a few shrubs lining the walkway. A small stack of firewood was piled near the porch -- practical, like everything else about the man who owned the house. A Hounds of Hell flag hung discreetly in the large front window, its placement more about personal pride than overt display.

Razor climbed off his bike and motioned her to

follow him as he opened the door to his house. The familiar scent of leather and cedar greeting her. The interior was as simple as the outside, masculine and tidy. It was way neater than she'd expected. He tossed his keys onto a side table and turned to her.

"I don't have a lot in the fridge," he said, his tone gentler now. "I can call for takeout."

Deva shook her head, her gaze on the rugged man who'd taken on her fight like it was his own. "Thank you," she murmured, her earlier defiance giving way to gratitude. "I'm not that hungry." But, for the first time all day, she felt a flicker of safety -- not because of the walls around her, but because of the man standing in front of her.

"You might not be," Razor told her. "But you're going to eat."

Razor didn't request or suggest. Even with her, he gave orders, and he expected them to be carried out. She might have enjoyed his domineering if not for the current situation she was in. Just now she wasn't in the mood to put up a fight. The day had left Deva exhausted.

"Is someone staying with my brother at the hospital?" Deva asked. Considering what happened to him, it wouldn't be hard for someone to sneak into the hospital and finish him off.

Razor cut her a look that said, *Really*? "They're taking shifts. Two at a time, twenty-four seven."

"How does that work with restrictions on visiting hours and all that?" Deva asked.

"It's not our first rodeo at Mercy General," he explained. "Last summer it was Ryder laid up in the hospital on the verge of death. We kept security there around the clock. One or two of the staff are usually brave enough to come recite hospital policy. None of them have the guts to ask any of us leave."

Deva understood. Razor, her brother, and the rest of the Hounds were all intimidating men. Saying no to them was an intimidating prospect.

"What happened to Ryder?" she asked.

"Long story," he said. "I'll tell you sometime when you're in a better place in life."

Going to a drawer in his kitchen, Razor pulled out a small stack of worn menus that offered take-out. Walking back into the living room, he handed them to her. "See if there's anything that strikes your interest."

Deva looked up from where she was perched on Razor's couch, reading through those menus, as a firm knock echoed from the front door. Razor, who had just returned to the living room with a couple of beers, muttered something under his breath, setting them on the coffee table. He shot Deva a glance as if to ask, *who's that* before crossing the room. He did a quick check at the living room window before going to the door.

When he opened it, a young woman stood on the porch, bundled in a coat against the cold. Her long, dark hair spilled out from beneath a knit beanie, and her cheeks were flushed from the cold. Deva recognized her immediately from the photos in Razor's shop. It was Jade Dock -- his daughter.

"Hey, Dad," Jade said, her voice a mix of concern and affection. "Thought I'd swing by and check on you, considering everything that's been going on."

A hint of a smile tugged at his lips. "Appreciate it, kid. C'mon in."

Jade stepped inside, brushing off the cold, and froze the moment her eyes landed on Deva. Her gaze darted from her father to Deva, seated comfortably on the couch, and the air in the room shifted slightly.

Deva sat up straighter, offering a polite smile, even as the back of her neck burned with self-awareness.

"Hi," Jade said, her tone neutral but not unfriendly. Her eyes were sharp, assessing, just like her father's. But there was no malice in them.

"Jade, this is Deva," Razor said, closing the door and stepping aside. "She's... going to be staying here for a little while. Things at her shop have been... complicated."

"Complicated," Jade echoed. "That's putting it mildly."

"Nice to meet you," Deva said quickly, standing and extending her hand. "Your dad's been great about helping us out."

Jade hesitated for only a beat before shaking Deva's hand, her grip firm. "You're Outcast's sister, right?" Jade's big eyes held sympathy. "Is he okay? Hero told me a little about what happened."

Deva nodded, feeling some of the tension ease. "He's in pretty bad shape right now, but they're saying he'll recover. Yeah, it's been... intense."

Jade gazed at her father, a flicker of amusement in her expression now. "Guess it's a good thing I came by. Wanted to make sure you weren't dealing with all this alone."

Razor shrugged, leaning casually against the back of his recliner. "You know me. I manage."

Jade rolled her eyes. "Right, because you're so great at letting people help you."

Deva couldn't help but chuckle at the familiar way Jade teased him. It was clear they had an easy, if slightly guarded, relationship. The awkwardness of her presence faded as Razor and Jade fell into a rhythm, their conversation turning to light updates about her job and the kids she worked with.

Still, when Jade's gaze flicked back to Deva occasionally, she saw something unspoken, like Jade was trying to figure out exactly what was going on between her dad and this woman sitting in his living room. But she didn't press, didn't pry, and Deva appreciated her grace in that.

When Razor asked to take Jade's coat, Jade paused. "I can't stay. I've got self-defense class in about half an hour. Take care of yourself, okay? And... take care of her too." She nodded toward Deva with a small, knowing smile.

Razor smirked. "Will do."

Jade's smile widened, and she stepped out into the night. Deva watched her go, a strange mix of warmth and nervousness settling in her chest. Razor closed the door, and when he turned back to her, his smirk lingered.

"She's nice," Deva said, feeling her cheeks flush slightly. Meeting his daughter had been as awkward as she thought it would be. But Razor's daughter was perceptive and charming. Deva hoped to talk to her again.

Razor chuckled. "Yeah. She is. Don't let her fool you, though. She's tougher than she looks."

Deva sank back into the couch. "Guess that runs in the family."

"What's that supposed to mean?" Razor's grin told her he didn't take offense.

"You're tougher than you look," Deva teased. "For an old guy."

Smoothing his hair back and putting it into a low ponytail with the band he pulled from around his wrist, he shook his head. "I'm not taking the bait until you get something to eat. Then you can bait me all you want."

"Threaten a girl with a good time," Deva said, focusing on the menus in earnest as he took a seat in his recliner. Even though the last two times they ended up in bed had been rough and exciting, it exhausted her into sleep. Deva was hoping he'd be interested in wearing her out again tonight, so she could get some rest.

Thinking about everything that happened reminded her of a question she'd thought of in her brother's hospital room earlier.

"Can I ask you something?" Deva asked. "Why do you call Jackson *Outcast*?"

Razor leaned back in his chair, his hazel eyes narrowing thoughtfully as he considered that. "Your brother's the kind of guy who does things on his own terms," he began, his voice carrying a rare mix of respect and regret. "Even in the club, he's always been the lone wolf -- takes the hard jobs, rides solo when he needs to. That's just who he is. We call him Outcast because that's how he made himself. It wasn't the club pushing him away -- it was him setting himself apart. He doesn't need people the way most of us do, and when you've been through what Jackson has, well, I can't blame him."

Deva frowned, her chest tightening at the weight of his words. "What do you mean, 'what Jackson's been through'? You don't think I know my own brother?"

Razor's tone remained serious. "I think you know him better than anyone. But sometimes you're too close to see the whole picture. Outcast's never talked about it with me, not outright. But I've pieced together enough over the years. Your dad wasn't around, was he?"

Deva shook her head. "No. He walked out when

I was a baby. Jackson was only six."

Razor nodded, as though confirming something he already knew. "And your mom... what happened with her?"

Deva exhaled sharply, the memories drifting in. "Yeah. She drank too much, couldn't hold down a job. CPS came when I was ten. Jackson and I were split up for a while but he fought like hell to get us back together. As soon as he turned eighteen, he ran right out and got a job and an apartment. He petitioned the court and got custody of me."

"That right there," Razor said, his voice steady, "is where it starts. He had to be the man of the house when he was just a kid, didn't he? Taking care of you while your mom spiraled. Then foster care... that kind of life leaves scars, Deva. Deep ones. Scars that make you feel like you can't trust anyone but yourself. You both carry those scars."

It was all true. Razor saw a lot. Deva swallowed hard, her hands tightening into fists on the table. "He didn't have a choice. He *had* to grow up fast. Somehow, he always managed... to keep me safe."

"Exactly," Razor said, leaning forward, his elbows resting on his knees. "That's why he's the way he is. Why he doesn't let anyone in. He's been looking out for you, for himself, for so long that it's just second nature. He doesn't lean on anyone because he learned early on that people let you down. He's been an outsider his whole life, doing what he can to survive. *Outcast.*"

Deva's throat tightened, her heart aching for the brother who'd sacrificed so much for her. "I never realized how much he's carried all this time. I mean, I knew, but I didn't... feel it the way I do now."

Razor nodded, his expression unusually kind.

"He loves you, Deva. That much is clear. And that's why he fought so hard to keep you safe. But let me ask you something. What do you think made him that way? What made him the kind of man who could survive all that and still come out the other side?"

The question caught her off guard. She stared at Razor, searching for an answer. "I don't know," she said quietly. "Maybe it's just who Jackson is. He's strong. He's always been strong."

Razor's lips curved into a small smile. "Yeah, he's strong. But that strength came from somewhere. Maybe it's because he had you to protect. Or maybe it's just in his blood. Either way, that strength is what keeps him going."

Deva sat in silence for a moment, absorbing his words. "I just hope he knows he doesn't have to carry it all alone anymore. Look what they did to him."

"He knows," Razor assured her. "But whether he lets anyone help him? That's up to him. You just keep being his sister, Deva. That's all he's ever needed from you. You take care of him too."

Tears gathered in her eyes just thinking about today. "Why did they have to do that to him? Why? I wish --"

"No," Razor cut her off. "They would have done far worse to you, Deva. That would destroy Outcast more than anything they could do to him, trust me. And that's not going to happen."

The sheer determination on Razor's face left no doubt. "Something else," Razor said. "Before you got to the hospital, Outcast said something. I could barely make it out. It sounded like... Anna or Anya? That mean anything to you?"

Anastasia. It had been years since she'd thought about her. Jackson's first love. They met her in the foster system, and she'd been a friend to both of them. Until they separated her from Jackson. Deva never knew what happened to Anastasia or what happened between her and her brother. She'd asked a couple of times over the years. Her brother's responses had been hard to read. She couldn't tell if his relationship with their friend was meaningless or it had hurt him so badly that he didn't recover and hence, didn't want to talk about it. "Anna -- Anastasia -- was a friend of ours, when we were in the system," Deva said. "I didn't know her as well because they split Jackson and me up. I've asked about her since but he never told me what happened."

Razor's expression was thoughtful as he considered her explanation. Then he said, "Pick out a restaurant, woman. The sooner we get something to eat, the sooner we can get to bed."

Deva grinned at him. The man knew just how to lift her spirits.

* * *

Deva

The next morning, Deva awoke early, warm in Razor's bed. The sun was just coming up and the handsome biker was spooning her, a heavy arm holding her to him. The soft cadence of his snoring and the warmth of his body were the perfect pocket of comfort, and she didn't want to leave. She knew the minute she got up and started getting ready for the day, she'd have to return to the nightmare.

No Mercy Ink couldn't have looked worse if it had been bombed. And the same assholes who did that to their store had savagely attacked Jackson and left him for dead. She was staying with Razor because he believed they were also a very real threat to *her*. And then all the other unanswered questions. Why was Victor Grayson doing all this? What was he really doing behind the scenes at his own so-called tattoo shop?

The sinful brush of Razor's lips and stubble over the back of her neck made her shudder. His chuckle was a deep rumble, the sound comforting. "Good mornin'."

When he continued the sensual chain of kisses over her neck, across to her shoulder, her thighs clenched. The movement reminded her of the soreness in her thighs and in other delicate places. That had her smiling, remembering last night.

Neither of them had worn anything to bed. When Razor ground his cock against her ass, she felt the full effect of it. And she wanted that. Right *now*.

Deva reached back to take him in her hand, to stroke and guide him where she needed him most. Razor read the situation the way she wanted, sliding with ease into her slick passage from behind. She welcomed the heat of him, the way he stretched her walls. As he slowly began fucking her, Deva clenched around him and moved her hips with his. The position put pressure on new points inside her and they eased into a slow, easy rhythm. Deva writhed in his arms, one hand moving to his ass to guide his movements, to make him understand that she needed more. The other slid down the front of her body, her fingers working her clit as Razor fucked her like they had all the time in the world.

A light nip of his teeth at her shoulder only made the fire he'd started in her body worse. Razor slowly burned her down, his hands and lips making the flames rise hotter. Deva loved the way his hand caressed her breasts, teasing the points of her nipples until she felt the ache all the way down to her pussy. Using her fingers just how she liked in her own wet folds only helped her come faster. It took her breath away.

"Feel good, darlin'?" His lips teased the sensitive shell of her ear as he tightened his grip on her. Holding her to his body with an arm that felt like a band of steel, Razor began to fuck her hard. No more romantic, easy sex. It was back to rough, claiming sex and the more he gave her, the more she wanted. His cock felt so good plunging in and out of her, the movements easy with the wetness from her excitement.

Deva planted a hand on the bed in front of her, bracing herself as his thrusts grew in strength and speed. His deep groans blended with the slapping sounds from their fierce movements, their bodies working together. Her breathy cries as he punched the air from her lungs had her vision fading to black along the edges. Mindlessly they chased their pleasure, but he made sure she got there first. Deva screamed as she came again, as he pounded into her with everything he had. When he reached his end, he pumped wildly into her until he was spent.

When his grip on her finally relaxed, Deva felt like she could breathe again. Razor rolled onto his back, and she collapsed where she was, no longer wanting to get ready for the day.

When Razor's phone hummed on the bedside table behind them, Deva's heart lurched in her chest as he went to answer it. Was it Jackson? Was he still alive? Had Victor Grayson's men made it into the hospital to finish him off?

"Yeah," Razor answered. A male voice spoke on the other end, but she wasn't sure who it was. "You think it's drugs? Guns?"

No mention of her brother. That was a good thing, right?

"We'll be there by noon," Razor said. "We're going to the hospital first thing and then I'll be with Deva at the tattoo shop. I want at least two guys with her, even if I'm there too, at all times. Is that clear?"

Razor wasn't playing around. But her brother needed the protection more than she did...

"I'll look at it then. Thanks, Snow," Razor said, ending the call.

Holding the heavy comforter to her breasts, Deva waited until his attention was back on her. "What's going on?"

Leaning forward, Razor kissed her forehead. "More activity at *Sinister Skin*. Snow's got some videos for us to look at when we get to your shop."

We. Deva liked that.

"I appreciate you trying to keep me safe," she said, watching Razor climb out of bed gloriously naked. Damn, Razor was *fine* for an older man. "But what about Jackson?"

That stopped Razor as he pulled on his jeans. "Darlin', in protecting you I'm not taking anything away from Outcast."

"We're going to the hospital first?" Deva was anxious to see if her brother was doing better, if he was awake.

"Yeah. As soon as we're ready to leave," Razor said, "we're going to the hospital first. I'm hoping Outcast is awake and can tell us what the hell happened to him."

Deva just wanted her brother to survive, to recover. But maybe Razor was right. If he was awake, what could he have to tell them?

* * *

Razor

The fluorescent lights in the hospital hallway felt too bright for the grim tension Razor carried as he strode beside Deva toward Outcast's room. Her smaller frame was tight with determination. Her shoulders were approaching her ears and every step she took was purposeful. But Razor knew her well enough by now to see the storm brewing just beneath her composed exterior. All he could hope was that Outcast was better today. If he was awake, maybe he'd have a story to tell.

When they stepped into the room, the rhythmic beep of monitors and the faint hiss of oxygen greeted them. Outcast lay still, pale against the stark white sheets, his body looking battered almost beyond recognition. The results of a beating always looked worse the next day and he did his damnedest to stay composed, though Deva's face almost crumbled at the sight. Razor hated the helplessness of seeing his brother like this. Worse, he hated seeing Deva dealing with this on top of what happened at *No Mercy Ink*. Since they started hooking up, her entire life was coming apart. Razor just hoped he wasn't making it worse.

The nurse stopped by to get Outcast's vitals and Deva asked her a few questions. Her brother was still sedated to keep pain and anxiety from hindering his recovery and Deva seemed encouraged by that news. Still, she seemed so small in the chair next to her brother's bed, holding his motionless hand in hers. Razor had been about to go find them some coffee when she abruptly rose from that chair, started looking around. Moving to the bedside table, she jerked open its single drawer and pulled out a plastic bag containing Outcast's personal belongings. Opening it, she fished out his phone.

Razor watched her move back to the bed, pressing her brother's finger to the sensor to unlock the device. He was about to tell her that the police had likely searched his phone already but then he remembered Axel saying it had been Dawson working at the scene yesterday.

"You're probably not going to find anything," Razor said, his voice low but firm. "Dawson was there. He probably already scrubbed anything that could point a finger at Grayson or his crew off there."

She held up a hand, her attention already on the phone. "Jackson might've left us something."

For a moment, she hesitated, her expression hopeful. The phone unlocked, and Deva let out a small, triumphant huff. "Barely any battery left," she muttered, scrolling quickly through texts, emails, and call logs. "Maybe there's something here."

Razor stayed quiet, leaning against the wall with arms crossed, his gaze flicking between her and Outcast. He admired her fire but couldn't shake the sense of foreboding gnawing at his gut.

"Wait." Deva paused, her brow furrowing. She swiped to the photo gallery, where a single video caught her attention. It was time-stamped the day before Outcast's attack. "What's this?"

She tapped it, and the screen flickered to life. The video showed nothing but darkness -- likely recorded from inside a pocket -- but the muffled audio was enough to freeze Razor in place. At first, the audio was unintelligible: footsteps on gravel, faint rustling, and muted voices. Deva adjusted the volume, holding the phone close to her ear. Razor moved to stand behind her chair.

"...I'm tired of playing games with *No Mercy Ink*," a woman's sharp voice snapped, her Russian accent thick. "This isn't working."

"Patience, Natalia," a man replied, his tone oily and confident. "We've got them on the ropes. We took the man off the table. His sister shouldn't pose much of a problem."

"Patience?" Natalia's voice rose, dripping with disdain. "We've wasted enough time, V. Either we threaten the girl and force her to sell, or we *recruit* her and take it. Needle can use the shop to bring in recruits. They do good business, their clients are mostly young, disadvantaged. Exactly what we're looking for."

The man --"V," as Natalia called him -- let out a chuckle. "Deva Crane might need... persuasion. Her brother's a member of a biker gang and by all account she's fucking their president. Probably she's thinking that'll protect her from me." The man snorted. "But you've got a point. *No Mercy Ink* would speed things up for us. It's going to take a while to get Sinister going."

"It wouldn't if you'd actually focus on Sinister's actual purpose," Natalia said. "Besides, I thought Sinister was going to be mine. All I've seen are your guns and... other supplies."

Razor's jaw tightened. The audio paused there, and he had to wonder where and how Outcast managed to get that recording. Natalia and V were lovers, and he was pretty sure V was Victor Grayson. Their plan wasn't just about acquiring *No Mercy Ink* -- it was about turning it into a hub for their human trafficking operation.

There was a long pause before Natalia added, her tone softer but laced with suggestion, "Just deal with the sister and let's get this over with. We've got a lot to do."

Razor's blood ran cold as he listened to Natalia's venomous confidence, but the recording ended before the pair revealed any specific actions.

When the recording finished, Deva stared at the phone, her hands trembling. "They're going to try to take it. They're going to try to take my shop. *Our* shop." Her voice cracked, but her rage pushed through the vulnerability.

"Deva," Razor began, his hand smoothing over her shoulder, "this is serious. They're dangerous, and you heard what they said --"

"Exactly!" She turned to him, her eyes blazing. "They're threatening everything Jackson and I have built. They think they can use my shop for... for that!" Her voice wavered as the implication of what Natalia and V planned settled over her. "We can't let them. *No Mercy Ink* isn't fucking going to be used by these assholes to prey on the vulnerable. No fucking way."

"I know," Razor said firmly. "And that's why *you* can't go back there. Not right now."

Deva's laugh was sharp and bitter. "You're joking, right? That's my shop."

"You think I like this?" Razor's voice rose, his frustration leaking through. "I don't want you sidelined, but I won't stand by and watch you get hurt -- or worse. It's *you* they're after."

"Razor --"

"No," he cut her off, his hazel eyes locking onto hers. "You heard what they said. They know who you are. Let us take care of this."

Deva rose from the chair and turned to face him, her jaw tightening. "I'm not some helpless little damsel, Razor."

"And I'm not saying you are," he shot back. "But this isn't just about you anymore. They sound like they have bigger plans for Mercy than *No Mercy Ink*."

Deva stared at him, her expression a mix of anger, fear, and reluctant understanding. "I just... I can't sit back and do nothing."

Razor stepped closer. His tone was gentle. "You're not doing nothing. You're trusting me to fight this fight for you. And I swear, Deva, we'll make them pay."

The room fell silent, the weight of their shared determination settling between them. For now, Razor knew he'd convinced her, but the fire in her eyes told him it wouldn't last long. Deva Crane wasn't the type to sit idly by -- and Razor wasn't sure he wanted her to.

Chapter Eight

Razor

By the time they made it to *No Mercy Ink*, more repairs were underway. The shattered front windows, a painful reminder of the earlier attack, had been replaced with reinforced glass that reflected the dim winter sun. It would be warmer in the shop now, which was especially good while working on repairs. Hero and Snow labored tirelessly, ensuring every pane was installed to withstand future trouble. Outside, the graffiti that had desecrated the shop's facade was power washed, but faint stains lingered. Deva's jaw tightened every time her eyes lingered on those persistent marks, but Razor assured her that Hero would figure it out. He was an auto body guy by day so he was good with paint. If he couldn't figure out how to get the remaining stains off the building, no one could.

Progress on the shop's interior was slower, but steady. The tattoo stations and furniture, tossed, ripped, and upended during the break-in, had been cleaned, then repaired or replaced. Crash came in around lunch time to patch up the drywall near the front door where the vandals had forced their way in. Only a faintly visible seam remained when he was done. Deva herself supervised the installation of the higher-grade security deadbolts on the front door, making sure it was done in a way that made her feel safe. Razor didn't make a big deal of it, but he inspected every detail pertaining to security himself, not willing to leave anything to chance.

The finishing touch was the state-of-the-art security system Snow installed, complete with well-concealed motion detectors and cameras. Razor took satisfaction in watching the live feed load on his phone, knowing he could keep an eye on the shop even when he wasn't physically there. He'd be able to verify Deva's safety whenever he wanted. Realizing how much he appreciated that capability caught him off guard.

But for all the progress, an air of unease hung over the shop. Outcast's absence hovered over them like a storm cloud, dark and unyielding, casting a shadow on every step forward. Deva busied herself with organizing what she could, but the strain showed in the furrow of her brow and the tightness in her voice. He knew she hated to admit to any weakness, but the events of the past few days seemed to have shaken her confidence. Still, she held herself together.

As the evening settled in, Razor urged Deva to lock it up for the night. She hesitated, her hand lingering on the reinforced door. Leaving the shop, even temporarily, felt like surrendering ground to Victor Grayson and his people. But with Razor's firm presence at her side, she relented, twisting the lock and securing the deadbolt.

"We're watching," he promised, his voice steady. "They try to do more shit, and someone will be here in less than three minutes."

Deva nodded, though the flicker of doubt in her eyes remained as they walked out into the night.

Outcast was awake when they arrived at the hospital, though he still looked tired and in a good amount of pain. His account of the attack was frustratingly thin on details. "A couple of guys in a black SUV," he rasped, his voice rough. "They ran me off the road, pulled over, and… well, you've seen the aftermath."

Deva sat at his bedside, her arms crossed tightly,

the tension in her posture mirroring Razor's grim silence.

"Did you recognize them?" Razor asked, barely keeping his anger out of his tone.

Outcast shook his head slightly, wincing at the motion. "No idea who they were. It was quick -- lights, impact, fists. I don't remember much else."

Deva's jaw tightened, her frustration visible. "What about the SUV? Did you get a plate or see anything distinctive about it?"

"Black," Outcast muttered, his eyes closing briefly. "Just black. Tinted windows. It was upscale, like... an Escalade or something. That's all I got."

Deva leaned forward in her chair, taking her brother's hand in hers. "I found a video on your phone. You can't see anything, but you were recording. Tell me about that."

Outcast rolled his ice-blue eyes. "I've never had a fucking secret from you, have I?"

"And you never will." she said quietly, her voice thick with emotion. "You were recording. How did you even get this, Jackson? Where were you?"

Her brother grimaced, his split lip making him wince as he tried to shift upright. Razor moved forward to help him, but Outcast waved him off, his eyes locking on Deva. "I was tailing one of Grayson's lackeys," he rasped. "I'd heard whispers about a meeting going down at the old rail yard outside of Mercy. Figured it'd be worth checking out."

Deva's heart clenched. "An old abandoned rail yard? Alone? Are you insane?"

Outcast smirked weakly, the gesture pulling at the bruises on his jaw. "There was an old warehouse out there. Figured I could get in, see if I could find out anything, and get out before anyone knew I was there.

Guess it didn't exactly go as planned."

Razor's hazel eyes narrowed. "What happened?"

"I parked my bike a ways off and moved in closer on foot," Outcast said. "Couldn't see much, but I could hear them. Victor and that woman -- Natalia, I think -- were talking near one of the old storage containers. The shit they were saying... it was bad, Razor. They're planning something big, and *No Mercy Ink* is right in the middle of it. Heard all of that before my dumb ass started recording."

Deva's stomach twisted. "Why would they target our shop?"

"They're not just targeting it," Outcast said, his voice growing more strained. "They want to use it as a front -- to funnel people for their trafficking ring. That's what they do. Tattoo parlors, vape shops. Natalia said they'd pressure you to sell, Deva, once I was dealt with. If you didn't... they'd make you comply." He shot her a grim look. "Figured that recording was the proof we'd need if things got worse."

It matched what they'd heard in the video. They'd already planned to go after Jackson first according to the recording. Someone saw him, and it just gave them an excuse to speed up their agenda. Now *she* was in their crosshairs.

"And then?" Razor pressed.

"They must've had someone watching." Outcast sounded frustrated. "The next morning, I was riding to work. I didn't see them until it was too late. Two guys in a black SUV ran me off the road. Guess they didn't like that I was poking around."

Deva swallowed hard, the weight of his words hitting her. "You could've been killed, Jackson."

"Yeah, but I wasn't," Outcast replied, his gaze

hard.

Deva glanced at the phone in her hand, the muted voices on the recording echoing in her mind. They had a lead now, but it wasn't just about the shop anymore. It was about stopping Victor and Natalia before they destroyed anyone else's life with their trafficking operation. They couldn't let him infect Mercy with his corruption.

Razor placed a firm hand on Outcast's shoulder, as much to reassure him as to steady his own rising fury. "Rest up. Let us know if you need anything."

"So, are you guys a thing now or what?" Outcast asked, his one good eye looking from one to the other.

Deva froze. She didn't know how Razor would answer that question. With everything going on, they hadn't had much time to talk about any of it. But Razor knew how he felt, and he wasn't about to play games with her or Outcast. Truth was best.

"We are," Razor said firmly.

Her big dark eyes were on him in a second, a thread of hope showed in her expression. It only strengthened his resolve. What he felt for her had been growing all the while. He wanted Deva for himself in a way he wasn't sure he'd felt before.

"Do we have any issues?" Razor asked him then, dead serious. If so, he and Outcast would be working shit out when he recovered. Honestly, as much as he respected his MC brother, whatever answer he got wasn't going to change his mind about Deva.

Outcast gave his sister a long look as color darkened her pretty face. Still, she seemed to like the way the conversation was going.

When Outcast turned back to Razor, he said, "It makes sense. My sister's strong. Not just any man can handle her. And not just any man is good enough for her. Glad it's you."

The sincerity of that answer had a smile playing around her full lips. That more than anything had Razor's heart skipping a beat. Just maybe little Deva wanted him as much as he wanted her. A good thing because Razor had no intention of letting her go anywhere.

Outcast looked tired, but his expression carried a silent gratitude. After giving his news, he seemed content to listen to Deva telling him everything that had been done at the shop, making Razor proud of the way he quietly supported his sister. Especially since Outcast had to be mad as hell about the entire situation and likely blamed himself for not being there to help out.

* * *

Razor

When they made it back to Razor's house, they were both dead on their feet. They picked up groceries after visiting Outcast at the hospital. The sound of Deva scrambling to put them away in his kitchen had him smiling. How she was still moving around when he could quite happily climb into bed right now, he didn't know. Razor had been restless since the attack on Outcast, every muscle in his body on edge as he sat in his recliner. It felt like they were waiting for the next shoe to drop.

The hum of his phone cut through the silence like a blade.

Razor glanced at the screen. It was Hero. His gut twisted. He didn't have a good feeling as he answered the call.

"What's up?" Razor asked, his voice calm despite the unease creeping in.

"Razor --" Hero's voice was ragged, frantic. "It's Jade. She's gone. I -- I can't find her, man."

Razor froze. "What the hell do you mean she's gone?"

"We were supposed to meet for dinner an hour ago. She never showed. I found her SUV, Razor. It's out near the hospital."

It was also near the strip mall where *Sinister Skin Studios* was located.

"The door's open," Hero went on. "Her keys are in the ignition, and... there's blood on the ground."

Razor's grip on the phone tightened, his knuckles turning white.

Hero sounded like he was beside himself, pacing like a caged animal. "I should've been with her," he muttered, his voice raw with frustration and anguish.

Razor felt the weight of his lieutenant's desperation, but his own focus was splintering. Memories of Jade's first kidnapping surged to the surface -- Babyface, the Cottonmouths, the knife he'd taken to the gut trying to get her back. Razor clenched his fists, the old wound aching faintly as if to remind him what was at stake. He was torn between leading his crew to save Jade and the growing need to protect Deva. And Deva refused to back down despite the danger she faced. The stakes were higher now, and Razor knew one wrong move could cost them everything.

"Stay there. Don't touch a goddamn thing. I'm on my way."

He ended the call, his mind already racing. As he bent down to put his boots back on, he saw Deva out of the corner of his eye. She stood in the doorway to the kitchen, her arms crossed and a worried look in her eyes.

"What happened?" she asked, her voice steady but laced with concern.

"Jade's missing," Razor said, shoving his phone into his pocket. "Hero found her car, but not her."

Deva's eyes widened. "I'm coming with you."

"No," Razor said firmly, grabbing his keys off the counter. "This isn't your fight, Deva."

"The hell it isn't," she shot back, stepping closer. "Jade's your daughter. She's part of your world, Razor, and that means she's part of mine. Don't you dare tell me to sit this one out."

Razor stared at her, torn between admiration for her fire and the gnawing fear of putting her in more danger. "Deva, I need you safe. I can't focus on finding my girl and worrying about you too."

"I *need* to help," she countered. "Don't make me fight you on this. You know I'll win."

She was fucking fearless. His jaw tightened, but he gave a reluctant nod. If Deva was with him, he knew for damn sure where she was and that she was safe. "Fine. But you stay close to me. No arguments."

Deva nodded, grabbing her coat as Razor called Snow, summoning the Hounds to action. He called Margot as he and Deva walked out to his truck.

They were there in ten minutes. The SUV sat skewed on the dirt shoulder of a back road not far behind Mercy General Hospital, its driver-side door wide open. Jade's purse lay discarded in the gravel, its contents scattered around it. Razor's boots crunched against the ground as he approached, his chest tightening with every step.

The recording of Grayson's voice played in his mind. The man had pointed out that Deva was hooking up with *him*. His heart squeezed in his chest as the realization hit him. Grayson's crew had already attacked Outcast, the one they could most easily hurt to get to Deva. It made sense that next they would take his daughter.

Margot was already there with Hero, in uniform and on duty, standing with Axel and Ryder. Their somber faces confirmed Razor's worst fear before he even asked. Nearby, Dawson lingered, visibly uncomfortable as he scribbled in a small notepad. Razor ignored him for the moment, his eyes scanning the scene for anything that might explain what the hell had happened to Jade.

Deva stood near the edge of the scene, her arms wrapped around herself, a mix of dread and determination etched on her face. Her gaze darted between Margot and the abandoned SUV. The tension in her body was palpable, like she was one second away from bolting forward to scour the car herself. Instead, she stood back, her gaze roving over the discarded purse and the telltale scuff marks in the gravel.

"Razor." Margot's voice was low and measured as she approached. "There are clear signs that she put up a fight. Her phone's missing. The tire tracks over there suggest another vehicle forced her off the road -- a larger SUV or truck from the looks of it."

Huh. "A black SUV ran Outcast off the road. He didn't get the plates, but he said it had tinted windows and that it was high-end, like a Cadillac or something."

Margot nodded. "We'll be on the lookout for that."

Guilt was etched in every line on Hero's face. Axel was kneeling by the side of the road, gesturing toward something on the ground. Razor's stomach twisted as he and Hero moved closer, seeing a dark stain on the gravel. *Blood*. Not much, but enough to freeze the air in his lungs.

"Found this over here," Axel said, standing as Razor reached him. "Could be hers. Could be someone else's." He hesitated. "It's not a lot."

Razor forced himself to nod, though his jaw was locked tight. His gaze shifted to the SUV, its door hanging open like a silent scream. He caught Deva staring at the blood too, her lips pressed together in a thin line.

"Razor." Hero's voice was rough, shaking him out of his thoughts. "They've got her."

"I know." Razor's voice was barely audible.

His vision blurred with anger as he turned to Dawson, shuffling awkwardly nearby, looking anywhere but at Razor. It was the wrong move. Razor's blood was already boiling, and seeing Dawson's evasive, nervous stance only poured gasoline on the fire. In three strides, Razor was on him, grabbing the deputy by the front of his uniform and slamming him against the side of Jade's SUV.

"You know something," Razor growled, his voice a low, dangerous rasp, his face inches from Dawson's. "You've been keeping secrets. Now my daughter is gone because of it."

"Razor!" Margot interjected, but he didn't let go.

Dawson flailed slightly, his notepad falling to the ground as he stammered, "I -- I don't know what you're fucking talking about!"

"Bullshit!" Razor slammed Dawson again harder, glaring at him with fury. "You've been covering for Grayson and his people, haven't you? What did they threaten you with, huh? What's worth more to you than my kid's life?"

Deva was at Razor's side in an instant, her hand lightly touching his arm. "Razor," she said, her voice surprisingly steady. "Let Margot handle this. Please."

Razor hesitated, his nostrils flaring, but he slowly loosened his grip. Margot quickly stepped between them, her gaze locking on Dawson.

"You'd better start talking," she said, her voice sharp and unyielding. "Because if you don't, I can't guarantee what he'll do next."

Dawson's face was pale, his fear palpable. "They're fucking blackmailing me!" he finally blurted. "Grayson's got stuff on me -- evidence of stupid shit I did when I was younger, my first precinct. If I don't keep quiet, he'll kill my career."

"Where would they take her?" Razor snapped.

"I don't know." Dawson's words tumbled out in a frantic rush. "He usually comes to *me*... I swear I didn't know they'd go this far. I thought -- I thought it was just about business, about Deva's shop."

Razor's gaze burned into Dawson for a moment longer before he released a breath, stepping back. "You're going to tell us everything." His tone left no room for argument. "Every single fucking detail about what you've done for them, what you know about their operation, and where the hell they could be keeping Jade."

Dawson nodded, his fear of Razor overriding whatever loyalty he'd had to Victor Grayson. "Okay," he muttered, looking like a man headed for the gallows.

As Margot led Dawson away to talk to him, Razor turned back to the SUV. Hero stood there looking more anguished than he'd ever seen the man. Razor placed a hand on his shoulder, steadying him.

"We'll get her back," Razor promised as Deva moved close to him.

And they fucking would. Failure wasn't an

option. Not this time.

* * *

Deva

Deva paced Razor's living room, her phone clutched in her hand. The tension in the air felt thick enough to choke on. She kept walking restlessly, crossing from the couch to the window and back again as if moving could somehow ease the anxiety gnawing at her. She kept glancing at her phone, flipping through contacts, her thumb hovering over the call button for Jackson, Margot, even Hero, but never pressing it. Would they find Jade in time to save her life?

She'd gone with Razor to comb every inch of the warehouse where Jackson recorded the video on his phone. Grayson and his crew *had* been there. There were clear signs of that. But the site was abandoned -- recently, from the looks of it.

Razor stood by the kitchen counter, his broad shoulders tense as he stared at his own phone. She could tell by his expression -- sharp, cold, dangerous -- that something was wrong. Really wrong. Every few moments, his jaw ticked, and his fingers gripped the edge of the counter like he was keeping himself in check.

Deva stopped pacing, planting herself in front of the counter. "What's going on, Razor?" she demanded, her voice quiet but firm. "You've been standing there for ten minutes, and you haven't said a damn thing. Is it Jade? Did they find her?"

He didn't answer immediately, just tilted his phone slightly so she could see the screen. The move made her heart hammer harder. "You're scaring me," she said, her voice cracking slightly despite her effort to stay calm.

Finally, Razor looked up, his hazel eyes blazing with barely contained fury. "I just got something. You're not going to like it."

Deva felt the floor drop out from under her. "What is it?" she whispered, stepping closer, her phone forgotten as her focus locked entirely on him.

He hesitated, his expression set in stone as he seemed to weigh whether to tell her. "Victor sent a message. It's about Jade."

Her stomach turned to ice. "Show me."

Razor hit play on the video, and the sound of Jade's terrified sobs filled the room. Deva froze, her heart slamming against her ribs as the screen showed Razor's daughter, restrained and visibly shaken. There was blood on her face, coming from her hairline. A woman's smug voice -- it sounded like Natalia from the recording on Outcast's phone, cut through Jade's pleas like a blade, dripping with malice.

"This is just the beginning," Natalia sneered in the video. "Sell *No Mercy Ink*, Deva. End this. Otherwise, you'll see just how far we're willing to go."

Deva's stomach twisted violently. The words were aimed at *her*, a direct punch to her gut. Razor's knuckles whitened as he gripped the phone, his jaw ticking with the effort to hold back the storm brewing inside him. But Deva couldn't hold back.

"Heartless bitch," Deva said, her voice rising. "This is about more than our shop -- it's about control. About breaking us."

Razor finally looked at her. "We're not the ones who are going to break."

Deva's guilt threatened to swallow her whole. Her shop, her dream -- everything she and Jackson had built -- was now a weapon in Victor's hands and Jade's life hung in the balance. But the guilt quickly morphed into anger, white-hot and unrelenting. "Send me that video," she said firmly. "We're going to find out where they've taken her."

She didn't wait for Razor to argue. Grabbing her laptop, she settled onto the couch and opened her brother's phone, its battery hanging on by a thread. Fortunately her charger worked with it, so she plugged her brother's phone up and played the single video he had over and over until Razor sent her the video of Jade. Her work as a tattoo artist had taught her precision, and her keen eye for detail was invaluable as she played the grainy video again. Razor stood nearby, his arms crossed, watching her carefully as she scrutinized the clip.

The video, though blurry, showed Jade restrained in what appeared to be a dimly lit room. Her terrified eyes searched the space around her, and Deva's heart twisted in sympathy and anger. Natalia's cold, taunting voice filled the air, urging them to sell *No Mercy Ink*, but Deva muted the sound. She wasn't focusing on the words right now -- she was searching for something else.

"Again," she said, her voice steady despite the turmoil churning inside her.

Razor hesitated, his gaze darting to the phone and back to her. "Deva, you've watched it three times already. There's not much to see…" With a heavy sigh, Razor watched her tap the screen to replay the video. Deva's eyes narrowed, honing in on every frame, every pixel.

"There," she murmured, pausing the video and pointing to the upper-right corner of the screen.

"What?" Razor leaned in closer.

"That light. It's just a bare bulb," she said, her

finger tracing the faint glow in the corner. "And it's dim. Like the kind you find in an old warehouse or industrial space."

Razor's jaw tightened. "*Sinister Skin Studios* has fluorescent lighting."

"But it's a start," Deva said, her eyes scanning the rest of the video. She unpaused it and let it play another few seconds before stopping again. "That wall. See the texture? It's metal -- corrugated. This isn't some backroom in a strip mall. They're keeping her somewhere bigger. Somewhere industrial."

Razor nodded slowly, his hazel eyes darkening with understanding. "It looks that way."

"There's something reflective on that part of the wall," Deva said, her voice thick with determination. She rewound the video again, pausing it on the moment the woman swung her phone away from Jade. "A logo, maybe? It's too blurred to make out here. I wonder if Snow could zoom in on it."

Razor crouched beside her, his broad frame filling her peripheral vision. "Maybe he could." He stared at the screen for a long moment before pushing away from the back of the couch. "All right. We start there. Sounds like we need to get our hands on a list of Grayson's properties here in Mercy. I'll get the Hounds moving. We've got no time to waste."

Deva nodded, her resolve hardening. They weren't just going to find Jade -- they were going to make Victor Grayson and Natalia and anyone who'd fucking helped them pay for every last threat they'd made.

* * *

Razor

The clubhouse meeting room was a hub of tense

energy, the scent of leather and motor oil mingling with the faint smell of coffee brewing in the corner. Razor stood at the head of the long wooden table, his hazel eyes scanning the group of Hounds assembled before him, some sitting, some leaning on the walls. Most of them in the Mercy chapter were crammed into the room, ready for battle. Maps, notes, and a grainy printout of the video from Grayson were spread across the table like a puzzle waiting to be solved.

"We narrowed it down to two possible locations," Razor said, his voice low but commanding. He pointed to a map of Mercy and the surrounding areas. "Hero, the twins, and I already checked out the old warehouse by the rail yard. The only other property Grayson unofficially owns that could be used for his operations is an old abandoned cannery on the outskirts of town. Both are properties tied to his associate Natalia Veska's crew. Thanks for the work on this, Snow. I know you worked on it for hours."

The white-haired biker nodded but stared intently at the photos. Razor appreciated him wanting to keep everything on track. Jade didn't have a lot of time. Hero leaned forward, his fists clenched. He'd never had much of a poker face and his misery was there for all to see. "Let's hit it. Tonight."

Margot, standing near the door in street clothes, nodded. "I won't have time to get the sheriff's okay on this. But Outcast's video should be enough to justify my going in."

It sounded risky to Razor, and he just hoped her participation didn't put her career in jeopardy.

Razor's phone buzzed on the table, cutting through the chatter. He glanced at the screen, then back at the group. "Snow's got live surveillance at the site. He'll be our eyes and ears remotely."

Deva, standing at the edge of the room, looked like a caged animal. Her hands were on her hips, her jaw set. Her dark eyes burned with determination. "What am I doing?"

Razor shot her a look, his brow furrowing. "You're staying here."

"No, I'm not." Deva stepped closer, her voice sharp. She had no way of knowing how out of line she was to just butt in on an MC meeting when she wasn't a member, much less talking to its president that way. Hell, even if she did, he doubted that she'd give a shit. "Jade is out there, and if there's even the slightest chance I can help, I'm going."

Razor's tone hardened. "This isn't up for debate, Deva. It's not safe."

"And you think I'm safe here, sitting on my hands while Jade is God knows where?" Deva snapped back. "We have an idea of where they have her, Razor, that I found originally." Deva's gaze shifted to Snow. "No offense."

Snow smirked but said nothing.

The room fell silent as the two stared each other down. Razor blew out a breath. Strong-willed as she was, if he didn't let her do something, she could get herself killed or possibly mess up the entire operation. She'd never forgive herself for the latter.

Hero finally broke the silence. "She's got a point."

Snow nodded his agreement.

Margot chimed in, her voice calm but firm. "Why not let her assist remotely? She can monitor from here at the clubhouse, run surveillance, and relay anything we might miss."

"I can set her up," Snow offered. "She can handle it. And it frees me up to be on the ground."

Razor exhaled sharply, running a hand through his hair. He liked this deal less the more it went on. Deva shouldn't be involved. He wanted to lock her ass in the clubhouse just to keep the unthinkable from happening to her. And Snow was always itching for a fight. But hell, what if Snow was right? Maybe she *could* handle his tech. And Snow was a lethal killer who would strengthen their attack.

Deva frustrated the shit out of him at times, but he admired her courage. Turning back to Deva, Razor nodded. "Fine. But you stay *here*. No arguments, no surprises."

Deva's lips curved into a small, victorious smile. "Deal, Prez."

Axel exchanged a knowing glance with Ryder, the faintest smirk tugging at his lips, as if silently applauding Deva for standing her ground against Razor. Beast and Crash, on the other hand, stayed quiet but visibly tense, their postures rigid, clearly uncomfortable witnessing anyone challenge the president so openly. Still, they seemed silently impressed by her resolve. That boded well for the future… if they could get Jade back safely.

"All right," Razor said, turning back to the table. "Hero, you're with me. Margot, get what you need from our weapons stash. Snow, you set everything up for Deva and she'll relay anything she finds to me. We're moving out within the hour."

The room buzzed with movement as the Hounds dispersed to prepare. Only Deva stayed behind looking composed and ready. Approaching his seat at the head of the table, she brushed a kiss on his forehead. "This will work."

It had to. He couldn't let himself think about what would happen to his daughter if it didn't.

Chapter Nine

Razor

The warehouse loomed in the darkness like a decaying beast. Its towering, rusted exterior was streaked with corrosion that gleamed under the scattered floodlights. The quiet hum of the lights buzzed on and off in a random rhythm. Razor crouched at the edge of the tree line, the cool metal of his binoculars pressing against his brow as his gaze swept over the grounds.

The perimeter was alive with movement -- gruff men in dark jackets, some pacing with restless energy, others huddled in tense conversation. Their postures screamed professional muscle, but the slouched shoulders and careless handling of their weapons suggested they weren't exactly hired for their brains. Razor noted the shine of a lit cigarette from one guard, its ember flickering in the dark like a firefly before being casually flicked to the ground.

His jaw tightened. They were here for intimidation, not discipline, and that made them even more dangerous. Didn't the dumb bastards know the law could easily light their asses up? A group this disorganized was unpredictable, and unpredictability got people killed. Razor lowered the binoculars and whispered to Hero beside him, keeping his voice down. "They're sloppy, but they've got numbers. We'll need to move fast before they figure out what's happening."

Hero crouched beside him, the grip on his pistol firm as he whispered, "Two at the west entrance, three patrolling. Looks like another pair near the loading dock."

Razor handed the binoculars to Margot, who

might or might not have been there with the approval of her boss, the sheriff. He sure as shit wasn't going to ask. She nodded and began marking points on a makeshift map. "There's no way they don't know we're coming," she murmured.

"Good," Razor growled. "They're not walking out of here if Jade's in there."

Hero's jaw tightened at the mention of Jade. His eyes were sharp, focused, but his body practically vibrated with restrained anger. "No, they're fucking not."

Axel and Ryder signaled from the far side of the group. Their rifles appeared to be slung casually across their shoulders and they stood ready, knowing danger could strike at any second. Beast loomed after them with several other Hounds behind him. His massive frame blended into the shadows like a silent sentinel, his sharp gaze never leaving the warehouse. Razor caught their signals and returned a sharp nod, then turned his attention to Margot, who stood nearby, her own weapon strapped securely across her chest.

"Margot -- you, Snow, and Crash cover the east side," Razor instructed, his voice low and firm. "Stay out of sight and don't move until you hear my signal. Hero and I will handle the front entrance."

Margot's steely expression didn't falter as she gave a curt nod. "Don't get yourselves killed before we even get inside."

Razor grinned. "Not the plan," he replied, his tone carrying just enough edge to mask the weight of his concern.

Snow adjusted the strap on his shoulder, his jaw tight as he exchanged a glance with Margot. "We'll hold position but make it quick. The longer we wait, the riskier this gets." His VP turned to give instructions to the men behind them.

Into his comms, Razor said, "Deva, check in."

"Here and monitoring," her sweet voice responded. She was where she was supposed to be. Now he could proceed.

"Move fast." Razor turned to Hero as he spoke. His second-in-command was already crouched low, scanning the terrain ahead.

With a final glance at his team, Razor stepped forward and Hero followed. Their boots crunched against the frozen ground as they walked. Razor braced himself for the shitstorm about to hit.

The guards patrolled with predictable rhythms, their shadows stretching ominously under the flickering floodlights. Razor held up a fist, signaling Hero to stop. Both men crouched low, their weapons at the ready as they scoped the front entrance -- a heavy steel door flanked by two guards.

Razor leaned toward Hero, his voice so soft it was barely a whisper. "Two at the entrance. You take left. I'll take right."

Hero gave a sharp nod, adjusting his grip on his rifle. Razor motioned for Axel and Ryder, who had moved into position to cover them from the far side, and Beast, now stationed with Snow, Crash, and Margot at the east. Their roles were clear, and Razor knew they'd execute them without question.

The plan was set, and Razor counted down with his fingers. *Three. Two. One.*

In unison, Razor and Hero surged forward, their movements swift. Razor's knife gleamed in the faint light as he closed the distance to the guard on the right, taking him down with a precise strike to the throat. Hero's rifle butt connected with the other guard's temple, sending him crumpling to the ground with a muted *thud*.

After the guards were neutralized, Razor pulled a small device from his pocket -- a portable breaching charge Snow had prepared. He placed it on the door's locking mechanism and stepped back, signaling Hero to cover him.

A low *pop* and *hiss* sounded as the device worked its magic, and the door's lock gave way. Razor pushed it open slowly, his weapon raised as he and Hero slipped inside.

The interior was dimly lit. The scent of damp concrete hung in the air around them. Rows of crates and industrial equipment created a maze of shadows, perfect for hiding enemies -- or captives. Razor's eyes scanned every corner, his ears straining for any sign of Jade. Behind them, Axel, Ryder, and Beast entered, securing the main floor as planned. Margot and Crash swept the east side, their movements precise and purposeful. Snow lingered behind, ready to offer cover. The team worked like a well-oiled machine, each step methodical, every shadow checked.

"Clear," Axel muttered, his rifle steady as Razor pushed the door open.

What they found froze them in place.

Inside the dimly lit room were rows of makeshift holding cells, constructed from rusted metal bars and plywood walls. The faint whimper of a young man broke the oppressive silence, and as Razor's eyes adjusted to the gloom, he realized the extent of the horror. There were at least a dozen young men and women; most of them looked barely out of their teens, huddled together in torn clothes and shackles.

"Jesus Christ," Razor muttered, motioning for the others to move in. "Get them out of here."

Ryder appeared at his shoulder, his jaw

tightening as he scanned the faces of the prisoners. "Margot, come here!"

Axel and Snow began breaking the locks on the cells while Razor moved through the room, assessing the damage. Most of the captives recoiled at first, a chorus of whimpers and screams as their eyes widened in terror. But Razor's gruff commands to help them escape seemed to cut through the haze of fear.

Margot walked up as the first of the young captives stumbled forward, their terror palpable in the cold, damp air. Her expression shifted -- sharp, focused, and blazing with determination. In an instant, Margot took control, her badge snapping into view as she stepped into the dimly lit room.

"I'm Deputy Donner," she said firmly, her voice steady, radiating authority and reassurance. "I'm with the Mercy Sheriff's Department. We're getting you out of here. Now."

Razor watched as she moved among them, offering a hand to a trembling boy and a calm word to a girl whose tear-streaked face tilted toward her in fragile hope. There was no hesitation, no doubt. Margot's fire burned brighter than ever, and Razor felt a swell of grudging admiration. She grabbed a handful of his men to help her, and Razor knew she'd make damn sure these kids weren't just bodies to rescue because they were lives worth saving. Ryder glanced at Razor for approval to go with her and he gave it with a nod. Ryder would waste anyone without hesitation who threatened his Margot or any one of those kids.

When they cleared the larger area, Razor heard something. A stifled cry echoed faintly from deeper within the warehouse. He froze, his heart pounding as he exchanged a glance with Hero. They moved toward the sound as quietly as they could. It led them to a heavy, padlocked door. Razor was ready for anything as he motioned for Hero to cover him. He retrieved a pair of bolt cutters from his pack, their sharp jaws slicing through the metal with ease.

Inside, the familiar-looking room was dimly lit by a single bulb swinging from a wire. Jade sat bound to a chair, blood streaked her face, but she was defiant even in her vulnerable state. Razor's heart clenched at the sight, and his voice was sharp but soft. "Jade. It's me."

Her eyes snapped up, relief flooding her features as tears spilled down her cheeks. "Dad... they're here - -"

Before she could finish, a loud *clang* echoed through the warehouse. Razor spun around, weapon raised, as shouts erupted from the other side of the building.

"Incoming!" Axel's voice roared over the comms.

Razor could have sworn he heard Deva over the comms. It could have been Margot, or both. The Hounds sprang into action, the stillness of the night replaced by the chaos of gunfire and the heavy thud of boots on concrete. Razor had two goals -- protect his daughter and eliminate every threat in the way. His instincts kicked into overdrive. He knelt beside Jade, working quickly to free her from the ropes binding her wrists and ankles. "Hero, cover us!" he barked.

Hero immediately positioned himself in front of the doorway, rifle aimed at the shadows beyond. The shouts and gunfire from the warehouse reverberated through the air like a storm crashing into their carefully laid plans. Razor cut through the last rope, and Jade slumped forward, her strength faltering after the ordeal.

"I've got you," Razor said firmly, slipping an

arm under her shoulders to support her. "Can you walk?"

Jade's voice was barely audible. "I think so."

Razor helped her stand, her body trembling but determined. "Hero, we're moving out."

Hero's eyes flicked back to Razor, then to the woman he loved. "You get her clear. I'll cover your six."

Razor nodded and steered Jade toward the exit. The sounds of conflict grew closer, the echo of boots and shouts signaling that the guards were converging. Razor's grip tightened on Jade as they ducked behind a stack of crates for cover.

Meanwhile, Axel's voice came over the comms. "Razor, we're pinned down on the south side. Crash is hit, but we've cleared the path to the vehicles. You've got to move, now."

"Copy that," Razor growled, his eyes scanning the area for the safest route out. He turned to Hero. "Stay with me until we clear the door."

Hero nodded, shifting to keep Razor and Jade protected as they made their way through the maze of crates and equipment. Just as they neared the exit, a figure emerged from the shadows. The guard raised his weapon. Razor didn't hesitate. With a quick, deadly motion, he fired, the shot echoing like thunder in the confined space. The guard crumpled to the ground. Razor kept moving, helping Jade along.

Outside, the Hounds were holding their ground. Beast's towering figure loomed as he unleashed a barrage of suppressive fire, keeping enemies away from their escape route. Snow was a blur of precision, his sidearm picking off guards with unerring accuracy. Razor was grateful he'd come along.

"Get her in the truck!" Axel shouted, covering

Razor as he and Jade sprinted for the closest vehicle. Razor opened the door of a black SUV, guiding Jade inside with a sense of urgency.

"Stay down," he commanded. He slammed the door shut and turned back to the chaos, his weapon raised.

"Let's end this!" Beast roared, stepping forward to unleash another round, providing cover as the rest of the Hounds regrouped.

Razor's gaze scanned the battlefield, making sure no one was left behind. His heart pounded, not just from the adrenaline but from the knowledge that Jade was safe -- at least for now. But this wasn't over. Not by a long shot.

"Did Margot get the kids out?" he rumbled into his comms, hoping like hell he hadn't sent them all into the slaughter.

"They're secure on the other side," Deva answered him. "I found them a safe route. The sheriff is on the way."

Thank fuck. Razor couldn't help smiling. His woman had really come through for them. With a final signal, the other Hounds piled into their vehicles, peeling out of the warehouse lot in a cloud of dust and the acrid stench of gunpowder. Razor sat behind the wheel, his hands gripping the steering wheel tightly as he glanced at Jade in the rearview mirror. Her eyes were closed, her breathing shallow but steady. Hero jerked open the door and scrambled into the back seat with her, taking her into his arms like she was all he needed in the world.

Hero's gaze met his in the rearview mirror. "What's the plan, Prez?"

Razor's jaw tightened. "The cavalry's coming for those kids we found. The rest of us are getting the hell out of Dodge."

* * *

Deva

Deva's fingers hovered over the keyboard as she monitored the live comms feed, her breath coming in shallow bursts. The weight of responsibility pressed on her chest like a heavy stone, but hearing Margot's voice over the radio, calm and clear, sent a ripple of relief through her. They hadn't been looking for the poor kids they found -- the ones Victor and his people had trapped and exploited. Although it was something they had planned for, Snow had left old blueprints of the warehouse with her, and she'd used them to get Margot and those young people safely out and away from the fighting.

Her heart ached, knowing the horrors they must have endured. Still, she was proud of her work. She wasn't out there storming the warehouse or kicking down doors, but she got to do something. When Ryder's gruff voice came through next, confirming the kids were out and heading for safety, she felt her shoulders loosen for the first time all night.

Deva let out a shaky breath, clutching the edge of the desk as she fought to get her emotions under control. Anger at the cruelty inflicted on innocent lives. Gratitude that Margot, Ryder, and the others had the skills to keep those young people safe. And a bittersweet satisfaction that, even from behind a screen, she'd been part of it. They got Jade out and she just prayed that Razor's daughter was going to be okay after being used as a pawn in Grayson's selfish game.

Deva yawned and stretched at the edge of the clubhouse table, the adrenaline of the night's events still coursing through her veins. The clubhouse was quiet now, but soon the Hounds would be flooding in, all amped up from their victory. She doubted she was going to stay up and listen. It was three in the morning. Exhaustion was hitting her hard. She just couldn't keep going.

She turned off the alarms so she wouldn't have to be there to do it when they all wanted in. They shouldn't take long.

"I'm going to call it a night," she murmured to no one in particular, grabbing her bag from where she left it by the door. She headed for Razor's room, happy in the knowledge that they were on their way back.

The moment she stepped into the dimly lit hallway, she felt it -- a presence. Before she could turn, a rough hand clamped over her mouth, and another locked around her waist, dragging her backward. Deva's muffled scream was swallowed by the darkened corridor as she thrashed against her assailant's grip. The faint scent of leather and smoke hit her nostrils as panic clawed at her chest. She caught a glimpse of two figures in black, their faces obscured by ski masks.

"Shut her up," one of them barked, his voice low and gravelly.

She was hit in the mouth and then something sharp jabbed her arm, and Deva's struggling grew sluggish. Her vision blurred, and her limbs felt like lead. She barely registered the faint sound of voices -- Razor's voice -- somewhere far away as darkness swallowed her whole.

* * *

Deva's head throbbed as she came to, the taste of blood coppery on her tongue. Her hands were bound behind her back, and the faint hum of fluorescent lights buzzed overhead. Blinking to clear her vision, she recognized her surroundings: *No Mercy Ink.* But the shop she loved was twisted into a nightmarish version of itself. Her tattoo chair was tipped over, her tools scattered across the floor like debris from a storm. Someone had come to destroy the progress they'd made on repairing the shop.

Then she saw the two people in front of her. They had to be Victor Grayson and Natalia Veska.

Victor exuded the kind of power that didn't come from brute strength but from the careful manipulation of others. He was tall and lean, pacing in front of her. His sharp suit was rumpled, his jaw clenched tight. His salt-and-pepper hair was immaculately styled, giving him the air of a corporate predator, and his clean-shaven face only made his angular features more striking. His eyes, however, were his most chilling feature -- steel-gray and utterly cold, devoid of empathy. There was a calculated cruelty in his gaze, as if he was always five steps ahead, deciding who to crush next.

Natalia leaned against the counter, her cruel beauty marred by a sneer, her arms crossed as she watched Deva with hawk-like intensity. Her jet-black hair fell in sleek waves over her shoulders, contrasting sharply with her pale, flawless skin. Dressed in a blood-red leather jacket and fitted black pants, she looked every bit the dangerous *femme fatale*. Her lips, painted in a deep crimson, curled into a sly, almost mocking smile. The woman's eyes were what made her truly dangerous -- dark and piercing. They held a flicker of amusement that hinted at her sadistic tendencies. Her beauty was striking, but there was nothing warm or inviting about it.

To make it worse, there were armed men scattered through the shop, waiting for orders that could come at any moment.

"Finally awake," Natalia drawled, her tone as icy as the glint in her dark eyes.

Deva swallowed hard, her throat dry. "Wish I could say it's a pleasure."

Victor snapped his attention to her, his eyes narrowing. "You think this is a joke?" His voice was cold, venomous. "Do you even understand the shitstorm you and your biker friends have stirred up?"

Deva forced herself to sit straighter, ignoring the ache in her shoulders. "If you're this pissed, I'd say we're doing something right."

Natalia chuckled darkly, pushing off the counter to step closer. "I see why he likes you. Bold. But you don't get it, do you? Mercy was supposed to be our fresh start. A goldmine. And you" -- she gestured to Deva with disgust --"and your pathetic shop ruined everything."

Victor stopped pacing, turning to face Natalia. "No loose ends," he said tightly. "The Hounds already know too much."

"They won't let you get away with this," Deva said, keeping her voice steady despite the fear curling in her gut. "They'll come for me."

Natalia smirked, her head tilting as if amused. "Oh, sweetheart, we're counting on it. But by the time they find you, it'll be too late."

Deva's mind raced, desperate to stall them. "Is that what this is? Some revenge fantasy? You two want to ruin Mercy just because you couldn't get control of it?" Her gaze shifted to Victor, then Natalia, looking for cracks in their confidence. "You think killing me will fix this?"

Victor's face hardened, but Natalia let out a laugh, circling Deva slowly. "It's not about fixing anything. It's about sending a message."

Deva's heart pounded as she worked to buy herself more time. "And what? You think everyone's going to fall in line after this? I'm no one. And you're delusional."

Victor slammed a fist onto the counter, the sharp sound echoing in the quiet shop. "Shut up! You have no idea what you're talking about."

Deva met his gaze head-on, defiance burning in her chest. "Then enlighten me."

Natalia scoffed but paused her pacing. "You're not worth explaining anything to. Let's just finish this."

Before Victor could respond, the distant growl of motorcycles echoed through the quiet night, faint but growing louder. Both Victor and Natalia froze, their gazes snapping toward the front of the shop.

Deva's heart soared. *They're coming.*

Victor's jaw tightened, and he hissed under his breath. "Damn it. Move her to the back. Now."

Natalia approached Deva but froze at the clatter all around them, an army of Hounds advancing.

"You should've stayed out of Mercy," Deva said, her voice steady despite the fear in her veins.

The sound of the shop door being kicked in sent a jolt through her, followed by Razor's voice, low and dangerous. "Where is she?"

* * *

Razor

They moved with purpose, their bikes cutting through the quiet night like harbingers of justice. Razor led, completely focused, scanning the shop for any signs of Deva. He barked orders over the comms, organizing the group into positions around the building.

Hero and Axel covered the back exit while Snow and Beast circled to the sides, making sure no one slipped away unnoticed. Razor, with Player and Wolf at his flank, approached the front entrance. The sight of the shop's dimly lit interior, shadows playing tricks on the walls, set Razor's nerves on edge.

"Deva's in there," he muttered through clenched teeth, gripping the handle of his firearm tightly.

Player nodded, his jaw tight. "Let's fucking go."

Razor listened cautiously, then kicked the door down. Inside, Grayson and Natalia were waiting, flanked by a few armed men. Grayson stood tall, his cold, calculating gaze meeting Razor's, while Natalia lounged against the counter, a mocking smirk tugging at her blood-red lips.

Deva was tied to one of the chairs, her face pale but her eyes blazing with defiance. The moment she saw Razor, her expression shifted -- relief flickered across her face, quickly replaced by determination. Razor caught her subtle nod, her way of saying she was holding on.

"You're just in time," Victor drawled, his voice smooth and condescending. "We were discussing what to do with Deva here."

Natalia chuckled, her dark eyes glittering with malice. "She's feisty, I'll give her that. Shame she got mixed up with you and your little biker club."

Razor's gaze flicked to Deva, then back to Victor, his voice low and dangerous. "Let her go, and maybe I'll give you the chance to walk out of here."

Victor raised an eyebrow, clearly unimpressed. "You think storming in here gives you the upper hand? This is *my* town now. I'm not going anywhere."

Razor's lips curled into a cold smile. "You sure about that?"

At his signal, the Hounds burst in from all sides, weapons drawn. Chaos erupted. Axel and Hero engaged Victor's men in a flurry of fists and gunfire, while Snow and Beast subdued the guards at the back. Natalia lunged for Deva, a blade flashing in her hand, but Razor was faster. He tackled her to the ground, disarming her in one swift motion.

Deva, freed by one of the others during the commotion, didn't hesitate. Grabbing the nearest tattoo machine, she swung it with all her might, connecting with one of Victor's goons who had been closing in on Razor. Grayson, seeing the tide turn against him, tried to slip out the side door, but Player and Wolf were waiting. Player slammed him into the wall, pinning him there with a knife at his throat.

"You're not going anywhere," Player growled.

While the dust settled, Razor stood in the center of the shop. They were tired and bloodied, but they'd fucking pulled it off. Deva clung to his arm, still holding up despite the ordeal. The Hounds had won this battle, but Razor knew the war wasn't necessarily over. Grayson's network ran deep. They'd need to be vigilant if they ever came back to Mercy. But for now, Deva and Jade were safe, and that was all that mattered.

"You okay?" he asked.

Deva nodded, her voice steady. "I am now."

The blare of sirens pierced through the tense air outside *No Mercy Ink* as Razor and the Hounds secured the shop. Flashing red and blue lights flooded the street, casting eerie shadows on the building's facade.

Dawson stepped out of the lead patrol car. The deputy's expression was grim but determined. Behind him, a team of other deputies fanned out, weapons ready. Holding up a hand, Dawson signaled for them to hold position. When his gaze met Razor's, a silent message passed between them. Dawson wasn't here to protect Grayson.

I'll be damned.

Inside the shop, Victor Grayson, his shirt torn and blood smeared across his face, tried to square his shoulders, but the weight of defeat was written all over him. Natalia, restrained by Beast, hissed like a cornered cat, her earlier confidence evaporated.

"Victor Grayson," Dawson announced as he stepped inside, his voice sharp and commanding, "you're under arrest."

Grayson's smirk faltered. "You sure you want to do this?"

"I am," Dawson snapped, stepping closer.

As Dawson cuffed Victor, Razor watched closely, ready to step in if the deputy wavered. But Dawson's hands were steady, his movements decisive. When he turned to Natalia, she sneered, baring her teeth.

"Go ahead," she taunted. "You think this changes anything? There's always someone else waiting in the wings."

"Let's hope they're smarter than you." Dawson snapped the cuffs on her wrists with a satisfying *click*.

The Hounds stepped back as the officers moved in, securing the scene and gathering evidence. Razor holstered his weapon, his shoulders relaxing slightly, though his eyes stayed sharp, tracking every movement in the room.

Deva stood close to Razor, hanging onto him, her body trembling with the aftershocks of the ordeal. When Dawson approached her, his expression softened. "You okay?"

She nodded, her voice low but firm. "I will be. Thank you."

Dawson nodded, glancing at Razor. "I owe you an apology."

Razor raised an eyebrow. "For what?"

"For not stepping up sooner," Dawson admitted, his voice thick with guilt. "But I'm done letting anyone control me. Whatever happens now, it's on my terms."

Razor studied him for a long moment before giving a curt nod. "About time."

As Grayson, Natalia, and their men were hauled out of the shop, their venomous glares aimed at Razor and Deva didn't go unnoticed. Razor stepped closer to Deva, his hand resting protectively on her back. "It's over," he said softly, hoping to keep her calm. In truth, he was still ready for anything.

Deva leaned into him, blowing out a long breath. "They busted up my shop. Again."

"We'll fix it. Again." Razor's lips curled into a faint smile. "But right now, call your brother. He's apparently worried as shit right now."

Chapter Ten

Deva

Jackson was being released from the hospital that weekend and she wanted to have a small homecoming party for him at his house. It was more like a Sunday social than a homecoming for a biker, but it would work. Deva got there just after dawn to clean despite Razor's protest that "It couldn't be that fucking bad."

Deva and Razor took her SUV and pulled into the gravel driveway of Jackson's house, her tires crunching against the rocks. The house itself was small and unassuming, a one-story structure with white siding, black trim, and a tin roof that reflected the overcast sky. A wraparound porch, slightly sagging in places, hinted at a charm that might have existed before years of neglect. Two mismatched chairs sat near the front door, one of them piled with motorcycle gear, while a stack of cardboard boxes leaned precariously against the wall. A pair of boots, dusty and worn, rested near the steps as if Jackson had kicked them off there and forgotten about them.

Inside, the house was just as she expected -- cluttered but not dirty. The faint smell of coffee and marijuana lingered in the air, a scent that was somehow quintessentially Jackson. His living room was an interesting arrangement of mismatched furniture -- a battered leather couch, an armchair that had seen better days, and a coffee table overflowing with motorcycle magazines, scattered tools, and a random assortment of gadgets he might've been tinkering with at some point.

The walls were sparsely decorated, with a few crooked frames holding photos of the Hounds, old motorcycle rallies, and one of Deva and Jackson as kids. A bookshelf stood in the corner, crammed with an eclectic mix of well-thumbed books on engineering, philosophy, and mechanics, all stacked horizontally in chaotic piles. A guitar leaned against the wall near the TV, its strings slightly dusty but not neglected. Interestingly, there was another photo of the phoenix tattoo, just like the one he kept at the shop. The tattoo displayed vivid colors across the white skin of a woman's back, framed and on his nightstand in the bedroom.

The kitchen was a functional mess, with clean dishes stacked haphazardly in the drying rack and random tools -- wrenches, screwdrivers, and even a motorcycle part -- occupying counter space that should have been used for food prep. His old coffee pot sat on the counter, still half-full, and a pile of unopened mail rested beside it.

Yeah, they had their work cut out for them. Still, despite the piles of clutter, there was something comfortable about the space. It felt lived-in, like every messy corner told a story about her brother. Deva sighed, running her fingers over a stack of books on the coffee table, smiling. It was Jackson -- bright, focused on his passions, and entirely uninterested in anything as boring as housework.

Deva half expected Razor to march right back into the living room, put his feet up, and watch TV. Instead, he was right there with her, cleaning the house. She tackled the kitchen while he worked on the living room. They had to laugh because although Jackson had tons of cleaning products, most had never been used.

After a good start, she'd sent Razor for supplies since some supplies he did regularly use, like laundry detergent and dishwasher pods, were low. Just then

Jade and Hero arrived. And she was grateful because things went a lot faster with more hands.

"How are you feeling?" she asked Jade when it was just the two of them folding towels and bedding.

"I'm fine." Jade shook her head. "I had a mild concussion, but Hero's kept me under lock and key for what feels like a week now. I'm glad to get out today. I was getting cabin fever."

Deva laughed with her. "Good. I'm just so sorry you got pulled into it at all."

"I'll live, and I did learn something," Jade explained. "I've been taking self-defense lessons from Margot for months now. I think I'm getting better at it. But all that preparation and I completely froze when those men ran me off the road and dragged me out of the car. I know it could have been so much worse, but still..."

"Yes, it could have," Deva told her.

"Dad told me that when he got to your shop that night, you were tied to a chair in there, but you were kicking ass and raising hell the minute Snow cut you loose."

It hadn't been entirely like that, and Deva didn't like the forlorn tone that crept into her voice. "Doesn't make me braver than you. They were after our shop, and they'd already been fucking with us. Wait until you see what Jackson looks like. We were already in the thick of it. We were expecting them to come after us. You weren't. And from what Razor told me, this is your second kidnapping. Give yourself some credit."

Jade nodded, expertly folding the comforter she pulled from the dryer. "Do you know that's how I met Hero?"

Deva listened intently, noting how Jade subtly praised Razor in her recounting. Deva had followed

Jackson to Mercy a few years ago, but she'd never truly grasped what unfolded in the shadows of the town. Jackson had always been fiercely tight-lipped. She'd been a regular at Emily Frost's bakery since she lived there. Still, she had no idea that the Mafia burned it to the ground in a calculated attempt to strike at the Hounds.

"I think I'd like to join Margot's class," Deva said. "If there's room."

"Is this a serious offer?" Margot said from the doorway. "That would give me a dozen students and that would be cool. We'd love to have you!"

Turning, Deva hugged the off-duty deputy. Margot, Sadie, and the twins had gotten there in time to help set up and they arrived just in time since the cleaning was done.

"Where can I put this?" Deva heard Sadie's voice from out in the hallway. When she made it out to her, she found the pretty redhead with a sizable crock pot in her hands. "Barbequed chicken wings."

"Bless you," Deva told her. It was a potluck, and everyone was bringing something. But bikers had pretty big appetites, and she sure didn't want to run out of food. Razor, who had returned with the supplies she sent him out for, assured her that there would be plenty.

Player showed up next with Crash and Helena, who Deva hadn't met yet. She thought the two of them had started dating around Christmas. Helena brought a couple of pies she made. Player, big and bombastic as always, showed up with two enormous roasts that he said just needed to be "warmed through" and a huge tin tub of what looked like the best homemade mac and cheese she'd ever seen. Snow and Emily arrived, bringing casseroles and baked goods, with Beast right behind them with his homemade bread.

"How are you feeling?" Deva asked Crash who was content to stay with Helena as she stashed tubs of whipped cream and ice cream in Jackson's fridge. She didn't miss the quick grin Helena threw him at the question. "I heard you got hit... What?"

Crash started chuckling. "I'm fine," he said. "Got shot in the ass."

Deva just knew he was never going to live that one down with his fellow Hounds.

When Razor and Hero left to go get Jackson, Deva was surprised it was early afternoon. They returned with him within an hour, and the timing was perfect. Everything was all ready for his homecoming. Not all Hounds and prospects were there because there wasn't enough room, and her brother was more of a loner than a social butterfly. On top of that, he had no idea what was waiting for him when he returned home.

Razor and Hero drove her SUV to the hospital to bring Jackson home. When they returned, Crash, who couldn't sit still for long, stood watch by the window and gave the signal as soon as he spotted them pulling in. The house buzzed with excitement as everyone gathered in the living room. The moment Jackson walked through the door, the room erupted into cheers and shouts of "Welcome home!" The energy was electric, a mix of relief and celebration, as their battered brother finally rejoined them.

After a week in the hospital, Jackson still looked rough around the edges but better than when Deva first saw him after the attack. His face was mottled with fading bruises, the deep purple and black giving way to yellowish hues. The stitched gash above his eyebrow was still swollen. Dressed in his usual clothes made him look less frail though. His sharp ice-blue eyes had lost some of their fire, dulled by painkillers and exhaustion, but his smirk, crooked and full of defiance, was still intact.

"Fuck," Jackson muttered, looking around. "You cleaned, didn't you?"

That had everyone laughing as Hero helped Razor get Jackson into his favorite recliner. Bandages peeked out from the edge of his sleeves and the neckline, covering the worst of the damage. His hands, resting loosely on the arms of his chair, were still scratched and scabbed from fighting back. His black hair, usually swept dramatically back, was in spikes all around his head, a reminder that even her big brother wasn't invincible. Yet, even battered and bruised, there was an undeniable strength about him that he'd always had and probably always would.

Deva approached his chair, meaning to give him a light hug to welcome him back. He took her off guard by grabbing her in earnest in a hug that compressed her ribs. "I'm so grateful you're safe, little sister. If anything had happened to you…"

The endearment brought on tears as he held onto her for a minute. "I wasn't hurt." Even if she had been, she wasn't about to tell him. "We're going to be okay now."

When he finally let go of her, she left him to listen to the tall tales of the others and how the rescue mission went. Everything he missed while he was stuck in Mercy General Hospital. Margot stayed in there too and it made her smile. Yeah, there were currently no female members of the Mercy chapter of the Hounds. But Margot seemed to fit right in, despite being the law, sharing her take on what happened once they found the young people Grayson and Veska had been trafficking.

"They're in good hands," Margot explained. "We coordinated with a few trusted contacts at the state level. They're being transported to a secure facility where they'll get medical care, counseling, and everything else they need to start putting their lives back together."

Hero, arms crossed, nodded. "What about their families? Do they have anyone looking for them?"

Margot sighed. "Some do, but others don't. It's going to take time to sort out who has someone waiting and who's completely on their own. The social workers I called in are some of the best -- no red tape bullshit. They'll make sure no one slips through the cracks."

Ryder, sitting nearby, glanced up. "What about Veska's network? Can they track these kids back down?"

Margot's eyes hardened. "Not a chance. The facility's location is classified, and we're making sure any leads that network might have are dead ends. They won't get near them again."

Deva and the rest of the "old ladies" got everything set up in the kitchen for the potluck. The storytelling didn't end while everyone took turns ducking into the kitchen for food. All but Jackson. Deva put together a plate for him, and checked in on when he needed to take his next meds. The men ended up back in the living room to eat with him while Deva and the ladies stayed around the kitchen and dining room area for their own visit. She found some old metal folding chairs in the basement, bringing them up so everyone had a place to sit. This time, Margot decided to join them.

"We have self-defense class on Wednesdays,

Deva," Margot said while they ate. "We usually start at seven. Like I said, we'd love to have you join us."

"I'd like that too," she admitted. "Especially with everything that's happened in the last couple of weeks."

"Are you with Razor?" Helena asked her, tucking a glossy lock of black hair behind one ear. "I'm sorry. I'm still new to this and I'm just trying to figure out who's who."

All eyes were then on Deva, and she had to laugh. Jade knew she was with Razor but honestly, she didn't know what the story was. Finally, she nodded. "Guess so."

"It works perfectly," Margot pointed out. "You with Razor. The president's old lady, from what I've seen, is like the president of the rest of the old ladies. Our leader, I guess."

Deva laughed at that. "Are you serious?"

Margot nodded. "And you did just that today with all of this."

The other ladies nodded or hummed their agreement.

"Yeah, that's not what I was doing," Deva told them. "But I really appreciate your help in pulling off this homecoming for my brother. It means a lot to both of us."

Margot and Sadie exchanged a knowing look and Jade just studied her, smiling.

They were all there visiting for a few hours before Razor stood, addressing everyone there. "Let's wrap this up. Outcast here needs to get some rest. Thank you all for coming out to welcome him back home. I'm hoping that you'll all make some time to help us get *No Mercy Ink* back on its feet. The fuckers did another number on the progress we had made when they came after Deva."

All eyes turned to Deva, including her brother's, making her the unexpected center of attention -- a place she'd never felt entirely at ease. Thankfully, every gaze carried warmth, appreciation, or welcome, easing the discomfort just enough for her to manage a small smile.

"I also want to thank you all for helping get Emily's bakery rebuilt," Razor continued. *"Whisk and Whimsy* is reopening the first of February. Thanks to Beast and Crash for leading that charge. It's a good thing the bakery is finished. Crash wouldn't be much help since he got himself shot in the ass during the rescue mission."

Crash shook his head because he knew it was coming, and he was good-natured about the laughter and the ribbing he took. Snow looked proudly at Emily who was beaming about the announcement. It was a big deal, because her bakery had been missed.

Deva half expected everyone to just grab their stuff and head for the exits but to her surprise, they started breaking everything down. Hounds stayed to put up chairs, gather trash. The other old ladies were already getting dishes washed and cleaning the kitchen. In no time at all the work was done. Only then did the Hounds and their ladies start filing out. By the time the sun was going down, it was just Deva and Razor left with Jackson, who looked ready to go to bed.

"Thank you," Jackson told her as he followed them to the door. Deva carefully hugged him goodbye before his attention turned to Razor. "Thank you for taking care of Deva."

Razor grinned. "Whether she likes the name or not, she's my old lady and that's my job."

Deva pulled a face. She most definitely didn't

like the term.

"I would have protected her anyway. For you," Razor added. "Always, brother."

Razor carried the rest of their things out to her SUV, but Deva lingered there with her brother.

"You look happy," Jackson told her. "I can tell you from what I saw today, the Hounds like you two together."

"I guess that's a good thing," she said. "I didn't know there was a vote or anything."

"No vote. But it's important. Razor's our Prez and you're *his*. That means the Hounds are obligated to protect you with their lives just like they'd protect him."

It took Deva a minute to realize her mouth was hanging open. "Seriously?"

"Yeah," he pointed out. "Helps me out too."

"Especially until you get back on your feet." Deva was still worried about him. "Maybe one day you'll find an old lady of your own. I guess I always thought you, Crash, and Player would just end up being old bachelors. But Crash found Helena. Maybe there's hope."

Her brother's smile didn't quite reach his eyes. "Maybe... Maybe I'll find her."

* * *

Deva

It had been maybe an hour since they returned to Razor's house when he found her by the washer and dryer, doing laundry. He threw her that charming half grin that always did things to her. The bastard knew it too. "What are you up to?" he asked in that sexy, deep voice. "I would have thought you got in enough housework for a whole week today at Outcast's."

"Jackson's." Deva sighed. "I still need to get my own laundry done so I can get back to my house."

That smirk evaporated fast. "What?"

"Well, the danger is past, right?" she asked. "Grayson and his assholes are done."

Razor went from sexy pose with one hand on the wall to leaning against it with his arms folded across the wide expanse of his chest and glaring at her. "The danger is *not* fucking past. What do you mean 'when I get back to my house'?"

She didn't mean to sound ungrateful. But she had her own home to deal with. "Thank you for letting me stay here," she said carefully. "I just need to get back home and check on things. That's all. Doesn't mean I'm leaving forever."

Oh, he didn't care for that explanation. "It's too soon. You need things from your house, I'll drive you over there to get them. You can do whatever it is you need to do. Beyond that, no."

Deva couldn't help but smile. "No?" She finished setting her load on the washer before she gave him her full attention. "What are you trying to say?"

"You know damn well what I'm trying to say, Deva," Razor said.

Was it wrong that she just wanted to make him say it? "I'm not sure I understand. Explain it to me."

He invaded her personal space, backing her against the washing machine. The intensity in his gorgeous hazel eyes took her breath away. "Didn't I already explain in front your brother that you're claimed? You're *mine*. And that means you live here. End of story."

Deva's brows shot up. "I do remember you telling my brother something like that in my presence and asking him if he had any problem with that, yes. I can't recall hearing about living arrangements."

"Goes without saying," he said, leaning in to try and kiss her. She dodged under his left arm, escaped his temporary trap, smiling as she did. "It's settled."

"Hardly," she said.

"Hardly, huh?" Razor's eyes were lit with amusement, but he wasn't smiling now, and she wasn't exactly sure how to read him. She backed away, out of the small laundry room in his house and into the kitchen. He stalked her, that intensity of his demeanor not letting up.

"You can tell Jackson and any of the other Hounds anything you want," she advised. "You can tell them I'm your old lady, whatever... But you never asked *me*."

Now the smirk she loved came back. "Wasn't aware I had to."

Deva shrugged, leaning back against the kitchen sink.

"You play the part very well," he said, moving closer. "I was kind of hoping you wanted it."

"Didn't say I didn't," Deva said. "But being asked would be very nice."

The full-on grin he flashed her at that had her heart racing. "I *could* ask. Or I could just make you beg me for it."

The last thing Deva expected was for him to upend her world by hoisting her over his shoulder and hauling her off to his bedroom. Her stomach complained a little because they'd all eaten a lot of food at Jackson's. But his words and actions had her body catching up quickly. The first sparks of pleasure raced through her blood. Razor carefully dropped her onto the neatly made bed at the center of the room. But it was his last careful action, and she was completely fine with that.

"Razor?" She watched as his fingers plucked at the laces of her ankle boots before swiftly tossing them off the side of the bed. "You're serious?"

"You're going to be singing for me, darlin'," he said, climbing onto the bed with her.

Deva felt lost in his shadow, sometimes forgetting how much bigger than her Razor really was. Straddling her, he pulled off his cut and his T-shirt, leaving her to watch, mesmerized. The beautiful expanse of muscles and tats had her thighs clenching together in anticipation. When he lowered his powerful body over hers, he planted his elbows on either side of her, caging her on top of the bed. Razor was so warm, smelling like her fresh linen and a deep, enticing scent that was just him. Hooking an ankle around the back of one of his thighs, and they were muscular too, she encouraged him, wanting more. *Needing* more.

And he gave it to her, grinding the heated length of himself into her belly, making her shudder in desire. Deva grinned at him. "Did you say something about begging?" she asked, breathlessly.

Razor's lips seared the tender flesh of her neck, gentle teeth nipping at her skin in a way he knew would make her crazy. "I did. And you *will*."

His lips claimed hers with a sweet kiss to start. It was gentle, soft. But it soon turned demanding, his tongue tracing the seam of her lips to gain entrance. Deva let him in, her fingers sliding into the long, sleek locks of his hair as he dazzled her with kisses that left her writhing beneath him. His hands were so careful, cupping her face and sliding into her hair. But as he continued drugging her with kisses, his hands slid lower, under her. The hooks of her bra didn't pose a challenge, and he whisked it off along with her shirt in one smooth motion.

Deva always appreciated the way his eyes lit up as his gaze moved over her breasts. Yeah, she'd been blessed there and while bigger boobs came with challenges aplenty, the way her man gawked at her bare upper body sent pride and lust rushing through her veins. It made her feel warm and worshipped.

Razor smirked, one full breast filling his hand. Deva pressed herself up into his palm as his lips blazed a trail down her neck and lower. His lips were soft, the rough of his stubble offering an enticing counterpoint. His tongue was a wicked tease on her skin as he made his way down to her neglected breast. He shifted down the bed as his hot mouth closed around its nipple. When he teased the peak with his teeth, he left her gasping.

"You feeling good, darlin'?" he asked in that deep, whisky voice.

She nodded her head when he hummed around her, his tongue a ruthless torment as it teased her flesh. His touches were tentative at first. But as her hands clutched in the gunmetal-colored locks of his hair, hanging on as he worked her breasts with his hands and mouth, raw need pooled low in her belly. Her thighs clamped around his slim hips so she could grind herself against him. Deva felt feverish in her need for friction and relief from the deep ache he'd stoked in her body. Her gasps and cries filled the room, a chorus he easily pulled from her.

When one big hand slid down to cup her through her jeans and ruined panties, Deva was pushed to the edge. But his touch was too light, too soft and the fucker did it on purpose. Lifting his head, he smiled at her. If she hadn't been so swamped with pleasure, she would have happily slapped him.

Razor was enjoying taking her apart. His fingers plucked at the front of her jeans, and with haste she helped him undo them and push them down. Her panties were a wet mess under there, but he dragged those down too, leaving cool, wet trails down her inner thighs.

Deva shivered, wanting him to hurry up in pulling the denim free of her feet, then tossing the jeans and her underwear away. Now he was getting to the good part. What she didn't expect him to do was to easily flip her onto her stomach, shoving a pillow under hips as he did. She had no time to prepare when he pressed his face into her wet folds from behind. As good as Razor was at everything else, Deva just hoped she survived as his lips and tongue worked to drive her wild. He held her hips in a punishing grip that didn't allow for any movement to make her situation even more desperate.

"You want to be my old lady now?" he muttered into her pussy.

Fucking bastard.

Deva sang for him. She just couldn't help it. Razor spent long moments lapping at her clit with his tongue and fucking her with it at turns. Most guys didn't know where to find that tight bundle of nerves, much less what to do with it if they did. Razor knew just how much pressure to apply and when, the slick swirls of his tongue crossing her eyes as release came up fast. Deva had never had a man bring her off like that, making her dance on the tip of his tongue. But he held her in place until tears spilled from the corners of her eyes. Until she *was* begging him, but she wasn't even sure what she was saying as the orgasm shook her like a rag doll.

He never stopped, either. When she came back around, he teased her opening with his tongue, with long, rough fingers reaching deep inside her. They slid in and out with deliberate strokes that kept her clenching around him, biting the pillow.

"You taste so sweet," he whispered, lapping at her clit intensely before stopping abruptly, letting currents of pleasure rush through her and start working her up again. "I could just do this until you agree to be my old lady... What do you think, beautiful?"

She'd been about to answer when the pad of his finger found what it was looking for inside her and she howled. More lashes of his tongue on her clit had it throbbing, had her writhing with nowhere to go to get relief. He controlled that and he wasn't letting up even as she kept a white-knuckle grip on the bedding beneath her. Just as she was about to blow apart again, her body shivering with need, he stopped.

The fuck?

Deva was dimly aware that he was shucking off his jeans behind her. Weakly, she tried to lift her head, to get a good view.

"See something you like?" he asked, climbing on the bed behind her, smoothing a hand over her ass.

Deva wiggled her ass. Shit yeah, she wanted that cock.

"Want to get a better look first?" Quick as anything, he climbed off the bed and came around to the side so that magnificent cock was at her eye level.

She didn't need anyone to tell her what to do. She got her hands on him, working him into her mouth with wild lashes of her tongue. She got him wet while the taste of him filled her. Deva wanted to do a good job, to make him hurt. She needed him in the worst way.

"Ready to be my old lady now?" he asked before pulling his cock free and claiming her lips with his own. The taste of her excitement blended with his own as they kissed, and her pussy throbbed now in desperation.

"Yes," she whispered.

"Not sure I heard you," he teased. Razor climbed back on the bed and her world spun as he flipped her onto her back like she didn't weigh a thing. The manhandling only made her want him more. Again, he claimed her mouth in a kiss. A dirty kiss, all lips and tongue. He groaned as her hands slid back up into his hair.

Razor pulled her flat under him, positioned himself between her quivering thighs. Deva sucked in a breath when the swollen head of him pressed against her entrance. *Fucking finally.*

The burn as he pushed into her was everything she wanted. The way her walls stretched around him as he slowly sank into her had her grabbing the bedding, clutching at his hair. Maybe it was how he'd dialed up her need, but it seemed to take forever for him to reach the end of her. His hips moved carefully, slowly, with a dirty grind once he couldn't go any further. Deva was already on the edge as he stuffed her full, inner walls quivering around him as she waited breathlessly.

More careful strokes while her heart raced. In and out. Finally, Deva just couldn't take it anymore.

"I need you to fuck me, Razor. I need it so bad right now..." She swallowed hard, moving her hips with him in hopes of encouraging him. "You can call me whatever the fuck you want... okay?"

Oh, that had him preening. Razor's grin widened

as he began to move faster.

"Yeah?" he asked, lips nipping at her jaw and neck.

"Yeah." It sounded far more desperate than she intended but she had no fucks left to give. With her arms and legs wrapped around him, she pumped her hips up into his thrusts. She loved the speed he was building along with the mild force of his movements. The muscles of his back and shoulders were slick with sweat, flexing under her hands. Razor wasn't holding back, and it was everything. His cock felt amazing, his weight trapping her between him and the bed, making her take him in wild abandon.

Her heart slammed in her chest and her pussy clamped around him hard. The room faded as she rode that wave, fighting to breathe. Fighting for *more*. Her nails carved grooves down his back while her hips moved with his frantically, riding it out.

Damp locks of hair framed his face above her as his huge form tightened, his weight dropping onto her as he neared his own end. His thrusts were fast and hard, just shy of painful. His thick thighs pressed hers wider as he pushed on, almost there. The growling sound he made when he came echoed in the corners of his bedroom. Pumping himself into her body, his movements finally slowed then stopped.

Dropping a kiss on her lips, Razor collapsed next to her on the bed. The rough chorus of their breathing was the only sound in the quiet of the room. Razor pulled her against him, holding her to his side while the two of them recovered.

"I told you I could make you beg," he said with a smile in his voice.

Deva shook her head, snuggling into him. "For some things. I guess..."

He froze. "You guess?"

"Next, you'll be wanting me to say 'I love you' or some shit," she teased him.

Razor shook as he chuckled. "Challenge accepted."

Jamie Targaet

Jamie Targaet is the author of the Hounds of Hell MC. She's anxious to introduce you to this club of gorgeous, dominant men and the lucky women who surrender to them. The ride is going to get wild at times, not going to lie. But there's thrilling action, scorching hot sex scenes, and all the feels.

Jamie writes erotic romance for Changeling Press, a little fanfiction on the side, and she's an aspiring horror writer in another life. She enjoys time with her family (including the fur babies). She likes good horror movies and shows, emo metal and classic rock, and time spent in other worlds writing and reading. She loves hearing from readers and is looking forward to hearing from you.

Hounds of Hell MC is part of the Hounds of Hell MC Multiverse.

Jamie at Changeling: changelingpress.com/jamie-targaet-a-227

Changeling Press, LLC

ChangelingPress.com

www.ingramcontent.com/pod-product-compliance
Lightning Source LLC
Chambersburg PA
CBHW071513260626
47170CB00002B/355